In the Shadow of a Dream

A Fareview Fairytale
Book 3

By Maci Aurora

In the Shadow of a Wish, book 1
In the Shadow of a Hoax, book 2
In the Shadow of a Dream, book 3

Coming Soon

In the Shadow of the Truth, the Novellas
In the Shadow of an Obsession, Book 4

The Accidental Seraph, Carran Hollow book 1

The Ring Academy: The Trials of Imogene Sol

The Messy Truth About Love

In the Echo of this Ghost Town
When the Echo Answers
The Stories Stars Tell

The Letters She Left Behind

In the Shadow of a Dream

A Fareview Fairytale

Book 3

By Maci Aurora

Mixed Plate Press
Honolulu, Hawaii
www.mixedplatepress.com

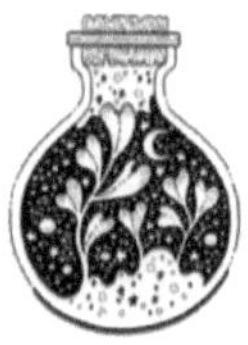

In the Shadow of a Dream
Fareview Fairytale Book 3
©2024 Maci Aurora w/ Mixed Plate Press
Honolulu, Hawaii

cover art: Sara Oliver Designs

ISBN: 979-8-9891543-0-2 (paperback)
ISBN: 979-8-9891543-1-9 (eBook)

About this book: *In the Shadow of a Dream* was inspired by a mash up of Grimm's Fairytales, "The Sleeping Beauty," "The Princess in Disguise," "Tom Thumb," The Robber Bridegroom," and "Maid Maleen.". It contains explicit sexual situations and is intended for mature audiences (18+).

DEDICATED TO

...those who are stuck...

and the way forward seems
impossible...

...find the bridge.

Author's Note

In the Shadow of a Dream is a reimagined fairytale filled with potions, magic, and true love, but even fairytales traverse dark roads and face scary monsters. While Brinna's story is a romance that focuses on that happily-ever-after, it doesn't preclude her (and others in her story), and thereby the reader, from facing some very real and possibly disturbing obstacles. It is important to share what could possibly be triggering for those who wish forewarning. If you don't want to know, please stop reading here, turn the page, and begin the story.

Brinna Fareview and her siblings have lived in a land dominated by men, where women are subjugated just based on their gender, and while Kaloma and its politics isn't as prevalent in this story, this loss of autonomy and agency has still occurred closer to home. Their mother, Scarlett, has been lying to her family, and is keeping them trapped. While her lies have been told with good intentions, they have resulted in a loss of power and choice for each of her grown children, unaware of her duplicity.

Scarlett's secrets reveal she has suffered at the hands of men. While none of it is glorified or explicitly described, this story touches upon loss of agency, entrapment, kidnapping, and incestual intent. None of these situations are graphically highlighted, but sometimes the allusion is enough. Please rest assured that I have done my utmost to care for the various characters (and my readers) in the narrative scope of these situations. My hope is that all scenes are presented with that

In mind. Please note, that given the fantasy elements, there are some dark creatures with frightening intentions depicting violence.

Thank you so much for being willing to take a chance on *In the Shadow of a Dream*. I hope you love Brinna and Luc's story as much as I enjoyed writing it, and that in all your endeavors, you are able to dream sweetly (and hopefully with some spice thrown in for good measure).

A Treatise on Magic

By Dorsha Romagil, Elcadian Oracle of the Magical Order

...After extensive research and expansive observation aligned with exhaustive testing, it has been determined that there are variations of known magic that can be categorized in two ways: rational magic and irrational magic [...]

Rational magic, for all intents and purposes, is of the natural world. This is the magic passed through the DNA of Elcadians via the godlight, traced back through the lineage to the origin of Elcadian beings. This rational magic potentially can be suppressed or heightened as with ascension when a godbeing takes their place within the natural order of their heightened powers. For example, while a godling is predisposed to the magic passed by their parents, the predisposition won't be fully realized until the ascension to power and passing of the mantle [...]

The second kind of magic—which requires further study—is irrational magic. This variation of magic occurs in two ways. First, this magic can be manifested through demon energy. While an argument can be made that this would, in fact, be a variety of natural magic, it does not occur naturally in Elcadia. Demon magic may occur within the natural sphere of demonic energy, the dark energy created has never been known to manifest in altruistic or positive means and has only augmented malicious intent. The second manifestation is through conjuring. Energy—demon energy, godlight energy and/or natural energy— is diverted, harnessed, and then manifested. This can be through spellwork as exemplified by sorcery but it can also be bodily harnessed much as ascended godlight is also carried within the body. The carrier would then be able to manifest the conjured power much as an Elcadian can manifest ascended godlight [...]

Once upon a time . . .

Before the spell was broken

Lucian Uraiahs, god of day and light, wasn't sure what to make of the woman singing as she traipsed through the snowy forest. The racing of his heart offered him a possibility he didn't want to acknowledge. This wasn't the first time he'd seen her. That had been in the meeting house in the tiny village of Sevens where she'd been sitting in a booth working with a needle and thread, smiling contentedly as she did. This was the first time he'd seen her in the woods, however, and he'd been there for some time.

Her sweet voice—a touch high with a gentle swell into nice round notes—carried a melody as she sang, *"My love, my love, where have you gone?"* The quiet woods with its snow falling in big, bright flakes made her song ethereal.

Evergreen trees flourished despite the cold, their branches heavy with snow, waiting like the naked deciduous trees for the return of warmth. Standing deep in the shadows, Luc would have been cold had it not been for his godlight, though observing the woman warmed him further, a fact he decided he would explain away after this awful business was over.

Snowflakes floated around the woman, muting sound as she pulled an empty wagon through the drift. There wasn't a path, but she made one as she walked.

"Where have you gone?" she continued to sing.

She was beautiful. It was hard not to notice the vibrancy in her cheeks and the sparkle in her eyes. Though not dressed in much more than rags, her boots were too big for her feet, and her coat was several sizes too large. She fought with the sleeves as she pulled the wagon through a drift. In the meeting house, she'd been wearing a lovely blue dress, and though she'd been thin, he wouldn't have guessed then at what appeared to be her impoverished circumstances. He'd only had eyes for her ready smile.

That smile had made him curious.

She smiled now with more abandon than in the meeting house as she sang, *"I'm waiting here for you."*

He couldn't fathom why she seemed so happy.

Since he'd completed his official Roam years before his ascension and continued to Roam well beyond it, he'd been across the Vasmost, traversing space and time as though searching for experiences to inform his own happiness. He'd been everywhere. He'd met others—happy, sad, in the throes of great joy, or the depths of dire grief—but he couldn't remember a time where he'd seen a smile like hers that gathered his breath and held it captive against his will. Nothing in his life had offered him the warmth and contentment of that smile—contentment that seemed misplaced. And that, he realized, was what gave him pause. The emotion that informed that smile was something he'd never felt. Content.

Hidden by the deep shadows of the winter forest, Luc watched and listened, guiding her with his power toward the meadow, toward the key, toward the trap. While he hadn't expressly created the ploy for her—it was set by a spell on a key—he was lying in wait for an unsuspecting person moving though this wood to succumb to the illusion. Who knew how much longer his brother Nixus would be trapped in that forsaken spell? The spell that was Luc's fault and the reason he was in these woods at all, luring an unsuspecting woman toward the enchantment with his godlight.

He had to make this right for Nix. Whatever it took.

Only the more time Luc spent watching this woman—whether it had been at that horrible meeting house where he'd learned she and the other women were forced to wait for prospective husbands, or in the immediate now, moving ever closer to the magical snare—he was unable to calm the way his heart spoke truth inside him. Ignoring its thumping persuasion, he continued leading her, dropping dollops of golden light along her path, telling his heart to bugger off with its selfish lies. He needed a final key keeper, and she was the first to come along. Who knew how long it would take to find another?

She sang another line— *"I dream, I dream, and sing this song. I'll prove my heart is true–"* —still smiling in spite of the snow and cold, in spite of her hunger, in spite of her empty wagon.

Luc didn't understand. Adding another drop of golden light, then another, he led her toward the meadow where he knew the key had appeared after the last key keeper's failure. He justified that luring her was an opportunity for her to wish for riches. It was clear she needed it.

But his reasoning drifted the longer he watched her. Though Luc wasn't a content man, the more he listened to her song, the more content he became. His heart quickened, pushing emotions through his chest that tugged his heart, tightening it in his chest—and to his surprise, enjoyment suddenly spiked his pulse with a possibility he didn't want to examine too closely.

Except, this was the final key keeper. This one *had* to break the spell when all the others had failed. Time to fix his mistake was running out. Understanding the parameters of the spell, coupled with the fact every keeper selected and lured by his goddess-cousin Poe had failed, meant this keeper was the difference between life and death for Nix and himself. If this last one failed…

He shook his head.

It wouldn't come to that.

Luc knew Nix. Luc understood the spell. He'd lure the right one where Poe had failed.

Though Luc accepted he was selfish—he'd done very little in his life that hadn't immediately impacted his needs and wants—he knew that he couldn't be this time. He tried to suppress the awareness that he'd failed epically at his first selfless decision by trapping his brother in that stupid spell. Obviously, he wasn't very good at it. Yet here he was trying to make another one, and his selfish heart was tempted away from his goal by a smile and a song. He knew the next key keeper—the right one—could not only save Nixus from the spell, but also Luc from having to sacrifice himself should it come to that.

Maybe this choice wasn't completely selfless.

"Oh Love, oh Love, come home to me. My arms are open wide," the woman sang, throwing her arms out to her sides. The sled's lead wrapped around her hips as she spun. Stuck by both the wagon's rope and the deep snow, she giggled, then hummed as she unwound herself.

Luc grinned, his heart jumping in his chest. He ignored it.

"*My Love, my Love*," she sang, quieter now as she tugged on the wagon once more, melancholy filling the notes. "*The fire I keep is burning bright, burning to keep me alive.*"

Luc's smile faded as he finally acknowledged the truth. This woman wouldn't break the spell. She wasn't the one. She was a dreamer, and from everything he'd learned about the spell, it would crush her.

Unable to overlook the selfish relief winding its way through him, he withdrew his golden power, collapsing the glamor he'd created to entice her toward the key.

The woman's humming stopped, her head tilting as she turned, looking around, clearly aware that something had changed. Her eyes scanned the shadows, and he suppressed the desire to reveal himself. Perhaps another selfless act when selfishly he was interested in meeting her to understand where she found the joy to sing as she did. But he doused his godlight—even though he was already hidden in a glamor within the shadows—and waited in the stillness.

She shook her head. "Don't be daft, Brinna," she muttered, then scoffed at herself. "There's no such thing as magic." Her humming resumed as she continued through the woods.

Brinna. Her name.

Luc stayed with her, following her back to a hedge where she disappeared. When she didn't reappear, he returned to the woods and Sevens, waiting for days until she did. He followed her to the meeting house of Sevens once more, and when three atrocious men arrived to claim his woodland fairy and her sisters, Luc was saved from making a very selfish mistake when her own father and brother arrived. He ignored the hope of seeing her in the woods again, of hearing her song, reminding himself repeatedly he wasn't there to watch her. He had a job to do.

Time to move on. As usual. Because that was what Luc did. It was who he was.

So he waited in the woods, and as much as he wanted to see her again, he hoped the next time someone came into the woods, it wouldn't be her. As if the stars answered his hope, the next human through the woods was one of her sisters. And this one, Luc decided as she walked through the forest with efficient purpose, was perfect.

He offered her dollops of sunshine, and where the woodland fairy sang, this one stopped, skeptical, and looked around. He was safe within his glamor in the shadows, of course, but he had the impression she could see through them. Despite what appeared to be her skepticism, his woodland fairy's sister ventured forth anyway, following his drops of sunlight in the falling snow, into the magical meadow. When she found the spelled key, she touched it and disappeared into the enchantment, and Luc took a deep breath.

Yes, he decided. *This one might break the spell.* He had hope, provided Nixus would get out of his own way, and Luc decided that perhaps he needed to visit his brother to push him in the proper direction.

But just before he left Sevens, the woods, and his singing woodland fairy behind, Luc paused, that ever-present tightening around his heart distracting his resolve. He contemplated staying, if only to see her one more time. He imagined running into her, speaking with her, wooing her. But it wouldn't do. He would ruin a woman like that. He carried too much wanderlust—too much like his father—and he didn't trust himself with another's heart. Not a dreamer like her. He couldn't afford to make another mistake.

With a deep breath, Luc closed his eyes, wishing himself from Sevens toward his next adventure. If he could just fill his meaningless existence with distraction, maybe his heart wouldn't remind him of the woman who'd written a song in his heart. So he disappeared from Sevens without any intention of ever returning.

Except...

Aurielle Fareview—sister to his woodland fairy—broke the spell, paving the way for Nix to drag Luc back to Sevens despite his resolve to never—and he was adamant, NEVER—to return. Which paved the way for two of the second-greatest mistakes of his life.

Err in Judgement No. 1

"I don't need to be there," Luc told his brother. "Father has forbidden me from leaving Sol."

"What Father doesn't know won't hurt him. Besides, he'd leave."

Luc gave Nix an impatient look.

Nix—though his intentions were good—seemed to think Luc needed to be out and intended to use his magic to transport him and obscure their whereabouts from their father. Luc couldn't blame his brother for his wanderlust. Nix had been locked up in a spell for ten years, but Roaming to Sevens? This wasn't wandering or sowing oats or any manner of things one did while Roaming, and Luc would know. He'd done it. Missed it, actually. Nix returning to the same place, the same woman repeatedly was… was… well, Luc didn't have a word for it, but it was certainly something tragic.

"You know that's true," Nix said. "Plus, you can get out for a bit."

"Me being there doesn't change a thing. Just come out with it. Why hide that you love her?"

"Auri's trying to figure out how to share the news with her overbearing mother. She's been stuck behind an enchanted hedge that hides their cottage. She has to sneak out to see me."

"Enchanted?" That intrigued him.

Nix's eyes widened and he wiggled his eyebrows, knowing he'd snagged Luc's interest. "You should see it."

It had been on Luc's tongue to tell Nix to go by

himself, but then the memory of his woodland fairy singing in the woods, and his desire to possibly see her just once more, overrode everything else.

"Fine."

The organic wall was indeed enchanted. While he'd seen it before, he hadn't studied it, too concerned with finding a key-keeper, but now he could. When he pressed his hands to the hedge, the pulse of magic flowed through his palms, though looking closer, he could see threads like thin wires of light woven through. The shrub was tall—at least twenty feet—and stretched as far as he could see. The magic wasn't powerful godlight but of a different kind—a spell— like the one he'd cast on Nix.

Luc snatched his hand back and shuddered, wondering why it existed at all.

"How do you find it?" he asked.

"Now, I follow the god-yoke threads I share with her," Nix said.

Luc frowned at the thought of the god-yoke, then frowned at the involuntary thought of Brinna Fareview. Just another thing he felt guilty about.

The horror of it. He couldn't fathom being linked to the same person for the rest of his existence. Seemed a ridiculous notion that there was a single soul that would connect to his. He decided it was natural to be unnerved by the idea of a god-yoke, but despite that, he owed Nix's little mortal Aurielle as much as he owed Nix. She had saved his brother. Saved them all from a demon bent on escape from the underworld. Everyone owed her.

Curious how this connection in conjunction with the spelled hedge worked Luc asked, "And before?"

"She had to show me where it was. But I still miss it sometimes." Then, before he had time to respond, Nix said, "I'm going to collect some flowers for Auri. Wait here," and disappeared into the woods.

Luc grumbled and turned back to look at the hedge once more, walking its length when he heard women's voices—sweet and lilting—coming from inside. He stepped back, searching for the elusive entrance.

"Remember when we were talking to Tarley the other day? About the man in the woods?" Aurielle— he knew her voice—replied.

"So romantic…" the other said, her voice soft and whimsical. Which left only two possibilities: Luc's woodland fairy or the other sister, the one with the dark, soulful eyes. "Why are we doing this again?" she asked.

He wondered which one was with Aurielle and suppressed any hope it might be his singer.

"Well, I've met someone." Aurielle snapped the words, because the other one seemed to be antagonistic about being dragged out into the woods.

He grinned at their bickering. Relatable.

"I have so many questions! You've been behind the hedge since–" The sister's voice cut off abruptly, then she shouted, "The Great Nap Escapade?"

"So," Aurielle said, drawing out the word, "you're

doing this for true love. And I promise, Brin, you won't have to wait long."

Brin.

Brinna.

He ignored the pitter patter of his heart in favor of frowning and pressed his fingers against his breastbone.

There were words spoken Luc couldn't discern, followed by Aurielle bursting from the hedge. She called out for Nix and disappeared across the road through the bramble.

"What if someone comes?" Brinna called, then groaned. "Annoying."

"Couldn't agree more." Luc couldn't see her; she was still hidden within the hedge.

She gasped. "Who's there?"

"The brother."

Her head—like a disembodied apparition— appeared from the hedge, turning to look for him. When she saw him, her eyes widened. It was the first time he realized her eyes were gray.

"Whose brother?"

He hummed but said, "Since we're both on lookout duty, we could make it interesting."

"Who are you, exactly?" she asked, stepping from the hedge.

Luc's breath stopped up, caught up by both disbelief and utter excitement. He was face-to-face with his woodland fairy—though he hadn't been sure why he ever thought of her as his—who stared at him as if he were something unbelievable. While he'd never intended to return, there he was.

"There you are," Luc said, finally finding his voice.

She demanded his name.

"Lucian," he said, turning slightly toward her, his shoulder leaning against the hedge—a terrible choice. He straightened and wiped the leaves from his shoulder.

"And you're not here to meet my sister?"

"Stars, no," he said, allowing himself to truly look at her as he shook his head, grateful, suddenly, that Nix asked him to be his unnecessary companion. "That would be my brother. Come closer." He gave her a slight grin. "I don't bite. Usually."

Her eyes narrowed. "I'm fine right here, thank you."

"You know my name, which gives you power. Will you not offer the same?" Though he already knew it, he wanted her to offer it freely.

"Brinna," she replied and disappeared back into the hedge.

"Wait," Luc called. "Where did you go?" The hedge didn't have an entrance. "Where are you?"

"Here," she whispered, as if daring him to find her. Despite the low volume, her voice reached him, and he wondered, strangely, if it always would.

He used his godlight to sneak through the magical threads of the hedge, and his arms passed through, allowing him to grasp Brinna. Using her as leverage, he pulled himself inside.

She squealed—a cute little sound that seemed as if she was trying to be quiet about it—and stumbled into him, her palms pressed against his chest. Heat seared his skin underneath his clothes where her hands rested.

"What are you doing?" she demanded. "Unhand me."

He did. Immediately. Swiping his hands over the place she'd touched to wipe away the sensation. He hated the added impulse of wanting to wrap her up in his arms.

Ridiculous. He told himself he was curious about this hedge, given he'd never seen anything like it on his Roam.

He walked deeper into an arched passageway that stretched out in front of him with no end in sight, as if it curled in on itself. Surprised by the muted light inside, Luc glanced over his shoulder, where Brinna now stood framed by an arched entrance.

She followed him. "What is wrong with you?"

His internal glow warmed the darkness inside the hedge so he could see her features, which pinched with her frown. He wanted to press his thumb against her mouth, run the pad of it across her lips, but he swallowed the urge instead and looked away.

"If I keep walking, what will I find?" he asked, ignoring her question for one of his own.

"The cottage. Where I live." She paused, then said, "You truly couldn't see me? That seems… unbelievable."

He hummed and looked around. "Perhaps if it

wasn't enchanted."

"Enchanted!" She scoffed, an unflattering kind of snort, but Luc found it… cute. "You must be mistaken."

He snorted back at her, incredulous. "I am not mistaken. Not about this."

"You don't make mistakes?" She offered a sharp laugh.

He'd begun to think this—trapping himself in proximity to her—was one. "Absolutely not," he lied. The very large mistake in his immediate past had nearly cost him his brother, but she didn't need to know about that.

"I highly doubt that." She crossed her arms, her dark eyebrows arching over her pretty eyes. "Now, why are you glowing?"

"Why is this hedge enchanted?" he countered, realizing he should have doused his godlight so his father wouldn't know, but he didn't with her attention finally fixed on him.

They stood facing one another, the hedge seeming to close in around them. He only needed to take a step, and he'd be close enough to draw her into his arms, lean forward, and kiss her. The shrinking hedge and his overpowering urge to touch her made him feel like he couldn't take a deep enough breath.

"How do you get out of here?" The shrinking hedge unnerved him, even if it was an illusion…Then he realized he couldn't see the opening any longer. It had disappeared. He was trapped.

"I need to go," he gasped.

She looked at him with confusion and concern. "Walk." She reached out and touched him once more, her fingers gripping his elbow. His skin burst alive, energy arcing and racing across his flesh until it collided between his shoulder blades.

"Right here," she said, gently guiding him in the right direction.

The entrance materialized.

"It's too tight in here." He rushed past her and stumbled out to the road, gulping breaths, trying to correct his thoughts. Embarrassing.

"Are you okay?" she asked.

Unnerved by her, by his attraction to her, by his embarrassment, he said harsher than he intended, "Of course."

"You just seemed…"

"What?"

"Upset."

He huffed again. "Ridiculous." But he was lying. He had been upset. Upset because he'd wanted more than he should. Upset because he'd looked like a fool.

"Time's up," he said, sending Nix a mental message that he was leaving, even if it would alert his father. And with a quick turn, he left, leaving Brinna standing there, resolving to never have to see her again.

Except…

Err in Judgement No. 2

Luc had sworn never to return to Sevens. He'd told himself any interaction with Brinna was a mistake and to stay as far away as possible. But there he was, in Sevens, attending a country dance.

Nix and Aurielle had gotten in a terrible fight, and though they'd separated for reasons unbeknownst to Luc, the god-yoke was wreaking havoc on his brother's system, dragging him back to Sevens. Luc right along with him.

So, despite Luc's resolve, he couldn't seem to escape the place. Worse yet, he was beginning to look forward to it. This awful little place was where Brinna was, after all.

Wait.

No.

Brinna Fareview. Absolutely not. She was a blight on his peace.

While he would do anything to get away from his banishment at Sol, visiting Sevens didn't seem to be the answer. After what had happened at the hedge, he hadn't been able to stop thinking about Brinna—but he didn't need chaos in his life. With a huff, he ran a hand through his hair, irritated that he was even thinking about her.

But Nix needed him.

Luc owed Nix, so he went.

Brinna was standing with her sisters; his gaze sought her out the moment he and Nix arrived.

"Lucian," she said curtly, a bright blush staining her cheeks. She didn't smile, which irritated him. He was aware how frequently she smiled otherwise.

"Brinna," he replied with equally false apathy. Two could play that game.

She looked away immediately.

As his brother whisked Aurielle out to dance, rather than ask Brinna—which Luc annoyingly wanted to do—he asked her sister Tarley.

Tarley nodded and let him swirl her into the throng of dancers. His gaze, however, returned to Brinna, watching them, a look she severed when she caught his gaze. She rolled her eyes instead and turned her head away.

Feeling devilish, Luc then asked Aurielle to dance, followed by Jessamine, and by the time he appeared before Brinna, her annoyance was a palpable creature with fangs.

"Would you like to dance?" he asked, offering her a grin.

She lifted her gray eyes to meet his. Even as much as she tried to shutter the look of hurt contained within by narrowing them, she replied in a huff, "No. I don't think I do," followed by a haughty shake of her head.

He shrugged, feigning indifference even though disappointment wove a new tapestry knitted with challenge inside him, lighting a fire in his gut. He hadn't had many opportunities to be a hunter, and that spurned his competitive drive to want to claim something even if he wasn't being honest about what it was. So, instead of walking away and leaving her be, he remained at her side.

Brinna, of course, rose to his challenge, remaining where she was. They stood side by side. Self-satisfaction bathed him each time a prospective suitor considered asking Brinna to dance before his eyes flitted in Luc's direction and veered away, taking the suitor's attention elsewhere.

Eventually she whirled on Luc, gray eyes shooting daggers that would've wounded at that range. "Why are you standing there?"

He raised his eyebrows at her with mock innocence. "Am I not allowed to stand here?"

Her mouth opened, then shut. Then she pointed at him. "No one is asking me to dance," she snapped, the tip of her finger poking his chest with each word. "Because of you."

That touch skittered like a skipping stone, shedding heat with each bounce, heat that slid through him with pleasant repercussions. He was suddenly relieved no one had asked her. "I didn't think you wanted to dance," he replied, glancing at where she'd touched him, smug for some reason.

She snatched her hand back and put both hands on her hips. "Who says I don't?"

Luc liked the vibrant way her face glowed in her ire, the way her gray eyes were bluer just then, but he hid the urge to smile, knowing instinctively that it would take whatever game he was playing with her too far. "You did. You said you didn't want to when I asked." He just wanted to win this battle, only he wasn't exactly sure what he'd be winning at this point. Perhaps her acquiescence.

She narrowed her eyes, her hands still on her hips. "I don't want to dance with you!"

"And why not?" He waved a hand at the dance floor as if he were presenting it to her. "Clearly you'd like to dance."

"Because–" She twisted away from him, her arms crossed over her heaving chest. She didn't finish her thought.

"Because?"

She refused to answer, refused to look at him.

"You're angry because I danced with all your sisters before you." He wasn't sure why he wanted her to admit it.

She gasped, her arms falling to her sides as she turned fully toward him. "I am not. I don't even like you."

He quirked an eyebrow. "You don't?"

She leaned forward. "I do not. You're arrogant, condescending, and rude."

He leaned toward her, his gaze dipping to her frowning mouth, rationalizing he was just trying to teach her a lesson as he leaned even closer to whisper in her ear. "Or maybe your pride is just smarting?"

He was hit with her scent, sweet jasmine with a warm layer of summer, and suddenly wondered if he was on the losing end of the game because he wanted to grab hold of her and whisk her somewhere else. He shook off the impulse.

She jerked back as if slapped, and instead of saying anything, turned and walked away.

That wasn't what he'd wanted. He watched her weave through the room and duck out the door into the night, noting a retinue of possible suitors notice the same thing, and for the first time in his entire life, Luc felt two emotions with which he was mostly unfamiliar before Brinna: jealousy and regret, at least where a woman was concerned.

He'd pushed her too far and didn't understand his desire to do it.

So, he followed her out. At least by being near her, he could make sure she was safe.

When he emerged from the meeting house, she wasn't in sight, but he caught a glimmer of her blue dress between the trees. Eventually, he stepped into a small meadow to find her looking up at the night sky. It was beautiful, the light twinkling across the expanse of darkness, and Luc liked that there were bits of his power mixed with Nix's to make something so dazzling.

But when he looked at Brinna, his breath caught, realizing her beauty superseded anything he might have ever created in the whole of his life. With her chin tilted up toward the sky, her silhouette created something otherworldly, as if she was a goddess herself.

His mind retreated into the memory of watching her pull that empty wagon, of her smile and her song. It was a time Brinna wouldn't remember, since Aurielle had changed their reality when she'd broken the spell, but he remembered the unexpected way being near her had made him feel… rattled.

"You shouldn't be out here alone," he said with irritation that didn't make sense. He'd won the battle of wills, after all. He should have felt superior, but he didn't.

She twirled at the sound of his voice and made a frustrated noise as she turned away once more. "I'm trying to get away from you."

"I've upset you."

She lifted her chin. "What are you doing?"

"Making sure you're safe."

"I'm perfectly fine." She glanced at him over her shoulder.

"I'd like to make sure, just the same."

She looked up, shivered, and wrapped her arms around her torso, turned away from him once more. "Suit yourself."

Luc removed his jacket. "Here," he said and draped it over her shoulders. "You're shivering."

Brinna looked from the jacket to him, and he had the impression she was at war with wanting to throw it at him or burrow into its warmth.

He looked up at the sky once more. "You enjoy star gazing?"

Her gaze shifted up. "I find comfort looking at them."

"There's a place I've visited where the stars sparkle in the night sky, and light dances across the sky like fluttering ribbons."

She took a deep breath. "That must be beautiful." She paused, then said, "I like the stories about them. I used–" But she stopped.

"Used to?" he asked, suddenly curious.

But she didn't continue, and though he was curious to know what she'd been about to tell him, he was content to let it drop.

A few moments later, he turned to face her, needing to find a way across the bridge he'd burned. "I wasn't trying to hurt your feelings, *mi alora*. Earlier… by waiting to ask you to dance."

She turned to look at him. "Mi alora?" she asked, using ancient *Ra'ha*, the language of the gods.

Confused, Luc tilted his head. "What? Where did you hear that? How do you know *Ra'ha?*"

"*Ra'ha?* You just said it. What does that mean?"

Luc swallowed and straightened, his heart skittering a haphazard rhythm in his chest. Why had he used old language, that particular phrase? With her? "I did?"

My heart.

Brinna nodded.

Rather than admit it, admit what it meant, because his heart was bumbling around inside his chest with a mixture of feeling—confusion, anxiety, anticipation—

he turned to face her. "I would like to make it up to you," he deflected. "May I have a dance? Under the stars?"

"Here?"

He saw she liked the idea by the way her countenance softened, so he took a step closer, anticipating her scent once more. "Yes. Here," he replied. "Allow me to make amends."

When she nodded, he dipped a hand under the jacket still draped over her shoulders and slid it around her waist to the center of her back, then folded his hand around hers. Chills raced across his skin, and he urged her a touch closer.

Brinna complied, and Luc, because he was still his devilish self, pulled her even closer until they were firmly pressed against one another. Then he danced with Brinna Fareview—his singing woodland fairy— with the music in the distance, in that little meadow under the stars. His memories of her careened around inside him, clashing with the feelings he had seeing her, the need he felt to remain near her, and the curiosity he felt to allow himself the pleasure of kissing her just once.

They danced.

"Brinna?" he asked, longing to see the sparkle in her eyes.

She made a soft questioning sound as she lifted her face.

His eyes dropped to her mouth, to that little divot in her bottom lip. Without considering the consequences, he leaned forward and pressed his mouth to hers, nipping at her bottom lip. She gasped, then relaxed into him, tilting her head, inviting the kiss to continue.

Their swaying stopped, the dance forgotten, and Luc slid a hand up her spine under his jacket draped over her shoulders, pressing her even closer.

Her hands wrapped around him; her softness pressed against his chest.

When she made a needy sound, his control slipped, and with his tongue, he explored that little divot until her lips parted, allowing him in. The moment she did, the kiss caught fire and he lost reason, as just a taste turned more substantial and wishful.

A shout and a laugh in the distance tore the kiss apart.

Brinna touched her mouth, a little sound of shock in the space between them.

Afraid of what he'd done, of the sensations crawling through him filling up the space inside of him with longing, he stepped back. "There. Obligatory dance given." He swiped his hands together and took another step away from her.

"Excuse me?"

"Just trying to keep my brother happy," he lied.

With a groan of frustration—and maybe hurt—she pulled his jacket from her shoulders and shoved it against his chest. Then without a word, Brinna walked back toward the meeting house, leaving him both happy she was returning to safety without him having to carry her there, and angry with himself for hurting her. Again.

He sighed, knowing it was for the better.

He would never return to Sevens again.

Never see Brinna.

And that was just fine with him. At least, that was the lie he told himself.

Brinna, third daughter of Tomas and Scarlett Fareview, stood near a wall in the courtyard at the Copper Pot Inn watching the revelry of the wedding party, uneasy at the prospect she no longer felt content and unsure what to do to change it. She was happy for her older sister Tarley, and Tarley's new husband, who had disappeared some time ago, but as the celebration continued that uneasy feeling grew stronger. Instead of overwhelming herself with such an unruly thought, Brinna straightened her skirts and focused on the beautiful spectacle.

The cold of the fall night—crisp and clear—

caressed her exposed skin. There were so many people in Sevens, strangers, most of them, dressed in an array of colorful finery glimmering in the flickering candlelight. Tall spires of fire offered both heat and light. Glasses filled with spirits glinted like fairy lights flitting through the forest as people moved, and the din of their conversation and laughter carried like notes swirling with the music over the cobblestones of the courtyard. People danced to the music, a flurry of movement like snowflakes riding a breeze.

It was romantic.

Brinna loved everything romantic—not that she had any experience in that department. But as much as she loved it, pressing the fingers of one gloved hand against her fluttering heart, she couldn't help but feel that perhaps not only would she never have this, but also that the moment Tarley left Sevens, a bit of Brinna's purpose would leave with her sister.

She had been her siblings' keeper her whole life.

Scanning the crowd, she looked for her family, her eyes skipping over strangers to her parents speaking with the groom's parents. The king and queen of Jast! In Sevens, of all places!

She found Jessamine dancing with a Jast soldier, though Brinna wasn't sure who since there were many. Not that she'd had any means to meet any of them. Scarlett had kept the family busy at the cottage with wedding preparations, preventing opportunities for socializing. "It's too dangerous," her mother had warned them, justifying the sequester.

Brinna's brother Mattias was across the courtyard, frowning at something—or someone—though she couldn't tell what or whom from her place. He just seemed to glower at the dancers in general. Since returning from his errand for the Queen of Kaloma and since the events in the meadow Brinna had only heard about, Mattias had been moodier. She wondered if perhaps he needed to talk about it. There'd been so little time to debrief the recent events, that Brinna had barely been able to make sense of them herself.

A few steps away from Mattias, Auri and her suitor Nixus Uraiahs danced together, twirling with the rest of the revelers. Nixus bent toward Auri to say something in her ear, and she offered him a secret smile as she moved closer. They lost all semblance of the dance steps and just held on to one another. Given Nixus's announced intentions, Brinna suspected there would be another wedding soon, which added to her own unease about her place in the world.

Considering her angst, she scanned the vicinity for Lucian—Nixus's brother—who was conspicuously absent. Brinna suppressed the urge to roll her eyes.

Figured.

Lucian was an escape artist. The last time she'd seen him had been a few weeks ago, and as it always was when they were together, it had been a disaster.

While sequestered, their mother hadn't been able to keep Lachlan or Nixus from Tarley and Auri, despite her best efforts. It was clear that Scarlett didn't exactly approve of either of the sisters' suitors but lacked the ability to do anything about it. Though Brinna didn't understand her mother's disapproval, it seemed excessive. Brinna could clearly see both men adored her sisters, but then their mother hadn't ever been one to relax her protective instincts. Brinna didn't think it had anything really to do with the men and more with whatever secret Scarlett was protecting.

On one such day, Auri had insisted Nixus be allowed to visit, but Scarlett had adamantly refused him admittance to the cottage. So Brinna had followed Auri under the guise of keeping her sister safe, but really wanted to see if Lucian had come with his brother. He had.

He'd been standing off to the side, leaning up against the trunk of a tree, the sunlight through the leaves drifting over his beautiful features. "Brinna."

She'd narrowed her eyes, annoyed at him for being so beautiful, but mostly for acting like such a cad. She'd still been smarting after the dance weeks ago. He'd been so rude, but she was resolved to take the high road.

"Lucian."

He'd grinned.

She'd gritted her teeth and looked away.

Auri and Nix had nearly disappeared down the roadway. "We're going for a walk," Nix had called and waved.

"Looks like it's you and me again on chaperone duty. Shall we?" Lucian had asked, stepping into the road, and offering his arm.

As much as Brinna had been tempted to accept his

gentlemanly offer—it was sort of chivalrous on his part—she'd just looked at him, untrusting. "Are you sure you aren't interested in asking one of my other sisters to accompany you?"

His grin had widened, and she'd hated that he knew how much his behavior had affected her. "Well, it would seem that you're the only one present."

She'd pressed her teeth together harder and started up the dirt road without him.

He'd laughed behind her.

She'd suppressed the urge to run ahead to leave him behind.

Within a few steps he was even with her, his stupid arm bumping hers. She'd hated that tingles raced along her skin every time it did, sending delightfully warm sensations through her body. Well, she'd wanted to hate them.

They'd walked along in silence, the breeze in the coupled with birds tweeting and warbling from their branches. Their steps had crunched along the roadway, and Auri's laughter had burst out like music as she and Nix had walked arm in arm up ahead.

Brinna couldn't appreciate there was music everywhere, her companion riled her so, but she had suddenly found herself hating the animosity that existed between them.

"Why do you dislike me?" she'd asked.

He'd come to a complete stop so that when Brinna had turned to face him, he'd been several paces behind her. "Dislike you? I don't—" His brow had furrowed as he'd shaken his head, but he hadn't been able to meet her gaze.

"Then why—"

"Don't be ridiculous," he'd said, picking up the pace and passing her. "I don't feel any given way about this or that."

"Are you saying I'm ridiculous?"

Lucian had suddenly seemed flustered, his mouth opening, then closing. He'd shaken his head. "I just forgot," he'd said, "I have somewhere… an appointment. I have to go."

Then he was gone, had disappeared in that strange way that she'd seen Nixus do, leaving her on the roadway alone.

He'd reappeared suddenly, grabbing hold of her. "Not safe alone," he'd muttered, and in the blink of an eye she was in front of Auri and Nix on the road, Lucian gone once more, leaving her more confused and annoyed than ever.

Now, she shook away her irritation and focused on what mattered. Her heart thumped with the rhythm of such a happy occasion, especially considering the chaos of late. With both Tarley and Auri losing their protective ribbons, the revelation that Nixus was the actual god of night and darkness, and that the horrid Dr. Rufus had been a horrible creature hunting Tarley for her blood, things had been stressful to say the least. Brinna had so many questions.

Grabbing hold of her own ribbon as if to ground her thoughts, she twisted it around her wrist, so the bow was on top. Her secret unease, which she was very good at hiding, receded some. Their mother was the only way they were going to get answers, and she'd promised to provide them after the wedding.

Mattias caught her eye as he skirted the dancers toward the inn. She didn't like that her brother looked so unhappy—especially on such a night when celebration was in order. He was only nineteen, which might have been a factor. Brinna remembered the morose way Sevens and the Whitling Woods sank their teeth into her thoughts when she'd been his age. The horrible feeling that she might be stuck forever when there didn't seem to be any other options. Perhaps they still did. And yet, as the party swirled around her, all the people, the vibrancy of both exemplified a broader world beyond where they'd been raised.

There was hope.

She started after her brother, if not to change his mind but to offer her moral support. That was who she was, after all. Jessamine was the perfect one, Tarley was the proper amount of sour to Brinna's sweet, Auri was the realist, and Mattias was the baby and the only boy. So Brinna slipped into her role as the nurturer and went to look for her brother. Her sisters might not need her, but maybe her brother still did.

After bypassing the throng of people and entering the dining room where the feast had been held, she scanned the room. Only Mattias wasn't anywhere to be seen.

"Evening, Miss Fareview."

Brinna turned her head and smiled at Horance, one of the proprietors of The Copper Pot Inn. "Hello, Mr. Rose. A lovely wedding, though I think we're long past evening," she replied with a smile.

He nodded, grinning back. "True enough."

"Have you seen Mattias?"

Horance glanced around, then shook his head. "Not for some time. Not since dinner."

Confused, because she was sure Mattias had only

just walked into the inn, she looked around once more, thanked Horance, and returned to the festivity outside. Spinning in place, she shivered, the chill of the night suddenly colder as she realized Mattias was nowhere to be seen. Worry climbed into her chest, adding to the weight of her unease, and she wondered if he might have left for the cottage. Knowing it would snap their mother's nerves, Brinna couldn't imagine Mattias going expressly against her wishes. Their mother had forbidden any of the family to be without one another for the sole purpose of safety—or so she'd said.

But Mattias was nowhere to be seen. He wouldn't have just left, would he? Could he be in trouble?

Her heart thumped at the thought.

With a glance at her parents, she considered interrupting them, but they were dancing, and her mother was smiling. It seemed such a long time since Scarlett had smiled. Brinna let them be, turning back to the darkness beyond the fire, and though she knew she shouldn't leave, her worry for her brother drove her forward. He shouldn't be alone.

"Mattias!" she called, wishing they'd lit the lanterns along the main thoroughfare of Sevens, but every lamp was currently being used at the inn. Her voice sounded muted, as if it hit a wall and dropped back into the dirt. She wasn't afraid so much as concerned for Mattias—and slightly annoyed at the inconvenience of having to look for him instead of finding an agreeable partner to dance with.

If she were being honest with herself, there hadn't

been anyone she'd been expressly interested in dancing with, even if there were some handsome fellows. Except for Lucian, who was expressly beautiful but horribly unapproachable. She ignored that she wanted to dance with him again; she refused to give him the satisfaction.

She hated that she'd waited for him earlier that day with that ridiculous hope fluttering inside her chest. Hated that she longed to see his golden face even knowing how aloof and uninterested he'd been the last several times they'd met. Except there was what had happened before the descent into the chaos of Tarley and the darkling. The dance she had shared with Lucian underneath the stars. She hated that she'd spent far too much time recalling that dance in the forest with him that had obviously met more to her than it should have. Hated that she'd dreamt of him nearly every night. Hated that of all the things she was looking forward to for her sister Tarley's wedding, it was the thought that he might be there.

So when Lucian Uraiahs had arrived at the wedding with his brother, Brinna had been standing near Tarley on the dais. The two men arrived like the strike of a match, a shift in the energy of the room grabbing her notice. Upon seeing them, Brinna had snapped her gaze forward, catching on the lace of Tarley's dress, trying to calm the racing of her heart. And as much as she told herself not to look, she hadn't been able to contain her gaze, allowing it to drift back to where he'd been standing. For just a brief second.

She'd realized her imagination hadn't been better than the real thing. Wearing a light suit—barely gray—with a white shirt and pink tie, he'd been such a contrast to his brother dressed in darkness. Such strange clothes compared to what she was used to seeing men wear in Sevens. He'd looked like a beautiful sunrise, his golden glow ever present. As she'd studied him, his bright, golden eyes had connected with hers, his dark brows shifting slightly along with a slight tilt of his dark, blond head.

She'd looked away as a flush had crept up her skin, and hated that he'd see, that he'd know.

Shortly after the start of the wedding celebration, he'd disappeared. Typical. Brinna hated that she'd been disappointed. What truly was there to be disappointed about? Lucian Uraiahs was an insufferable, pompous stiff-neck, too prideful for his own good.

So, that left all the other agreeable gentlemen to meet, she supposed, and she would just have to dance with them all. Once she'd returned with Mattias. How was she to meet the love of her life without opening the door to find him?

Her dainty new boots crunched over the scree of the roadway, and she pulled up her skirts to keep them from dragging along the dusty ground. "Mattias!" she called again. She'd made it to the middle of the village where the meeting house stretched out across the street beyond the green. She could see the shadowed outline of the large tree and turned to look back at the inn, wondering if perhaps Mattias hadn't left. Thinking that this—venturing out into the darkness alone—was careless.

A raven squawked.

No longer walking, Brinna stood at the center of the village and yelled for Mattias once more. No answer. No Mattias.

Yes. It had been silly to venture out by herself. There were so many places in the inn to check first.

She turned back.

A resounding crunch against the roadway called her attention, and Brinna looked over her shoulder. A man was illuminated by the faint light from the inn and the intermittent moonlight shining between the clouds. She couldn't see him clearly but could tell he was pale, and his lips appeared to curl with a smile, though its shape was unsettling. He smoothed his gloved hands over the dark wool of his jacket—a nervous gesture. "Hello?"

Had she dreamed this? It felt... familiar somehow.

Brinna's heartbeat quickened both with excitement and trepidation. He had a nice voice. How many times had she imagined meeting a handsome stranger in Sevens? Too many to count, though in her dreams, the faceless suitor hadn't been found in the dark, but often overwhelmed her with light. She squinted now too, only it wasn't because of the brightness, but rather the fact she couldn't see clearly in the dark.

He started toward her, his steps nearly

imperceptible on the roadway.

Brinna remained fixed to her spot, turning toward him. "You're late for the party," she said.

The man smiled wider, and now that he was closer, she noticed his ink-black hair shimmered blue when he moved, like a crow in the sunshine. His skin held a bluish hue tinted by the shadows of the night. "Perhaps you might help me find my way?" he asked. His voice was rather alluring—deep and resonant— and Brinna, despite the discomfited perception coating her rational thoughts, her irrationality seemed to take control.

He smiled, his teeth bright behind his smile.

Brinna tilted her head, considering him, feeling a strange sensation run the length of her spine. It wasn't pleasant, culminating in her belly, and she took a step away from him with an impulse to run, even if propriety insisted on hospitality. With another glance back at the party, she considered leaving the man to fend for himself, only she wasn't one to be rude. "The wedding is just that way. I can show you," she told him, and waited politely as he approached.

"Brinna!" A new voice cut through the night, the sound cracking just a touch behind her invitation like an echo. "No! Run!"

Brinna swiveled in place, looking at the shadows of the tree on the green once more as a man emerged from the darkness moving swiftly toward her, too quick to even to make him out albeit for the light he emitted.

Something hissed.

As if in slow motion, she turned back to the stranger, registering the change in his face, now sharp and angular with hollowed dark eyes, the whites swallowed by darkness, blood-red mouth lined with sharp teeth. It reached a clawed-hand out for her— "mine," the voice hissed, no longer alluring, but terrifying in its other-worldly sound grating against her ears. Cold rushed toward her.

She leaned away, opening her mouth to scream when a rush of warmth hit her like a wall. White-hot heat banded her waist, rushing up her back to her neck drawing her into its safety. It was followed by a flash of a bright light before everything turned white around her, blinding her. Then everything disappeared

Brinna

Not quite prepared for what had just occurred in the dark of Sevens, Brinna's imagination seemed the safest place to retreat, so she decided she must have been dreaming.

The bright light.

The warmth.

The sensation of both being suspended and sinking.

A heavy weight banded around her waist and a resistance at her back affecting the air fighting to move through her lungs.

It all pointed to that alternate reality.

She'd spent a lot of time in her imagination over

her twenty-five years of life. Certainly, living in a tiny cottage in the woods with a family of six other people required a healthy dose of imagination. She'd conjured all sorts of adventures. Some stories made her the hero, while in others she was the villain. Sometimes, she was the damsel, and sometimes the savior. She'd constructed tales where she went to battle with an evil wizard or found buried treasure. And that was when she was awake. Her dream world was even better, vibrant and detailed, filled with fantasy and worlds where it was safe to explore, to be someone else, someone without all the expectations about who she was supposed to be.

"Are you okay?" a deep voice asked.

The resistance around her eased and she was turned, a tender grip around each of her arms.

When Brinna opened her eyes, Lucian Uraiahs, was holding her. His head was bent with its dark, honey hair, obscuring what she knew to be a breathtaking face. He seemed to be looking for something on her person, which didn't make sense.

But a dream? Yes. That made sense. He'd never be holding her like this in reality. He was an arrogant snob, even if he was beautiful. Tall and sinewy, wide shouldered with a tapered waist, skin tanned by the sun. Brinna loved meeting him in her dreams, which happened quite frequently, even if it was all she had.

When he looked up, his eyes met hers. Such beautiful eyes, their golden intensity streaked with amber striations. "Are you bit?" he asked, dimples hinting in his cheeks even as he frowned. His wide hands slid up her bare arms until he was standing before her, inspecting her shoulders, her neck, her face.

Bit?

Dazed and unsettled, Brinna took a step away from the golden god and wrapped her arms around herself under her cloak. She shook her head. "I'm dreaming."

It was the only explanation.

First, it was daytime. Golden light gilded Lucian's beautiful features. Hadn't it just been nighttime? Second, this version of Lucian looked concerned, interested. In her limited experience with him, that wasn't Lucian Uraiahs. Aloof, condescending, even. In reality, she'd only ever seemed an obligation, to him.

Stars, he was beautiful, and her breath struggled against that awareness as he tilted his head to the side, studying her. She smiled. "I am really good at this. This is going to be fun."

Lucian's eyebrows, a shade darker than his golden hair, lowered. "Excuse me? Good at what?"

Confirmation she was dreaming. The real Lucian Uraiahs would never condescend to be confused.

She looked him up and down, smirking at having the upper hand. This was why she loved her dreams because she'd never have the upper hand in reality. Her eyes caught first in the varied hues of his hair, hanging around his face, then roved over the hint of golden stubble gracing the strong planes of his features.

At her perusal, his eyebrows rose over his glittering eyes.

She continued over the contours of his throat, revealed by his loosened tie and the undone top buttons of his shirt. Her eyes slid across his broad shoulders, still covered in the sleek gray fabric of his suit jacket, then down the plane of his chest. When she got to his pelvis, she tilted her head, then allowed her gaze to travel down his legs, shown off in the slim fit of his trousers. Finally, she dipped her gaze to his dapper shoes, displaying his ankles and the golden skin on the tops of his feet.

"Seen enough?" he asked.

She'd had dreams like this before. Gorgeous man. Exotic, warm location. The promise of something physical to release her pent-up frustration. Looking at this masculine conjuring, excitement swept through her at this realistic manifestation of Lucian. He was so detailed, and as often as she'd dreamed of him, he'd never have been standing with her looking so perplexed.

No. The Lucian she knew would smirk at her, offer her sarcasm. Then he'd run away.

She stepped toward him, pressed both palms against his chest, then spread her fingers wide.

His muscles tensed under her touch. "What are you doing?"

"I haven't ever created one to look as perfect as you. But it makes sense. You are magnificent."

"You're in shock." He grabbed her hands and removed them, but didn't release her.

The warmth of his touch sizzled up her arms. She

looked from his hand wrapped around her wrists up to his face. "Shock? No. I'm just dreaming."

He squeezed her wrists. "This is real," he insisted.

"You'd never be here with me. Not for real."

"What?" He released her, then. "That isn't true. I'm with you here, now. For real."

She laughed softly. "But you're different from the others I've dreamed up. They're usually darker. More dangerous."

"Wait." Lucian's brows dipped again. "I'm very dangerous."

Her eyes snapped up to his, and she laughed. "Oh. Really? You look more like I've conjured someone from the realm of Elysian in need of wings. Maybe I should add some."

He tilted his head. "You think you've conjured me? Where do you think you are?"

"In my dream, of course." She paused and looked down at her clothes. "I'm wearing what I wore to the wedding. Hmm." Then she looked up at him once more, tilting her head. "My dreams don't usually talk back. They just do what I want."

His eyebrows twitched, and his surprise seemed to give way to something different. "And what is it you want? Usually?"

"You're a curious conjuring of Lucian. I wish you were this curious in real life." She grinned at him. "Sex, of course."

This admission—which Brinna would never have said in her waking life, especially not to Lucian

Uraiahs—seemed to stun him momentarily. He cleared his throat and shoved his hands into his pockets. "And how does that usually occur? Do you remove your coat first?" His eyes went to her hair and lingered there, then dropped to her hands as she unbuttoned her dark blue cloak.

His face was serious for the moment as he watched her, weighted with something new Brinna decided was desire. She could feel the tension, how sensual it felt to hear the slide of her clothing as she removed it. To feel the heft of his gaze. It increased the pace of her heartbeat, of the breath moving through her lungs. She drew the cloak from her shoulders.

"This feels more real than my other dreams. I don't usually have to remove my clothes; they just sort of fall away. Perhaps this is one of those kinds of fantasies."

His eyes jumped from the cloak in her hands to her face, and his intensity connected somehow to the beating of her heart, as if it were a power source increasing its rhythm which in turn heated her blood.

His dimples deepened as he spoke. "And what kind of fantasy is that?"

"The slow kind. The kind where we watch one another pleasure ourselves and–"

His eyes widened, and his hands came up in front of him. "Whoa," he interrupted.

She draped the cloak over her arm and fingered the velvet. "I don't think I've ever noticed the feel of fabric before. In a dream." She lifted her feet and twirled a booted ankle. "The sensations feel–"

"Real?" Lucian asked.

Brinna straightened as she set her feet back on the floor and admired his form, though the gray jacket obscured much of it. "Exactly." She stepped toward him until there was but a breath between them, then looked up.

His regard was as palpable as a touch. "And in these dreams," he asked, his voice low and husky, "do you usually undress the object of your fantasy?"

"Well, no. Sometimes he undresses me. And sometimes his clothes are just gone." She snapped her fingers.

"But it's not the same in every dream?"

"Oh. No. I like variation."

His eyebrows rose. "That's—" But he couldn't seem to find the words and swallowed, clearing his throat as he did.

"Keeps things interesting," she said, then took a moment to look around. She frowned. "I can't remember talking so much in a dream. Or being so aware of each moment. I feel like in the ones I like most, there's very little talking."

"You don't like talking."

"Oh. I do. I love it. Especially dirty talking." She smirked and offered him a wink. "In my dreams, there's more acceptance of forgoing that nicety, and just getting to the good stuff."

He threw his head back and laughed, dimples deep.

She loved his laugh, like summer-day fun at the river. She noticed the line of his neck, the flow of it as it disappeared between the white collar of his shirt. Then she frowned again. This was a very strange dream. "We should probably get on with it," she said, laid her cloak over the back of a nearby chair, and began rolling her gloves from her arms. "The worst kind of dream is getting all that way to the sex part, and then, utter disappointment at not getting the full experience because I wake up."

He cleared his throat. "Full experience?"

"Right." She waved her hand about between them. "When the head of dream man's co—"

"Wait!" Lucian reached out and pressed his hand against her mouth, startling her. "Stop."

His skin against hers felt so real. She tested the taste with the tip of her tongue: salty and earthy. She wanted another sample, but he snatched his hand back, and she laughed, loving this dream.

"I may be a god, but there's only so much I can take. I'm not that altruistic." He paused and took a deep breath, his cheeks a tinge darker, then glanced at his palm before fisting his hand. "This is real. I'm real. You're real." He pointed at her, then swirled his finger around between them. "Not dreaming. Don't you remember?"

It was her turn to laugh. "Remember what? None of that proves this is real. First, we barely know one another. Knowing those things only reinforces that you're up here." She tapped her head. "You'd never be talking to me like this in real life. You're aloof, supercilious, and always leaving me behind."

"I am not." He frowned. "I do not."

She laughed. "You are and you do!"

"You were looking for Mattias–"

Wait.

She had been. She'd been at Tarley and Lachlan's wedding. Had she fallen asleep? "How would you know–" The face of a monster filled her mind, and she swayed on her feet as the fear that had been absent now flooded her chest, filling her lungs, and making it harder to breathe. "Oh–" Her eyes jumped to Lucian standing in front of her. "Wait." She shook her head.

He fisted his hands at his sides. "I think you should sit," he said, then waved a hand at something behind her.

Shaken, she looked over her shoulder and realized she was in a sitting room of sorts, only the space was giant; at least ten of her family's cottages could fit inside it. And it looked nothing like any room she'd ever seen in her whole life.

Beautiful couches—several of them—the color of bare bones, were placed around the room. Plush rugs covered bright, slick surfaces reflecting light. There were no walls but rather a wide expanse of clear windows without mullioned panes glowing with a bright expanse of brilliant blue, the sun gilding the room. She had the sensation they were floating in the sky.

This had to be a dream.

Her breath snapped in her chest at the spectacle. There were so many things she could have said. Things like *what was that creature? Where am I?* And to Lucian, *why are you here? Where am I?* But what came out was: "It's daytime." As if that proved it was a dream.

Lucian's hand pressed gently against her lower back. "Come. Sit."

She moved where he'd directed, stepping down and sitting stiffly on the edge of one of the couches. Her gaze drifted to the windows. "But–"

"Brinna."

His concerned tone snapped her gaze to his.

He swiped a hand over his face, his palm stretching over his mouth, then sighed.

She swallowed and recalled the creature's face, its horrible teeth. The snarl. Her gaze jumped from a button on Lucian's jacket to his eyes. "That wasn't real?"

Her brother and sisters had tried to explain. She'd had dreams of feral creatures, but that... thing... she'd... Brinna covered her face with her hands with a sob. "I'm not dreaming?"

"That was a darkling."

She gasped behind her hands.

"I brought you to Elcadia. To Sol. There wasn't time–"

She swiped her cheeks with her fingertips and looked at Lucian, who was now crouched down in front of her. The light, the heat, the stronghold had been him. "My family–"

"I summoned Nix. He knows."

"Is it going to hunt... Tarley?"

Lucian looked down at his hands, then back up. "I don't know. It went after you. It could have just been intent on killing. But you offered it help before I transported us here. It may have imprinted."

"Does this mean I can't go home?"

Lucian took a seat on the table in front of her, his thighs protectively caging hers between them. "To be safe, probably not until we've spoken with Nix. Learn if anything happened after I turned us here."

"But Mattias. I couldn't find him. What if–"

Lucian shook his head. "I'd been standing under the tree for a while. I never saw Mattias pass by."

"This isn't a dream?" she asked.

He shook his head.

Her skin heated and she covered her face, appalled at her behavior. Stars, she'd been so forward. With Lucian Uraiahs. "I think you should take me home."

"I can't do that, Brinna–"

"Why?"

"It isn't safe. Not if it has your scent. Not if it wants to hunt you."

She jumped up from her seat. "But my family! They need to be warned."

"Nix is with them. He won't leave them if they aren't safe."

She sank back onto the seat and folded over with her head between her knees. "Wake up, Brinna. Wake up." But she couldn't. This was real, and her imagination—no matter how adept—wouldn't be able to get her out of this mess.

Watching Brinna kicked up worry inside of him. She was an emotional tempest, trying to seduce him moments before folding into a storm of fear and shock. Now bent over herself as she sat on the couch where he'd led her, he shouldn't have let her go on about it being a dream for so long, but damn him, he'd been so interested to see where she'd go with it. But it was Brinna, and he was way more than just curious. He was desirous.

No. No, he informed himself. He wasn't. She was a blight. He just had to keep reminding himself of that, only doing so was getting more difficult.

He slid forward to the edge of the table, a touch closer to her. "I can imagine you're overwhelmed..." he started, wanting to comfort her but sorely lacking the ability. When had he ever needed to make anyone feel better? Better yet, when had he ever wanted to?

She raised her head to look at him, her tear-streaked face distracting and tugging on something inside of him that felt very uncomfortable.

"And that perhaps you're overcome with relief at my benevolent intervention," he continued. "It's because of Aurielle–"

Brinna straightened and narrowed her eyes, now frosty. "Auri?"

Luc swallowed, worried that perhaps he wasn't saying the right thing, but like a rock rolling downhill he continued his course. "And I appreciate your gratitude, but it really isn't necessary."

"You think I'm feeling grateful?" Her voice was icy. "Because you're obligated?"

"Obligated?" He preferred the Brinna who thought they'd been in a dream, her voice warm and sensual. He wasn't sure why she'd suddenly turned cold. He'd saved her. "Of course you're grateful. Otherwise, you'd have been a darkling's meal."

Brinna slowly got to her feet and glared down at him. "You arrogant ass. My family is in danger, and you think I'm sitting here thinking about what you did?"

Luc regarded her—stars, she really was gorgeous, and just then looked like an avenging angel. He liked it but shook his head.

"I need to go home." She picked up her skirts and climbed up the step, passing her cloak, before spinning in place with a nervous energy she couldn't seem to keep contained.

His eyes narrowed. "I can't do that." He stood.

She whirled back to him. "Excuse me?"

"I owe your sister. And if your life is in danger, then I must do what I can."

She crossed her arms over her chest. "You owe… Auri?"

He took a step closer. "A long story, but yes. Taking you back is a terrible idea. Not without more information. I can't in good conscience—even if I've only just seemed to acquire one—take you back to your death."

Brinna's crossed arms unfolded and fell to her sides. "You're abducting me?"

"No." Luc shook his head, throwing his hands out. "No!"

"Then you're being heavy-handed," she snapped, her eyes tracking him as he moved closer.

Her ire was tinder for his own, and he lashed out. "For wanting to keep you safe?"

"Yes."

"You'd rather I pretend to be a voiceless fantasy you can fuck?" He was too close to her, her silk bodice close to his chest, and he chastised himself for imagining running his hands up her sides to feel the slick fabric, her curves under his palms.

Her mouth dropped as her cheeks reddened. "How awful of you. I would never–"

"Except for in your dreams." He liked the red of her cheeks, and his body tingled, flaring to life, thinking all the ways he would explore that blush, incite it further. But he was as irritated as he was turned on.

Brinna crossed her arms over her chest once more and looked away, cutting off the connection. "Take me back."

"Fine," he snapped, grasping her arms. "That's what you want?" The room faded to gold, then flashed white before the dark forest materialized around them.

It should have been easy to leave her there—she'd asked for it—and it would eliminate the temptation of her being so close. But it wasn't. She'd be in danger. He'd never been able to leave her knowing danger lurked. And besides, the thought of leaving her tugged on his chest like threads pulled taut, as if she'd cast a line and snared him. As much as he was a solitary creature, he hadn't wanted to bring her back to the forest—a realization that confused him as much as it irked him.

Brinna rustled her fancy skirt, running her hands over the fabric as if to press out any wrinkles. Straightening her bare shoulders, she wrapped her arms around herself, then shivered. Luc remembered her cloak was still draped over the edge of the chair where she'd set it.

"Thank you." She wouldn't look at him.

Even though he wasn't supposed to, Luc extended

his golden glow to bring her inside a bubble of warmth and light. "Brinna."

"I can see myself home." She turned and walked away, her boots crunching through the woods, leaving him and the warm light behind.

"Brinna," he called, his ire cooling rapidly. Those strings tugging on his heart pulled harder as he watched her walk away.

She ignored him. When she was nearly swallowed by the darkness, she hesitated.

He could hear her breath whipping through her in short gasps. When a crashing sound cut through the dark forest, followed by a screech, she jumped.

His anger—gone now—had refined into a different feeling, something more patient and compassionate, leaving him to contend with its unfamiliarity, but also something more fearful. He knew he couldn't —wouldn't— leave her there. "Brinna," he repeated, quietly, hoping she would come willingly.

She turned, shivering, and snapped, "You couldn't have whisked me to the cottage?"

He shook his head, unprovoked by her hostility. "I can't find it. Only Aurielle has ever led Nix there." Brinna had led him there. Once. He paused, and she faced the forest once more, her back to him. His gaze caught on the softness of her neck, the tendrils curling around her pale skin, and he had the urge to go to her and gather her in his arms, offer her comfort. But he didn't. "Brinna? Please give me some time to take care of the darkling. Then I'll bring you back, I promise."

Still, she remained where she was. "Everything looks the same."

He glanced out at the forest, sensing something in the darkness, and cast a brighter light, reaching out further to make sure Brinna was inside the boundary. He could raise the sun, but it was too soon. "Will you return with me? Where it's warmer." He sighed. "I'm sorry for getting angry–"

She whirled around. "Because I'm just an obligation, right?"

Luc straightened and finally recognized the words he'd spoken the night he kissed her as they'd danced. Recognized the lie. He'd hurt her, he realized. He shook his head. "It was wrong to say."

"But still the truth," she said, her back to him once more, and Luc wondered if there was more to it than just this careless lie. She hugged herself, rubbing her arms. "How long will it take? Taking care of the darkling?"

He didn't know, so he didn't say. "I'd like to get you somewhere safe. We can talk about this there."

With a sigh, Brinna turned back. "Fine."

Rather than giving her time to change her mind, Luc closed the distance and held out his hand. For a beat she just stared at it, but then placed her hand in his. The moment Luc pulled them into the portal, another ghastly screech sounded—closer—as they left the forest behind.

Returning to Sol was strange. While it served as his

god-seat, he hadn't spent much time there, at least not until his father had sequestered him. Prior to that, Luc's use of Sol had been as a stopping off place between Roaming, trying to free Nix, and whatever else he could find to occupy his time. But since being forced to stay, he'd had to come to terms with being alone with his thoughts, alone with himself. Which was torture.

And yet, seeing Brinna in danger, where to take her, he hadn't hesitated. Sol had called to him then as much as it did now as it materialized around them. Only now, he was returning with someone and wouldn't scurry off again, and that filled him with a feeling he couldn't name and decided it was best he didn't try.

Somewhere between Brinna taking his hand in the woods and the return, Luc had her in his arms. The proximity of her had him remembering her earlier actions, her unfettered and unabashed belief that they'd been immersed in a fantasy inside her mind, which resumed playing like a fevered dream in his own. Even with fabric layers between them, he thought about her hands on him, and his pulse quickened, her brazen look and words effervescing like warm sunshine in his bloodstream. Recalling the way she'd removed her cloak lit a fire at the base of his spine.

He frowned at an ache that compressed his heart. Nope. Nope. A blight.

Brinna opened her eyes, glancing at him quickly before looking away. "Oh." She jerked out of his embrace and took another step away. "I don't…"

His heart stalled and pinched as he studied her. He'd seen beauty, a feat impossible to forgo when Roaming. But he couldn't remember the sensation of his body feeling both lost and found because of it.

Brinna's beauty made him feel that, as if he should both hide and step out in order to be seen. Her round cheeks were currently tinged pink, her mouth pursed. He knew that when she smiled, she had a tiny divot in her right cheek near the corner of her mouth. When she smiled—which she often did except with him—he felt as if perhaps he'd been cast in the fiery depths of Lexa's Underworld, because all of him burned. His eyes dipped to her lips now, and noted the bottom one was fuller than the top. Kissable.

Kissing her invaded his thoughts. He'd kissed her before.

Fuck. He wanted to do it again.

Kissing was ridiculous to ponder, so he cleared his throat. "We're back," he said and reminded himself that she disliked him—he'd made sure of it. Maybe he was the blight.

"Yes." She turned and looked around, then wrapped her arms around her body as if holding herself together, still in the gown she'd worn to her sister's wedding. With a shiver, she picked up the discarded cloak.

"Would you like something to change into? I might have something more comfortable."

Her eyes darted back to him. She offered a partial smile—one that didn't create that divot—and nodded.

"Thank you."

He started toward the hallway and glanced over his shoulder to make sure she was following as he led her to one of the sky bridges that connected each wing of Sol to the central atrium of the villa. The corridor arched above them. Made of metal and glass, the bridge between wings always made him feel as if he were walking in the sky. Though technically that was true, since Sol hovered in the heavens, suspended above Elcadia. The sun's light was waning, drifting toward sunset, and cast a golden glow through the corridor.

Brinna gasped, then squeaked behind him.

He turned to find her still at the opposite end of the corridor staring down at the transparent floor, the expansive landscape of Elcadia far below with intermittent clouds drifting between them.

"What is it?"

Her eyes jumped from the floor to him then back again. "That… I… we're…"

"In Sol," he said and walked back to her. "This is my…" He stalled on the word.

Her eyes jumped back to him.

"It's my home," he finished, realizing that though he hadn't made it much of one, it was still the truth. "It's perfectly safe." He grinned and offered his hand. "I promise."

She took a tentative step onto the glass floor toward him. "Earlier, I thought maybe it was on a mountain. Attached to the land."

He chuckled.

When she was close enough, she reached out and grasped his hand. The contact sent a current zipping through him.

Ignoring that sudden heat, he led her over the bridge toward the atrium. When they stepped from the glass hallway, he had to stop and wait for her. She hesitated, looking over her shoulder at the floor once more.

"It isn't going anywhere," he said. "You'll cross them so much, you'll get used to it."

"How is this possible?"

"Godlight," he said and dropped her hand. He had no reason to keep hold of her. And he didn't appreciate the way his body was betraying him by wanting to keep touching her; he regretted the loss of the connection. Rather than acknowledge the initial pang, he ignored it.

"And that is what exactly?"

He hummed, trying to figure out how to explain it. "Every god is born with godlight. It's like–"

"Magic?"

He led her into the central hub of Sol. "Power, yes, but it's also asleep, sort of, until ascension."

"Oh my stars," she breathed.

He looked over his shoulder. Her head was tilted up, taking in the expanse of the atrium, which arched so high it was difficult to make out the details of the ceiling. He stopped and looked up with her, examining Sol through her eyes, and realized he'd stopped looking at it with awe a long time ago.

But seeing her reaction, he realized it was rather

amazing. The domed ceiling arched high above them, but this far down, it resembled the open sky through the glass. Add to that the verdant foliage of the greenhouse, the creek running through the wooded grove and gardens at the center, the flowers, the trees, the pathways, the doors. It really was stunning.

"How many people live here?" she asked and turned in place.

"None."

"But all the doors."

Luc glanced at the twelve doors spaced out around the circumference of the atrium. "Those are Elsewhere Doors."

"Elsewhere Doors?" She repeated it like she was trying out the words.

Luc turned and walked to the nearest door, then opened it. The stretch of sun-bleached earth beyond the threshold had Brinna bringing her hand up to shield her eyes as she gasped. In the distance, an azure stretch of water undulated under a bright blue sky. Tall. narrow trees bent, heavy with leaves that resembled an open hand fluttering in the soft breeze.

"What is this place?" Her airy words were filled with awe.

He knew she wasn't talking about what was beyond the door. "Sol is..."

"Spectacular."

He grinned, pulling the door shut and nodding to the rest of the doors. "The doors represent the twelve gates to the twelve circles of Vasmost."

Watching her, he enjoyed when she turned her gaze up to meet his with unadulterated delight even as her brows bunched with confusion.

"I don't even know how to make sense of what you just said. Vasmost?"

He laughed, delighted by her and the look on her face—absolute enchantment—he couldn't remember ever seeing, even when she sang. "Easiest explanation: the cosmos. And behind each one is a place I discovered during my Roaming."

"And what do you do with them? The Elsewhere Doors?"

"Visit, I suppose."

"Really? That's it?"

"My responsibility as god of light is to control it—across the many tiers of the cosmos. The doors offer passage to each circle, allowing me access."

"Oh." She looked at the door, then turned toward him. "What's Roaming?"

He wasn't sure why he found her curiosity so endearing, but his heart thumped, and it made him smile. "A rite of passage for a young god."

"Like ascension?"

He nodded and shut the door. "Right. The Roam happens prior to Ascension, but yes." He started across the atrium again. "This way."

"And what is ascension?" Her boots tapped on the floor as she followed him.

"When a god takes their place in the order of Vasmost." He glanced at her and found she was still looking up, turning, her face open with awe and curiosity. His woodland fairy. He cleared his throat and had to glance away to recenter himself. "Their godlight takes its place in the order of things."

"What sorts of ways does a god prove they are ready?"

There was too much to explain, so he stuck with the basics. "Emotional control, command over their power and mastery of it, intellectual cognizance of their role." Luc felt his throat tighten knowing he'd failed despite his ascension. He'd fucked it all up with that stupid spell and trapping Nix.

"Your home is beautiful," she said.

"I love the morning light in here," he admitted as they meandered down one of the pathways.

When they reached the next skybridge, he stopped, waiting for her in case she wanted his help across, hoping she might want to hold his hand again, which seemed a silly thing to want.

As she turned from the atrium back toward him, she stopped.

"Another glass hallway?"

"Another. There are several."

She offered him a smile.

Luc held out his hand. "If it makes you feel better?"

She glanced at his hand, her smile bloomed brighter, this one truer than the last, and took his hand. Though he couldn't explain to himself why, her doing so felt like an accomplishment.

Once through the skybridge, Luc led her down the

hall, then stopped and opened another door, this one to a suite of rooms. "For you," he said and stepped back so she could enter. "I'm just across the hall," he said and pointed.

Brinna walked into the first room and turned, taking it all in, her eyes wide. "This is. Wow. And I don't have to share it!" She turned and grinned, her eyes bright.

The main room was expansive, though he hadn't ever thought about it. A wall of windows with an inset door offered a view of the balcony profuse with greenery and blue sky beyond. The large bed was clothed in ivory, the bed frame and tables fashioned of metal and light wood. There were sconces for light and clean walls devoid of anything. A plush rug stretched between the bed and a chaise lounge, a large mirror opposite. It was a rather sparse room. But that didn't seem to bother Brinna, who moved in deeper.

"Yes. All for you," he replied, unable to contain an answering smile. "You share a room?"

She walked through the room. "You haven't been to the cottage. It has two bedrooms."

"How many of you share your room?" Luc watched her touch the fabric of the bedspread, then stop at the windows to look out.

"Four of us. Jessamine, Tarley, Auri and me. Mattias sleeps in the living room."

"I would kill my siblings."

"I've been tempted a time or two." She glanced over her shoulder and grinned, then turned back toward him.

"I doubt that," Luc said. "Tarley perhaps."

She laughed, but then her smile faded. "And now Tarley's married."

"And Aurielle soon?"

Her eyes flashed to his, and she nodded, her smile absent.

Unsure what to say because he didn't like the way she'd sort of wilted, he tilted his head toward another room. "Here's a bathing room."

"A bathing room? There's a whole room, just for bathing?"

He glanced at her. "You don't have a bathing room?"

She barked a laugh.

"I take that it's a 'no.'" He lifted an eyebrow and opened the door.

Her swift intake of breath made him look at it again through her eyes, but he wasn't sure what was so inspiring about a bathtub, a shower, and a water closet.

"Is that a place for bathing?" she asked, walking to the shower encased in glass and stone. "It's so beautiful."

He chuckled as he stood next to her. "Yes. This is where you turn on the water." He reached past her, his shoulder brushing hers. "Step back or you'll be doused." Then he turned the knobs. They watched the shower come to life overhead. When he looked at her, her eyes were gigantic with surprise. They flitted toward him. She held her hand out to feel the water and grinned as if he'd shown her a room full of riches.

"Like a rainstorm. But it's warm." She laughed with delight.

Who was this woman? His woodland fairy. He should have remembered, recalling her poverty, thinking about the rudimentary conditions of her village, that of course she didn't have running water.

He turned off the shower and turned. "Through here," he said, leading her to a closet. "My sister Innes leaves her things sometimes, so I stash them in here. I think you might be able to find something to wear."

Brinna walked through and touched the fabrics with her fingertips as though afraid she might hurt them. "They are so beautiful. She won't mind?"

"Innes has probably forgotten they are even here." An awkward feeling gripped him as he watched Brinna. An intense longing, which was strange. He needed to flee. "Well… I'll just–"

She turned then. "Lucian?"

He paused. "Yes?"

"Thank you. For intervening. I didn't mean what I said earlier. I'm grateful. I know you saved–" Her throat closed around the word as she choked on a sob and covered her face with her hands.

Without considering the choice, Luc closed the space between them and gathered her in his arms. "You had a scare, Brinna." His hands moved across the silk of her bodice to offer her comfort. "You're safe here. I promise."

Then she wrapped her arms around him, holding

onto him as though she might disintegrate into nothing if she didn't. And while that would have terrified him at one time—maybe still did—with Brinna, it seemed right, somehow.

After she'd spent her tears, she stepped away and swiped at her eyes. "Thank you."

He accepted with a quick nod, feeling like he didn't deserve it since he'd been an ass earlier, which was more of the same for him. "How about some tea?" he asked. "And perhaps you're hungry?"

"I could drink some tea." She offered a teary smile.

Struggling to look at her, he glanced at the open door. "Do you think you can find your way back to the main room?"

"If I don't show up, you can come looking for me."

"Okay." He nodded, his gaze on something he wouldn't have been able to name over her shoulder.

"Lucian?"

Her voice, his name as a question, drew his gaze back to hers.

Her cheeks darkened. "I'm sorry to ask, but could you help me? With my dress's buttons?"

His heart constricted in his chest with awareness, heat spreading out toward his limbs.

Brinna turned, offering him her back. "My sisters helped me, earlier. I can't reach–"

"Right. Sure." His eyes drifted to the back of her neck once more, to the golden swirls of her hair teasing the skin there. "I'll just…"

He fumbled with the top closure, his racing

heartbeat making it difficult because for some reason his hands were trembling. He leaned back, opened his hands wide, fisted them, then resumed his task. When the first button was finally unfastened, he slid his fingers to the next, released it, then to the next, his heart thumping erratically inside his chest as each released button revealed more of her.

She sighed, and Luc couldn't help but let his thumb brush her exposed skin as he slid his hands to the next button. Chills formed on her skin as vibrant heat raced across his, connecting with his heart, blooming with fiery awareness. He imagined leaning forward, pressing his lips to the naked skin of her shoulder.

He didn't.

Perhaps this is one of those kinds of fantasies.

Luc shook his head and took a deep breath.

"Are you okay?" Brinna asked, turning her head, tilting it to look at him.

He gave her a quick smile and a nod. "Perfect. Almost done."

She held the now gaping dress against her front. "I think I can do the rest. Thank you."

Luc pulled his hands away and cleared his throat. "Right. Yes. I'll go and put on the tea."

As he retraced their steps to the living room, he replayed unfastening her dress on a loop in his mind and walked across the now darkened skybridges in a kind of daze. She had a constellation of beauty marks on her shoulder that trailed down her back. He imagined kissing each one.

By the time he reached the kitchen, he simply stood in the room staring at the windows, having forgotten what he was supposed to do. His thoughts were filled with Brinna, his singing woodland fairy, noting the sun kissing the horizon cast the sky a similar shade to Brinna's hair.

The sound of moving air jolted him back. He pressed his fingers against his chest and turned away from the windows. *What the hell was wrong with him?*

Nix swirled into the room still clothed in his black wedding attire. "Luc–" He strode toward him. "Where is she?"

"Safe." Luc crossed the room to put on a kettle of water. "Did you find it?"

Nix shook his head and shared the dramatics of corralling all the Fareviews at the wedding. "Then I finally got the family to the hedge around the cottage. They are safe there, for now. Tarley wasn't pleased. Neither was her husband."

"Can you blame them?"

Nix didn't answer, which Luc decided was because the answer was obvious. "You could bring them here."

What the fuck, Luc? he chastised himself.

Nix laughed. "Good one. Lucian Uraiahs offering Sol as a refuge."

"Right."

Stop!

"We both know there's enough room."

Nix's eyes narrowed. "You're serious?"

"Until we can deal with the darkling."

Nix looked at him, his dark gaze measuring him. Luc turned away to avoid it.

"I will suggest it, but Scarlett–"

"We can send Tarley and her new husband through an Elsewhere Door for time alone." Luc looked over his shoulder at Nix, who was grinning. Knowing he'd made Nix happy made Luc feel content, a somewhat foreign feeling he'd felt more tonight than he had in his lifetime. He didn't dwell on it. "I know the perfect place for newlyweds."

"Who are you and what have you done with my brother?"

B
rinna struggled to make sense of the nonsense that had become her life.

She'd been standing in the center of Sevens looking for Mattias.

There'd been a horrible creature she'd mistaken as a man.

Lucian Uraiahs had intervened, saving her, and whisked her away to his home floating in the sky where there was something called Elsewhere Doors.

How was this not a dream?

And now she was in the bathing room where water

flowed from the walls, standing in a smaller room within staring at beautiful garments she couldn't have fathomed existing in Sevens. A set of trousers and a shirt. A knitted sweater so soft she was certain it had been crafted with threads of a cloud. A dress that sparkled, every available surface covered in gemstones. A shift of silk. Brinna blinked, sure she had yet to wake.

Then there was Lucian's touch.

Her chest constricted then disintegrated, recalling the sensation of his fingers against her skin as he'd unfastened her gown. Even now chills raced through her, heating everything and making her feel breathless and achy, as if she'd only just awoke from a pleasurable dream. She swallowed, desirous of his touch once more, then shook her head of the thought. It was Lucian, for stars' sake! Lucian might be offering his hospitality, and maybe she'd dreamt about him, but she did not want his touch. Dreams weren't real life, and her traitorous body was a liar.

Having stripped out of everything she'd been wearing, she washed under the rainwater spigot, then slipped into the beautiful shift the color of a hot-summer-day sky. The fabric slid across her skin, whispering secrets as it did. Decadent and sensuous, she ran her hands along the fabric, sure she was still dreaming. Thinking about Lucian's touch was added proof. The shift made her feel exposed; she was so used to multiple layers. Underclothes. A chemise. Corsets. Underskirts. The dress. A cloak. She pulled out a light gray sweater, a comforting texture in her hands, and shrugged into it. It was a hug, and she desperately needed one from her family, needed to know they were safe.

As she left the bathing room, she glanced at her reflection in the mirror. Oh. Her hair was a fright. She stopped and pulled all the pins releasing the length, then found a brush. Smoothing the strands till they flowed over her shoulders down to the middle of her back, she reached for a pin, but then hesitated with a sigh. Putting it up again felt overwhelming. Letting herself to be so undone was strange, but for the moment, it was all she could manage.

Settling herself with another deep breath, she left the bedroom and started back through the corridor. When she reached the glass hallway, she hesitated. The sky outside was a vibrant blue, deep and moody, as if still holding onto all the motion from the day, but the interior skyway glowed with ambient golden light still, filaments of artificial light—strange lamps—running along the sides of the walkway leading the way. On the other side of the glass corridor, she could see the greenery of the park Lucian had led her through. If she stared straight ahead and didn't ponder that she was walking through the sky in a glass passageway, she could imagine it was just a hallway like any other.

She sucked in a breath and darted across the expanse as quickly as she could, bursting into the massive atrium, drawing in a new breath only once she was over. Lucian had cut through the massive green space at the atrium's center—a woodland dotted with foliage and a stream that Brinna could imagine enjoying—but she didn't think she would be able to find her way through by herself yet.

Yet?

She shook her head and skirted around it, noting the Elsewhere Doors. When she reached the next glass walkway, she hurried through to find she was in another corridor much like the one she'd come from. Had she gotten turned around?

With quick steps, she returned to the doorway she thought was her room and pulled at the door. An oppressive heat slammed into her. Not her room. Inside was… a lake. A giant body of water in the ground… in a floating house. Brinna closed the door, blinked, and opened it again. The pool—still there— was surrounded by lush greenery, fragrant flowers, and wooden platforms with reclining chairs flanked by green plants. A waterfall resounded at the far end. A wall of glass framed the entire wall opposite the door where she stood offering an expansive view of the waning-sun sky and everything beyond, including the corner of another wing of villa.

Her breath hitched—this place was massive. A floating village.

But she wasn't moving in the wrong direction, so she closed the door, and dashed over the glass bridge to make another turn, moving past another set of Elsewhere Doors. Wishing she had more time to explore, she suppressed the impulse to open one and peek, and instead continued forward, looking for the bridge back to the main room.

She passed over another skybridge—another wrong turn to more bedrooms—and backtracked into the atrium once more. By the time she crossed the only glass corridor she hadn't been across, she didn't rush and took her time to look out at the darkening sky, awed by the beauty. The house floated amidst the clouds, dark shadows of mountains hinting below them. Though she couldn't now see, she was sure on a clear day, she could see the landscape beyond.

When she heard voices, she turned and started toward the main room.

"You're serious?" It was Nix. Brinna's heart burst with joy, knowing he'd have news.

"You're offering Sol to Auri and her family?"

Moving too quickly, Brinna tripped on the hem of the dress, which was a touch too long.

"Brinna is already here." Lucian's voice. "We both know there's enough room."

She pulled up the silk, bunching it in her hands so the hem wasn't a danger as she held her breath at the sound of Lucian's voice. The depth of it reverberated through her chest, especially as he said her name.

"At least until we can deal with the darkling," Lucian added.

Something whistled, followed by the thump and scrape of metal against metal, the cadence matching the sudden pace of Brinna's heart at Lucian's words, his kindness.

"I will propose it, but Scarlett–" Nix said, cutting

through the other sounds.

"Just ask. We can send Tarley and her new husband through an Elsewhere Door. I know just the place for newlyweds."

Brinna's heart melted in her chest at Lucian's thoughtfulness. Moving quietly, she made her way toward them, enjoying the exchange.

"Seriously, who are you and what have you done with my brother?" Nix laughed.

Brinna smiled, lifting a hand to cover the sound of her near giggle.

There was a pause, then the quiet words she couldn't quite make out from Nix.

"What?" Lucian exclaimed. "Absolutely not."

"Well, she's lovely. I could see–"

"No. She's Aurielle's sister."

Brinna stopped, her back rigid, her heart frozen along with her breath. Were they talking about her?

"Exactly."

"I don't fool around with mortals anymore, Nix. Especially not ones with their heads in the clouds."

Brinna's mouth fell open as her heart plummeted into her belly, burning up as it did.

"When has that ever stopped you?"

There was a silent pause, which communicated enough quite loudly. Then Lucian said, "You can rest assured, Nixus, I have no intention of crossing any romantic boundaries with Brinna Fareview."

Brinna pressed her teeth together. As if he could!

But her cheeks heated, recalling what had

happened earlier. The brazen way she'd spoken to him thinking she'd been dreaming. The way she'd touched him. The way her body had responded to his touch. And now to learn hers had been unwelcomed.

She pressed her hands to her burning cheeks, knowing she never would have done something so bold had she been in her right mind. Lucian might be handsome, but so far, his personality was a sieve leaking most of the good parts out and leaving behind the egregious.

Except he'd just offered up his home. To her family.

Which confused her. Which Lucian was he?

She straightened her spine and smoothed the fabric of the shift, reminding herself that his offer was the right thing to do. He had the space. Her family needed help. With a huff, she started forward again. Lucian Uraiahs was doing the bare minimum.

"Good. Good," Nix said. "I don't want—"

"She isn't my type," Lucian interrupted, his voice clipped and impatient.

Her step faltered as her heart cooled, hardening with hurt. What a horrible thing to hear. It punched a hole in her already strained self-confidence. There was nothing to be done but endure it, so with a deep breath, she reminded herself she didn't care what Lucian thought and pulled the sweater tight around her as walked the final few steps through the corridor.

"Brinna," Nixus said brightly when he saw her, his dark eyes assessing. "Are you alright? There weren't any bites?"

"None," Brinna replied. Though she could see Lucian from the corner of her eye, she didn't look at him. "My family?"

"Safe at the cottage. I'm going back now to let them know you are safe."

"Mattias?"

"He's with them."

Brinna released a sigh and closed her eyes for a moment, relieved. "Thank the stars. Maybe you can take me back with you?" she asked, hoping to get away from Lucian.

Something clanked in the kitchen, and Brinna finally turned her head, her body tensing in anticipation of Lucian's condescending looks.

But that wasn't what greeted her. He'd removed his jacket, and his white shirt was open at the collar, the sleeves rolled up to reveal his forearms. His golden gaze took her in, his face tight with tension before he frowned as he wiped something from the counter. She hated that she found him so alluring and refocused on Nixus.

"Lucian" –Nix glanced at his brother– "offered Sol as a place to stay for your family," he finished.

She turned toward Lucian once more, chastising her stupid heart. "That is generous of you." Her words sounded forced even to her own ears, which bothered her because she didn't want him aware he affected her. She looked at Nix, focusing on his face and movements though she wanted to look at his brother watching her from the kitchen. "Or you can just take me home."

Lucian cleared his throat, smacking whatever was in his hand down on the countertop. "I don't think that's a good idea."

Brinna leveled her gaze on Lucian, hoping it communicated disinterest instead of hurt. "And why is that?"

"I haven't had a chance to search the woods around the cottage," Nix answered, drawing her attention away from Lucian once again. "I think that should be done first, before returning you."

"That makes sense." She drew the sweater tighter around her and swallowed the threatening tears.

"Do you think they will come?" Nix asked, a hopeful note in his voice. "Brinna?"

Having lost the thread of the conversation, she looked up, hoping Nix couldn't read her emotions. "What?"

"Do you think they'll come to Sol?"

She cleared her throat. With a hum as she tried to organize her thoughts around the question, around the moment, she finally answered, "Getting my mother out of that cottage would be a miracle."

Nix nodded. "That's what I thought too." He glanced at Lucian, then back to her. "She was a mess when I left. She'll be relieved to hear you're safe."

"You can talk her into it," Lucian said. "You could talk a wood nymph into the sea."

Brinna tried not to roll her eyes.

"I will be my most charming self," Nix said, "but Scarlett is something entirely beyond my understanding."

"Her will of iron?" Brinna asked.

"And then some. I'm not sure I'll ever find a way through her defenses." Nix smiled.

"When you discover it, please do let us know." She answered Nix's smile with one of her own.

He laughed before saying, "I'll return, then."

And in the blink of an eye, he was gone.

Brinna wasn't sure she could ever get used to that.

"Here," Lucian said, reminding her where she was and who she was with.

With a fortifying breath and a reminder to not be affected, she whirled around. He was closer than she anticipated, holding out a steaming cup.

"Oh." She stopped short to keep from knocking into him and spilling the cup, then made the mistake of looking at his face. The corners of his eyes softened as they dipped from her face, leaving a trail over her form before stopping at her feet, then jumping back up.

"I wasn't sure how you liked your tea, but I do have milk and sugar."

Brinna reached out and took the offered cup. "Thank you." Her fingers brushed his, a jolt zipping across her skin and radiating up her spine, collecting around her heart, then flooding it. "Milk would be nice," she added politely even as she bristled inside, not wanting to warm to him.

Lucian turned and led her back into the kitchen. Brinna noted his feet were also bare, and they were as beautiful as the rest of him. Irritated with her thoughts, she frowned but decided that he wasn't her type either, even if he was pretty. And she could be cordial, a gracious guest.

"You were able to find your way," he said, glancing over his shoulder.

"I got lost a few times." She looked around at everything but him, set the cup down, and ran a hand over the smooth countertop. Theirs at home were wooden, which her father had to resurface once a year. On the stove-top where the tea kettle rested, a barely perceptible blue flame heated the water. The stove at the cottage was a dark, potbelly, metal beast that used wood and fire to heat the surface. There was a sink, but like in the bathing room, knobs rather than a pump activated the spigot. This kitchen had cupboards lining the wall, whereas at the cottage, dishes and linens were stacked in a cabinet with glass doors, goods were stored in jars, sealed containers or in the pantry between the kitchen and her parents' room.

"This place is so…" she paused. What could she say? She couldn't even fathom it. "Like a dream," she finally said. The realization that this was Lucian's life made her feel even smaller and backward in comparison. No wonder he didn't see her as someone desirable. She knew nothing. Came from nothing.

Instead, she reached for something she did know. "Do you cook?"

"Some," he said, opening the door of a contraption to reach in and pull out a container. "During my Roaming, I spent time in a place where food, and how it was prepared, was an artform. I learned basic things before I grew bored, so there are a few things I can do. But cooking for one isn't enjoyable. I usually make myself easy things to eat." He set the container on the counter.

"What is that?"

He lifted the container again. "Please don't tell me you don't know what milk is."

She frowned. "I know what milk is. What was it inside?"

His brows compressed, and he looked at the milk and then over his shoulder. "It's an icebox of sorts. You don't have an icebox?"

Perplexed and curious, she skirted the counter, then Lucian, and pulled open the door. A burst of cold air touched her skin as a light came on to reveal an array of items. It was a wonder! Her parents had a wooden ice box with an assortment of doors and latches. Definitely no light. "Not like this. Where's the ice?"

"It runs on sunlight." He reached past her and shut the door.

"Sunlight? Heat?" She stared at him, knowing she must have looked like the idiot she felt like.

"The power collected from the light is turned into energy needed to make the icebox cold, the lights turn on, and the water warm."

She didn't truly understand but knew there wasn't

anything like that in her cottage or in Sevens. She wasn't even sure there was anything like it in Kaloma. Aware she probably seemed even more ridiculous, she schooled her features. "We don't have that in the cottage."

Lucian made a humming sound.

Brinna felt judged, though she couldn't say if it was because of Lucian or because of her own insecurity. "You must have seen many things while Roaming."

"So many things." He smiled and leaned a hip against the counter.

She wanted to ask him to tell her, longed to hear his stories, but his dismissal of her reverberated in her mind, so she didn't. Silence crept between them, and she moved back to her tea and took a sip. "Thank you for the tea."

"It's my pleasure."

She tried to reconcile the hurtfulness of his earlier words with his actions, but she couldn't make them align. He'd been kind. Saved her. Gave her a place to stay, clothing to wear. Offered a place for her family to find refuge. Made her tea. Comforted her.

She shivered.

"Are you still cold?" he asked.

She pulled the sweater tighter around her. "No. I'm comfortable." Though that wasn't exactly true.

She noticed the way his throat moved as he turned away, the way his shirt stretched across his shoulders as he replaced the milk in the icebox. She looked away and took another sip of her tea.

"When do you think Nix will return?" she asked.

He leaned against the counter; his hands pressed behind him to frame his hips. "After he makes sure you're safe. Your family is safe." His jaw tensed, working underneath his skin, but she couldn't decipher his tension. "It could be in the next thirty seconds, thirty minutes, or thirty days." Then he turned and reached into a cupboard. "Nix has always been unpredictable."

Brinna followed the line of his shirt where it was tucked into the trousers that curved around his form. She hated that she noticed that her body tightened as if anticipating action, so she looked down at her tea. "That's inconvenient."

Silence descended between them once more. She disliked the awkwardness of it, though what was to be done? It was clear she was an interloper, and even if he was kind and hospitable enough to offer her this place to stay, he didn't want her here. By his own admission.

But then why offer a place for her family, she wondered.

Self-consciousness descended on her like a storm cloud, and it made her annoyed and tetchy, which was never a good idea. It made her do stupid things to overcompensate for her insecurities. Things like chatter, and work to make someone happy, which is what she found herself wanting to do with Lucian.

"The darkling–" she started.

"Nix should–" Lucian said at the same time.

They both stopped speaking. Her eyes met Lucian's before she glanced back at the cup of tea in her hands.

"I'm sorry," he said. "Please."

"Are darklings common?" she asked.

"Truthfully, other than knowing about them, I don't have much experience."

"And Nix?"

His eyebrow rose like the arch of a question mark.

"As the god of night and darkness?"

"He's familiar—like me—but darkness isn't synonymous with dark beings."

"Point taken." She took a sip. "I supposed a dark creature could be just as likely to walk in the light."

"Unfortunately."

Silence descended once again.

She snuck a glance at him as he sipped his tea, following the curve of his jaw with her eyes and noted the stubble starting to shadow the skin there. She tracked the way his throat worked as he swallowed his sip, then let her gaze dip to the hollow at his throat. Then, because she couldn't help herself, she looked at his mouth, the teacup gone.

He smirked.

Her eyes jumped to his.

He tilted his head, which was both inquiring, arrogant, and Brinna ruffled with both embarrassment and annoyance.

"Thinking about your fantasy?" he teased.

"No." She studied the interior of her teacup.

"A shame," he said and chuckled.

She let out a frustrated groan and stood, wanting

to spit out that she wasn't his type but sputtering the beginning of an excuse instead. "I didn't realize–"

And her skin heated once more, recalling it. Touching him. Speaking crudely without concern for any sort of propriety ingrained in her since birth. He must think her foolish and garish, and she could feel herself wanting to prove him wrong but knew that would take her down a path that would ultimately prove him right. The memory pushed the pace of her heart a little faster, recalling the feel of his taut body, the rich fibers of his jacket on her fingertips, about telling him such intimate details of her thoughts. She needed to change direction immediately, otherwise she might say or do something impulsive.

He grinned. "It's alright, Brinna."

"As if I need you to tell me that." She scoffed and raised her chin, then strode away from him across the room to the windows with as much confidence she could exude. To tease her so dreadfully was boorish, but it wasn't any more than she deserved. She wished she wasn't so oversensitive that she couldn't laugh it off with him, but she mostly just felt ashamed. She'd bared a secret she'd only alluded to even with her sisters.

Looking out at the now dark sky, at the stars sparkling beyond, she took a deep breath, calming her heart, except it wouldn't stop. She wished she could take it back, especially now that she knew she wasn't even his type.

As much as she wanted to be optimistic, she

couldn't find the mettle to take a deep breath and believe that things could definitely be worse. That might be true, but at the moment, this felt as bad as it could get.

Luc

Luc ground his teeth together to keep from saying something flirty to Brinna. As much as he wanted to travel this path with her, he'd reassured Nix that he wasn't attracted to her. It was an exploding star of a lie, but he also knew it would only serve to complicate things. Brinna was the type of woman who would want a lover to stay. And that certainly wasn't him.

Her back was to him as she stared out the windows at the sky, still dark before the stars appeared. Fuck, she was gorgeous. Her smile—when it was real. The way she moved in the space around her, natural and unpretentious. Her energy. She was like the warmth of the sun, and he wanted to bask in it. There was something about her he liked immensely, and that was why he'd forced himself to ignore his attraction.

Only he couldn't lie to himself about his attraction to Brinna anymore. She might be a blight on his peace, but she was one he wanted around more and more.

He pressed his fingers against his heart, annoyed at the pinch he felt there, then took a deep breath and closed his eyes, recalling the way her hands had felt on him earlier. The way her eyes and words had teased him. The way his body had responded, wanting to grab hold of the back of her head and kiss her, to render them both senseless. But he'd known better than to succumb to that temptation, just as he'd always known. He couldn't. For Nix. For her. She deserved better.

There were so many times he'd wanted to kiss her—the one time at the dance included when he'd actually succumbed to the temptation, he'd fucked it up. But not just then, even the first time he'd met her—after the singing-in-the-wood version of her in a varied web of space and time—he'd had the opportunity to be a different version of himself and hadn't. Brinna Fareview had a way of tying up his mind and his tongue and rendering him his basest self.

He stood staring at her across the great room of Sol as beautiful now as the first time he'd ever seen her. She looked like a goddess in that blue silk of a dress slipping around her curves like a caress, her gorgeous hair flowing over her shoulders, her feet bare, her kissable lips turned down in a slight pout, those gray eyes flashing at him with annoyance. She hit every nerve in his body.

Since he'd met her, Luc had only been his worst self. Or maybe, this was just who he was. He refused to allow himself to ponder Brinna's allure because he knew his pondering would complicate things. He'd act on it, and he wasn't able to be uncomplicated. Not with his sequestering.

Damn Nix for even bringing it up.

Now he couldn't seem to stop looking at her.

Fuck.

He needed Nix to return with Brinna's family immediately, otherwise he was going to be tempted to push boundaries that he knew were necessary. He wasn't trustworthy.

He owed Nix. He owed Nix. He owed Nix.

He swallowed.

"Lucian." His father's voice boomed through the space.

Brinna twirled. "What was that?"

"My father. Brace yourself." Before he finished, his father materialized.

Ur, dressed as he always was in one of his impeccable suits—this one a dark blue with a light gray shirt and dark gray tie—glanced around until his golden-brown eyes landed on Lucian in the kitchen.

His countenance communicating his displeasure, Ur unbuttoned his jacket and put his hands on his hips.

"You left. Again," he said without preamble. "I believe I made it clear you weren't to leave." His gaze bounced around the room. When he caught sight of Brinna, his hot gaze jumped back to Luc, full of assumption and accusation, his brows arched high. "That's why you left?"

"No, sir. This"–Luc held a hand toward Brinna, watching the exchange– "is Brinna Fareview."

His father either didn't recognize her surname as Nix's Aurielle or he didn't care. Probably the latter.

Luc added, "Aurielle's sister. The mortal who saved Nix."

"You left and accessed your magic, then brought a mortal to Sol?" Ur shook his head, seeming to ignore the information in favor of the focus he wanted. "I had hoped, Lucian, that confinement to Sol would be enough of a punishment, given your poor choices."

"Perhaps I should go?" Brinna said.

"No," Luc said at the same time Ur said, "Good idea."

Brinna padded back across the room to set her cup in the sink. "Thank you, Lucian. I'll see myself back to my room."

Luc bowed his head slightly as he watched her go. When she was gone, he said, "First, Father, I'm a grown ass man."

"Who makes rather childish decisions."

Luc sighed. Ur wasn't wrong, but Luc didn't need reminding.

"And your punishment for that spell business was

imprisonment here. What part of imprisonment means leaving?"

"Nix asked me to go."

"Oh. So the brother you trapped—the very reason I've sequestered you here—asked you to leave, so you go?"

"What did you expect me to do? Tell him no? What if he needed help in the mortal world?"

Ur let out a frustrated noise. "Damn him. He's after the mortal— or whatever she is."

"Can you blame him? The god-yoke makes it rather difficult not to."

Ur scoffed. "I'm not here about your brother."

"I did it. I left. I went with Nix to the mortal realm. There." Luc held up his hands. "Is that what you want to hear? There was a monster who went after Aurielle's sister. So I used my power and you caught me. Like it or not, we owe Aurielle for Nix's life. For mine. For Lexa's."

Ur walked into the living room and sat down, leaned back, and set an ankle on the opposite knee. Cool, calm, collected. Luc had always admired that about his father. There were things he hated about him, like his wandering eyes and the way he fought with their mother, who had her own wandering eyes. But when it came to everything else, Ur could assess a situation as if he owned it and only had to speak his will to see it as it should be. He had his faults, but nearly costing the universe something wasn't one of them.

After a moment, Ur took a deep breath and said,

"You're my oldest son, Lucian. I need you to—"

"To what?"

"Grow the fuck up." Ur set both feet back on the floor and leaned forward. "I need to pass my mantle, and I want it to be you."

"Lexa said 'no'?"

Ur sighed again. "I asked her. She said she doesn't want it. Probably best. Her role as god of the Netherworld means she's involved in all kinds of questionable activities. That kind of power might be a conflict of interest." He paused. "Nix wants to marry a mortal—"

"Probably not a mortal."

"Whatever she is." Ur waved a hand. "And he thinks you're better suited."

"So I'm your third choice." Luc scoffed, not sure why that news surprised him, considering what he'd done to Nix.

"You've always been my first choice. I asked the other two because I knew you'd refuse." Ur stood and started back toward him. "I agree with Nix and Lexa. The god of the Cosmos—of the Vasmost— needs to be bigger than their immediate wants, Lucian."

"Well, that isn't me, now is it, Father."

Thunder shook Sol as lightning streaked beyond the glass. Ur's electricity sparked between them; his look menacing. "Enough."

Light buzzed at Luc's fingertips to challenge his father's ire. "Enough what? Refusing you?"

With a twist of his hand, Ur grabbed hold of Luc's

power, and pulled, yanking the golden light from every fiber of Luc's being. Bright tendrils of gold bounced across the expanse of the room to Ur, putting Luc's power in his father's fist.

"Is this what it will take?" Ur shouted. "Stripping you of your power? Banished to Sol isn't enough? You need to be powerless too?"

"Just take it," Luc shouted back. "I've never deserved it anyway. And that's what you think, right? I've done nothing but abuse it. Give it to someone else."

"Who are you?"

"Not someone who deserves to be the god of day and light."

"Fine."

With another twist of Ur's fingers, Luc's power drained completely. He was nothing. Empty. A man.

Ur—looking suddenly more sad than angry—dropped his hands to his sides. "You will remain here at Sol."

"I've nowhere else to go."

"When will you stop running, Lucian?"

When Luc didn't reply, Ur sighed. "When you are ready to accept who you are and who you are intended to be, I will restore your power."

"What if I don't want it?"

"You will. Mark my words, Lucian, you will." And then he was gone, taking Luc's power with him.

Though it was supremely comfortable, Brinna tossed and turned in the gigantic bed. Without Auri's warmth, Brinna struggled to relax into her exhaustion. It wasn't that she was cold, exactly, but the emptiness of the bed matched an emptiness pulsing through her heart. She'd never felt this alone before, and it surprised her that she missed her sisters, missed the feel of Auri next to her in bed. What would she do when Auri was gone? Married?

She'd thought she would like to feel independent, the possibility of just being Brinna, not a sister of

Jessamine, Tarley, Auri, and Mattias. But *being Brinna* up until then had meant never being alone. She was the helper, the nurturer, the one who built and maintained emotional bridges. She told stories and entertained, offered kindness and shoulders on which to cry. She'd assumed alone would mean she could exist for herself, but now she felt like she didn't know who she was without them. And maybe that was more frightening.

"Sleep. Sleep," she whisper-chanted. But when she shut her eyes, it was Lucian's face she saw. Such a lovely face. Her eyes flew open, and she grunted in frustration. She was angry with him, hurt—he was the last thing she wanted to think of. But when she closed her eyes, his face was exactly where her mind took her anyway, the light around him bright and warm. Strangely, the closer she got, the farther he drifted from her. It was day, then night, then day again, and as the sun waned, the darkling's terrible face with its wide mouth full of teeth and blood, loomed between her and Lucian.

She cried out and lurched up in the bed.

Dreaming.

Her heart raced, thrumming its strong rhythm at the pulse in her neck.

Just a dream. She'd fallen asleep despite feeling like she might never find it.

A knock pounded at her door. "Brinna?!"

With a screech, startled, she flung herself out of bed onto the floor to hide.

"Brinna?" The door opened. "Are you alright?"

Lucian's voice.

She knelt, looking over the bed at Lucian's shadow in the doorway. "Oh stars." She took a deep breath and pressed her forehead against the mattress. "You scared me."

"I heard you call for me. I thought–"

"I did?"

"Yes."

She didn't remember doing it. "I had a nightmare," she admitted.

"Are you okay?"

Using the bed as leverage, she rose to her feet with a shiver and cleared her throat. "Yes. I dreamed of the darkling." She shivered again, crossing her arms over her chest.

The brilliance of the stars in the windows beyond did little to light the room, so she reached and pulled the chain next to her bed. The lamp cast a soft glow, illuminating Lucian across the room. His honey hair was the same mess of waves it always was, but the rest of him looked as undone as she'd ever seen him. The buttons of his ivory shirt were misaligned exposing tanned skin and an enticing dusting of hair across his chest, his pants loose around his hips, perhaps unbuttoned, as if he'd only slipped them on as he rushed from his room.

Her cheeks heated, and she looked down at the bed with its rumpled sheets. That didn't help—her flush deepened, spreading warmth across her body.

You aren't his type, she reminded herself.

"I'm sorry for barging in. I thought…" He sighed and ran a hand around the back of his neck. "I don't know what I thought. It isn't like anything can get you here. You're perfectly safe."

"I'm sorry for waking you." Unable to help herself, she let herself study him. She'd always thought Lucian a beautiful man but seeing him like this made her stomach feel as if it were falling down, down, down between her thighs.

Pressing his shoulder against the doorframe, he crossed his arms over his chest, his gaze roaming. She noticed, and wondered how it would feel to touch that tanned skin, that dusting of hair. She tightened her hands into fists to keep from thinking about it.

"Having difficulty sleeping?" he asked, his eyes finally meeting hers.

She forced herself to hold his gaze. "Yes." Heart fluttering, she released her arms and smoothed the gown at her sides. "Actually, I am."

Lucian cleared his throat and looked down at his feet.

Reflexively, she glanced down as well.

Her gown was transparent.

Her cheeks burning, she crossed her arms over her chest aware it did little to hide the rest of her. "I'm not used to so much space or being by myself." She shivered again, only this time it wasn't because of the darkling, nor because she was cold. Instead, she felt like there were bubbles inside her, rising toward the surface and making her jittery.

"Are you cold?"

"A little," she lied.

"I can warm–" He paused. "I can get you another blanket. I'll just–" He pushed away from the doorframe.

"Stay?" she asked, then pressed her teeth together, not sure what she was doing, as if she'd been possessed and something else spoke through her. In what world was it ever a good idea to invite someone into her bed? To her surprise, the thought of Lucian wasn't repulsive, even if he was usually such a jerk. Even if he didn't like her.

One of his eyebrows rose.

"I mean–" she started. "I was scared. It's nothing. Forget I said it. Thank you. Good night." She bobbed a stupid curtsy, then wanted to melt into a puddle on the floor for doing it. There hadn't been a moment in front of Lucian Uraiahs where she hadn't been obnoxiously annoying, crying, or horrifyingly forward. She dropped her face into her hands and sighed.

He stepped into the room, shutting the door behind him—surprising her. "I'd be happy to stay until you fall asleep."

"You would?" She peeked at him through her fingers. He'd stopped in the middle of the room. "I mean… I thought…"

"What did you think?" His brows drew together.

She'd given him an out, and yet he was still there. "You've never stayed. With me." She dropped her hands to her sides, and his eyebrows drifted up. "You always leave…" she added, flushing once more at the insecurity tapping out her heartbeat. "You must think I'm ridiculous."

His eyes scanned her, starting at her face, roving down, then back up again. When his gaze found hers once more, she shivered, but this time with anticipation.

"That is the last thing I was thinking," he said, now standing on the opposite side of the bed. He lifted the bedding but didn't move. "In. You've had a stressful and frightening day. I think you're entitled to some care." He offered her a warm smile.

Hardly believing this turn of events, she climbed back into the bed. When she'd settled herself, he covered her then sat on top of the covers next to her, his back against the headboard, his long legs stretched out in front of him and crossed at the ankle.

She noticed his bare feet. Tanned. The nice way they were put together, the bones, veins, and sinew. They were straight, perfect. Rather lovely—like everything about him— which was a strange thing to think about feet.

"Is everything okay with your father?" she asked, turning her focus away from his feet to the fabric of his pants, instead. She followed the lines of his legs, noted the way he filled in the fabric, the fullness of his thighs.

Her belly tightened and her breath hitched against a hook of awareness in her chest.

"Not really. But there's little to be done about it.

Tell me what you're afraid of."

"Huh?" she asked, not truly having heard him over her heartbeat pounding so loud inside her ears. Her eyes traveled higher, and she attempted to politely skip over his groin, but not before she noted the way his misaligned shirt hung open. The panels split, to drape over his hips, giving her a glimpse of his flat stomach and the trail of hair that disappeared under the unbuttoned fabric of his pants.

"Your nightmare?"

"Oh." Her cheeks heated further, and she skipped his face altogether, pretty sure he'd caught her looking. Instead, she rolled to her back and stared at the ceiling, tracing the ornate swirls of plaster with her eyes as she tried to get the image of him out of her mind. "It was about the darkling. All those teeth." She shuddered.

"It can't get you here."

Brinna laid her arms over the coverlet, her hands resting on her stomach as she traced the raised whorls in the fabric's pattern. "You know, right before you swooped in to save me from that abomination, I'd been thinking about how I needed to get back to the party to dance with as many partners as I could." She tipped her head to look up at him. "Isn't that silly?"

He met her gaze but didn't say anything, his mouth unsmiling but not unfriendly. There was an intensity in his gaze she couldn't decipher.

"Twenty-five years I've lived in Sevens," she continued, "and in a single day my sister Tarley gets married to a prince, I get attacked by a darkling, and then I'm saved by a god. If I were a calculating sort of girl, which I'm not, even that seems highly improbable as odds go."

"So it would seem."

"Were you frightened of the darkling?"

"Frightened?" He paused and stared straight ahead; his fingers threaded over his belly. "Not for me."

A bead of warmth bloomed in her chest but was clipped with sharp confusion and the incongruence of the man lying next to her. Earlier, there'd been an awkward silence between them; now, it didn't feel so awkward but instead alive with awareness. Unsure how to manage it, she eventually said, "This is nice. Talking like this. We don't usually do this. My sisters and I chat when we go to sleep, and usually Tarley gets angry and tells us to hush up. Auri and I are always whispering to one another."

"What kinds of things do you whisper?"

"Stories. Secrets."

He hummed. "Stories and secrets," he repeated.

Brinna rolled to her side to face him; her hands tucked under her cheek. "Have you ever laid in bed telling stories and secrets?"

He smiled and plucked at something on the bedding between them. "I don't think I have, actually. I like to do other things in bed." He grinned.

Brinna blushed and glanced away only to find her gaze drawn to that intriguing line of hair on his stomach. She forced her eyes to the bedspread. "You should definitely tell secrets. Puts me right to sleep."

"I'm not sure whispering stories and secrets in bed would put me right to sleep. There are other things I can attest to." He was still grinning at her when she glanced at him again, and warmth spread across her chest down into her belly.

Was he flirting with her?

"Perhaps you should tell me a secret?" he said.

She cleared her throat. "I think I already revealed enough secrets to you today."

His eyes caught hers, and he laughed quietly. "You're right. You did. I liked it."

"You did?"

He nodded.

"I think it's only fair if you tell me one of yours." Brinna smiled at him, enjoying this sudden ease, even if she wasn't his type, even if he'd been pretentious and condescending. For the moment, she needed this more than to be angry with him.

"Secrets are power."

"I promise to never use a secret against you."

Lucian looked away, his grin fading, and she watched his features harden, as though whatever was on his mind was difficult and painful. But when he turned to look at her once more, his mask had been restored.

"What was that?" she asked.

"What?"

"That angry face thing?"

His eyebrows bunched together. "You should

probably go to sleep."

"Except you owe me a secret, and whatever happened on your face said you have many."

"When you've seen what I have, it's impossible not to." He linked his fingers together over a slice of skin visible under the misbuttoned shirt.

Brinna swallowed once more, suddenly imagining licking that visible skin. "From your Roaming?"

He made a sound of affirmation, then turned to look at her.

"A secret is only fair, Lucian," she said lightly, teasing, grateful he couldn't read her mind.

"You know gods don't play fair, right?"

"How would I know that? I've never known one."

One side of his mouth curled up. "Alright. One secret. Let's see." He paused. Then he grinned, his eyes dropping to meet hers. "I have never met anyone quite like you."

"Horrible secret. Doesn't count. Try again."

His smile shifted. "I like this."

"What?"

"Talking with you."

"Not fighting, you mean." She grinned.

He chuckled, then his smile faded. "Okay. A secret." He turned his head away, looking straight ahead. "My father took my powers."

"What?"

"I wasn't supposed to leave Sol and I did."

"To go to the wedding?"

He nodded.

"If you hadn't been there–" Her gaze collided with his and held, cognizant of what would have happened if he hadn't been there.

He was the first to look away. "Well, there are consequences."

"Could I talk to him? Perhaps explain how chivalrous you've been… for me."

"Chivalrous?" He grinned, though it seemed more to himself than to her. "That isn't something I've ever been accused of being before." There was a long pause. "My father wouldn't put much weight on the word of a mortal."

"What now?"

"He wants me to wait here in Sol and reflect on what a horrible god I've been."

"Horrible?" This didn't seem to add up to Brinna. Sure, Lucian was an unapproachable ass, and he'd been arrogantly rude on multiple occasions, but horrible didn't seem quite right, anymore. In fact, since he'd brought her to Sol, he'd been rather… wonderful, aside from the "not my type" comment, which had wounded her pride.

"I trapped my brother in an enchantment that lasted 100 years for him—I won't bore you with the details of it—but he would have died in there and night would have been lost had your sister not saved him."

She sat up, the blanket pooling around her hips when she did. "Wait. Auri? This is why you believe you owe her?"

He nodded, his eyes tracing her face, then dipping

lower before jumping back up. "I deserve the solitude and the stripping of my power."

Brinna flopped back against her pillow. "The Great Nap Escapade."

"What is that?"

So Brinna explained it to him. Eventually, Lucian scooted down on the bed, his head on the pillow next to her as he filled her in on his side of the story, explaining how Auri had saved the world.

"My sister? Auri?"

He chuckled again, and Brinna realized how much she liked the sound. "Yes. Auri."

They talked deep into the night, sharing, laughing, finding a new common ground that hadn't ever existed between them. It felt so natural. She liked it. Liked talking with Lucian Uraiahs, who smiled easily and was so much more than she'd ever given him credit for— even if she wasn't his type, which she decided was okay even if it hurt her pride. Eventually, she yawned, and though she fought the exhaustion so she could keep talking with Lucian, somewhere between words, she fell asleep.

A small wooden door decorated with swirling metalwork brushed with a turquoise patina and heavily flourished with green vines laced with white blooms stood in Luc's way. A floating gateway between him and where he knew he needed to be. But he didn't recognize the door. With a knock and a push, the door unlatched and swung open like an invitation. He pushed it open all the way and peered inside.

Beyond, it wasn't unlike the woods where he'd once seen his woodland fairy—only it felt thicker somehow. Warmer. There was no snow. The woods leaned into summer, overflowing with green leaves and bright blooms. His mind recalled his singing sprite, trying to remember her name—which seemed important—but it flitted away like a hummingbird as he ducked through the small doorway. He pushed through the foliage, looking for that something he was there to find, though he wasn't exactly sure what that something was. He just knew he needed to walk forward.

Her.

He was looking for her.

Flowers bloomed as he walked, a profusion of colors: white, yellow, violet, green, red. Tiny pink blossoms rained around him, creating a lush pink carpet on the forest floor. Ahead, a curtain of vines and blossoms obscured the path. When he reached them, he pushed them aside and walked through. The jaunty song of a creek trickled somewhere nearby, and the buzzing whispered laughter of sprites sounded from the bower of the trees.

Luc continued, traveling deeper into the woods, though to call it the woods didn't feel quite right anymore. There was something magical about it, comfortable, as if he were still in Sol walking through the solarium. Though while the greenery was lush and beautiful there, it didn't look like this. He was sure he might be lost, yet he didn't hesitate to continue on, sure that he was supposed to find something.

Her.

He was looking for her. Always looking for her.

The thicket thinned and opened overhead, and Luc walked into a magical glen framed with trees and foliage as if they were walls. Flowers bloomed. Butterflies flitted from blossom to blossom. Pink petals still rained gently around him. Under the bower, with low branches dripping with vines and flowers and framed in a thicket of black and white aspens was a dais. A woman reclined on a chaise made from the forest, waiting.

Her.

Luc's breath caught, then released. "I found you."

Brinna.

Her gray-blue eyes met his, and she smiled. "I wondered if you'd come."

She looked like the woman he'd come to know, but different somehow, as if she had her own light, a faint glow that drew from the pink blossoms, the foliage, the music of the forest, as if she were truly a woodland fairy whose sole purpose was to share her beauty with the flowers. She swung her legs off the chaise and stood, the gauzy, aquamarine gown draping around her shape. He caught a glimpse of her creamy thighs through the side slits that rose to her hips as she walked toward him, his eyes traveling up over her waist, cinched with a gold belt, to the shadowed outline of her breasts and nipples under the sheer fabric, to the lines of her neck up over her face until he met her gaze.

"I found you," he repeated. "Look at you."

She smiled, the pleasure touching the corners of her eyes and brightening them. Luc realized he hadn't seen her smile with such abandon in a long while, and thought it was a shame. It did something otherworldly to her face.

"I can only see you," she said.

"Do you still sing?" A dumb question, but it was always on his mind.

"Still?"

"The first time I saw you, you were singing." He hummed a few bars of the song he remembered.

She tilted her head, listened, and smiled. "It does seem familiar." Then she glanced over her shoulder. "Walk with me?"

"Where are we?" Luc followed her as they started through the forest. It made way for them as she led them through, as if the forest obeyed her, moving, adjusting, blooming, changing to create a cleared passage.

She looked over her shoulder at him, her copper hair loosely braided and threaded with blossoms, wispy tendrils framing her face. "I suspect a dream."

"Like the dream you told me about?"

She didn't blush like he thought she might. In the waking world, she would have. Now, however, she tilted her head to regard him without any artifice. "Not quite." She smirked. "You wouldn't have any clothes on." Her gaze raked over him, almost as heavy as a fingernail's touch scraping along his skin.

He shivered. "Why am I here?"

"Why not?" she countered.

She took his hand in hers as they walked. It was a

chaste touch, but Luc still noted the energetic pulse arcing between them, the promise of that connection falling into place.

But he knew nothing of such promises. Had never given one. Hadn't received one. Had mocked those who might try. Abhorred the thought of being god-yoked like Nix. And yet—this touch sent bright heat through his body, reminding him of desire, and warm heat to his heart. making it beat a little faster, a little stronger with new awareness he wasn't prepared to acknowledge.

He wanted to resist it, but then Woodland Fairy Brinna looked at him with all-knowing eyes, "Why are you afraid?"

"I'm not afraid, I'm a g–" But his throat closed on the word. He'd once been a god. Now, he was just a god without his ascended power.

"Once upon a time," she said, stopping and releasing Luc's hand.

They were at the edge of a lake. The gray-blue surface stretched to the horizon as far as he could see, reminding him of Brinna's eyes. Frothy waves rolled in, lapping at the pebbled shore, dappled with a variety of colors. The steely gray sky threatened a coming storm.

He'd been there before, or somewhere like it during one of his many Roams. Then after, when he'd realized he'd failed to free Nix from the spell the first time. He'd used his own blood, just like he was supposed to do with a simple blood spell, but it had failed, revealing he hadn't actually helped to cast a simple blood spell. The clarity of what he'd done to Nix filled him with absolute shame, so he'd run, and ended up at a lake like this in the seventh circle. Luc remembered standing lakeside, shouting into the storm at his failure and stupidity and the piercing accusation of what he'd done to his brother.

"Why are we here?" he asked, wanting to leave.

"You tell me. You made it. I've never seen anything like it. Sevens has a river, but I've never gone all the way to Silver Lake."

"I made it?" He looked at the view again.

She nodded. "Do you feel like running now?"

A gentle breeze drifted off the water, lifting the tendrils of her hair and cooling his skin. Luc couldn't help but notice her nipples pebble underneath the fabric hugging her form.

"Why?" He resisted the urge to reach out and touch her.

"Isn't that what you do? I believe you told me that once, and I've witnessed it." She tilted her head to regard him and waited.

He opened his mouth to argue, but no words came out. He blinked, and they were in the glen once more, Brinna reclining on the chaise, Luc standing at the edge of dais looking at her.

"You're different here," he said.

"How so?" she asked, shifting and offering Luc room to join her on the chaise. He did, perching on the end and twisting so he could look at her. She reclined, stretching out her legs, one hand resting on the arched wing of the chair.

"You seem happier. Freer. More… you." He looked down at her foot pressed against his thigh, and unable to resist touching her, laid his hand over the top of it, his skin connecting with hers, his thumb pressed into the arch. His heart picked up speed, and he could feel it in his throat, hear it like a pulsing ocean in his ears.

She plucked a berry from a bowl next to her and popped it in her mouth. "There is freedom in dreaming. We aren't beholden to the expectations of the beyond."

Luc understood her words but got stuck watching her slip her fingers inside her mouth and suck the berry juice. His insides quickened. "Yes," he managed to say, only he wasn't exactly sure what they'd been talking about, only remembered she'd been about to tell him a story.

"Why do you leave?" she asked.

"I like adventure. The novelty."

"Do you?" she asked.

Luc wanted to lash out and tell her "yes" but then swallowed it. He knew it was a lie. It was because he was afraid of being alone with his thoughts. Shame, guilt, and failure were horrible monsters that pointed gnarled fingers at him and chained him up with doubt. It was impossible to get away from them—except when Roaming. There, they were kept at arm's length. But he didn't feel like admitting that to Dream Brinna. Truthfully, he wouldn't admit that anyone, not even himself in his waking life.

"So the story?" he asked, trying to distract her.

"You want to hear one?" She ate another berry, then offered him one, which he took from her open palm.

"Yes."

"Once upon a time there was a witch who cast a spell on a maiden who'd wandered into her woods."

"Is that you?" he asked, the berry bursting pleasantly in his mouth.

"You'll have to decide if I'm the maiden or the witch," she said with a devious smile and ate another berry, her pink tongue curling around the fruit.

He felt it in his groin and distracted himself by taking another offered berry. "Tell me more."

"The witch trapped the maiden in the forest to steal the maiden's youth and beauty for herself. But the maiden was cunning and made a deal with the witch."

"What sort of deal?"

"She knew the witch hadn't known the pleasure of a man, and so the maid said that if she could lure a man into the meadow and receive pleasure from him—" Her lips closed around another berry.

The sweetness of the berry he'd eaten was vibrant on his tongue as he squeezed her foot with his palm before running his hand over her ankle up to her rounded calf. "What?"

"And if she could, she would be free."

"That doesn't seem like a difficult prospect."

Brinna hummed. "One would think, but men are

very selfish creatures. The witch knew this. Knew that a woman's pleasure was often left to her own devices. So she thought she had a good chance of gaining the maiden's youth and beauty for herself by requiring the deal to be *true* pleasure by a man's doing." Brinna smiled, and her eyebrows rose over her eyes with a challenge. "Do you think you are capable of offering true pleasure?"

True pleasure? Luc pondered the question a moment, knowing he knew how to offer pleasure. But it felt like a trick. "True pleasure?" he clarified but ignored the instinct that there was more meaning embedded in the words. "Are you offering to let me practice?"

She laughed, and it hit him in the solar plexus, radiating down to his groin.

Luc found he was enjoying Brinna, longing to make this time last. He knew it would end, somehow, as if there was someone at the door deep in the forest calling him back.

"Would you like to practice?" Brinna asked as one of her hands skimmed the roundness of her breast, stalling over her nipple, pinching over the fabric and rolling it between her thumb and finger.

His breath caught.

"In the story, the maiden has learned many ways to please herself." She shifted, spreading one of her legs open, then slid her other hand from her knee up her thigh to the keystone of her body. "But has never known true pleasure from a man. But I find practice is a reward." Her hand slipped under the thin fabric of the dress in between her legs.

He watched her with greedy eyes, his belly tightening as hot tendrils of desire shot through his back and blood rushed to his cock. The front panel of her dress obscured the view he wanted to see, but the sight of her relaxed thighs, the movement of her hand underneath the fabric of the dress as she caressed her sex entranced him.

"Are you sure this is a story about her pleasure and not his?" He squeezed her foot.

She mewled a soft sound, as gentle as the falling blossoms raining around them, and arched her back her hips rocking forward. "Both." She moaned the word, and her head fell forward, eyes closed, lips parted with a gasp.

Luc's body tightened, blood surging to his groin as he watched Brinna spin her fantasy for him, touching herself, moaning, moving under her own ministrations.

"Look at me," he ordered and pressed a hand against the hardness in his pants, the thought of pleasure with this woman louder now than the voice in the distance wanting to pull him back.

She lifted her head, eyes open, and focused on him.

His hand tightened around her ankle.

Brinna bent her knee and drew the leg he was holding toward her chest, pulling him toward her. "The maiden was lonely." She gasped, her breath moving in rapid pants, her gaze never wavering. "Can you give me true pleasure, Lucian Uraiahs?"

Luc moved up her reclined form until he leaned over her, one hand against the back of the chaise, the other near her head, entranced by the sight of her face amid her pleasure under him. "Come for me, *mi alora.*"

"She. Waited. And. Waited." Each word from her mouth was a staccato rhythm to the energy he knew was building between her thighs. She drew in a harsh, throaty breath, gasped, then tipped her head back, arched toward him, throat exposed, mouth open in ecstasy, offering a soft cry as she came.

Luc held his breath while he waited, moved by such a beautiful sight, trying to recall a time he'd ever experienced watching a woman's pleasure in wonder. She shuddered, gasped, and shivered as she fell from the rise. He ran a hand up her thigh, over her hip, around the curve of her waist, the fabric catching against his palms.

When she raised her head, her gaze bright with desire, she asked, "Join me?"

The voice in the distance grew louder.

Luc looked over his shoulder but knew that wasn't where he wanted his attention. He wanted to hide from whoever was calling him back to the door, so he returned his gaze to Brinna beneath him. "Is that what you want?"

She smiled. "Since the moment I laid eyes on you."

"I am rather easy on the eye."

She laughed, but her smile faded. "I want your true pleasure, Lucian."

His heart faltered, then expanded at her words.

Had anyone ever been interested in his true pleasure? He'd been through the pleasure-rite as a young god-of-age and had been taught the ways of pleasure. Throughout his Roam, he'd experienced many ways to find pleasure, to offer it.

But he couldn't remember anyone concerned with him, not in any of those interactions. He wasn't sure what to do with that.

The voice was calling for him once more. *Luc! Luc!*

And he knew the voice. It was Nix.

"I promised my brother."

She frowned. "Right. And I'm not your type."

"What?" he asked, confused. "No. That's not—"

With fingertips against the front of his shoulder, she pushed him back and ducked out from under him. "Perhaps it's for the best." She started to walk away.

"What is?" he asked, grabbing her by the waist and pulling her down onto his lap, her back against his chest. His engorged cock pressed against her backside. He thrust his hips up, against her. "Does that feel like you're not my type?" he asked, his lips against the skin of her neck, an arm clamped around her middle.

She moaned, leaning against him, her head falling against his shoulder as she rocked her hips with his, rubbing against his erection. "That feels… so real."

"Stars, Brinna," he said, holding one of her hips as she rocked, helping her move. He sucked in a breath at the sensations her body ignited. "I want to be inside you. I think about you all the time." The words surprised him with their accuracy, the honesty.

"More." She turned, straddling him, her knees framing his hips as she worked at the fastening of his trousers.

"I thought you said clothes were just gone. There wasn't the need to undress."

"I want this to last," she replied. She reached into his open trousers and took hold of his cock.

He groaned. "Fuck. Yes." His head fell back against the chaise. "That feels so real."

"Look at me," she ordered.

He lifted his head, then his eyes from where her hand held him, meeting her intense gaze as he lifted his hips and shimmied his pants down until his cock was free.

Brinna reached between them, grabbing hold of his flesh in her tight grip, and rose onto her knees over him. She slipped her thumb over the moisture on his head and slid her hand down to the base and back up. He groaned, hardly believing this to be real.

With deliberate slowness, she lifted her thumb to her mouth and licked his essence from its tip.

"Fuck, Brinna. What are you doing to me?"

"How do you like it?" she asked. "I want to know."

"Brinna." He reached out and grasped the back of her neck, pulling her down and pressing his mouth against hers, grateful, suddenly, this was a dream. It had to be. Because he didn't care about his promise to Nix. His lips melded with hers, his tongue sliding into her mouth, meeting hers, needing more connection. It felt so real.

"I want to be in you," he said against her mouth, then grasped her hips, needing to feel her body sheathing his.

She drew back. "She's moving through the woods. Hurry." She kissed him with ferocity, absolute need, moving against his cock. Her mewling moans, little words said between kisses, gasps for air fueled Luc's own desire.

"Who?" he moaned into her mouth, their kiss somehow changing the chemistry that made him, as if it were casting a spell to hold him hostage. "Fuck, Brinna. I need you—" And when he said it, he knew that need extended back and back to the beginning.

"I hate it when we don't get to the good part." Brinna bunched the fabric of her dress up into her hands. He helped her lift her skirt, and though he was looking down at her, he couldn't make out her form under all that fabric. "Hurry."

Luc grasped the base of his cock as she adjusted over him. He was poised to enter her as the slick heat of him slid against the velvet of her. She moaned, but the moment he thrust—

He blinked.

He was lying in bed on his side, fully clothed, facing Brinna—and as hard as a fucking rock. His heart raced inside his chest, its rhythm echoing in his ears. Trying to reorient his mind from the dream, he took a deep breath to remember why he was in bed with Brinna.

She'd had a bad dream.

They'd been talking.

Obviously, he'd fallen asleep.

And he'd dreamed about her.

Fuck. The sensations from the dream stuck to his skin and skittered through his body, his cock alive with all the sensations as if he were an emerging adolescent once more in the throes of a wet dream.

He let himself look at her, chastising himself that this in and of itself was crossing a line. He'd crossed it the minute he'd walked into her room as she'd stood there in her transparent nightgown afraid of a nightmare. He'd crossed it the moment he hadn't left. Her company was a balm that somehow filled some of the emptiness plaguing him after what his father had done. It was as if he'd needed her soothing.

So he'd stayed.

And he'd fantasized.

His heart was racing, his body still hot with the hazy remnants of the dream as he recalled what Brinna had said about the disappointment when she didn't get to the good part. It made him smile as he looked at her peaceful face, soft in sleep. Except she looked… upset, somehow, a crease between her eyes, her pouty lips even poutier because they were turned down in a frown.

Then she blinked.

When her gaze connected with his, she blushed.

He had the sensation that she knew exactly what he'd been dreaming, what he'd been thinking. But that was impossible.

"Good morning. Sleep well?" he asked.

She nodded.

He had the compulsion to lean forward and kiss her, which made his heart freeze, then crack with the tension. Unable to stay near her and not fantasize about crossing boundaries, he rolled away and got off the bed, doing what he could to hide his erection.

"I'll go and get some coffee and breakfast together," he said without looking at her. And without waiting for her reply, he made his escape. When the door closed behind him, he leaned against it, bent forward at the waist, breathing quickly—too quickly—as if he were a young god before his sex rite, excited by the prospect of first times.

I want your true pleasure, Lucian.

Just a dream.

He rubbed his forehead and pushed away from the door, resolved to remind himself who he was. Lucian Uraiahs. He might not have his god powers anymore, but he was born of gods. And Brinna was Aurielle's sister. And Nix had expressly forbidden him to cross any lines with Brinna. So he wouldn't. He couldn't. He owed Nix. He just needed to get Brinna Fareview home to her family and out of his life as soon as possible.

Resolved, he moved through Sol, and as he walked down the hallway, he lied to himself that he hadn't felt absolute peace waking up with Brinna beside him.

After Lucian disappeared through the bedroom door, Brinna rolled onto her back with a sigh and frowned at the cedar ceiling. Everything—from the dream, to being in a god's home, to the terror of the day before—was surreal. All of it crashed against her insides, pooling around in her mind and gut, making her feel slightly nauseous.

She turned her head and looked to where Lucian had been the night before. The sun shining through the windows illuminated the stark bright white of the pillowcase, brightening everything about the room: the white walls, the wooden ceiling, the soft bedding. The indention in the pillow beside hers was still visible, proving he had been there and wasn't a figment of her imagination. He'd sat with her, and they'd talked until they'd fallen asleep.

Then she'd dreamt.

A vision of a woodland fantasy flashed in her mind's eye now.

Raining pink blossoms.

A gauzy dress.

Pleasuring herself as Lucian watched.

"*Does that feel like you're not my type*," he'd said in the dream—which wasn't real, she reminded herself, but something her own subconscious perhaps wanted to hear.

But the recollection still made her cheeks and body heat now. She could feel that desire pooling, rushing like liquid heat to important and pleasurable places. The truth was it had been his words she had wanted to hear.

The kiss.

The physical need.

His body pressed between her legs.

Then gone—over at first touch—leaving her breathless and yearning. She pressed a hand between her thighs for relief and thought about Lucian lying next to her only moments ago, watching her with those pensive, golden eyes.

She took a shaky breath.

Just a dream, and she knew she should be grateful that was all it had been. But as she worked over the memory of it, she noticed differences about this dream from others she'd had, though she couldn't put her finger on exactly what. She was used to dreaming and used to the lingering effects of a dream nagging her to pay attention. Mostly her dreams were impressions, as if they were pictures pressed into parchment in a single color, allowing awareness but without discernable details.

This dream, however, had been vibrant with detail and somehow unfamiliar. The color, the striations of petals, the fragrance of flowers, the sound of a creek, the sweetness of the berries on her tongue—and Lucian. There hadn't been anything missing in him. It was as if he'd walked into her dream, a full, complete version of himself, then took her to places he seemed to recognize.

He was a god. Could that be something he could do, she wondered?

How might she bring it up?

But if she did, then he'd know she'd dreamt about him.

The heat in her cheeks grew more intense. No. She couldn't. Not after embarrassing herself.

But then she remembered what he'd told her. His father had taken his power.

She sat up, pressing her fingers to her face to subdue her dramatic reaction to something that had only happened in her mind. The dream hadn't been real, and it wasn't as if she hadn't had pleasure dreams before. Even ones about Lucian. She'd had lots of them. Loved them. She just hadn't ever had to look the object of one in the eye the next day. She imagined seeing Lucian later and the heat in her body intensified.

"It was only a dream," she reminded herself out loud. "My dream. He doesn't know."

Heartened by that realization, she flung the covers off, made the bed, and went into the glorious bathroom. Lucian was making breakfast, and her stomach growled. She hadn't eaten since the wedding. Somewhat reluctantly, she finished showering, then slipped back into the dress and cozy sweater.

It was time to face Lucian.

Retracing the route from her bedroom, she found her way to the glass skyway. Today, she felt brave, enough to stop and admire the view. Below her, clouds drifted between her and the bright, verdant landscape below, a patchwork of varied greens. Breathtaking mountains reached toward the house, capped in clouds and snow. In the distance, the sapphire ribbon of a river meandered like a serpent through the landscape. Standing in the sky was incredible and surreal.

She left the walkway behind and entered the atrium, still awed at the spectacle of a wooded forest in the center of a house. Instead of skirting it, however, like she had the night before, she followed a path into the garden. The trees, the greenery, the blooms reminded her of something. The deeper she wound along the path, the more the impression tightened and strengthened. The trickle of water—the sound—hit her with how much it resembled the magical glen from her dream. Though there weren't any pink petals showering the space, it was eerily similar. She turned in a circle, unclear how that was so.

"That doesn't make sense," she whispered.

But dreams were strange things, she knew. Unruly and very rarely straightforward. She decided she must have unconsciously stored away the information when she'd walked the garden with Lucian the night before.

When she reached the entrance of the path, she looked at the three doors directly in front of her. The day before, Lucian had opened one to reveal the sea. She wondered what she might find if she opened another. It was probably a terrible idea, but she didn't think Lucian would keep monsters behind Elsewhere Doors. No, he'd said they were places he'd been during his Roaming. Besides, he hadn't told her she couldn't or shouldn't open them.

Curious, and telling herself that just one peek wouldn't hurt anyone, she walked to a door and turned the knob. Opening it just a touch. she peered through, then threw it open wide with a gasp. A gray-blue lake stretched out to the horizon as far as she could see. At her feet, dappled pebbles of in a variety of colors lined the shore as frothy waves lapped toward her.

It was the lake from her dream. *Her* dream!

"What the—" She breathed the words like a curse, knowing. "How?"

And yet she'd never seen the lake.

Until now.

She shut the door and leaned against it, her heart

beating an errant rhythm in her chest, unable to explain what she was seeing and how it was in her dream. She could explain the gardens—she had walked through them, even if it had been rushed and dark—but the lake behind the Elsewhere Door? That, she couldn't explain, and it made her feel like she might not be able to catch her breath.

A muffled noise drew her attention away from her unanswerable questions. She left the Elsewhere Doors behind and crossed to the atrium to the glass bridge she knew would take her back to the main room. The din of boisterous and happy voices drifted through the hallways toward her, sounding like... Auri!

Brinna hurried over the glass walkway—ignoring the view this time—not exactly ignoring it; she thought about how amazingly beautiful it was as she dashed through the hallway, bursting out into the great room. It smelled of something delicious. And—

"Auri?" She froze. It wasn't just Auri but also Mattias along with Nixus. "Mattias! You're alright!"

Mattias, looking hale and huge as usual, turned toward her. His brow collapsed over his hazel-gray eyes. "Of course I am!" The look on his face indicated he thought she was being intrusive, as usual.

Brinna rushed forward and grasped his face, making sure he was real, patting his shoulders and arms. "I'm so happy to see you. I looked for you–"

He shook her off like he usually did, even though she knew he appreciated the attention. "Stop."

"You disappeared."

His brown brows crashed together with confusion. "I'm right here." He grinned and held his arms out wide.

She hugged him.

He hugged her back, then pushed her away.

"What are you wearing?" Auri asked, her head tilted and studying Brinna's outfit. "Is that a nightgown? Nix told me you were fine, but I insisted I see for myself. Has Lucian been nice? You've been nice, right, Lucian?"

"It's not a nightgown. It's a dress." Her cheeks heated, thinking about Lucian seeing her in a transparent nightgown the night before, about waking up next to him, about her dream. "He's been a perfect gentleman," she added and glanced around, looking for him.

She found him in the kitchen, just like the night before, pouring hot liquid into a cup. Her heart bounced around inside her chest, drawing in the image he made. He'd showered too, his golden hair damp and wavy around his face. He hadn't shaved, so the stubble made his jaw look even more defined. His dimples, one on each side, cut into his cheeks as he gave her an impish smile. He wore a simple cotton shirt—a pleasing gray—that hugged his lean torso, with short sleeves so she could see the definition in his arms as he pushed a cup toward her. "Coffee?"

Without saying a word, she disengaged from her sister and padded across the floor, for the first time wanting to be in the glow of his presence.

"I added some milk," he said, quietly. "I took a chance since that's how you took your tea."

Her heart surged, expanding. He'd remembered. She nodded and lifted it to her lips, taking a deep breath to inhale the comforting aroma. "Thank you." She offered him a grin to match the bouncing of her heart. "I do like a spot of honey in my coffee. Do you have some?"

"I do have honey." Lucian whirled around in the kitchen, going to a cupboard.

"Stars, honey. I do love honey," Nix said loudly.

Auri choked behind Brinna, and she looked over her shoulder at her sister, whose eyes were wide in her red face.

"Did I say something funny?" Brinna asked.

"No! It's just that honey is my favorite," Nix said. "Always on the hunt for honey with Auri."

Auri giggled; her hand pressed against her smiling mouth.

Nix tapped her back, grinning at her. "Are you alright, my love?"

She nodded, her cheeks blazing red. "Fine," she choked again. "Just swallowed wrong."

"Remember that time–" Nix started with a wide grin, grabbing the back of her neck.

"Nix!" she gasped and pressed a hand over his mouth. "I swear to you, you will pay."

His grin widened as he leaned forward and spoke words only Auri could hear. Her blush grew fierce. Brinna had the feeling she was witnessing something she wasn't supposed to be, which seemed to be how Mattias felt as well because he said, "What's happening?" then frowned.

"Nothing," Auri said, smiling.

"My brother is being a pest to your sister," Lucian explained.

Brinna turned to look at him once more, watching as he pulled plates from a cupboard and placed them on the counter.

"And my brother made someone else coffee." Nix's dark gaze jumped from Lucian to Brinna, his hands still on Auri as if he couldn't keep them to himself. "I don't think I've ever seen Luc do something nice for someone else."

Lucian huffed and poured himself a cup. "I do nice things," he muttered.

"He does," Brinna defended, then waved a hand around the room. "Obviously."

Lucian cleared his throat. "For example, I made everyone breakfast."

Auri tilted her cheek into Nix as he leaned to kiss her. "That is very kind, Lucian, but we just came to collect Brinna."

"So soon?" Lucian asked, setting down his cup and grabbing a plate. "I'm sure she's hungry." His gaze jumped to hers, sizzling the base of her spine.

"I am starving," Brinna admitted, suddenly not wanting whatever peace had occurred between them to end, afraid that as soon as she left, it would.

"Mother and Father are waiting," Mattias said.

"And she's promised to finally tell us the truth."

Brinna turned back toward her siblings. "Now?"

Auri nodded.

Brinna looked over her shoulder at Lucian, holding a plate of something he'd made.

Her glow fizzled as she looked from the plate Lucian set on the counter then to his face, his dimples gone.

"It is overdue," she admitted. "I don't want to keep everyone waiting."

Lucian still wore that thoughtful look she couldn't decipher, but his focus was on the plate. "Is it safe?" His eyes jumped up to hers, then to Nix. He frowned. "She shouldn't go if it isn't safe."

"I scoured the woods, and the darkling seems to have vanished—for now. We'll portal to the edge of the hedge. Scarlett insists the creature can't get through the hedge. So yes, it's as safe as I can make it." Nix took a sip of his own coffee. "Do you want to come with us, Luc?"

Lucian shook his head. "Can't. Father visited."

"Oh." Nix set his cup down.

"I don't want to talk about it."

His powers had been taken. Brinna remembered his confession the night before, but she ignored the impulse to go to him, to wrap him in her arms and offer comfort. It was her way, after all, only this desire wasn't born from keeping peace in the ranks of her family, nor about the order of things, but rather about Lucian and what he might need. It felt different, somehow, more honest.

The night before, he'd revealed the secret with such nonchalance, but now the news seemed weighted with the reality of having lost his power. It made her wonder about his usual indifference about so many things—her included—and how much of that was real.

"Well" –Nix clapped his hands together- "are we ready?"

Brinna was, and she wasn't.

She glanced at Lucian, her heart a heavy rock inside her chest as if she'd missed something very important and was only now discovering it much too late. Except she couldn't identify what it was.

"Yes," Auri said, grabbing hold of Nix and smiling up at him. "I'm ready for the truth."

"Me too," Mattias added.

Brinna walked around the island of the kitchen and set her cup in the sink. Then she turned to face Lucian. "I should change."

"Keep it. Innes won't notice. And I'll have Nix return your dress. Later," he added.

She looked up at him. "Lucian…"

He seemed to want to step closer, his body leaning toward her, but then didn't.

She tried not to be disappointed.

"Thank you. For everything."

He swallowed, nodded, but didn't reply.

Brinna walked back through the room to her siblings and Nix, then turned to look at Lucian, who'd followed. It wasn't a breath later that Lucian and Sol faded from sight as she felt as if she were falling and standing still simultaneously, the Whitling Woods along with the hedge coalescing around them. She pressed a palm to her heart, suddenly sharp with an ache she didn't quite understand and didn't know how to process.

"I will never get used to that," Mattias said and started through the hedge, disappearing into the darkness inside.

"Auri—"

Brinna watched Auri step close to Nix and grab hold of his jacket. He leaned closer, and Auri whispered words meant for only him.

He grinned, turning his head slightly into her and kissing her cheek. "Get your sister inside," he ordered. "I'll return with Lachlan soon, after you've had a chance to talk with your mother. Then you're mine." He faded away still holding Auri's hand.

Brinna followed Mattias through the hedge, Auri a few steps behind. Brinna glanced over her shoulder at her sister, who was talking.

"I hate being apart from him," Auri said and pressed her fingers to her heart, her eyes glistening with tears.

"It's temporary," Brinna offered and thought of Lucian, which didn't make sense. They'd made peace, but the inexplicable desire to turn around and go back was extreme. She wouldn't need to see him again unless it involved Nix and Auri—so why did the thought of that make her feel so sad?

When they reached the cottage, Scarlett was setting tea service out on the table along with food. Tarley and Jessamine were near her, setting platters of food down as well.

Brinna's stomach rumbled.

"You're here!" Her mother's exuberance was a bit too animated. She rushed from the table to wrap Brinna in a tight hug. "You're safe."

Brinna's belly rumbled with hunger again, but she hugged her mother back.

Scarlett pressed her palms against Brinna's cheeks, her gray eyes scanning Brinna's face as if searching for some change. After she let go of Brinna's cheeks, her mother took her hands, checking for the ribbon that was ever-present. Brinna's gaze jumped to Tarley and Auri, who'd lost theirs.

Scarlett finally smiled. "My family is all together. Again."

Brinna turned to her sisters clumped together near the table, to Mattias flopped on the couch. Their father had stalled in the doorway to the backroom, but now resumed his walk, moving to kiss her before crossing to the hearth to add wood to the fire.

"I'm so relieved," Scarlett added as she picked up the tea pot once more and filled the cups on the table.

"Well, I'm safe," Brinna said. "Thanks to Lucian." She plucked at a scone and popped it in her mouth.

Jessamine dried her hands on her apron. "Why weren't you with us?"

Brinna glanced around at her family; their eyes

heavy on her as they waited for an explanation. "I was looking for Mattias. I was worried about him, but I didn't want to bother anyone. Everyone was having so much fun."

"Worried about me?" Mattias asked.

Brinna nodded. "You looked like you were unhappy, and I watched you walk into the inn and followed to talk."

His brows folded together. "You followed me?"

Brinna nodded and took another bite. "You weren't there, so I thought maybe you'd left for home."

"We asked you not to leave the inn," her father said.

"They said not to leave the inn," Mattias echoed. "Why would I have left?"

"I know, but I couldn't find you," Brinna said. "And I wasn't thinking. I'm sorry."

"We heard the screech of the darkling–" Jessamine shuddered.

"I'm supposed to be leaving for my honeymoon," Tarley grumbled, getting to the point of things. "Lachlan will be here soon. Let's get this over with."

Jessamine followed Scarlett as she poured the last cup of tea. "It's time for the truth, Mother."

Scarlett set the teapot down and swiped her hands over her apron. "Yes. I owe you that, but the story isn't a pleasant one. Sit. Take some tea with me first so we can think of happier things, like being together. That we're all here. Safe." She paused, her eyes jumping to Tarley, then back down at the table.

Brinna took her seat next to Auri and watched the rest of her family take their usual places around the table. Her heart thumped, ready to hear the story their mother had been withholding from them, but also afraid. Afraid because she knew whatever it was, she had a feeling it was going to change everything.

Her mother seemed nervous. Brinna supposed she could empathize with Scarlett's anxiety about sharing the story she'd withheld from them for the whole of their lives. While Brinna loved her mother and respected her reasons, she along with her family was ready to hear it.

But the silence stretched on, and in the strained atmosphere, she wished she were at Sol breaking bread with Lucian instead. A strange desire.

The clink of the dishes as they drank tea seemed overly loud as each of them nibbled on scones and pastries arranged on plates around the table, the only sounds giving the cottage life. Worse, the longer Scarlett remained silent, the more strained Brinna's siblings grew. Especially Tarley and Auri.

Scarlett sat in her usual place at one end of the table, Tomas at the other. Brinna had taken her usual place between Auri and Tarley, which was why she could feel their tension so acutely. Jessamine and Mattias sat across from them.

Jessamine caught Brinna's eye, her dark brows coming together with confusion and a flick of her gaze at their mother and back to Brinna.

Brinna shrugged, unsure, then jumped when the fire cracked loudly in the hearth.

"Mother–" Tarley started, her strained patience lacing her tone. "You promised. The wedding is over."

"Yes. I did." Scarlett set her teacup in its saucer, and Brinna detected a slight rattle of the porcelain.

Scarlett wiped her hands with her napkin, then her mouth. "I'm not sure where to begin."

"Start with the ribbons," Jessamine suggested, laying a hand over Scarlett's forearm. Scarlett reached over and patted Jessamine's hand, then ran a thumb over her ribbon.

"Auri was right," Scarlett started, then stopped, leaning back in her chair after picking up her cup once more and taking a sip. This time she kept the cup between her hands.

Brinna took another sip of her tea, glancing at the herbs floating inside, a nice zip of cardamom and lemon with a touch of something sweet.

"A protection spell?" Auri reached and touched Brinna's ribbon. "From what? Why magic? None of it makes sense."

"One thing at a time," their father said. "Let her go at her pace, yes?"

Scarlett paused, her eyes hopping between them as she seemed to consider what to say. Brinna followed her mother's gaze glancing from Tomas to Jessamine, who exuded the patience she always did. Tarley shifted in her seat with contrasted impatience. Mattias watched Scarlett expectantly, his mouth full of scone. Their father took a sip of his tea, watching Scarlett over the top of the cup as he sipped. Auri narrowed her gaze, communicating her displeasure.

Brinna took another sip of her tea and set the cup down, turning the dish so the handle was just right. "Mother?" she prompted after Tarley sighed next to her.

"You must know," Scarlett said, "everything I have done has been to protect you."

"From what?" Auri asked, exasperated now, a great heft to the words.

"Him." Mattias took another bite of his second scone.

It looked delicious, and Brinna was so hungry. She took a bite of the one she'd put on her plate, the cinnamon, sugar, and butter flavors bursting on her tongue. She was famished and polished it off.

"Does anyone need more? Tea? Maybe some more scones or fruit?" Scarlett stood.

"Enough with the food, Mother," Tarley snapped and set her cup in the saucer with a clank. "You're stalling. I don't have the time or patience for it."

"Agreed," Auri added.

Scarlett sank back onto her chair, then glanced at the table, watching Jessamine take another sip of her tea.

"Keep going," Auri said. She lifted the cup to her lips, sipped, then set it down.

Scarlett nodded, then glanced at Tomas, and back to her own tea. With her hands clasped under the table in her lap, Brinna watched as Scarlett hunched in on herself.

Brinna gulped down the last bite of scone she'd practically inhaled, worried suddenly. Her mother looked… withered, and that was not who Brinna knew her mother to be.

"Mother?" she asked, taking another sip of tea to wash down the scone.

Scarlett's gray eyes flashed up to Brinna's. She offered a short smile as if to reassure her, then looked back to her own teacup. "This isn't easy." She took another sip, turning her head to glance out the window.

"It's okay." Brinna tried to comfort her. "We love you, and whatever it is–"

Scarlett looked back at them and shook her head. "You say that. But–" She stopped, pressing her lips together into a thin line. Shaking her head, she adjusted in her seat before taking another sip of her tea.

They all did, a chorus of sips, waiting.

Scarlett cleared her throat, rubbed her hands over her skirt, then stood, picking up the tea pot and walking around the table, refilling each of their cups. "I wasn't born in Kaloma."

"Wow?" Mattias looked around, eyes wide. "I didn't know that." He reached for a cut of crispy shortbread and took a bite, his obvious enjoyment convincing Brina to take some.

"Where were you born?" Jessamine asked.

"In a land very far from here."

"How far?" Mattias looked up from his plate.

"A different home—not Sevens?" Tarley tilted her head, then looked around the table with a forced smile, as if she were trying to put Scarlett at ease. "Imagine that." She adjusted her teacup, spinning it around in front of her. "We could have grown up somewhere else. I might not have met Lachlan." She took a sip.

"That's hard to imagine," Auri said, then took another drink. "Not meeting Nixus."

"Does it have a name?" Jessamine asked.

Scarlett hesitated and swallowed. "I can't remember the name," she said, dragging out the words as if searching for them. "It has been so long–"

Auri's eyes narrowed. "Who doesn't remember the place where they grew up? I will remember Sevens and these woods for the rest of my days."

"It isn't important to the overall story," Scarlett said, her eyes jumping to Auri as Auri stifled a yawn behind the back of her hand.

Brinna yawned, as did everyone else around the

table. "Yawns are contagious," she said, hoping for the levity that usually graced their time together at this table. But no one joined her.

"Tell them what's relevant," Tomas said, then covered his mouth as he, too, yawned.

"There was a king there," Scarlett said. "Where I grew up."

"A king?" Brinna asked and stifled another yawn behind her palm. The stress of the last few days must have been catching up with her. A woozy weight moved through her body, weighing her limbs like she was being held down. Brinna lifted her hand, thinking to reach for her tea, and watching it as if it belonged to someone else.

"Yes." Scarlett nodded. "And I remember it being beautiful," she added.

"I feel weird," Tarley said, and her voice drifted as if realizing something. "Wait. I've seen this…" Tarley stood abruptly, stumbled, and pressed her palms to the table, her accusing gaze on Scarlett. "Mother?"

"Like a dream–" Brinna said, yawning once more before turning toward Auri. She was moving so slowly—as if she were submerged in water. With a shake of her head, she looked across the table.

Jessamine's eyes widened. She looked down at her cup before her dark eyes flashed to Scarlett's. "Mother. You didn't." She shook her head as though trying to clear it.

"Mother," Tarley said. "You did." Then she slumped back into her seat and fell forward hitting the table with a crash, followed by Jessamine and Tomas.

Brinna turned to look at their mother, who sat watching. The only one of them not yawning. "Oh. Mother. No." It was the last thing Brinna remembered before everything went black.

The Spell

A drop of this potion— two, three, or four—
will call to the Deep Sleep and close the door,

to slip into Dreamland locked up nice and tight,
with a magical beastie guarding with might.

One whose heart is bound and pure
Can face the beastie and endure.

A true heart to be veiled from sight
to reach the dreamer bound to endless Night.

Upon True Love's kiss, the spell will break,
and into True Love's arms, the dreamer will awake.

L uc welcomed the quiet at Sol after Nixus whisked away the Fareviews, at least that's what Luc told himself. But after thirty minutes of telling himself it was what he wanted, it felt cloying and uncomfortable. He was listless and achy. Brinna had caught his eye just before she'd effervesced back to her circle, and Luc returned to it in his mind over and over.

At first, he'd decided her look had meant nothing. Then he'd decided, it was just her being friendly, a *thank you* of sorts. Then a question. What did that look mean? Had Brinna meant something by it? Then later:

what if it meant something? How would he ever know? Did he want to know?

With a frustrated groan, Luc slammed shut the book he'd been trying to read. He wandered Sol, making sure everything was in working order. He spent time in the atrium, pruning the plants. He even stopped at the doorway of the room where Brinna had slept, the bed—though made—not quite as perfect as it had been before she'd slept there. He'd checked the doors to Elsewhere, none of which he could cross into—he learned—without his power.

Eventually, he flopped on the couch in the living room and stared out at the sky beyond the windows, contemplating the purpose of his existence. His father was controlling the light for the time being. Luc watched the sun trek across the sky, wondering if there was anything different, wondering if he was truly necessary.

He doubted it.

Eventually, he rolled over, his face toward the cushions, and drifted to sleep.

When awareness found him, he was standing at a door, feeling like he'd been there before, though he didn't recognize it. It wasn't a door to Elsewhere—tall, narrow, and true—but rather a small one, round and wooden with an ancient-looking patina of moss glazing its surface. It seemed to be suspended in front of him, and he could neither turn around or go around it; he couldn't even see beyond it. Only the door existed, so he turned the brass knob and stepped through.

He was standing in the woods. A forest covered in winter white, and it was snowing. Everything was in shades of black, white, and gray. The impulse to shiver pushed against his awareness, but he realized he wasn't cold. Unsure where he was supposed to go, he walked, his shoes moving noiselessly over the terrain, though a glance over his shoulder, he discovered he was still leaving footprints. When he looked forward, the forest remained noiseless, locked in the muffled acoustics of a snowfall.

"Hello?" he called out and felt as if his words dropped into the snow at his feet, traveling nowhere.

Suddenly there was a rush of sound like a vortex of wind, and a voice called, "Lucian?"

Luc spun where he stood, certain it was Brinna's voice, but the forest was empty. "Brinna?"

"I'm here!" she cried out.

"I can't see you," he answered, turning around once more, sure she was just within arm's reach.

"I'm behind the hedge."

"Keep talking." Luc started forward. "I'll find you."

"I'm stuck. Trapped. She trapped us!"

"Who?" he asked. Though he didn't know where Brinna was, he started running. "Are you in danger?"

The dreamscape stretched endlessly so it felt as if he were running in place. "Brinna?"

"No. I'm safe. I think–"

Then, suddenly, as if he'd stopped moving, a small green dot—the only bit of color he could see—rushed toward him until it stopped at the tips of his toes. He tilted his head up and saw he was standing outside a brilliant green hedge that stretched as high as he could see and as long in both directions. Thick with massive leaves, vines as thick as his thigh curled in and out of one another with thorns so sharp it seemed impossible to squeeze through.

"I'm at a hedge," he told her.

"At the cottage?"

He'd seen that hedge before, stood inside it once with Brinna. This was not that hedge. Of course he must be dreaming because Brinna was... where was she again?

"I can't see you," Luc said, and reached out, curling his hand around a vine. A thorn pricked his finger. He pulled it back, a bead of bright red blood welling at the tip, dropping to leave another drop behind. A blood-red flower sprouted where it had fallen, blooming wide and bright, and in the blink of an eye it sprouted a fat thorn as the petals shriveled and fell away.

Luc snatched his hand away. "Brinna?"

"Lucian!" Her voice suddenly sounded so far away. "Lucian," she repeated, now clear and close, as if she were relieved to see him. As if she were–

He turned and there she was, dressed in a dress and sweater that weren't enough for the cold.

She rushed forward and threw her arms around him. "You're here." The sensation of her against him was... so real. The solidity of her body, the binding of her hold, the wet of her tears against the skin of his neck, her familiar scent invading his lungs.

He wrapped his arms around her, his palms slipping over the silky fabric, and drew her in closer. The proximity affected his ability to breathe, though in a good way. He hadn't even realized he'd barely been drawing breath without her.

"Where else would I be?" he asked, her hair tickling his skin.

Brinna's arms tightened.

"Lucian!" A different voice, somewhere behind him.

"No!"

And suddenly Brinna was ripped from his arms.

"Lucian!" Her scream cut off abruptly as if a door slammed shut.

Luc's eyes flew open as he gasped. The fabric covering on the couch was the first thing he saw. Asleep. Fuck. He'd been asleep. He sat up, rubbing the sleep from his eyes and shook his head. Unsettled, he attempted a deep breath to clear the dream from his body, but it lingered like tree sap on skin.

"Luc!"

He jumped up from the couch and spun to find Nix striding across the room toward him. He looked terrible. His brother's usually impeccable attire was haphazard, his hair a fright as if he'd been yanking at it so it stood on end. "Auri's in trouble." He paced.

Luc sank back onto the couch. "What do you mean?"

Nix's arms flew out to his sides. "I don't know.

She's just… I can't feel her." He tapped his chest. "No. I can but it's…" He swallowed and shoved his hands into his hair, pulling.

"Brother," Luc said, his heart still racing with the strange dream, pulsing against his waking mind. He took a deep breath. "Why don't you sit for a second. Breathe. Tell me what happened. She can't just be gone," he added. "They're safe at the cottage."

Nix flopped into the closest chair, his elbows to his knees, his hands still holding his hair. "No. Not gone. But there's something wrong with the cottage. No. The hedge."

The hint of something important tingled at the base of Luc's neck. "What do you mean?"

"After leaving Auri at the cottage, I returned with Lachlan to the inn. You know" –he waved his hand around– "so they could have their family conversation."

"You and Lachlan?" Luc chuckled. "That sounds… engaging. I can't imagine what you talked about."

"What it's like to be a god," Nix said, jumping up again and pacing. "He bored me with details about his royal highness…ness. But that's beside the point. When we went back, Lachlan can usually find the entrance to the hedge, whereas I can't—it's the magic that blocks me—us. It doesn't block him, well, not anymore because of Tarley, I guess, that and he's mortal."

"You're rambling."

"Sorry. He couldn't find it."

"Couldn't find what? The hedge?"

"No. The hedge is there." He made an incredulous snort. "There's no entrance."

The giant hedge from his dream appeared in Luc's mind. Surely a coincidence. "Why?"

"That's just it. The hedge is… different, Luc. It was like a behemoth had grown in its place, completely changed. We hadn't been more than a couple of hours. And the thorns."

Luc's gut tightened. "What did you say?" His heart compressed with awareness, though his mind wanted to doubt what he was hearing even as snapshots of his dream resurfaced.

"I don't know what... It's hard to explain. Like being in the spell. Like the enchantment. It must be. The hedge that was around the cottage has changed, and neither Lachlan nor I can get through. My power was useless. As usual." Nix sunk onto the couch and put his face in his hands. "If something has happened to Auri–"

"Can you take me?" Luc asked, needing to see it for himself, to calm the pressure that was compressing his innards, making him feel like he might implode.

Nix stood. "Yes."

Sol drained away, and the Whitling Woods formed around them, the fall foliage hinting at the coming winter. Reds, oranges, and yellows vibrant in the deciduous trees, and the evergreens offered deeper shadows. The air held the bite of the coming winter.

Luc reached for his light, recalling too late it was gone. He crossed his arms over his chest, instead. Around them, there was a flurry of activity. Soldiers bustling to and fro erected tents, built pens, and lead horses with wagons, making a camp.

"What is this?" Luc asked.

"Lachlan. He's freaking out."

"He did just get married, and his new bride is…" Luc turned, and the words caught in his throat before his breath unhooked. He sucked in a ragged gasp. "Holy fuck."

The hedge—the one he'd been in all those months ago—reached high into the sky, stretching as far as the eye could see. The broad leaves had grown and were wrapped with vines upon vines like coiled snakes. And there were thorns. It was the hedge from his dream.

"I wish I could agree that it was something holy," someone said.

Luc looked to the speaker. Lachlan—the crown prince of some random neighboring country—stood next to him, looking up just as he'd been, just as Nixus was on Luc's other side. Lachlan looked about as good as Nixus, his hair a mess though perhaps a touch more put together. No god-yoke, Luc figured.

"This is from the Netherworld," the young prince said, hands on his hips, then pointing at the monstrosity as if it would yield to his command. "And I need it gone. I need my wife–"

"My guess is that our sister wouldn't agree this is from the Netherrealm," Luc said. "But we'll certainly ask her."

"Did you try anything yet?" Nix asked Lachlan.

"We tried burning. Fire is useless. Chopping makes it grow back thicker."

"Anything else?"

"Climbing is too dangerous. And it seemed to respond to blood. A soldier bumped into it, got stabbed by the thorns, then sucked inside where he was… consumed. After that, it sprouted new thorns." Luc looked at Lachlan, who shuddered. "I can still hear him screaming."

"That's pleasant," Luc replied.

"We'll try Lexa's fire," Nix said. "And she can fly, maybe get over the top?"

Silence drifted through and around them, binding them up in their worry.

"This is… unfathomable," Lachlan eventually said. "I just don't understand it."

While Luc didn't really have a heart, he did feel for the young prince, his bride now missing behind this monstrosity. And for his brother, whose god-yoke would certainly be an issue. Luc had seen many things in his life wandering, but nothing like this.

After telling Lachlan they were going for Lexa, Nix returned them to Sol.

"Are you… okay?" Luc asked. "I mean, I know you're not okay, but …" His words drifted away, not sure how to process what he'd seen.

"I can't talk with her. I don't know what to do."

"You're a god, Nixus."

Nix looked up. "And what good has it ever done me? What good is it doing now? I can't talk to her. I can't feel her. I can't fix the god-yoke." He tapped his chest. "I can't fix it with my powers. I am powerless."

Luc swallowed his initial comment on being powerless. It wouldn't help. Instead, he took a deep breath, wishing he had better words of wisdom for his brother. He didn't. He was fresh out, and perhaps he'd never had any to begin with. He'd bungled being a god so badly he was trapped in Sol without an ounce of his power.

But then—he'd dreamed about the hedge before Nix had told him. Luc opened his mouth to tell his brother, then closed it, unsure of himself, doubting what he'd experienced. How could he dream of Brinna and the hedge? He didn't know how to explain that to Nix. He didn't know how to explain that to himself.

"What about Father and Mother?" Luc asked instead.

Nix stood with a frustrated sigh, his hands in his hair again. "Father isn't exactly a paragon of compassion when it comes to helping mortals."

"We both know she isn't mortal. It's an impossibility. Perhaps you can appeal to his love for you? It isn't like you can control a god-yoke," Luc replied. "You could agree to be his replacement."

"No. He doesn't want me anyway. He wants you."

Luc rolled his eyes. "We both know that's a terrible idea."

"It isn't," Nix said, though his tone was distracted.

"Maybe Mother could help. She controls the seasons. She could cast winter early, freeze the hedge."

"It's an enchanted hedge," Nix said. "If my power didn't work, I'm not sure hers will either. Besides, Mother isn't prone to helping mortals any more than father."

That was true. "So we'll just try Lexa's dragon fire?"

Nix nodded. "We'll probably be making the same point. Enchanted."

"Who set the enchantment?"

Nix looked up, his eyes widening and his hands leaving his hair. "That's the question!" He snapped his fingers and pointed at Luc. "The right one." He stood.

"Who has the most to gain by trapping the Fareviews behind the hedge?" Luc mused.

Nix stopped, holding up a finger as if he'd thought it through, but then put it down and began pacing again.

Luc watched his brother, silent as his steps took him back and forth. After a while, Luc looked down at his own feet, unable to watch Nix, trying to recall the specifics of his dream. Brinna had been behind the hedge. She'd said she wasn't in danger, but that she'd been trapped by *a her*—a woman. He looked up at his brother. As ridiculous as it was going to sound, he owed him—

"I'm going to tell you something."

"Luc. I don't need a confession. I need—" Nix stopped and leveled a hard stare on Luc. "What happened with Brinna?"

Luc shook his head. "No! No!" He had no intention of confessing his sex dreams to his brother.

"What is it, then? But it better be helpful to this specific scenario. I don't want to hear about a weird rash you had to have healed. You know what will happen to Auri and I."

"I know." He'd seen the effects over their forced separations. The way Nix faded, becoming a ghost of himself. The despondency, the sadness, the listlessness.

Nix swiped a hand over his brow. "What is it, then?"

"I dreamed of the hedge," Luc confessed. "Right before you arrived. Giant. Green. Vines. Thorns. The works. In the dream I pricked my finger, and the blood made a thorn grow."

Nix sat down. "How? How is that possible?"

"I don't know. Truly. I don't." But he suddenly thought about the night before, the detailed dream he'd had of Brinna, of nearly fucking her. And now this dream. How real she'd felt in his arms. How when he'd awoken both times, it was as if they were memories rather than the conjurings of a dream. He had no intention of telling Nix about the first one, but it did seem a strange coincidence. "I heard a voice on the other side of the hedge."

"A voice?"

Luc nodded. "It sounded like…" He paused, worried that his brother might put together that Luc was feeling some type of way for Brinna, but given the situation, that seemed a minor issue. "Like Brinna. Saying they'd been trapped. By an unspecified *her*."

Nix whirled to face the windows. "You dreamed of the hedge and of Brinna speaking to you from the other side?"

The sun had begun to fade in the sky, casting Nix's face in golden light. Incredulity was the first emotion on his face, then it shifted, morphing into the hope of possibility. "And she said they'd been trapped by *her*?" He took a deep breath as he pondered something, then turned back to Luc. "For argument's sake" –Nix's gaze reconnected with Luc's– "let's say it's real. I know someone who's spent a lot of time protecting what's behind that hedge."

"Their mother." Luc's eyebrows arched high. "You think Auri's mother would have trapped them inside?"

"I think it's time to find out exactly what Scarlett Fareview is hiding. And you're going to help me."

rinna tried to come up for air, panicked, and thrashed for the surface. *No. No. No!* Her mind rebelled. She could feel the weight pressing against her chest, afraid she was going to take a gulp of air and that liquid would be the only thing filling her lungs. She was stuck, drowning in the thick, viscous substance holding her captive. With her eyes open, all she could see was a blurry haze of gray, as if she'd been dropped into the deep of nothing and nowhere.

Then she couldn't hold her breath any longer; she opened her mouth and screamed, "Help!"

Nothing filled her lungs, her breath moving in and

out as it should, but the word she'd screamed drifted like a leaf, wobbled, and fell, fading as it disintegrated in the deep gray that held her captive.

Not underwater, then, though that was how she felt. Slow, floating, weightless, though there was pressure pushing against her body. Frightened, she curled into a ball and cried. *Help. Help. Help*, she sobbed to the rhythm of the word chanted in her mind. After she'd spent her tears and the fear waned, the word changed. *Think. Think. Think.*

A dream.

This was a dream!

"Wake up," she told herself, then repeated the command, but nothing happened. She remained where she was. If it was a dream, it wasn't like any other dream she'd had, much like the one she remembered having of Lucian recently—how real that had seemed. Was this real?

Concentrating, Brinna forced her mind to focus on what she knew. What she could remember. But grasping onto those memories was difficult, as they were distant and wrong, somehow, a mismatched pattern of movement, light, and sound she couldn't reassemble, making her feel nauseous. She pictured Sol. Of looking at Lucian one more time before— before what?

Brinna uncurled her body, drifting in the strange liquid-like state, and shut her eyes. She needed to remember something. Though there was no reason to know it, she was sure it was the only way to unlock the gray.

"Hello?" a resonant but substantive voice called out.

Brinna's eyes flew open, and she dropped from the jelly that held her onto the ground with a thud, thick, gray liquid raining around her, until she was in a puddle. She touched her silk dress—the one she'd worn at Sol. Completely dry. When she looked around, she was outside the cottage.

Home. She was home! She stood and started back toward the cottage. Her family would know what was happening.

A dream, her mind reminded her.

"Lucian!" she screamed, then spun back toward where she'd been and noticed the hedge. It had always been large, looming like a massive wall around the cottage, but it had been beautiful, with bright white flowers and broad green leaves. Now, however, it rose so high she couldn't see the top, and any passageway through it was gone. The white flowers were withered, the leaves dull and gray, now tightly woven with vines accentuated with impressive thorns.

Something's not right. Her mind was trying to tell her. She bent forward and groaned, clutching her stomach.

"Brinna?" the voice called out, far away but ringing like a vibrant bell. It was Lucian's voice.

She gasped for breath as the pain in her gut eased. Images rushed through her like phantoms. The darkling. Sol. Lucian. His father. Her dream of Lucian. Nix and Auri and Mattias at Sol to bring her home.

Sitting around the table in the cottage. Her family assembled as they drank tea. Waiting for their mother to tell them… something. Then Tarley had fallen forward onto the table. Followed by Jessamine. Then their father, and Brinna hadn't been able to keep her eyes open as the darkness of unconsciousness had rushed toward her.

"I'm here!" she cried out to Lucian, grasping onto one of the vines. Color leached back into the plant where she touched it.

"I can't see you."

Brinna pulled her hand back, the color fading. She looked at her hand, gray like everything else. "I'm behind the hedge."

"Keep talking. I'll find you," he said.

She didn't understand why she'd conjured Lucian, but she wasn't going to be picky.

She spun back toward the cottage and realized it was drained of color and life, filtered in shades of gray. She thought back to sitting at the table, to the tea, and bent forward again as a pain struck her once more. "I'm stuck," she gasped. She thought of Jessamine looking at their mother and saying, "*You didn't,*" just before she'd collapsed.

"Trapped. She trapped us." Brinna's heart tightened in her chest as the pain in her stomach faded, and she looked up at the hedge once more. Her mother had done this! Rather than tell them, she'd poisoned them.

"Are we dead?" she asked and closed her eyes,

allowing her mind to move. It floated away from her, flying toward the cottage, then into it, finding her family. Her parents curled together, asleep in front of the fire. Mattias in her parents' bed. Asleep. Through the cabin and up the steps. Each of her sisters, herself, tucked into their beds. All sleeping peacefully, or so she believed. When she opened her eyes again, she was in her dream body.

"Who? Are you in danger?" he asked. When she didn't answer, he called her name again.

"No." She turned back to the hedge. "I'm safe. I think–"

"I'm at the hedge," Lucian said.

"At the cottage?" Brinna rushed to the hedge but didn't touch it.

His voice was faded on the other side. "I can't see you."

Brinna shut her eyes. *Think. Think. Think.*

"Brinna?" Lucian's voice carried through the hedge, the warmth of it grabbing hold of something inside her.

"Lucian?" She opened her eyes, and there he was, standing an arm's length away in beautiful, vibrant color. "Lucian!" She rushed forward, into his arms, and the terror of being alone receded.

His arms wrapped around her, pressing her close. He was so real. The strength of his back shifted under her hands, the scent of sunshine—warmth and citrus and clothes fluttering on a line—filled her senses, the strength of his body molding to hers. She tightened her hold around him, afraid of letting him go.

The sound of tearing paper interrupted her contentment, her peace, followed by the pins and needles of a limb reawakening as blood rushed back.

Lucian was ripped from her grasp.

"Lucian?"

There was no answer.

"Lucian!" she screamed.

He was gone.

He wasn't real, she reminded herself. *You're in a dream.*

You're in a dream!

No longer on the opposite side of the hedge, she turned back and walked across the meadow toward the cottage. *I'm in a dream,* she told herself. Color bloomed around her as she walked. When she touched the doorknob, color spread across the wood, returning it to the color she knew. She stepped inside, bringing the color with her, where her parents remained the same as before.

If they were asleep, then there had to be a way to wake them?

Brinna doubled over again, pain shooting through her belly. "Poison," she gasped. She looked around for something, anything, considering all the ways she'd ever woken from a dream. Pain. Fear. Sex. The pain was immense, powered by the fear pulsing through her.

And yet she remained asleep, remained where she was in the dream.

I'm dreaming, she thought, breathing through it, and

the pain waned.

As it subsided, she took the stairs, color invigorating the cottage as she went, and hurried into the room she shared with her sisters. At her bedside, she reached across Auri and nudged her own sleeping self. "Brinna," she said and shook her own shoulder, but Sleeping Brinna didn't respond. Nothing. She nudged Auri next. Then Tarley and Jessamine.

This was a dream.

And Brinna was a dreamer. She didn't know if there were any rules, so she closed her eyes, and when she opened them, she was in her mind's version of Sol. It wasn't exactly the same, the edges muted and hazy, though it was vibrant with color—oversaturated colors, making the details obscure.

"Lucian?" she called.

"I'm here," he said from behind her.

Brinna whirled around to face him. It wasn't quite Lucian, but rather a replica of him. A variation of the man she knew, as if he was the copy of an image of the Lucian she'd been with in her dream before. That confused her since she knew dreams to be shades of truth. But everything else about this dream felt different somehow. "Can you help me?" she asked.

"No," he said, and burst into thousands of butterflies that fluttered away.

Sol melted away, dripping down to the ground, returning Brinna into the room of the cottage where she and her sisters lay asleep. She wondered if she could get beyond the hedge. With a thought she was, standing on the outside of it in her version of the Whitling Woods, the bows of the trees bright with verdant greens. In the next thought, she was back in the cottage standing between the two beds where she lay with her sisters.

It wasn't like any dream she'd ever had before—more coherent. Perhaps it wasn't poison in the cups, but a potion. A sleeping potion. She looked around at her sleeping sisters, then returned to the main room of the cottage and crouched down near her mother.

"What did you give us?" she asked, but Scarlett didn't stir.

Brinna wondered why she'd taken it with them. They were all trapped there. Asleep. And while Brinna had always been the fixer in their family, she had no idea how to fix this.

Later that night, after the sun had gone down and Nix had left to talk their sister Lexa into using dragon fire on the hedge, Luc stood in his bedroom staring at his bed. Confusion and concern plagued his thoughts with an unanswerable question. How had he dreamed of the hedge before he'd known about it?

He spent the rest of the evening contemplating his dreams, considering and wondering if he'd ever had the sort of dream to predict something would happen, but couldn't remember having had that occur. He'd had strange dreams twice in a row now, and that made him wonder if he'd have another that night? Though truthfully, he was too keyed up to sleep.

So he laid on his still-made bed, still clothed, his legs crossed at his ankle, and thought about Nix. They'd planned a trip to the Library of Oracles if things with Lexa didn't pan out. As much as he wanted to help Nix, Luc wasn't sure how much help he'd be without his powers, though there was one positive: his father wouldn't know he'd left. Luc pressed his fingers to his twinging heart, a slight discomfort reminding him he was without his powers. He wondered if he was suffering the effects.

His bed felt strange, for some reason, but of course he hadn't slept in it the night before. He'd been in bed with Brinna, platonically, of course, though what had happened in his dream certainly hadn't been platonic. His dick twitched as he recalled it, but then he felt ridiculous. He reached down and adjusted his semi-hard cock. Dream Brinna had been so uninhibited with him, and he'd really fucking liked it.

He wondered if she was behind the hedge with her family in the midst of a wild domestic squabble that would be cleared up in the morning. That the hedge—under duress of a Fareview battle—had grown and would disappear, and all would go back to normal, so they'd only have to worry about the darkling. He thought of Nix and Lachlan and their restless energy under the stress of being separated from the women they loved, both focused on solving the problem. Perhaps they just needed to take a breath and wait.

He punched his pillow, adjusted things to get more comfortable, then settled into his bed, knowing he'd need sleep. A hint of anticipation swirled in his gut at the thought of dreaming of Brinna again, but he also realized that was unlikely. One couldn't control their dreams. Yawning, he laced his fingers over his stomach, wondering at dreams and godlight. Maybe a god could control their dreams—not that he had his powers any longer, but that was something to… maybe something to…

His eyes fluttered open. He was standing in that strange in-between space where nothing existed behind or around him except for the door. Round, wood, ancient. He'd been at this door before and in the next thought, he knew he was asleep. He pushed open the door and walked through.

Once more, he entered the woods, though now it was vibrant with fall colors. Leaves drifted around him like snow.

"Brinna?" he called, his voice sounding hopeful, if tentative, in his own ears. Would he be so lucky to find her here once more?

"Lucian!" Brinna answered.

He whirled at the sound of her voice to see he was already standing outside the hedge, and Brinna was only an arm's length away. She appeared as she had the last time he'd seen her here, in that blue silk dress that skimmed her gorgeous curves. Now her copper-gold hair was loosely braided. Then she was in his arms, hers curled around his shoulders. Chest to chest, his arms wrapped around her, pulling her in tight, his hand skimming across the silk fabric of the dress at her lower back.

It all felt so familiar.

"How are you here?" she asked.

"What?"

She drew away, leaning back to look at him. "Where are you?"

It was a confusing question. "Here," he answered, though it sounded as if he was asking her a question.

"No. Not here, here." She left their embrace. "Where were you before here?"

Luc tried to concentrate on her question, but his mind focused on watching her move. He thought about missing the sensation of her in his arms. He was empty now.

"Lucian." She grabbed hold of his face.

"Huh?" He blinked. "What?"

"Where are you?"

He blinked again to focus on her question and realized he couldn't recall being anywhere other than there with her. He pictured his bed, his pillow. "In my room. Sleeping. Wait—"

"We're dreaming," she said and turned away, walking a few steps into the woods. "How are we dreaming together?"

The woods suddenly shifted, the colors clear and bold as if they had been painted over one, two, three times to make them somehow brighter. The evergreens were vibrant with light green tips while the darker boughs popped with over-saturation. The deciduous trees—the orange, red, and yellow leaves—were so bright it was almost difficult to look at them. When Luc turned his head to look at Brinna, he had to refocus his eyes, squinting to see her properly. She, too, was so bright.

He held up a hand to shield his eyes. "What are you talking about? Where are you?"

"What are you doing?" She put her hands on her hips. "Inside the cottage. Sleeping."

He shook his head, trying to shake his thoughts back into place and blinked more, the color regulating so he could focus. "Sleeping?"

Brinna nodded, her eyes widening. She took several steps back toward him. "Mother. She gave us all a sleeping potion. I'm sure of it."

Suddenly, this weird dream paralleled reality a bit too closely. "Your mother? But why? I'm dreaming right?"

She ignored his question, pacing instead as she chattered. "We got to the cottage, and she'd promised to tell us the truth. She insisted on the tea. Next thing I know, I'm asleep."

Luc followed her movement with his eyes. Focusing on her was easier than the unfiltered light around him, the color regulating and making it easier to see. "Wait. You're asleep." He rubbed his forehead. "This is a weird dream."

She reached out and pinched him.

"Ouch." Luc rubbed the soft spot on the underside

of his arm. "What was that for?"

"A test." She tilted her head, and Lucian noticed the loose tendrils of her hair skimming her neck as Brinna tucked a lock behind her ear.

"How is it that you felt that?" she asked. "I've spent my whole life dreaming, and I have never once felt physical pain in one. The suggestion of pain, yes, but actual pain?"

She was right.

"We're both dreaming," she said. "Together."

"That's impossible."

"Why?" She began pacing again. "It would seem impossible for there to be a monster in the woods, or gods who control day and night. It would seem impossible for Tarley—a poor woman from Sevens— to marry a prince, or for Auri to have saved a god from a spell."

She was right again.

"Why not?" she asked. "For the sake of argument."

Luc nodded. "Okay. I concede."

She stopped pacing and faced him. "Whatever is happening here is different. I've been trying to work it out since we met before—"

"Wait. Before?" He had trouble following her. "What are you saying?"

"I don't know. I can't make sense of it. But weren't we standing in this exact spot earlier? It feels too coherent, too detailed."

"It was—"

"Snowing," she finished.

His breath stalled, then restarted, but it was rather ungainly if you asked his lungs. "How did you know—" He tilted his head and studied her. Her brows were drawn together over those expressive gray eyes, her mouth gathered into a contemplative pout. "Was it in color?"

"No."

His eyebrows arched over his eyes, but the surprise slid around inside him. She knew it had been snowing, knew it hadn't been in color. That didn't mean she was real, however. She could still be a product of his own subconscious. "You're implying that this is real? That when I touch you—" —he reached out, slid his fingers into her hair at the back of her head, and smoothed his thumb across her cheek. Her mouth parted as she drew in a heavier breath— "that you're actually feeling it."

She hummed a noise and stepped away from his touch with a sharp gaze—a very Brinna action— then looked down at the ground and crossed her arms over her chest. "I just told you I don't know, Lucian. What part of I don't know means I know?"

"You don't have to be sarcastic."

"You're right. Sorry."

Luc narrowed his eyes. "The real Brinna would never apologize to me."

She huffed. "Yes, I would!"

"But that is definitely how the real Brinna would say that." Luc was enjoying this dream immensely. "How can we determine if we're real or just a figment of the dream?"

She seemed at a loss for a moment, then spun back to face him. "We have to tell a fact to one another, and then the next time we see each other, share it."

"Defeats the purpose. Could still be a part of my subconscious." He tapped his head.

She sighed and brought her finger to her chin, tapping. Luc watched her pace back and forth, completely engaged in the moment—dream or not. Tap. Tap. Tap. She whirled around. "I have it."

"Hit me."

"Sort of."

"Wait. What?"

Brinna held up a finger. "Can we agree that when we dream, anything that causes physical sensation–"

"Physical sensation?" Luc was afraid to add to that, and he recalled his hand grabbing her hips, the feel of her soft heat on his cock. He cleared his throat. "Like?"

"Like when I pinched you. Or falling."

Right. Her mind was elsewhere. "Okay. What am I agreeing to?"

"That under normal dream circumstances, you'd wake up."

Luc nodded, not sure he liked her trail of thought. "Okay. Sure."

"So then, we have to do something physical to one another—and if we experience the physical sensation, then the other person is most likely real."

Luc smirked.

"What?"

He scoffed but didn't elaborate. "Okay. I'll agree with you for the sake of trying to determine if we are dream people, that if the other is able to make us feel something physical, then we're really here."

Her eyes narrowed, but she continued. "We should probably put some parameters on it. You know, to keep it clear."

"Oh. Parameters. Okay." He grinned. "Like 'no kicking the groin."

Her eyes dipped to his pelvis, then back up.

Luc enjoyed the blush of her cheeks. "Just in case."

"That's probably an excellent parameter. No maiming."

"Why? Would you want to maim me?"

"No!" She bristled, her head shaking emphatically. "Of course not."

He wasn't sure if that disappointed him or not. He'd never been opposed to a little pain. "Do you have a parameter?"

"Well—" she tapped her chin again— "I'd rather not be hurt... you know... like your kicking rule."

"But anything else goes? You know, for the sake of the experiment?" Luc rubbed his hands together, deciding to enjoy this little dream experiment. What did he have to lose? Nothing. He was dreaming.

She hedged, then said, "Yes. Okay."

"But it should probably be more than a touch, right? Or a pinch since we've already done that. Something a bit more drastic." His mind delved into another moment engaged in finding pleasure with dream Brinna. That had pushed him awake. "And what proves that you're real? That we're really here? Together?"

"Okay. Something more than a pinch or a touch. Nothing harmful, and the proof is if you remain here in this dream. That you don't wake up. That you feel it." Her eyes searched his face. "You first?"

"I think ladies first," Luc said, smiling, interested in knowing what she would do. "You can demonstrate what you mean."

She turned her back to him, obviously thinking as she tapped her chin.

"Having trouble?"

"Sort of. I'd really like to maim you."

He laughed. "I thought you didn't want to."

She glanced over her shoulder and smiled, her tongue dipping out to curl up to her upper lip.

Luc's belly bottomed out, and his cock nudged inside his trousers. Fuck. That look. "Maybe a kiss?" he suggested.

"I kiss in dreams all the time," she said, slowly.

"All the time?" He waited, and when she didn't respond, said, "But do you feel the kiss?"

She didn't answer, but she turned toward him and swallowed. "This is real, Luc."

He tilted his head. "Prove it to me."

"Fine," she said and walked toward him with purpose. He admired the sway of her hips, the way her dress flowed with her movement. When she stopped, just before her toes met his, she tilted her head up. Luc had to look down to meet those gorgeous gray eyes. His heart bobbed, excited at the prospect of kissing Brinna.

She reached out—never taking her eyes from his—and placed her open palms on his abdomen, then slid them up over his shirt. He definitely felt that, and his heart bounced around erratically inside his chest. It wasn't the suggestion of her touch but the exacting pressure of her hands on him. Her fingers splayed, and damn, if he didn't feel every bit of that in gorgeous, life-like detail.

Her gaze darted from his eyes to her hands, and he watched her track them, feeling all the delicious friction between her movement, his shirt, and his skin. Though he wished his shirt was gone, it remained—which seemed strange, since dreams often obeyed.

Her palms curved over his chest, then paused when they met his rigid nipples, which she brushed with her thumbs.

She tilted her head to look at him.

He smirked.

She smirked back, then pinched his nipples. Hard. And twisted.

"Fuck, Brinna!" he yelled, slapping his hands over his now stinging nipples. "No maiming!"

She grinned, ducking away from his possible retaliation. "That wasn't maiming!" She laughed, and despite the pain, he liked that sound. "That was a demonstration."

Unable to help himself, he smiled. "Brinna

Fareview! You are monstrous."

She shook her head and laughed again, and he noted the beautiful lines she made—her neck, her jaw, the plait of her hair, her shoulders, her hands pressed against her belly. Her vibrant color pulsed with her joy so that he had to squint again. "Never forget it, Lucian Uraiahs. Now do you believe me? You're still here. You felt that. And you remember it."

"Fine. I'll suspend my disbelief. And that still hurts."

Her eyebrows arched. "And yet, you're still here."

"You wouldn't let me do that to you," he groused.

"Lucian!" she breathed, but her cheeks heated, and Luc wondered if maybe she might enjoy it.

He straightened, still swiping at his nipples, but they were feeling infinitely better now that she was blushing. "So I'm here. You're here." He took a breath and decided to come clean. "I dreamed of being here earlier. Of this place. Of you. I woke up because Nix called me from my nap to tell me about the hedge." He waved a hand at the monstrosity. "How did I know about this before knowing about it?"

"I was in that dream with you. You asked me if I was safe… your voice brought me out."

"I don't understand."

"I don't either, Lucian. But this really seems like it's happening." Her eyes searched his face before she turned slightly away. "The question is, whose dream are we in?" She tapped her chin, then pointed at him. "We both need to think of a neutral place—not a place the other would know—and we'll think of it at the same time, to see if the dream takes us."

"Okay. I get where you're going with that."

"Here." She held out her hands. "I feel like we need to be connected."

Luc looked down at her outstretched hands, stepped closer, then took them. The image of Tarley and Lachlan standing this way at their wedding flitted through his mind, and his heart jumped as his chest warmed. It was such an unbidden and ridiculous thought. So he focused on the feel of Brinna's hands in his, how small they were. How smooth and soft she felt against his own skin.

"Close your eyes," she ordered.

Luc did.

"Okay. Now think of your place."

He tried to, and when he next opened his eyes, they were standing in a bedroom. *Nice Luc*, he chastised himself. The room was cast in sunset colors, a gentle sea breeze wafting through open windows. Panels of sheer fabric moved with the air. He remembered the place from Roaming. It was on an island in the middle of an aqua sea where the tranquility had made him feel… different. Better.

"Oh," Brinna gasped. "Yours, then." She released his hands and stepped back, turning to take in the room.

Shame felt hot, accusatory. "I'm sorry. I didn't–"

"It's beautiful," she said with an expelled breath.

His shame melted away, and he smiled. "Look

outside," he said, grabbing hold of her hand and leading her to the balcony beyond the open windows. The vista beyond offered an aqua swath of blue ocean that stretched out beyond them as far as the eye could see. Hovering on the horizon, a burning sun. Breaking waves intermittently washed the white sand. People walked along the shoreline, hand in hand, and buildings rose around them in colorful relief: pinks, blues, whites, yellows, greens, all cast in the golden light of the setting sun. It was beautiful, a favorite of the places he'd ever spent time, one he'd come to often when he needed space to think.

Brinna gasped, her hand squeezing his. "I've never seen anything like it."

Luc studied her face, enamored with her awe. "It is beautiful."

Without dropping his hand, Brinna leaned against the balcony to look down. He held tight to her hand, sobered suddenly at the thought of her being hurt.

"Tell me how this is possible," she said, straightening and turning to face him, her hand still in his.

Feeling guilty because his own wishes were at odds with Nix's, Luc released her hand and walked back into the room, where he took a seat on the edge of the bed, elbows to knees as he stared at the terra cotta floor. "I don't have an answer. I'm a little taken aback, and I've grown up around gods."

Brinna's bare feet appeared in his line of sight. "You're a god."

He looked up. "Was."

She waved a hand, then sat next to him. "Still are."

Luc felt the outside of her thigh press against his and tried to ignore the enjoyable sensation that fluttered through him from that connection.

"I've had dreams before that seemed like they were telling me something, and they turned out to be true. Like when Tarley was in danger. But this is different. Not like those dreams at all."

"How?"

"This is… well, besides being in someone else's dream, those dreams were disconnected. As if I were just an observer. This…" She glanced at him then down at her lap, and he wondered if she was as aware of their touch as he was. Then she said, "You're so real," and he thought that might be so.

His heart picked up speed as the other dream—the sex dream—flickered in his thoughts, and he slid his hands over his thighs to keep them busy. "When Nix was caught in the spell, I was able to visit him, to cross between our realm and the enchantment." He pondered it a moment, staring at the curtains moving back and forth in the soft breeze. "Maybe it's a little like that?"

"Magic?"

He nodded. "I don't think I would have been able to do it without Nix allowing it, of course. And I think maybe because I was the one who'd trapped him—my blood—maybe that played a part too."

A slamming door somewhere caught Luc's

attention, and he turned his head to look for it.

Brinna grabbed his thigh. "No. Stay with me." Her voice was panicked.

Luc glanced at her hand on his leg and slid his hand over hers, wrapping her fingers with his. "I'm here." An unfamiliar need to stay unfurled in his chest.

"I'm afraid it isn't for long, Lucian. And when you're not with me, I'm alone." Her eyes filled with tears, breaking Luc's heart. "My family—everyone sleeps."

"Brinna–" But he stopped, not sure what he'd intended to say.

The beachside getaway dripped away, melting into the greenery of a summertime forest appearing around them. A faint trickle of water bubbled as bursting pink blossoms rained around them. Luc looked down at their joined hands and saw he was sitting on a chaise. His head snapped up to Brinna next to him.

He'd brought them to the sex dream!
Shit.

Brinna jumped to her feet and spun away, putting distance between them. "Oh. Oh!" She pressed her fingertips to her red cheeks. "Oh."

"Wait. You know this place?"

Her eyes jumped to his. The color in her cheeks deepened, and she looked away.

"That was real too?" he asked. "Whoa." He shoved his hands into his hair. "How?"

"That night—"

His eyes met hers, remembering every single

sensation. The kiss. Her skin. The sounds she'd made when she came. His mouth popped open, then shut, but a few beats later, his eyes on her face, he said, "It was a very memorable dream."

Brinna's cheeks brightened, and she fanned them with her hands. "You remember—"

"Every fucking thing." He expelled a gusty breath. "Fuck. That was… I haven't stopped thinking about it."

"Maybe we should try and forget that happened."

"Sorry, Brin. Can't. Won't," Luc replied.

"I'm not your type," she pointed out. The fact she'd brought it up again told Luc he'd hurt her.

"If I remember correctly," he said, smirking. "I set you straight on that point. In fact, you were hard-pressed against some sturdy evidence." The memory of his cock against her sultry heat warmed the space in his chest, and he had to take a couple of deep breaths to subdue the muscle memory in his groin.

She covered her face with her hands. "I'm so embarrassed."

As much as he wanted to chase the feelings they'd shared, Brinna's struggle stayed him. While his first impulse was usually to chase the discomfort away with humor, he found he didn't want to run from it. He wanted to jump into the moment and face something real with her. The impulse frightened him.

"**B**rinna," Lucian said, his voice gentle, which was simultaneously comforting and unnerving.

Her skin was so hot. Everything was hot. It had been one thing to think it was a dream, to allow herself to let go so completely, but learning it had been real, that Lucian had experienced that secret side of her, again—it was mortifying.

"You shouldn't feel that way," he said.

"But I do."

Lucian's hands wrapped around her wrists, and he pulled her hands from her face. "Why?"

"I wouldn't have done that in real life."

One of his knuckles curled under her chin, forcing her to look up at him. Though it was a struggle to meet his gaze, she did. "Why?"

"It was a fantasy."

"Yes." He offered her an understanding smile. "It was."

She remembered he'd been just as into it as she had.

"And so what?" he said. "It also happened to be real—which neither of us could have predicted." His eyes searched her face, settling on her lips for a heartbeat before jumping back to her eyes. "Was it so bad?"

Her first impulse was to lie in order to protect herself, his prior behavior making her feel insecure and somehow less-than. Only in their last several interactions, that hadn't been how he'd treated her. He'd been patient and kind, protective and honest, which made him worthy of her trust. What then, exactly, was she protecting herself from?

So instead of lying, she said, "No. It wasn't."

Her heart was in her throat at the admission.

He swallowed, and she watched his throat work, before he cleared it and plucked a pink blossom from her shoulder, twirling it between his fingers. "We can just keep thinking it was a dream." He glanced at her lips again, then looked away, dropping the blossom and taking a step away from her. "If it makes you feel better." He swiped his hands on his trousers.

She looked away, trying to ignore the disappointment coursing through her at his dismissal. But then, he seemed to be wanting to make her feel more comfortable. And that was… that was… she wasn't sure. She thought that would be what she wanted, but realizing it was real, ignited something new inside of her when it came to Lucian, a spark she wanted to feed.

An awkward silence stretched between them.

"If everyone's asleep," Luc said, breaking the silence, "are you able to dream share with your family?" He changed the subject, as if it were somehow safer.

Except Brinna couldn't forget that they were there together and that the dream had been real.

"Maybe your mother will give you answers about how to break the spell? If she really did this?" His voice brought her back to the topic.

Another door slammed.

Fear grabbed hold of Brinna's heart, and she clamped a hand around Lucian's. "Not yet. Please."

His golden eyes gave her comfort, his hand squeezing hers. "I'm not going anywhere. And if I do, you have my word, Brinna, I'll find you."

She tried to reconcile that with what she'd always thought of Lucian. "But you've always run from me."

His mouth opened, his eyes just as wide, before he shut his mouth and shook his head, his eyes dropping so his lashes fanned his cheeks. When he looked at her again, his gaze was steady and sure. "You have my word."

As he said it, the magical glen melted away until they were standing in a glass skyway of Sol, between the atrium and one of the wings. The deep blue sky was streaked with pinks as the sun rose.

"I'm sorry. I'm just afraid," she admitted, surprised at herself. She'd rarely offered unfiltered truths to Lucian, and now couldn't seem to stop.

He drew her into his embrace, and she relaxed against him, letting his strong arms make her feel safe. "We both know that I won't remain asleep, but I promise you, Brinna, I will return to you."

"I hate being afraid—"

"It's okay," he said, squeezing her harder. "Natural, I think, considering these outlandish circumstances. I'm not feeling so confident either."

She leaned back to look at him, and he smiled. This smile reached his eyes, and she realized he didn't smile that completely very often, with his golden eyes sparkling that way. Her gaze dropped to his lips, and she remembered kissing him and imagined doing it again. With a quick rush of breath, she put some distance between them, rattled by her desire.

"You brought us to Sol," she said.

Lucian turned and looked around, then hummed a sound. "I guess I did."

"Home." She smiled, then thought it strange that he seemed slightly stunned.

"Yes." He crossed the skybridge and walked through the hallway into the great room.

Brinna followed and surveyed the room. The

couches, the tables, the kitchen, the wall of windows, the plants, the fireplace—everything as she remembered. "I've never been out of Sevens. Goodness. Dreaming with you, I've already seen several wondrous places." She named them using her fingers as she did and turned to find staring out the windows at the sky beyond. She wondered what he was thinking but couldn't even begin to guess.

Instead, she walked to the counter and leaned over, facing his back. "Why do you think we're dream-sharing?" It seemed the most obvious question. "Do you think it's because of your god powers?"

"Except I don't have them." He remained at the windows, his hands in his pockets. "I didn't have them the first time either," he pointed out. "If it was just about godblood, why aren't you sharing with Nix?"

She hadn't thought of that, and started to say, "I don't like—" but clamped her jaw shut at what she'd almost admitted, confused by it. Had she been about to admit she liked Lucian differently than Nix, after everything they'd been through? After hearing him admit he didn't like her in that way? (Even if it was a fact he'd refuted in their dream?)

Lucian, turned to face her, and with uncharacteristic grace, didn't push her to finish the thought. Instead, he said, "I think this is your doing, somehow."

"But your godlight would exist without your powers, right? It's a part of you since you're born with it."

"Yes. That is true."

Brinna pushed away from the counter, unnerved by Lucian's unwavering observation, and started to pace. "That explains why you might be able to connect in a dream, though? You're a god. But I can't fathom how I could."

Lucian crossed the room, and she ignored how close he got, skirting him as she paced. But as she turned to retrace her path, Lucian stood in her way. He gently grabbed her shoulders to stop her nervous movement, and anxiety burst inside her chest, fluttering like a sparkle of fireflies.

"Except," he said, "your sister."

Her gaze met his, that sparkle of fireflies bursting with light inside her. "Auri?" They'd spoken of Auri, of the spell and enchantment, of her saving Nix before. "Because she saved you?"

"I haven't told you the rest." He dropped his hands to his sides, and Brinna missed the warmth of his touch.

"There's more?"

He nodded and turned to sit on one of the stools at the counter. "There's this rare bonding that happens between some gods. But for some reason, your sister and Nix, they share it. It's called a god-yoke."

"But how? Does that mean—" Brinna's mind raced, trying to put the pieces together.

Lucian was nodding. "Her having godblood—you having godblood—that would be the only way it would make sense."

She wanted to voice *how*, but she realized she knew. "Our mother." Brinna stood thinking about all her mother's secrets, walked a few paces then spun back. "But why hide that?"

"Why would you hide something like that?"

Brinna worked through it. "Anger. Shame, maybe?"

"Fear," Lucian added.

"Danger."

"Those are some strong motives." Lucian swiped his hands over his thighs, then stood once more.

"You're right. I need to figure out if I can get into her dreams. Maybe I can figure out how to fix this."

At the sound of a slamming door, she jumped, her heart lurching. She knew what that meant.

Lucian glanced over his shoulder. "I'm getting pulled, Brin."

She went and stood in front of him, putting her hands on his arms. "I'll be okay," she said, searching his handsome face.

"Yes. You will be," he said, swiping a loose strand of her hair back and tucking it behind her ear. "You're strong."

The urge to kiss him hit her hard enough she had to look away, hopeful he hadn't seen. Though she wasn't sure she believed his words, the way he said them made her want it to be. She nodded.

"Next time," he said, though she could hear he was unsure whether to make that kind of promise.

She understood. There was no way to ensure she'd

see him again in this in-between world, and as quickly as she thought it, he was gone, and Sol with him as if she'd blinked it away, leaving her in the room where her body lay with her sleeping sisters.

Brinna sighed and glanced around the room, suddenly weary. She considered taking a moment to rest, the tug of something gray and threatening kept her from it. *You're strong.* Lucian's words echoed in her mind, so she resisted the impulse and focused on what she might be able to do: get into her family's dreams—however that worked. And she knew exactly where she'd begin.

She made her way down the narrow stairs into the main living quarters of the cottage to where her parents were lying asleep. The main room of the cottage was bright with a fire, the light frozen in time but not the heat. Brinna wasn't sure if it was truly cold or if it was her broken heart.

Looking down at her parents laid out on the wooden floor together, Brianna was filled with love, but deep disappointment as well. Her father was on his back, head propped on a pillow. He looked so peaceful. Her mother was on her side, head resting on her husband's shoulder, her hand on his chest. The last to sleep, Brinna figured, after having taken care of the rest of them.

It hurt to realize that her mother had betrayed them this way. Brinna was sure her mother had a reason—just as she and Lucian had discussed—but couldn't fathom something good enough to hide it from them.

She knelt next to them, angry tears now filling her eyes. "Why would you do this?" she asked and swiped her cheeks.

But her mother didn't answer. Of course, Brinna hadn't expected her to.

"Did you know?" she asked her father. But he remained silent, as she knew he would.

Her gaze jumped back to her mother. "I need to talk to you," she whispered.

Scarlett's face remained unresponsive. Brinna reached out, caught a lock of her mother's auburn hair with her fingertip, and hooked it behind her mother's ear. As she did, her fingertip brushed the skin of her mother's cheek, and Brinna's vision flashed, like lightning brightening the sky for a brilliant moment as her consciousness was pulled through space and time. One moment there, then gone.

Brinna blinked, then looked at her hand. "What was that?" she said aloud and reached out again.

The same sensation occurred. This time, a scene shimmered around her for the moment they were connected. Everything turned vibrant, then vanished when Brinna drew away.

I'm in a dream, Brinna reminded herself. *This is a dream within a dream.*

This time, she reached out and grasped her mother's hand, and she was dragged through a swirling vortex of light and sound.

It stopped, on a scene of Scarlett in the woods,

though the forest didn't look realistic, rather like someone had taken varied colors of clay and smeared them to create a moving landscape. It undulated around her, but Scarlett looked like herself. She was dressed in a strange dress that appeared old-fashioned to Brinna. It was filthy, the lace accents dirty, the hem was coated in muck, and a dark cloak clasped at Scarlett's throat. Beneath her dress, her belly protruded, heavy with a baby. Still, she walked, pulling an ox behind her as she hummed.

"Mother!" Brinna called and stepped toward her, then bumped up against an invisible wall. It shimmered with opalescence, rolling with waves as it resettled. She hit it with her hands, the sheen of the wall quivering under her force. But it didn't break, just adjusted. "Mother!"

Scarlett continued walking with the ox behind her, humming a tune, oblivious to Brinna pounding on the invisible wall between them. And though Scarlett kept walking, it seemed as if she was walking in place. There wasn't any forward movement, just the clay-like landscape shifting around her.

Scarlett stopped and checked the ox. "Are you sure you're okay?" she asked the animal.

The animal looked at her with big, brown eyes. "I've grown thirsty," it said.

"Let's look for water." She nodded. "Yes. Water is very important."

"But this potion might be more helpful," a bird— a raven— said from its perch on the back of the ox.

"I don't trust your potions," Scarlett said and started walking in place again, continuing with her song.

"Mother!" Brinna pounded against the shield between them, but there was nothing to be done to break it or to get her attention.

Unlike her ability to interact with Lucian, she seemed to only be an observer inside her mother's dream. *It must be the spell*, Brinna thought, trying to work out the difference, but was unsure. She knew they both must be dreaming somehow, since they were both asleep, but whereas Brinna could Dream Walk, her mother couldn't. And perhaps it was the magic keeping Brinna from her mother's dreams? Except this reminded her more of her normal dreams, the distance, and the observation.

"Do you think he'll find us here?" Scarlett asked.

"Perhaps you can hide like you've hidden me?" the ox replied.

Brinna stilled, focusing on the words, the images, realizing that dreams rarely spoke straightforward language. They often operated in symbols.

"Hide," Scarlett said, sounding doubtful.

"In plain sight."

"Why do you need to hide, Mother?" Brinna asked, but her mother continued humming, unable or unwilling to hear her.

The dream shifted, the clay sliding away until Brinna stared into the depth of nothing, then at her mother's sleeping form.

Brinna pulled her hand away, wondering what she'd learned, but nothing felt reliable or true. The nebulous *he* again. Hiding. It all felt much the same.

She stood and walked back and forth across the cottage, considering what she'd seen. What she knew. What had her mother told them?

The red ribbons were protective spells.

That she wasn't from Sevens but from somewhere else.

Brinna considered what her family had experienced at the meadow that day. What had Tarley said? There were ravens who'd spoken to their father. She looked at her father, wondering where he'd been in the dream. Her mother had been pregnant. Who was the ox? The crow?

She needed more.

"You're not hiding from me, Mother," she said and crouched again at her mother's side.

With a touch, Brinna was pulled into a new scene, still an observer behind the transparent wall. Now, she stood in a town square—or the hint of one—the colors and people just a chaos of moving swirls, hints of themselves in the dreamscape. But there was Scarlett, her hood pulled up, hidden among them though clear and vibrant to Brinna's eye.

"Here ye! Here ye!" a herald called, and the crowd stilled. "The king has issued a time of mourning for the queen."

Everything turned dark, still there and swirling but now in shades of gray. Scarlett was still there, still clear, but now her hood was off, and she walked among them, though no one noticed. Tears ran down her face, eventually becoming chains that bound her body. She floated up into the sky, and the town square was gone, a stone room taking its place.

Scarlett stood in the stone room in chains. The sole window offered light, and she tilted her face toward it, tears shining on her face. She was alone. Alone. Alone.

Brinna pulled back, her heart racing in her chest and her cheeks wet for what she'd seen. That level of loneliness had felt like death, but what did it mean? Brinna wasn't sure, but she tucked it away inside her mind like clues to buried treasure.

She turned to her father. "Your turn," she said and reached out to touch him, then blinked into his dream.

Separated from him just like her mother, Brinna stood inside the woods, though where her mother's landscape had been muddy and shifting, her father's was clear and radiant with color. He walked through the woods carrying his ax, humming. When he looked up at the sky, Brinna followed his gaze, realizing that the trees were so large, the plants, the flowers. Giant. It would have made him tiny, which seemed such a strange thing considering how large her father was. For some reason, this made her feel sad, as if this smallness was how he saw himself.

He stopped, looked around. "Scarlett?" he called and frowned, turning in a circle. "Scarlett?"

"Father?" Brinna asked, pressing her hand against that transparent wall. "Can you hear me?"

But he clearly couldn't, continuing to call for Scarlett as he started through the gigantic forest once more.

Brinna disconnected from him, then leaned down to kiss his cheek. "I love you," she said.

In her dream, his eyes fluttered, as if he'd heard her. It gave her hope. She waited, holding her breath as if it might be gifted to him, but he stilled once more, and remained so.

She stood and sighed, resolved to visit each of her siblings. So she turned away from her dreaming parents, and went to look for Mattias.

Luc

Luc woke to streaks of sunlight sneaking through the window filter over the floor-to-ceiling windows. He sat up and swiped a hand over his face, the stubble on his cheeks scratching against his palm. Bending forward, he stared at his feet, pressing them against the wooden floor, then wiggling his toes to ground himself in the sensations. He looked at his fingers and wiggled them too, afraid perhaps, that he was losing all sense of what was real and what wasn't.

He sighed and wondered how he would know. He could see he was in Sol—but he'd been here in his dream with Brinna. He could feel the way his body moved now, but it hadn't felt so different in the dream. In the dream, he'd held her—he could still hear the sound of her voice, the lapping of the sea against the shore beyond the bedroom he'd conjured. Now that he was without her, he noticed that ever-present hint of discomfort in his chest, and his brow furrowed at the sensation.

He supposed he shouldn't be surprised by something magical like being connected to Brinna in their dreams, considering he was in a home suspended in the heavens. He thought of Brinna, her fear, but also her resolve. She'd pinched him. Luc could still feel the sting of his nipples and pressed his palm against them. He smiled. Real. He couldn't think of a single god with that particular power and wondered: even if Brinna carried godblood, why she would possess the power to walk in dreams?

Needing the normalcy of something mundane, he pressed the button and the tint within the windows changed, allowing unfiltered light through. He stood and walked to the window, still dressed in the same clothes from the day before. He'd slept deeply, and yet still felt exhausted.

Out the window, Sol looked as it always did, the structure suspended like a cloud in the sky above the Elcadian realm subject to his—now his father's—power. Unchanged. The clouds drifted past in the blue sky and the sunlight was bright and crisp. Far below the rolling hills of Elcadia, a patchwork of agricultural lands gave way to the edges of the city. A ribbon of river wound through the landscape and cut around the city, widening as its length disappeared toward the sea in the west. Everything familiar. But he felt stripped.

He wanted to get back to Brinna.

What if he couldn't?

The thought flustered him. He could lie to himself and say that it was for Nix and Auri, but it tasted wrong, where it never had before. Now, the truth was that he wanted to be near Brinna. He wanted to help her. And that didn't make any sense to him. When did he ever want to run toward rather than away? Brinna had called him out on it, and it had floored him. He'd never felt so exposed.

With a sigh, he turned away from the window and headed for the bathing room. He needed to speak to Nix, knowing his brother would be interested in what he'd discovered. Reaching for their godlight tether, he tried to summon his brother, only to find the tether missing.

"Fuck," Luc muttered, realizing he couldn't summon anyone without his power. He was truly trapped in Sol.

Eventually he made his way to the kitchen to make himself an espresso. As the pleasant aroma filled the space, his mother's voice rang out across the expanse of Sol's living room. "Lucian?"

He glanced over his shoulder. "Good morning, Mother."

Aiah smiled at him and drifted toward the kitchen;

her cinnamon tresses dressed around a crown of fall leaves to denote the season. Her dress flowed around her, gossamer panels of shades of orange, green, red, and yellow drifting like leaves falling from a tree. "You didn't answer my summons, and I got worried."

"Father took my power. I can't."

She stalled. "He did what?"

"Took my power."

She cursed. "When I get my hands on him…"

"It is no less than I deserve," Luc said. "But it would be nice to be able to summon help should I need it."

She continued to mutter.

Though his parents had been paired for their lifetime, a marriage of convenience, their partnership had been tumultuous at best. Luc had a host of half-siblings across the Elcadian realm—maybe even beyond it—both by his father and mother. Though turbulent, there did seem to exist a sense of partnership and camaraderie between them, even if it was hard to predict which way the wind blew from one minute to the next. If his mother's glower was any indication, it wasn't a peaceful wind at the moment.

"Deserve is an ugly word, Lucian," she said and sat down on a barstool at the counter. "Make me an espresso." She tapped the counter with a fingernail.

Amused, Luc huffed through his nose. He set the espresso he'd made for himself in front of her. "I'm here. Safe and sound," he said, though he didn't bother to hide the sarcasm as he turned to make another cup.

She took a sip of the coffee and made a sound of contentment. "Delicious," she said. "Now, that is a beautiful word."

"How about devious?"

She set the cup down in the saucer with a clink. "Devious? Are you being devious?"

"No. Just thinking of other words that begin with the letter D. How about di–"

"Lucian," she warned. "I'm not in the mood."

She was never in the mood for fun, especially in the fall and winter, but he didn't say that. Instead, he finished brewing his espresso and enjoyed the first sip, then leaned over the counter toward her, his elbows on the cool marble.

"I'll assign some piskies to come up. Clean the place, bring food, serve you."

"I don't need—"

She raised a hand, indicating she wasn't open to discussion. "No. Without your power you can't summon. You'll need someone for that. You won't be able to leave, see to your needs. It's a hopeless business, and absolutely barbaric," she said in a huff.

"Hopefully Sol will remain intact under their care," Luc said, then shrugged, knowing he wouldn't change his mother's mind.

"Tell me what happened with your father."

"I told you what happened. He stripped me of my power. He said he'll keep it until I give him what he wants."

She clapped her hands against the marble. "That's

it then. Give him what he wants."

"Can't. He wants me to agree to take his place."

Her eyes grew in circumference, and a smile spread across her face. "Why, Lucian," she said with pride. She stood and skirted the edge of the bar. "That's wonderful news." She clapped her hands together. "God of the Vasmost, god of all. There could be no one better."

A lie. Luc closed his eyes. "I refused him, Mother. It's why I'm standing here powerless."

"Well, change your mind," she said, patting his arm.

He opened his eyes to study her once more, noting the threads of silver in her hair. When had that happened? "It isn't that easy."

"Of course it is."

"I'm not—"

She waved a hand. "Lucian…" She tittered after saying his name and returned to her seat to gather her cup and saucer, then walked into the living room, where she sat on a sofa facing him.

"What?"

She took a sip, then set the tiny cup on the table in front of her. "I'm going to use that awful word. Do you think your father *deserved* his place as god of the cosmos?"

"Yes?"

"No! Good gods, no. No one does. Deserve is this term that either elevates beings far above their station into the realm of entitlement or drags beings deep into the realm of repudiation. One must rise to the occasion of their station, serve their function as best they can, and seek to find a replacement who will surpass their efforts. No being is perfect. You understand?"

He did, of course, but he didn't quite believe her. He'd only ever seen his father as true and just—Ur's relationship with his mother notwithstanding. "I used my power to trap my brother, and it nearly killed him. Nearly released a demon into the universe. Tell me, Mother, does that sound like a candidate for the highest order of the gods?"

"Not your power–"

"Same difference. Rationalized the use of dark magic to do it."

She patted the seat next to her. "Come here, Son."

"I'm not a boy, Mother."

"Then stop behaving like one and come sit next to your mother."

He complied, if only to get her moving and in hopes she'd summon Nix for him. He sat next to her, and she wrapped an arm around his shoulders.

"Your father has gotten up to a lot of mischief." She snorted. "So much. I've nearly killed him on many occasions, and had his power not been greater than mine, may have succeeded once or twice."

Luc turned his head to look at her, noting the strange nostalgia on her face at the mention of killing his father. "I'm going to try and not be disturbed by that."

She cleared her throat. "The point being that he's

not perfect. Neither of us are. You aren't. Nixus isn't. No one. We are doing the best with what we're given. Your mishap with your brother–"

"Mishap? Mishap!" He stood. "That wasn't a mishap, Mother."

"Was it your intention to trap him for eternity?"

"No, but–"

"Did you intend to release that demon?"

"No, but–"

"A mishap. A mistake on your part, Lucian, but not a defining one. Not one to determine what you *deserve*. Think of it as a learning opportunity." She reached for her cup and took her last sip. "That was lovely," she said as she stood, then ran a hand over her skirt before straightening it. "I will talk with your father." She reached up and pressed a hand to his cheek. "Reconsider your position, yes?"

He wouldn't, but he agreed to appease her.

"Do you need anything?" she asked.

"Nix?"

She nodded. "I'll send him." Then in a swirl of color, she was gone, leaving Lucian alone once more.

Alone in Sol.

Alone with his thoughts.

He wrestled with his mother's words, wondering at but discarding their truth. He'd made an unforgivable mistake, failed at being a god so terribly that he'd been stripped of his power—he'd rationalized away that his father had only stripped him because he'd refused to capitulate.

And yet, it had only been after being stripped of his power that he'd truly seen Brinna. Stripped, he'd finally longed to stay. Stripped, he wanted… something, even if he couldn't quite name it. While he might not be altruistic, he figured with his unexpected ability to dream with Brinna, he could begin to make up for all the ways he'd hurt her. Provided he could find a way back.

He wandered each wing of Sol, ruminating, watering the garden, ruminating, fluffing the pillows in the living room for the tenth time, ruminating, then sat and watched the sky beyond the windows. Finally, Nix arrived.

"Thank the gods," Luc said, jumping to his feet.

"Why can't you summon me? Mother sent me." Nix strode across the room and flopped onto a couch.

Luc met him and pushed Nix's shoes off the arm of the couch. "No power."

"Even to summon?"

Luc nodded.

"That's terribly inconvenient."

"Tell me about it. What did you find out?"

"Dragon fire is useless. Can't fly into it either. And you? Any more dreams?" Nix's brows rose over his dark eyes.

Luc sat on the sofa across from his brother. "Yes."

Nix sat up, scooting to the edge of the seat. "You have news."

"Sort of," he said. "I saw Brinna."

Nix flopped backward. "How is that supposed to

help me?"

"I think–" He paused knowing it was going to make him sound… foolish. "I think it's real."

Nix sat forward once more. "What do you mean?"

"I mean, I think the dreaming is really happening." It was Luc's turn to sit forward. "I'm not sure how to explain it."

"Don't try, just explain."

"She knew what I was seeing. Exactly. And she pinched me, and the dream didn't end."

"She pinched you?" Nix's body shifted, and his eyebrows scrunched over his dark eyes. "That makes it real?"

"See. It sounds too wild to be believed."

Nix leaned back again and sighed. "We're gods–"

"You are."

"We're gods," Nix repeated. "I was trapped in a spell. We've seen demons and darklings. I can kill someone with the flick of a finger. There have probably been wilder things, yes? So Brinna being in your dreams doesn't seem all that wild." He paused, glanced at Luc, then plucked at his pants. "Did she say anything about Auri? Is she okay?"

"Brinna said everyone is asleep. That Scarlett gave them a potion."

Nix sat back up. "I knew she was responsible." He looked out at the window a moment, then back at Luc. "Why Brinna? And the dreams?"

"Not sure, but she said she's always been able to dream. To see things with them."

Nix tilted his head. "Auri said that about her." Nix stood, and it was clear he was pondering, thinking it through. "But why you?"

Luc shrugged, unwilling to reveal the first time it had happened, especially considering Nix's request that Luc not cross any lines with Auri's sister. "If I could hand it over to you, I would. Take it."

"Feels like it confirms they're godblood."

"That's what I thought too," Luc said. "Even if they had magical abilities as sorcerers, it wouldn't explain your god-yoke."

"And what is Brinna's plan?"

"She's going to try and connect with her mother's dreams—try and get some answers."

"And how will she get that information to you? Dreams?"

"It would seem that's the only way."

"Will it happen again?

"I don't know."

"Okay." Nix nodded. "Okay." He paced a few steps, then turned back before his head snapped back to Luc. "What if you can't get back in? You know, to see Brinna?"

"I don't know, but it sure would be nice to know if this is a thing. This Dream Walking thing."

Nix nodded.

"I can't leave here to find out."

"But I can." Nix closed the distance between them and hauled Lucian against him into a hug. "This is the best news I've heard all day. Thank you."

Luc wasn't sure how it was good news, other than he was able to communicate to a Dream Brinna that may or may not have been real—even if she seemed to be. He didn't argue, though, more content to have made Nix happy for once. It was, after all, the least he could do.

"You look pale," Luc observed, tilting his head to look closer at his twin. It was clear that the separation between his brother and Auri was already taxing him. "Do you think the spell is making your separation more intense?"

"I'm fine," he said, swiping a hand over his chest as if to check. "I'm fine."

"No. Brother. I can see you're feeling—"

Sol faded around them as Nix conveyed them away, the rose-gold of Elcadia proper appearing in Sol's place. The tall spires and steep rooftops dripped into the alabaster marble and limestone of the buildings around them. Cobblestone streets paved the way into the old heart of god city.

"Don't." Nix cut him off and waved a hand and started walking. "If we want to change the current circumstances—and we both know I need to in order to save Auri—we need to solve the larger problem. Lexa thinks the Library of Oracles is probably the best place to go."

Luc nodded. "Okay. Didn't you already visit? When you were searching for the god-yoke cure."

"I don't need to be cured, Luc." Nix scoffed. "I'm quite content being yoked to Auri."

"As your current pallor suggests. You look like you might fall on your face." He reached out to grab hold of Nix's arm to keep him from it and ignored the weight he felt inside his body.

His brother shrugged out from under his touch. "I'm fine. Yes. I visited the Oracles, but it was a dead end."

Luc could tell Nix wasn't telling him the whole of it, but he also decided he would step back from the discussion for the time being. Nix was stubborn and nagging him wouldn't help.

They walked in silence for some time, the quiet hum of the city moving around them.

"Does father know?" Luc eventually asked. He figured Ur would have tabs on him.

"Know what?" Nix asked.

"That you've removed me from Sol?"

"Why should he? He isn't your keeper, or mine."

"That sounds reminiscent of the god of the Vasmost." Luc smiled. "You should reconsider your position, brother."

"Absolutely not. Besides, he discounted me for falling in love with a mortal."

"Prick."

"Right?" Nixus looked over at him with a dimpled smile. "Besides, he'd discount me for anything. He wants you. You know I don't want that job. You're the right god for it."

Luc scoffed and looked down to watch his steps, shaking his head. "Not a god anymore."

"Easily rectified."

When they reached the library, Luc followed Nix up the wide steps and through the wide, ornate, dark wooden doors into the gloom of the interior. The decorative lamps buzzed with Oracle magic rather than solar energy in order to protect the contents of the Elcadian treasure trove. Luc's eyes adjusted to the dim light as their footfalls echoed against the marble entry echoed in the expansive foyer. Several doorways branched off the vestibule, and at its center stood an oracle wrapped in blue robes offsetting his dark complexion, waiting as if he'd expected them. He probably had. This one was in training, denoted by the empty chain around his hips lacking the keys of knowledge.

"Gods." The acolyte greeted them with a dip of his shorn head. "Welcome to the Library of Oracles. How may I guide you?"

Luc looked at Nix and froze, not sure how to ask for guidance. Finally, Luc said, "We're trying to ascertain someone's identity."

The acolyte blinked, though Luc knew it wasn't because he was confused. The Oracles had an unnerving way of communicating, as if they operated with a hive mind that was linked telepathically.

"Do you have any information about this individual that could guide us?" The acolyte asked.

"Her name is Scarlett," Nix said.

"Wait." Luc stopped him, putting a hand on his brother's shoulder. "I would bet that isn't her name. If she's godblood and in hiding, right?"

"Right."

"No family name?" the acolyte asked.

"Unknown," Nix said. "What do we know?"

"She's using magic to remain hidden."

"This isn't much to help a search, but Sister Prudence in the Hall of Records will help you." The monk bowed. "This way."

They followed the young acolyte through one of the entrances, the archway over the door marked with ancient symbols denoting *Ra'ha*—the old language of the gods. This one read *Rumaha Alora Maiah*, which roughly translated meant *to be enlightened*. Lucian hadn't spent any time there beyond what had been required of him as a child before his ascension, but when they emerged into the gigantic room, he felt transported back to the awe of his boyhood, a feeling he'd forgotten.

The arched ceiling faded away into the open cosmos, the darkness home to distant, sparkling stars, the ribbons of galaxies, gasses, and ether as spellbinding now as he remembered. The physics of the room didn't make sense, considering they were walking through a building since it appeared far more expansive than the exterior of it suggested, but he supposed the physics of Sol didn't make sense either.

"That never gets old," Nix said next to him, looking up at the sky.

Reacquainted, Luc agreed, recalling that he'd once loved this place. He smiled, remembering a time when he and Nix raced through the library trying to find all the nude artwork, competing for who could find the most. They'd gotten scolded by an acolyte, who'd then told their father.

They followed the acolyte through the long room past a series of floating orbs denoting the twelve different universe systems at various intervals of time. As a boy, all he'd had to do was touch one and the orb would expand, rotate, shifting to the selected time period. It occurred to him, suddenly how much this place had had a hand in how he'd Roamed.

The acolyte led them through the hall and up a set of stairs, followed by another.

"In the labyrinth," Nix said, "I made a smaller version of this library."

Luc turned his head to look at his brother. They hadn't spoken much about his time there. "Yes. I recall. But warmer."

"Did you know that there were Elsewhere Doors there too?"

Luc shook his head. "Like at Sol?"

Nix nodded.

Luc didn't have time to ask his brother why that was so, because the acolyte stopped before a tall, thin woman dressed in a matching blue robe. She had a sort of ageless quality aside from her wide, expressive, brown eyes. Her hair was short, and unlike the younger acolyte, her belt held a plethora of keys that rattled when she moved, denoting her place in the order. She dipped her head toward them in acknowledgement.

Gods," she said, but her eyes locked with Luc, and he knew she sensed the emptiness of his power inside of him. He disengaged from her knowing gaze as he watched the acolyte who'd led them take his leave.

"A hiding god is your only clue?" Sister Prudence asked. "You have asked me to uncover a single word in a library filled with words." She waved her hand around them.

"Yes," Nix said. "We know. Probably unascended."

"Unascended?" she asked, tilting her head. "But perhaps with the gift of her forebearer."

"If we knew her forebearer, and what sort of gift to look for." Nix glanced at Luc.

"A her?" Sister Prudence asked.

"Yes," Luc nodded.

"Finding her is really important," Nix said.

She tilted her head. "Why?"

It was a revealing question, Luc decided, though perhaps more so for Nix. But his brother was silent, as if he weren't sure of the answer. So Luc said, "He is god-yoked, and his match is locked in a sleeping spell, separating them. We haven't discovered the means to get through its magic."

"Magic." She hummed. "What kind?"

"We aren't sure," Luc answered.

Sister Prudence turned to Nix, her dark brown eyes full of knowledge. "You are fading?"

"I'm worried for her. My match," he admitted.

"Because if you are fading, she is also fading."

Nix nodded.

"Without the means to break the god-yoke, we thought finding the connection between the clues and the magic is our best chance to reunite them," Luc added.

"There is a temporary means of ending your suffering," she told Nix.

"To end the god-yoke? I thought–"

"There is no end to a god-yoke." She tucked her hands into her long sleeves. "But there may be a way to prolong the fade."

"What is it?"

"Sever the memories."

"What?" Nix took a step away from her.

"Remove them, and your essence will forget the god-yoke's existence. At least until you can reunite with your match."

"Will I remember?"

"That, I cannot answer."

Nix shook his head. "No."

She paused, her eyes sliding to Luc. *And you?* her voice said inside his head. *Would you make the same choice?*

"Excuse me?" Luc asked, shaken and unsure if what he'd heard was real.

"Luc?" Nix asked, confused by his outburst.

"I'm okay. Sorry. Just in my head."

"How old is this unascended god?" Sister Prudence asked.

"Living. A generation removed," Nix answered.

Luc reached out to touch the bookshelf near him, sliding a finger along the books to feel the grooves between them to test if this was real. He pressed his palm to his chest to feel his heartbeat and waited, worried that perhaps it wasn't there, and he was imagining everything.

"What is wrong with you?" Nix whispered to him.

Luc straightened and swallowed, shoving the hand that had been on his heart into his pocket. "Nothing," he replied, but he knew he was saying it equally to himself.

Without a word, Sister Prudence turned and started through another archway, which led to more rooms and shelves upon shelves of books. "The Hall of Records would be a place to begin our search. Each godblood is recorded upon birth and death and any pertinent information is marked for the soul's life. Like for you, Lucian Uraiahs."

"Excuse me?"

"Like your betrayal of your brother, your subsequent banishment, and the loss of your power."

Lucian pulled up short, swallowing as Sister Prudence continued. Nix stopped and turned to look at him, indicating with his dark head to keep up. "That's recorded?"

"Yes," she said. "You should research your father sometime. It's quite an extensive list."

"I can imagine," Luc replied and shared an eye roll with Nix.

"It might surprise you." She stopped at a long, low shelf stacked with pale tomes. The white coverings were faded and marked with repetitive use, the edges frayed and worn. She indicated they were marked by eras, then pulled a set of ten books. "I will collect the rest."

"Well," Luc said. "We better get started."

They carried the books to a nearby table, and Luc sat, pulling a thick book toward him. Inside were names upon names, dates, ascension and relinquishment, marriage, yoking, progeny, accomplishments, disgraces, an index of lists without any context offered. Lives reduced to facts without a story.

Luc could imagine his: Lucian Uraiahs, first son born to Ur and Aiah. Ascended age 25. God of day and light, betrayer of his twin Nixus. Then it would say: lost his power at 32 and faded into mortality where he died at 92. He swallowed, hating that was what his legacy would be. Instead of dwelling on it, he reset by asking Nix if he'd found anything.

"No."

Luc flipped another page. "If she's in hiding—where do we even start? Without her name, it's impossible."

"Search for all the unascended entries." Sister Prudence pointed at an entry. "Unascended gods are rare, but this is where you will find the marker."

Luc went through entry after entry. Eventually, he found his father—Ur Musaama. His entries stretched on and on, not all of them heroic or exemplary.

He could feel Sister Prudence watching him and when he met her eyes, she said, "Ur has acquired much knowledge."

"You could say that." Luc skimmed through the list, some things positive and many not. "It is a wonder he ascended as god of the Vasmost," Luc said quietly, flipping the page to another set of entries still related to his father. He thought of his mother's words earlier: *One must rise to the occasion of their station, serve their function as best they can, and seek to find a replacement who will surpass their efforts. No being is perfect.*

"You judge him?" Sister Prudence asked.

Luc shook his head. "No. I'm just surprised. I didn't know."

"Your sire has acquired a wealth of knowledge from which to serve, yes? This perspective—both sides of a coin—adds to his honor, making him a valuable god."

Luc swallowed and turned the page considering this.

He and Nix spent the remainder of the day moving through each of the books Sister Prudence deposited, but each time they came up empty handed. A handful of unascended gods, but none of them matched.

"Night is coming," Nix said. "Maybe Brinna has news?"

The thought of seeing Brinna constricted Luc's heart in the cavity of his chest, which made little sense. Why would he look forward to sleep, to dreaming? "Perhaps." He pressed his fingertips to his heart, rubbing the discomfort and his worry away.

He looked up to find Nix watching him. "What?"

Nix shook his head and returned to reading.

Sister Prudence stopped at the vestibule, not crossing the threshold into the entry. "Magic," she said and stopped, tilting her head in that strange way, her eyes seeing something beyond them. "Time." Her wide brown eyes jumped to Luc's, then to Nix's. "I will confer with my brothers and sisters." Then she turned and left.

"Time?" Luc asked. "What does that mean?"

Nix shrugged.

They left the library and stood at the top of the steps staring out at the Elcadian night. The buildings glowed golden in the midnight blue of the night sky, the spires, the building faces lit up like sparkling treasure. The city and people moving to and fro faded around them as Nix whisked them back to Sol.

The familiar surroundings of Luc's sky home reappeared and wrapped around him like a hug, which seemed strange to recognize considering he usually longed to leave it.

He squeezed the bridge of his nose and stifled a yawn. "I don't know how those monks do it all day. I feel exhausted."

"Good. Hopefully you'll find Brinna then." Nix's subdued and exhausted response worried Lucian.

"I don't think I will find her. I think she will find me."

Nix nodded. "Tomorrow then," he said and faded from view.

Luc ate and rushed through his bedtime routine, anxious to get to sleep, but when he finally settled into bed, he struggled to settle his mind. He was tired, could feel the way it seeped into his bones and eclipsed any other sensation. But when he closed his eyes, he rolled to one side, then the other. He took several deep breaths and counted to one hundred and twenty-seven, but the more he thought about not sleeping, the more anxious he became.

"Brinna?" he whispered. "I'm sorry, I can't seem to fall asleep." He was breaking his promise to be there. So he spoke with her, first out loud, then silently, until somehow, he drifted into the deep chasm of sleep.

B rinna, sitting on the floor next to the bed where her body was lying next to Auri, looked up the moment she felt Lucian slip into sleep. It was a vibration, as if there was an invisible web between her and Lucian, pulling her from the deep gray that was trying to suck her deeper into the spell.

She scrambled to her feet and raced down the stairs and out the cottage door. But rather than being spit out into the meadow within the hedge, she found herself standing in a library.

She twirled in place. It was beautiful, filled with so many books there would be no way to read them even in a thousand lifetimes. The ceiling wasn't a ceiling at all, but the dark blue sky filled with planets and stars. It moved gently, mimicking the true sky. The room was layers upon layers of books. There were golden lamps and suspended, glowing orbs, tables and chairs, sculptures, stairs, and so many things to see and touch. Brinna pressed her hand just under her throat.

"Lucian?"

"I am here," he said, stepping into view.

She took a fortifying breath, grateful to see him once more, her link to something tangible to keep her from the spell's grasp. Except she realized her relief was something more. Her heartbeat knocked an excited rhythm inside her, making it difficult to find her next breath, and awareness of him raced across her skin. For so long, she'd been telling herself that she didn't like Lucian. She could see that it had been a lie, but had it always been a lie or had her feelings changed somewhere along the way?

He offered her a subdued smile, and she thought he looked exhausted, weighted with worry.

"What is this place?"

He looked around. "My version of the Library of Oracles. In Elcadia."

"That's where you're from?" she asked.

"Elcadia. Yes." He hummed an affirmation as he walked toward her. "I spent the day here with Nix, looking for unascended godblood—since we've never heard of your family."

"Did you find anything?" She bent to look at a

sculpture, a man carved in stone with an oversized, erect appendage. Straightening, Brinna stepped back quickly, right into Lucian. His hands centered her, the warmth of them curling around her arms.

His eyes sparkled as he looked at her, even though he looked tired. "Nothing that fits." He looked at the sculpture. "You know, I visited this place on my Roam—an ancient city in twelfth circle—where every sculpture was some version of this. And when I was a godling, I spent time here looking for all the… colorful art. Nix and I made a game of it." His gaze jumped back to her, as he grinned. "Does this *ancient civilization* interest you?"

Brinna narrowed her eyes, feeling that he was setting her up somehow. "It does."

He grinned wider, as if her answer energized him, then he tucked her arm into his and led her through the library. They stopped to look at different sculptures, works of art, many of which depicted gigantic phalluses, female genitalia, and sex acts, Lucian telling her stories about what he'd thought as a boy.

"Are you trying to tell me something, Lucian?" she asked, straightening from a sculpture where the stone woman had her legs bent and splayed open, waiting.

"Subliminally?" He arched an eyebrow and smiled. "Were you able to Dreamshare with your mother?"

"You didn't answer my question, and this isn't subliminal." She laughed, and he joined in, the lightness in the moment giving her strength. "Yes. I was able to dream with my mother." She filled him in on what she'd seen as they walked. "It's different than dreaming with you, though. It feels like a dream—difficult to decipher—instead of... this."

"Less real?"

"Yes," she said as she looked around, thinking this looked like a fantasy rather than something tangible. Yet here she was with Lucian. "I can't communicate directly with her, only try and guess at the meaning of her dream."

He drew her a touch closer with his arm. "How are you?"

She wasn't sure why the question made her throat close. Why it made her feel like she might drown while simultaneously making her feel light as a feather on a breeze. Perhaps she wasn't used to anyone asking her how she was. She cleared her throat and blinked, a glowing orb over Lucian's shoulder blurring. "Um. I'm–" But she couldn't finish the thought. Her eyes jumped to his golden ones, and his handsome features pulled into something resembling concern. "I don't–"

"I'm here," he said with a reassuring squeeze.

"I feel myself being tugged away from what's real," she admitted.

He stopped and turned to face her; his brows drawn together. She watched his throat work as he swallowed.

"I think I understand," he said. "Today, I was... afraid that perhaps I'm losing my grasp on what's real. When I was here—in the real library—with my brother today, that felt more like a dream than this. Being with you feels more authentic somehow." He looked away as if ashamed to have admitted it.

Brinna took one of his hands in hers, unsure what to say but needing to feel him, needing to comfort him, to take his comfort.

Lucian laced his fingers with hers and looked around the library, then back at her. "I remembered something today. Something about being here."

"Yes?"

"I loved it. Loved coming to the library. I'd forgotten it, but it played such a huge part in inspiring my Roam. Do you think that's strange?" He looked at her once more.

"What? That you loved this place? I love it."

He smiled but shook his head. "No. That I'd forgotten."

Brinna looked around, then back at him. "No. I think we lose sight of things sometimes. Things that are so important at the time, but then other things take precedence." Her words struck a chord inside of her. What had *she* lost sight of? "I think there's always a way back, even if we have changed."

He nodded. "I read about my father's life." His voice carried something she couldn't decipher.

"And?" she asked, curious, and started walking once more, her hand in Lucian's. She reveled in the ease of being with him and feared when it would come time for him to leave.

"His life is filled with missteps and misguided choices. And still…" His voice faded away. He shook his head, but his eyes drifted back to hers. "I think I thought he was more than he is."

It made her think of her own parents. Her mother. "Does that make you sad?"

He shook his head and gave her a short smile. "I think it makes me think differently, but not in a negative way."

Brinna blinked, and the dreamscape had changed into the woods.

"Wait," Luc said, looking over her shoulder. "Oh."

"Where are we?" She turned in place and recognized it—the Whitling Woods—though different in Luc's mind. Her eyes connected with various details, the snow piles, the boulders, the tall evergreens and naked, reaching branches. A sound and movement captured her attention, and she turned her head to see a young woman—no! It was her, only different— walking into the meadow, pulling a sled.

"That's me," she whispered and looked over her shoulder at Lucian. She didn't wait for his answer and watched the different version of herself, noting the bedraggled state of her clothes. How thin she looked. Hungry. But she was smiling and singing. "I don't remember this," Brinna said, looking over her shoulder at Lucian once more. His eyes were on that singing Brinna, a look on his face she couldn't interpret.

He shook his head. "You wouldn't. It was a different version of you. Of me." He nodded toward a different area of the meadow.

Brinna turned, scanning, and spotted a different

Lucian lurking in the shadow of the trees, watching. Suddenly, Lucian's heat closed in behind her as he transferred her hand to his other.

"It isn't what you are thinking," he said, his voice soft. She could feel the soft graze of his mouth, the gentle movement of his breath against her ear. Eager energy raced across her skin. "I admit I know it looks bad."

Enjoying the closeness, and desirous of more sensations swirling inside her, Brinna took a step back, nearer to him. She tilted her head to invite him closer, her heart jumping higher into her throat, constricting with longing. "You were watching me?"

Lucian wrapped their connected hands around her front, pressing their hands against her belly and closing the distance so that the front of his body fit against her back. Then he slid his hands up her arms to her shoulders. "I was looking for a key keeper. To break Nix's spell." He moved her hair, exposing her neck.

"Auri."

Lucian made another one of those humming noises, then she felt his warm breath on her neck, raising chills, blissful ones, on her skin.

"But that isn't Auri," she whispered.

"I saw you first." She felt his touch, just the hint of one, skim from the nape of her exposed neck down to her shoulder.

Her breath caught, but she was somehow able to say, "This was before the spell? A different time?"

He hummed again, his touch retracing its path. "I

listened to you sing."

"But I didn't find the key?"

Lucian stilled, then disconnected, and she missed his proximity. He cleared his throat. "I didn't go through with showing you where it was."

She turned around, facing him. "Why?"

His brows arched over his golden eyes. "I don't–" He took another step back.

Brinna stepped toward him and grabbed his hand. "Stay. Don't run, Lucian. Stay here, with me."

He swallowed; his gaze nearly tortured with whatever was moving through his thoughts. Then his features relaxed, as though he'd come to an internal understanding, and he stepped closer, crowding her, his hands framing her face. His eyes skipped over her features, tracing them with his gaze. "I didn't want you to find it."

Brinna reached out and placed a hand over his heart, just as hers thumped wildly and heated with bright warmth. She could feel the furious rhythm of his own under her palm. "Why?"

He laid his hand over hers, and his heat burned up her arm, sizzled through to her spine, and raced down to heat the very center of her being. "I'd trapped my brother, and instead of leading you to the key like I was supposed to, I closed the way, blocking you from it. Trapped Aurielle instead."

"You didn't answer my question."

But he didn't add anything, just swallowed the words, looking down at their hands over his heart.

"Why, Lucian?" She wanted—no, she needed to know the answer.

She recalled that first shared dream—the hunger and desire between them. Then she thought further back, to the first time she remembered seeing him outside the hedge. The irrationality of the moment, the warmth between them. How he'd left in such a rush. The disappointment she'd felt after he was gone. She'd denied that feeling.

Then the time he'd asked her if she sang, how he'd disappeared in a hasty flurry. The starlight kiss. She looked back at this version of herself moving through the forest, singing, then looked back at Lucian and repeated her question. "Why?"

The landscape dripped away like droplets of water, making way for a new dreamscape. She was standing just outside the hedge as it had been before, her hand still pressed against Lucian's chest. His eyes were on her.

"This is when we first met." She smiled and stepped away from him to look for the opening in the hedge. When she found it, she walked inside. "I thought you hated me."

"I was rather rude," he replied.

She knew what he was doing, trying to distract her from her question, and whirled to tell him that she wouldn't forget, but Lucian was right behind her.

"Why were you rude?" she asked.

"I remembered you, from before. Remembered the way I felt."

She took a step closer to him, her heart racing with an unanswered rhythm. "How did you feel? Why did you lead me away?"

Lucian swallowed as the hedge's tunnel rushed past them, the dreamscape changing as it did, until they stood inside a glass skybridge at Sol facing one another. Stars sparkled in the night sky surrounding them.

Brinna was afraid he wasn't going to answer, but then Lucian took her hands in his.

"I wanted you for myself."

Her breath caught, surprised at his admission.

"Even then," he admitted. "I'd never felt nervous in my whole life. Not even the day my father escorted me to my rite of passage pleasure ceremony. Excited, yes. Not nervous."

She wanted to ask what he was talking about but didn't risk the question, afraid to bring an end to what he was telling her.

"I hid the way, because I wanted you for myself. Then I felt guilty."

"How come?"

"I'd trapped my brother. How could I keep you from possibly breaking the spell because I selfishly wanted you for myself?"

He wanted her! She smiled, unable to contain the fresh joy coursing through her. "It turned out to be the right choice," she said, her voice soft. "Auri broke it."

His eyes searched hers. "But they were yoked, and now he's in pain. And…"

She took a step closer to him. "And?"

"And I really want to kiss you. Like I did the night of the dance."

Brinna's heart sputtered to life inside her chest. "To kiss me?"

Lucian nodded, and his eyes caught on her mouth.

Nerves fluttered inside of her. Though this was a dream, it also wasn't—not really. And though they'd kissed before in a dream—done so much more—she hadn't known it was real. So she turned away and walked across the bridge into the atrium where the night sky was dark overhead. The torches were lit in the central garden and sconces glowed around the room. It was so romantic, and her heart swooned, longing for that connection, but for some reason she feared it and couldn't decide why.

"Maybe we should talk about something else. Something related to solving this problem," she said, grabbing hold of Tarley's bite and Auri's efficiency.

Lucian's footsteps tapped on the floor behind her. "Do you have anything new to add?"

"No."

"Good. I want to talk about this."

She turned, walking backwards along an atrium path. "I think you're going to wake up." She didn't want him to but said it anyway, deflecting.

He laughed. "Not yet." He followed her. "Tell me, Brinna. Your dreams—"

"You promised not to use that against me." She turned her back to him once more.

"I don't want to use it against you. I want

to…Brinna? Would you please stop?"

She did, took a deep breath, and turned to face him. She could feel the heat moving beneath her skin. He'd stopped several paces away, the golden torchlight lighting his beautiful face and the greenery around him.

"You asked me to stay. You asked me to confess. Why are you running now?"

And she knew, suddenly, why she was deflecting. "I'm afraid."

She could have lied to him, but for so long, she couldn't remember when someone had asked her how she was, how she felt, what she felt. She knew her family loved her, but they were stuck in their own lives. She'd spent so much time taking care of them, understood who she was—if she'd ever known beyond it—defined by her relationship to them.

But Lucian asked. Lucian saw her. Without a doubt, she wanted Lucian for herself, and it was frightening. Though this was as real as it could get, it still wasn't. They were dreaming. She was stuck in this spell. This was her new reality, and there wasn't a way to hide from it. She didn't even know if there an escape.

"What are you afraid of?" he asked and took a tentative step forward.

"I'm afraid that…"

He drew closer.

She swallowed, trying to find a way to articulate it. "Afraid that even if this is real, it isn't." Her eyes jumped from his chest to meet his gaze. He was close enough to touch, but she didn't.

"I thought we established this is real," he said.

She nodded. "Yes. But, what if... I give in to what I want, and it changes things?"

"What you want?" He grinned. "Do you want me?"

"I think you know I do."

Lucian reached out and smoothed a lock of her hair. His skin against hers felt so good, she leaned into it.

"What we... shared... was exceptionally pleasant," he said.

She couldn't help but smile, then closed her eyes and hummed with pleasure as his palm pressed against her face.

"You aren't curious?" he asked.

She opened her eyes to meet his gaze. If the rush of heat through her was any indication, she was more than curious. "It would be a lie to say otherwise."

Closing the distance between them, Lucian held her face between his palms and tilted her head so that she was looking into his eyes. "I am interested in you. You are interested in me," he said. "This is a world where we don't have to second guess our choices. No consequences."

"I don't want to lose you." The words lodged in her chest, and she had to gasp a breath, grabbing hold of his wrists to keep herself steady.

"I'm here," he said.

It hit her that if they never broke the spell, this is

where she was stuck. Forever. She wanted Lucian. She wanted love. She wanted sex. She wanted more life.

"We are both here."

He wasn't wrong.

His thumbs traced the curve of her cheeks to the edge of her mouth. His golden eyes deepened in color, laced with a mysterious darkness that spread as the darkness in his pupils widened. "May I kiss you then, Brinna? Where am I able to kiss you but in my dreams?"

She couldn't deny she wanted to kiss him, and he was right, they were dreaming, together. So she moved closer, sliding her hands against his chest. "Please."

Lucian smiled and leaned toward her, waiting just a breath before his mouth touched hers, then closing the space between them. His lips were soft but sturdy, offering and taking in equal measure. The kiss was delicious and sweet.

She'd kissed a boy once, behind the meeting house, when she'd been fourteen. Her romantic notions had written stories about what the first kiss would be, and it had been utterly disappointing. Her only other kiss had been with Lucian outside under the stars, and that kiss had both lifted her toward the heavens, then slammed her back to the ground in its aftermath. Though she recognized this was them walking a dream together, this kiss rewrote her romantic stories. This kiss was everything she thought a kiss was supposed to be. It was reverent, worshipful.

Lucian's hands slid from her face, one grasping the

back of her neck, the other angling across her back, his palm splayed above the curve of her bottom, holding her even closer. He tilted his face, and she mirrored him, holding his shirt in tight fists to keep him close. When his tongue caressed the seam of her lips, requesting entrance, she allowed him in, and the kiss shifted. Where it had been chaste and restrained, the tangle of her tongue with his whipped up a storm between them.

She moaned, releasing his shirt and sliding her hands up around his neck, sinking her fingers into the silky hair at the nape.

More. She wanted more.

"Brinna," he whispered as his hands grabbed her hips, drawing her tighter. His mouth owned her, craved her, led her deeper toward her own desire.

Closer. She wanted to be closer and rose onto her toes as her insides flooded with want. Her belly drifted over his erection, the knowledge of his desire making her feel powerful and needy.

Touch. She wanted to touch him. Gliding her hand down, she moved, grazing his chest, his abdomen. He tensed under her touch.

"Is this okay?" she asked, nibbling at his lip.

Lucian tore his mouth away, his breath moving quickly. "Stars, Brinna–" He groaned when her hand pressed against his cock, still hidden by his trousers.

Brinna searched his face, shaped with blissful torture, his eyes dark with desire.

"Don't stop."

He kissed her, his mouth dominating her once more, but a door slammed, and tore him from her arms, leaving her standing outside the cottage in the dark.

Alone. Again. Each time felt more final that the last, and she swallowed against the fear growing in her chest.

"Lucian?" she called, but he was gone.

"Time," Lucian shouted, sitting straight up in his bed as if he was coming up out of a pool of water, oxygen deprived and wet with perspiration. He was hard as fuck. But it wasn't time on his mind or rushing across his skin like an actual memory. It was that kiss.

"Fuck me," he moaned and flopped back onto his bed. That kiss. He pressed his fingertips to his lips, wishing it had been there in his bed, wishing that when he'd had the opportunity the night of the dance, he'd done a better job of it. But as with most things, he'd been a coward. He palmed his cock, needing to take care of it, then gave up with a frustrated groan and got up. He'd have to face another day without Brinna. It put him in a foul mood.

When Nix arrived, he looked about as good as Luc felt, though maybe worse, pale, a shade of his usual itself.

"I'm worried about you," Luc said the moment he laid eyes on his brother.

Nix ignored him. "You should talk. You look like shit. Did you dream of Brinna?" he asked, walking across the room to the windows. He stopped, his arms crossed in front of him.

"Yes."

His brother paused. "Did she say anything about Auri?"

"She said she would try to Dream Walk with her…"

Nix looked over his shoulder at Luc and nodded.

"I thought of something," Luc said. "Brinna made me think of it, well, the spell."

Nix turned back to the window. "What about it?"

"The Oracle said something about magic and time yesterday, as we left. Then, my dream… well, it reminded me of the spell." He thought again about standing in the woods with two Brinnas.

"The spell where I was stuck?"

"Yes. That spell. Auri's wishes changed things outside the spell, but it got me thinking that there's another version of Auri, of you and me, of Brinna, where Auri's wishes didn't change things. The Vasmost and its circles. The layers of alternates."

Nix turned to fully face Luc. "So you mean perhaps we're looking in the wrong era?"

"A possibility if magic is involved. If she is in fact from our godlines, we might still find her…"

"I hadn't considered *that* possibility." Nix walked toward Luc, a bit more vigor in his step. "Let's go."

Sol faded away, and soon they were ensconced at a table in the library with Sister Prudence, once again surrounded by tomes as they searched indexes and lists for a clue.

"Brinna said maybe there's royalty involved. It was in her mother's dream."

"We don't keep records like that," Sister Prudence said, setting more books on the table. "That would be mortal records, and their keeping isn't as thorough."

"But…" Nix's voice faded, then he looked at Luc, his dark eyes sparkling with hope. "Father wanted to disown me for falling in love with Auri, thinking she was mortal."

"Right." Luc had a good idea where his brother was going with the thought.

"What if our unascended god was unascended because they were disowned?" Nix mused.

"Good thinking, Nixi."

"Don't ever say that again, Luc."

"I kind of like it."

Nix rolled his eyes, and they settled in to look.

After several hours, Nix stood. "I'm going to grab another set."

Luc watched him walk away, worried, then turned to Sister Prudence. "You know yesterday, when you mentioned prolonging the fade?"

She looked up from her book and offered her undivided attention, her wide, knowing eyes unnerving.

Luc suppressed a shudder by looking at his current page, thinking of her telepathic question to him. "How would that work?" He turned the page and skimmed the information, sliding his finger down to keep his place.

"Severing the memories?"

Luc looked up and nodded, then lowered his voice. "He won't do it."

"But?"

"Just in case."

Her eyes flitted to where Nix had disappeared in the stacks. "Perhaps he would do this for his match rather than for himself, then you would not be faced with such a horrible choice, Lucian Uraiahs? Betrayal doesn't seem to fit you very well."

He dropped his gaze from her too perceptive one. "How would one do it?" He turned another page. "Please don't say a spell."

"No. Not a spell. A god. It's an *oblitorium* and is sanctioned by the god of the Vasmost and performed by an Oracle of the Highest Order."

The slam of books on the table made Luc jump. "Anything?" Nix asked.

"No," Luc said, feeling guilty for going behind his

brother's back but resolved he would talk to Nix about it later. After this task. Besides, he knew Nix wouldn't listen to reason. Not when it came to Aurielle.

"I have an idea," Nix said as he took his seat once more. "If we don't find anything in these books."

"Do share."

"Lexa. If anyone is going to be able to know magical beings with powers, she would."

"Or she'd know others who do."

"Right."

"Maybe we could find a way for me to Dream Walk," Nix said nonchalantly as he turned a page. "Then I could see Auri."

"That is powerful magic," Sister Prudence said. "Not to be dabbled with cavalierly."

"What do you mean?" Luc asked, his eyes jumping to Nix and back again.

"There are different kinds of magic," she said, "or powers, I should say. Gods for example, like you, have natural magic. It is whole and ordinal, defined but omnipotent. It is passed down in the bloodline, transferred, but fixed and awakened by ascension. You, Nixus, for example, have a duty to your power to the night and darkness, shadows, and death. You wield absolute power, but there is balance. You aren't able to cross the boundaries of Lucian's power."

"Yes. We learned this as godlings."

"This is rational magic. But there is also irrational magic, a means to split, distort, steal, and hoard power. This power can be natural, but it can also be conjured."

"But energy is fixed," Nixus said. "I might have absolute power of night and dark, but to create power from nothing–"

"Yes. This is true, but there is irrationality. Things like disturbing the natural boundaries, such as time, would tap into those irrational planes of power."

"We cross space and time all the time," Nix said. "We did it to come here."

"I did it when I Roamed," Luc added.

"Yes. But still natural. Time and space are defined by rationality and rules. Your godlight allows you to tap into this power. But to disturb that natural order, it must be–"

"Conjured," Nix finished for her.

Sister Prudence nodded. "Or stolen. Dream Walking," she added, "is an irrational magic. There isn't a godblood that has ever wielded that power naturally, and none that I have ever come across in my research, but I have read of that kind of power being conjured."

A prickle of awareness traveled down Luc's spine. "But how could it be possible that two gods—neither of whom have conjured a power like Dream Walking—like Nix, for example, do it?"

Prudence paused, her head tilting as she measured Lucian with her gaze. *Can you think of nothing?* her voice asked, though her mouth didn't move.

"A god-yoke," Nix said, staring off into space, unseeing. Then he looked at Luc. "In the spell, Auri and I could communicate with one another without ever speaking."

"Still?" Luc asked.

"No. Not since, but maybe those god-yoked could?"

Luc stood abruptly, knocking over his chair. It hit the tiled floor with a bang.

"Luc?" Nix asked. "Are you okay?"

He was agitated, but he wasn't sure why. He and Brinna weren't god-yoked. It was impossible. Illogical. It couldn't be—but he realized he was pressing his fingers against his heart. Again.

You look terrible, his brother had said.

Fisting his hands at his side, Luc told himself he was just exhausted. He didn't have his powers. That was it. Rather than entertain the idea further, he picked up his chair. "Sorry. I just got a little ahead of myself."

Nix's dark eyes were on him, a little too shrewd for Luc's comfort, so he bent over the book and forced himself to focus.

Seemingly unaffected, Sister Prudence continued, "It could also be a combination of stolen, natural power spelled with demon spite, for example. Irrational magic is dangerous and volatile. It takes as much as it provides."

Luc's finger stopped as he stumbled on a name. "Wait. I might have found something." He leaned over, to take a closer look.

Nix joined him. "What is it?"

"Alea Maximora, daughter to Maxim, god of fire, and Ora, goddess of healers."

"Healers?" Nix said, his tone hopeful. "That's—"

"Look." Luc pointed at the entry. "She ascended, then was disowned."

Sister Prudence stood and joined them. "Godblood disownment?" She flipped the book closed to look at the cover. "The fifth era. That's quite some time ago."

Luc reopened to the page.

Nix crowded him to read, then pointed at a line. "It says she married a Zollah Cumbria. Is that a godline?" He sifted through the tomes on the tabletop. "Fifth era?" He pulled one and opened it, skimming the pages, then looked up the name. "No Cumbria."

"Disownment is so rare," Sister Prudence said.

"Could this be the one?" Nix asked.

"Says here that Zollah Cumbria was mortal," Lucian said. "Look. They had a daughter. Azleah."

Nix's head snapped up. "What did you say?"

"Alea had a daughter named Azleah, and" —he calculated the years in his head— "thirteen years later, Alea died. Azleah disappeared at seventeen. That's where the entry ends."

Nix moved over to look once more. "I know that name." He stood. "Shit. After the meadow at the inn. Tarley said it when she confronted her mother, asking who *Azleah* was."

"Did Scarlett answer?"

Nix shook his head.

Luc looked down at the entry again. "Godblood. Proof—if we can connect them. Do you think this could be her line? The fifth era? But how?"

"How is Brinna Dream Walking?" Nix asked. He grinned. "Maybe we've found our best lead yet."

"I will see if we have any more information on those names," Sister Prudence said and left the table.

Lucian watched her disappear through the stacks.

"So, Lexa's later?" Nix asked. "She might have some connection to the human records we need."

It meant delaying dreaming with Brinna, which Lucian didn't want to do. It wasn't about the kiss—Okay. It was—but it was also about the new, nagging idea running under his skin that he wanted to deny.

He pressed his fingers to his heart, then retracted them quickly when he saw Nix notice.

Not dreaming meant Brinna would be left alone, and that, he didn't like. But if it got them closer to breaking the spell, she would want that. So he nodded, knowing he was bound for trouble either way.

Auri's dreamscape was unsettling. When Brinna entered, the dark landscape was strangely rounded and hazy at the periphery, while at the same time appearing sharp and dangerous at its center. Still unable to cross into Auri's true consciousness, Brinna discovered she could walk over the surface of the dream. Her footsteps were like opalescent ripples on water, still apart, a disconnected observer.

"Auri?" she called out, hopeful, though she knew Auri wouldn't respond.

The dreamscape rushed past her, pulsing until it

was apparent her sister's dream was complete darkness with only a pinpoint of light in the distance. Brinna kept walking, looking for Auri in the oppressive dark, but no matter how far she walked, the pinpoint of light seemed the same distance, if not further.

"Auri?" Brinna called once more, just in case.

A lump appeared, a shade darker than the darkness, so Brinna moved toward it. But the closer she came, the more the thing moved, until she realized it was Auri.

Her sister stood and glanced over her shoulder. She looked fierce, wearing darkness like a shield, her frown deep, but she was also no more than a glimmer of her true self, stooped and weighted with a burden Brinna couldn't identify.

"Auri?"

Though Auri looked in Brinna's direction, her sister's focus wasn't on her, but on something behind her.

Brinna turned.

A horrific monster loomed, giant and hideous. Its face was filled with a multitude of eyes and its distended mouth overfilled with too many teeth, dripping blood. The monster hunched, its bent legs ending with split hooves and claws. Its skin oozed pus and gore.

Brinna put a hand over her mouth, gagging, then screamed.

Neither the creature nor Auri responded. As with her mother's dream, Brinna was merely an observer. It didn't help her terror.

"You don't belong here," Auri yelled, turning.

"You have something that's mine," the creature said, its voice a horrible manifestation of anger that scraped against Brinna's ears. She cried out, covering them in a desperate attempt to block the horrid sound.

"I sent you back," Auri said, her voice somehow so brave that Brinna longed for that feeling herself.

"Oh, young goddess. You know nothing."

"Goddess." Auri straightened, clearly disarmed. "What?"

The creature advanced, its horrible form drawing to close to Brinna for comfort. She shrank back. Its giant claws tapping against the rocky ground.

"That magic lingering in your blood," it rasped. "Sweet, tasty magic I will drain from your body."

"And what is this magic?" Auri yelled, somehow now wielding a sword.

"Godblood." The monster sniffed. "And something else. A taint of... darkness."

Auri straightened and tilted her head. "Nixus?"

The monster scoffed. "No. Something borrowed. Taken." The creature advanced another step. "But you are alone, sweet godling. I will suck the marrow of your godlight and use it to break free."

"Run, Auri!" Brinna screamed.

But her sister couldn't hear her.

Instead, a bright light flashed, the creature screamed, and Brinna squeezed her eyes shut.

When she opened them again, Auri, wilted and

withered, collapsed onto a sandy shore like the one Lucian had once shown her behind an Elsewhere Door.

"Auri!"

Brinna ran forward and dropped next to Auri's unmoving form. Her sister looked like a plant whose roots had failed, her skin pale.

"Nixus?" Auri whispered. "Are you here?" She rolled to her back and looked up at the sky, seeming not to care the waves lapped at her legs partially submerged. Or she was too weak to do anything about it; her pallor was awful, so pale. Her hands stretched out to her sides, her body covered in a shroud of dark gossamer and water.

"Auri?" Brinna asked. "I'm here. What can I do?"

But Auri didn't answer.

And in that moment, Brinna felt her absolute powerlessness. She'd spent her life being there for her family, helping them, comforting them, listening to them. And now, when it mattered, she was… nothing. Tears stung her eyes.

"I'm glad you brought me here. It will be easier this way. To fade," Auri said.

The fading. Lucian had spoken of it. Brinna's heart took a tumble, tripping against her chest as it tried to find purchase inside her chest.

"It's one of my favorite memories, Nix, realizing that I loved you." Auri brought her hands together at her heart, one of her hands circling her wrist where her red ribbon would have been. "I think this is where I lost it," she whispered and smiled at whatever she was seeing.

Brinna gasped, pulling herself back into the cottage and reaching for her own red ribbon. Still there. Auri's was gone. Tarley's was gone. Jessamine's was there—different than her own. Hers oldest sister's was woven with multiple threads, though she wasn't sure why.

Brinna turned and looked at Auri.

Just as in her dream, she was deathly pale, her brow pinched as if she was in pain.

"I'm going to help," Brinna told Auri, but she didn't know how.

She stood and raced through the cottage—the only one able to do it—to her mother, and blinked her way into Scarlett's dreamscape, screaming, "Mother! End this! Please. Something is wrong with Auri."

But Scarlett was bent over in her version of the garden, tending dead plants. She didn't hear Brinna, didn't flinch, just plucked dead leaves again and again.

Brinna removed herself and tried her father's dreamscape. "Father?" she asked.

She stood inside the cottage, but it was empty, the front door flung wide open. She left and walked outside, where everything was gigantic once more. Blades of grass were huge trees; gravel was a canyon.

"Father?" she cried, afraid to walk further for fear of getting lost, but then remembered she could leave the dream. So she stepped into the dense forest to find Tomas and wandered until she knew it was hopeless.

She closed her eyes. "Father, I need you." When

she reopened them, Tomas stood in front of her, looking up at the sky.

"I'm small," he said, fretting. "So small. Always small. I will not find my way. Scarlett? Where are my children?"

Brinna pulled herself from his dream and screamed, "I can't do anything!"

With a frustrated sound, she stalked to the back room to check Mattias's dream and watched as he battled a knight in dark armor, a relentless warrior. Over and over, her brother was struck down, blood blooming across his belly. Mattias would look up, flicker away, only to return healed to face the knight once again, a cycle that repeated with her brother's feral cry at his inability to change it.

Brinna left him to visit Tarley's dreamscape. Her older sister sat at the edge of the river in the woods holding a pile of clothing against her breast, crying. "I've lost him. I've lost him. I've lost him," she sobbed, again and again, then adding, "I should have seen it coming."

Brinna leapt from Tarley's grief into Jessamine's dream.

Her oldest sister was in a room of a sparse cottage, kneeling on the floor next to an indecipherable lump, her apron bloody. At a knock at the door, Jessamine looked over her shoulder, fear flashing on her face.

She hesitated, then stood and slowly moved across the wooden floorboards. When she reached the door, she twisted open the doorknob. Standing on the other side was an old woman and an old man, their skin sagging on their faces. They were dressed in tattered rags, their bodies emaciated. The old woman smiled a toothless smile and held out a teacup as the man offered her an armful of wood.

As Jessamine reached for the cup, a conspiracy of ravens attacked the door, wings fluttering, whipping up a frenzy of chaotic noise. The cup crashed to the ground, shattering, and the birds plucked at the couple's eyes, skin, hair as they screamed, "Daughter! Daughter! Help us!"

Jessamine cried out and jumped into the fray. The ravenous black birds pecked her apart, only to have the dream begin again—Jessamine kneeling on the floor once more.

Brinna blinked back into the cottage and whirled around, looking for a solution.

But there wasn't one.

Tears streamed from her eyes, and she sank to her knees. A sob followed by another bubbled up from inside her, until she was nothing more than a crying mess on the floor between the beds where she and her sisters slept. Stuck. She was stuck, they were stuck, and there was nothing she could do to fix it.

She screamed, a howl of absolute pain and hopelessness.

With her face in her hands, Brinna cried, "Lucian? Where are you? I don't know what to do."

He didn't answer; she hadn't expected him to.

And for the first time, Brinna allowed the deep gray

of the spell to take her, drawing her into its viscous power.

"You're brooding," Lexa said, filling Nix's tumbler with the amber liquid Luc knew his brother liked. "You both are."

Luc looked away from their sister's astute observation and glanced around the bungalow nestled below Alabastrine, their family home in the heart of old Elcadia City. Lexa was rarely in residence, spending most of her time beyond them in the Netherrealm where she was most comfortable, where her dragon form was protected at the heart of the labyrinth, and claiming she wasn't keen on what up-worlders did with their time. "Boring lot," she'd said once.

"I don't brood." Luc took a sip of his drink.

"Beg to differ, little brother."

Luc pushed a sound through his nose and sat back. "You haven't done much with the place." He rested an ankle on his knee and smirked at Lexa.

"Why should I? I only come to visit Nix."

"I'm hurt," Luc replied with a tone like smooth gray sky.

"And why would that be? Was it jealousy that had you trapping your twin, Lucian? So you could take his place as my favorite?" She smirked back.

They both glanced at Nix, waiting for him to join in the repartee, but he was ruminating with focus elsewhere. Luc's smile faded, worried for him.

"Ha. Ha," Luc said with very little intonation. "I get it. I screwed up."

Lexa looked from Nix to Luc, her brow furrowed. "How are you doing now, since Father has taken your power?"

Luc huffed at her then took another sip of his whiskey. "Fine."

She took a sip of her drink, watching him too closely. "You don't look it." Lexa had a way of seeing through to the heart of him. And she was right. The discomfort in his chest had grown more insistent, turning toward pain, and he wondered if this is what his father had promised, claiming he would beg for his powers back. The only relief he found was when he slept. Dreamed. Which made him return to what he'd wondered in the Library of Oracles. Could he be god-yoked with Brinna?

He was relieved when Lexa turned her golden gaze on Nix.

"Why are you brooding, Nix? Your human grow tired of you?"

His brother came back to himself, shot her a glare, and took a sip of his drink.

She chuckled.

"For the record, Nixus," Lexa said, grabbing her flute of champagne and flopping into an overstuffed chair near a dark window, "I like Auri."

"She hasn't grown tired of me."

"She will. And I will be waiting." Lexa licked her lips and grinned.

Nix groaned, rolling his eyes and pressing his hand to his pale forehead as he shook his head. "Why are you like this?"

She snorted. "I'm like this because I enjoy being like this." She shrugged. "And, better you learn this now—women need more than a man is able to give them."

"Fair enough. But I am no man," he said with a glint of his usual arrogance, but it slid away as quickly as it had surfaced.

"We might have found something." Luc set his tumbler on the table. "A name, but it isn't in any of our records."

"With the Oracles?"

"Right. Auri and her family are most likely godblood."

"Makes sense considering the yoke," she said with a grimace. "Have you checked with Father?" Her eyes darted between Luc and Nix.

"He won't intervene. Mortals, unless we can prove otherwise. We need to find this piece of the puzzle to prove it."

"Ask him for your powers back."

Luc shook his head. "You know he's exacted a price."

"Of course he has." Lexa took a sip, then smoothed a perfectly manicured hand over the satin of her black pants. "You should acquiesce."

"I can't."

Lexa's concerned gaze jumped to Nixus, and she arched her eyebrows. "What if it could save your brother?"

"And what gives you the impression my power—Father's power—would make any difference? It won't impact the yoke."

She shrugged. "Who knows what this spell requires, but what if your powers could break the spell?"

"Yours can't. Nix's can't. It's unlikely. Besides, I can't agree to his demands."

"Which are what? Taking his place?"

His silence was affirmation enough.

Her eyebrows arched, and she smirked. "I don't envy the position." She took a sip, then pointed her champagne flute at him. "But Father's powers as god of the Vasmost probably comes with some omnipotent perks."

"You denied him."

Her smirk deepened. "I can't be trusted with power like that. Besides, I was always his second choice." She gave him one of those looks he hated.

"That isn't why we're here," Luc said. "We have two options. The human link and–"

"–the magic," Nix finished. "Irrational magic." He drained the rest of his drink. "We wondered if you might be able to help."

Lexa nodded at his whiskey. "Feel like getting drunk? I can take you somewhere where you can drink yourself into true oblivion while pursuing your investigation." She arched an eyebrow.

Nix stood. "Let's go."

"It's a demon bar."

"You never cease to amaze me, Lexa," Luc said, standing. "You'd think you'd have enough of them in the Netherworld." He flicked a hand. "Lead the way."

After walking the streets of Upper Elcadia, they came across their triplet brothers Eitan, Lior, and Pax who joined their journey into Underworld, the city under the city.

"Thank you for that help, with Auri's brother," Nix said to the triplets.

"Of course." Lior swung his brown hair out of his eyes. "It was an easy task. The kid didn't really need us."

"But it brought Auri peace of mind," Nix told him.

"Did you tell him?" Eitan elbowed Pax.

"Tell him what?"

"About the kid disappearing." Eitan looked at Nixus. "Just there, then gone" –he snapped his fingers–"then there again."

"That's right," Pax said. "It was strange, but I forgot about it."

Luc met Nix's eyes.

He knew why. *Irrational magic. Time*, making their theory and this trip feel even more important.

They followed their sister down into the caverns below the city, using the set between two buildings of the Elcadian Justice Hall Square. The stairwell was carved from the rocks rather than built and spiraled down into the dark.

Like the caves beneath Alabastrine where the entrance to Lexa's lair began, the whole of Elcadia was nestled on top of caverns—an entire city below as the one above. Only unlike Lexa's caves, which looked like…well, caves, Lexa spirited them into what resembled a buried crystal city, a great cavern carved from the expanse with great round pillars of white crystal etched with art.

"I don't know why I haven't come here more," Luc said drolly.

"Your head is always in the clouds," Lexa joked.

"Hilarious. God of the sun and light."

"Was. Was the god of sun and light." She grinned at him. "And I'm an underground kind of gal. I like to be under all kinds of things." Her tone was bright.

"Lexa. Don't," Pax begged.

"Don't be so uptight," she said. "In fact, I don't think this field trip is for you, young brother. You're much too sensitive for the likes of a demon bar."

"I'll decide what I'm too sensitive for," Pax groused.

"Now, now." Eitan put a hand on Pax's shoulder. "We're here on a mission, and this is the place to do it."

"You've been?" Lior asked.

"Of course," Eitan said. "It's all about who you know, brother."

"And who do you know?"

Eitan grinned a devil's smile. "More than you'd guess."

"On that note," Luc said, "let's focus."

"About that," Lexa said. "Let me do the talking. I'm the god of the Netherworld. More gravitas among this crowd."

They wormed their way through throngs of creatures: nymphs, witches, fae, cats and unicorns—in their human-like forms versus the animal ones—seraphs, vampires, gods, demigods, wizards, and even a smattering of lesser demons. Lexa stopped in front of a storefront, the crystal walls carved to resemble one from above ground—though if Luc were being honest, the translucence of the crystal that changed color from clear to aqua was even more beautiful than the granite and marble above. An ornate wooden door hinged with a copper patina waited for them.

Lexa turned and looked at the triplets. "Best

behavior. I've no intention of vouching for you if you act like asses. Got it?"

"Got it," Lior said.

Pax nodded.

Eitan snorted. "As if."

Inside, it was dark, but crystal chandeliers hung at intervals across the expansive space, each caging creatures holding torches. They were dressed in very little, black leather strips covering various parts. Music blasted throughout the space, and at various beats the creatures would shift inside their cages.

"Are those humans?" Nix asked Lexa, following her through the crush of patrons, weaving between bodies so he had to shout the question over the din of the establishment.

Lexa looked up, turned, and looked at him, then nodded. "Willing."

"You brought us to a sex club?" Luc asked.

She laughed. "Not specifically a sex club. What did you expect of a demon bar?"

He shrugged. He wasn't exactly innocent—he'd been to a few sex clubs in his Roaming, though no demon clubs. "Who do we need to ask about the magic?"

"First, brother," Lexa said, "relax. I have it all under control."

"That's what I'm afraid of."

Luc trailed Nix, who followed Lexa until they reached a cordoned off area. His sister leaned into the fae woman at the entrance and whispered something in her ear. The woman smiled, a blush creeping across her cheeks, before she stepped back to allow them passage. Before long, they were seated with Lexa, Pax, Eitan, and Lior in a booth in the VIP section of the club.

"Will this do?" Eitan asked, his hand coming down onto Nix's shoulder with a crack.

A succubus arrived at the table with a fanged smile. Red leather stitched with ornate black thread wrapped around her form, leaving very little to imagination. "Eitan." She winked and ran her pink tongue over one of her fangs.

Luc looked between her and his brother, who leaned back and rested a hand on the top of the seat cushion.

Eitan smirked. "Delia."

"What can I get you?"

"Two things," Lexa said, commanding the vampire's attention.

"Ms. Uraiahs." She nodded her head in deference.

"I need" –Lexa looked at her brothers, then back at the waitress– "two bottles of your best lazuli, and is Ozland here?"

Delia nodded. "I'll be back." Her gaze returned to Eitan before she left the table.

"You better watch your back," Pax said. "She's going to show up while you're sleeping."

"Been there, done that." Eitan reached out to squeeze their brother's shoulder. "You should try it. Might break up some of that tension, Pax."

Luc sighed. Perhaps this had been a terrible idea. He wondered if Brinna was alright, his heart squeezing at the thought of missing her, of not meeting her in their dreams. He wondered how she was holding up, if she'd learned anything new.

The strangeness of the way his thoughts tumbled over one another in relation to Brinna hit him hard, his breath locking up as he looked around. At one time, this place—a place that he would have sought during his Roam—would have been enough to occupy his thoughts. But now, he was thinking about Brinna, about wanting to be with her.

Fuck, he thought, realizing he wasn't sure he could explain that away, or that he wanted to.

What if he was god-yoked to her?

Was that such a terrible thought?

He glanced at Nix, who resembled death warmed over, and thought perhaps it was. Only he knew, his brother wouldn't wish it away, even for all the pain he was in at the moment. Nix just wanted Auri, and there was something very powerful in that.

The owner of the bar was a reformed demon, though Luc used the word 'reformed' loosely in this demon's case. Ozland was a hulking beast, on two legs with two arms like any man, tall and chiseled, shaded with charcoal gray skin and bright green eyes like a cat's, with a smooth flicking tail and a sharp, pointy end to match. The bar wasn't Ozland's only foray into the darker side of the Elcadia Underground, according to Lexa, even if what he dabbled in wasn't exactly demon business.

When he arrived at the table, he grinned at Lexa, his pointy teeth sharp. "Goddess," he said in a tone that suggested he was intimately familiar.

Lexa's eyebrows rose over her eyes. "Oz. Still on the straight and narrow?"

"For now," he replied. "Come to coax me off?"

"No," Lexa said, "but if I ever want to sample your wares, I'll be sure to let you know."

Luc and his brothers groaned.

The demon threw back his head with a raucous laugh. Then he pushed into the booth to sit next to her, taking the time to look at the rest of them. "And these are?"

"A handful of my brothers," Lexa said and introduced them.

Oz's thick black eyebrows rose over his green eyes, the dark slits of his pupils widening. He offered Eitan a nod, but his eyes stopped on Nix with interest. "God of night and darkness? It would seem, if rumors are true, that you have only returned to the realm."

Nix nodded but remained reticent. Luc could understand, considering the last interaction they'd had with a demon.

"As talkative as your sister, I see." He grinned at Lexa.

She chuffed at Oz's assessment, which struck Luc as odd. Was this Lexa unsettled? He couldn't be sure since he'd never witnessed it.

"We're here for information," Luc said.

Oz's eyes narrowed, his pupils constricting to a slit. "Where's your power?"

"Gone," Luc said.

Lexa cast a dark stare at Luc and kicked his shin under the table. "My brother, it would seem, has lost his sense of propriety," she said. "What he means is he's enjoying the place."

Oz dragged his gaze away from Luc's, turning his head to look at Lexa. "One can offer allowances under certain circumstances." The demon's gaze raked Lexa.

Lexa's eyes narrowed, and she tilted her head.

Luc and his brothers leaned away from their sister, knowing that look.

"Are you insinuating something, Oz? To the goddess of the Netherworld?" She placed her elbows on the tabletop, lacing her fingers, and leaned forward, her gaze on the demon.

"If I am?"

Lexa hummed and paused, a duration of silence stretching long enough to make it full of threat. "I have this amazing room in my maze, filled with all kinds of toys I enjoy."

Oz's gaze widened, intrigued.

"I like to hear unruly creatures scream and beg for mercy when they cross me. And not in a fun way."

Oz swallowed.

"But here's what you should know, Ozland. I don't deal in mercy. I don't deal in favors. Not when you cross me. You have this" —she waved her hand around indicating the club— "and everything else, because I let you. Are we clear?"

Oz grinned, his eyes alight with something feral.

Without turning her head, she said, "Ask your question, Luc. I don't give a fuck about propriety anymore."

Oz, still grinning, turned his head to Luc, adjusting in his seat. Luc wasn't sure if the demon was frightened or aroused by his sister. The latter made him cringe, but he ignored it for the question. "We're looking for access to human histories."

"Human histories are a messy business," the demon said. "Besides the name, you'll need their realm and time-period. Terribly antiquated record keepers."

"What about by magic?" Nix asked.

"What kind of magic?"

"Dream Walking," Nix said.

"Irrational magic, then. This kind of magic often contains a signature, which allows you to track the sorcerer who cast it."

"How would we find that?" Nix asked.

"It would take another sorcerer to identify it."

A dead end, Luc thought and sighed.

"Do you have the human's name?" Oz asked.

"Zollah Cumbria."

Lexa's head snapped to Nix. "What was that?"

"Zollah Cumbria."

She took a deep drink of her bright blue beverage, then set it back down on the table. "You're in luck. Zollah Cumbria is in the Netherrealm." She shuddered. "You better drink up."

Time was strange there, as if it were both stopped but moving quickly at the same time. As Brinna drifted in the dream current without that connection to reality, she felt as if she was losing all sense of herself. She could feel the thread holding her there, a slim, fragile thing that might snap with the slightest pressure, though she couldn't be sure what sort of pressure might destroy the tether. Considering the idea of letting go, she drifted into the current, but knew somehow that if she did, she wouldn't be able to find her way back. She wouldn't find Lucian again, which made her achy. So she held on, because of him, his promise, and the knowledge that the only way to help her family meant she couldn't let go of what was real.

Yet, she could feel the persistent tug to sink into the mire of the deep sleep.

"Lucian?" she called.

But there wasn't an answer.

Her mind slipped, the tether wobbly, the shimmer of gray around her trying to draw her deeper. She felt the distance between her and Lucian and attributed it to her fear of being in the spell, fear of what would happen if she slid into that deep sleep with the rest of her family. Would she disappear? Would she cease to be? Would she have perpetual nightmares, as they were? She couldn't get Tarley out of her mind, her absolute grief of missing Lachlan playing out in as a crazed woman at the river washing her hands until they bled and watching the drops of blood coalesce into a creature who turned on her sister. Tarley would scream, and the dream would slide away before starting once again.

That was where Brinna was headed… lost to her nightmares. Only she had the ability to Dream Walk, for some inexplicable reason.

You're strong.

With a shout, Brinna resurfaced from the deep gray that wanted to keep her. Breathing hard and with her head in her hands, she said aloud into the deep gray of the sleeping world—as if it were Lucian speaking to her— "Brinna. You're strong. Stay."

When she looked up and the room where she was

asleep with her sisters coalesced around her, giving her something concrete once more. The wooden floor felt smooth under her. The single mullioned window flickering with the flame from the glowing lantern illuminated the rough-hewn beams holding up the thatched roof of the cottage. The two beds—one at her back, the other before her—were pressed against opposite walls, both filled with her sleeping sisters. Alive.

Her family. They were her purpose to hang on. She had to save them.

She'd spent much of her life feeling as if perhaps she was the odd one out, the one without a purpose. Only right then, she realized while her waking life had been spent nurturing them, loving them, being a bridge, now she was a bridge between the sleeping world and the waking one. Almost as if she'd been made for this moment.

She could do this.

With a fortifying sigh, she stood. "Back into Mother's dreams," she said and started down the steps, stopping only when she'd reached her mother. Brinna placed her hand on Scarlett's cheek, closed her eyes, and fell into her mother's dream.

The strange conglomeration of her mother's mind coalesced around her, the swirl of things moving and shifting like thick paint sliding over a surface, revealing colors and shapes. Trees squiggled into being, thick, wide, and covered with foliage, hinting at the woods. It was dark but for a single lantern held by Scarlett, alone in the darkness.

"Baba?" she called out.

"Mother?" Brinna asked, testing the barrier, but it remained between them, reminding her she was only an observer.

A brilliant light—different from the rest of her mother's dream, more cohesive and real—coalesced from somewhere in the woods, so bright it hurt to look at it, but Brinna forced herself to do so, shading her eyes with her hand. A shadow appeared at its center, diffusing the radiance. As the shadow grew, the light dissipated until only a woman remained— a breathtakingly beautiful woman. She had an ethereal quality, her hair long and white, her form bathed in that brilliance. She seemed to float among the forest as if it were a part of her and she a part of it.

"Scarlett," she said. "Again?"

Scarlett's hand fell to her flat stomach, and she nodded with a smile. "I'll need another ribbon."

The woman chuckled. "It would seem our Tomas is making good on my orders. The others?"

"Healthy. Robust. But Brinna never cries. Is that... normal?"

"And that is your only complaint? Is she eating?"

Scarlett nodded and smiled. "She is a fat thing. Happy."

"Then all is well." The beautiful woman held out her hand. In her palm was a swirling light twisted up with violet iridescence. It shimmered until it became what looked like a ribbon—a red one, in her open palm. "You remember the spell?"

"Yes, Baba."

Brinna lifted her wrist and looked at the ribbon tied there—a ribbon she couldn't remember ever being without. When she looked back at the dream, the beautiful woman was now old and bent. Her white hair was a ratted mess upon her head, her body clothed in rags. She leaned against a wooden staff in her hand.

"And what will break it?"

Scarlett nodded. "Yes. I remember. It will be sometime before that happens. They are small," she said. "Maybe he'll stop looking before then."

Baba harrumphed and shuffled to a rock, where she sat. "You tell yourself that, Scarlett, if it makes you feel safer behind your hedge. But the throes of true love will come before you are ready for them, and it will be as if you have built a house of cards."

The hand-painted forest blew away as if it were a house of cards, leaving the two women amid a blank canvas of gray. Baba still sat as if on her rock, cane in hand, though Brinna couldn't see that there was a rock there holding the old woman up any longer. Her mother stood facing the woman.

"There isn't another way," Scarlett said.

"There is always another way, child. This path—" Baba sighed and shook her head. "I see sadness on the road before you. You will try so hard to control…"

"Safe. I'm trying to keep us safe."

"You will lose them."

"How can you say that?"

"Look in your heart, Scarlett. You aren't without power. It will tell you."

"The magic is gone." Threads of light exploded from Scarlett like yellow ribbons, five of them, and at the end of each satiny thread, a beating heart.

"That isn't the power to which I refer. Besides, magic is never gone. You've just given it away. But seek your heart—"

"A mother?"

The old woman nodded. "That will never be removed from them. From you."

Scarlett covered her face with her hands. "I need to keep them safe."

The dream slammed shut, everything disappearing into the black as if Brinna had closed her eyes, shutting it out. She came back into consciousness, removed her hands from her mother, and fell back. "What does it mean, Mother?"

The world around her faded into gray once more, leaving Brinna to cling to that tether. She considered what she'd seen, unsure what was real, what was a symbol, and what was dream logic. She didn't know how to decipher any of it.

"Lucian?" she called out, testing the vibration of their shared web.

But there was no answer.

With a sigh, Brinna entered her mother's chaotic dreams once more, hoping to find the answers she needed. There, at least, she would remain safe from the Deep Gray.

He hated the caverns of the Netherrealm, but it was even worse without his powers. It was dank, cold, and dark. All the things he loathed. He wanted to complain about it, and under normal circumstances, he would have, but at the moment, Nixus's pallor, his own aching body, and the promise of information that might be able to help them was enough for Luc to keep his mouth clear of complaints.

But to keep his mind occupied, he worked to keep his brother and sister talking.

It made the trek more bearable and reminded him

they weren't actually residents of that grisly landscape—not him and Nix, anyway. Over the River of Sorrows, he had considered jumping into its dark waters, but Lexa had lashed both he and Nix to the boat. On the Plains of Chrysanthemum, the bones stretched on and on, even as he and Nix hung from Lexa's talons as she flew over them, and he wondered if he was losing all sense of reality or if he was in a morbid dream.

He missed Brinna.

Finally, Lexa touched down on the other side of that expanse, setting them gently on a new landscape smoking with sulfur.

"And where are we now?" Luc asked, smoothing out his clothing. "Dammit, Lexa, I'm wrinkled."

She snorted. "You're about to enter Pyre Canyon. And you're worried about wrinkles?"

"I don't like the sound of that," he said. "It sounds… hot."

She laughed. "An understatement."

"We should get going," Nix said, his normally witty repartee nonexistent.

It worried Luc.

Rather than say something that might get his brother to laugh, he nodded. "Yes. Let's get this over with." He looked at Lexa, back in her non-dragon form. "Is Cumbria burning in this fire?"

She shook her head. "Unfortunately, he's deeper in the Netherrealm. The fires of the pyre would have been too kind."

Luc didn't like the sound of that.

"How much further?" Nix asked.

"Down the Dismal Rapids and over the Falls. Then it's into the Malevolent Marshes. We'll fly over the Nefarious Sea to the Verge, and there we'll find the Edge."

"Good goddess, Lexa," Luc snapped.

"Now that, I have never been called, unless I'm using my tongue."

"Lexa," Nix said with a groan.

She laughed.

"Can't we just portal there?" Luc asked. "Time is of the essence, and you've described a fucking quest."

"Oh." She tilted her head. "I thought you wanted a hero quest." She patted down her pantsuit. "You're both trying to be heroes, yes?"

"No. We're trying to break the spell and fix Nix," Luc said, but then, maybe he was lying. He thought of Brinna, aware of the twinge in his chest, wanting more than anything to find a way to help her. Originally this had been for Aurielle and thereby Nix—at least that's what he'd rationalized. But he realized when it came to Brinna, it had never been about Nix. It had always been about him.

"I don't need to be fixed," Nix said. "I need to get back to Auri."

"Forgive me for wanting to share my home with you both. But whatever–"

"Don't be like that, Lexa. You've never wanted me in your realm," Luc replied.

"But now I do. You've no light and are at my mercy." She grinned, and he could swear he saw her dragon's teeth.

He groaned. "Way to rub it in, sister."

She held up her hand. "Fine. You want instant gratification?" The landscape drifted away, throwing them into the dark, and when the movement stopped, Lexa said, "Don't move." She paused.

The scree under his shoes informed him that the landscape was rocky and uneven, though he couldn't see it.

"Your light would come in handy right about now, Luc," Nix said.

He couldn't agree more, though it didn't help to wish for it. He couldn't cast anything, couldn't call on anything. He shivered, and the sound of falling rocks made him freeze. "Lexa? What is the Edge?"

She snapped her fingers, lighting a fire between them, then opened her palm so the fire grew brighter. Then she tossed it, making more and more until globes of fire hovered in midair, lighting the landscape.

They stood at the ragged edge of a ravine, the bottom obscured by a dense fog swirling around them, muting the sound. Incoherent muttering drifted like the fog, reaching Luc's ears, and filling his head with every dark thought. It smelled terrible, and Luc covered his nose.

"What is that?"

"It isn't bottomless," Lexa said, as if in answer to his observation. "It's a literal shit lake down there."

Luc gagged.

Beyond where they stood were smooth pillars of stone rising from that formless nothing, and on each stood a soul, chained to the precarious surface. There was no relief there. No sitting, no lying down, only standing precariously to maintain one's balance, smelling that awful stench.

"Do they jump?" Nix asked, his sleeve pressed against his mouth and nose.

"They try," Lexa replied.

"Into a shit lake? Gross," Luc said behind his sleeve.

"See the chain?"

Luc noted the manacle shackled around the limb of a soul on one of the closest pillars.

"They jump," Lexa said, "and the chain catches, pulling out the limb from its normal position. Painful to just hang there with a broken limb."

The screams were clearer then—far away but present.

Luc shuddered. "Why is Cumbria here?"

"You will see," she said.

"How will we find him?" Nix asked.

Lexa snorted and lifted her voice. "Zollah Cumbria. Present yourself." The floating pillars shifted, moving, shuffling, the souls clinging to their precarious perches with shouts and curses. When they stopped moving, one pillar floated closer to the edge, though not close enough for the prisoner to find a way from his perch.

The prisoner was strange—a man, or it had been once, only now it was as if it was made of four sides. One of the sides looked at them, its wild eyes devoid of color but for red ringing its irises. Its hair was a horrible mess of white with traces of copper. The creature looked like a beggar, ragged clothing hanging off its form. It licked its lips when it saw them, but then its eyes unfocused, looking through them.

"Where is she?" it asked. "Where is my Alea?"

"Alea Maximora?" Nix asked.

The creature yelled at them, its mouth open wide, its jaw distended. Then it chanted, "She is mine! Mine! Mine!"

"Not you," Lexa ordered. "You are the shade."

The creature screeched at her, before its head and body twisted, attempting to align the head with the torso that Lexa wanted, all while the pillar swayed in the expanse.

Eventually the shifting stopped, and a man, a real man, stood before them. He was handsome, with auburn hair covered with a crown of silver and sapphire, and gray eyes—familiar eyes—sad. He was dressed in fine garments, his hands at his sides. He was young, though not too young to have been unaware of the world.

"You called, Mistress of Death?" the man asked Lexa.

"Zollah Cumbria, these are my brothers, gods of light and dark."

The man nodded.

"Did you know Alea Maximora?" Luc asked, cutting right to the heart of why they were there.

The man's features collapsed with emotion, his body twisting again, until before them was an older man, the crown still on his head but his body and face ravaged by grief. "You say her name. Do you know my wife? Is she here?" His eyes—filled with desolation—bounced around.

A king?

Lexa looked at them, then back at Zollah. "Was your wife a goddess?" she asked.

His eyes jumped to Lexa's. "Where is she?"

"Not in the Netherrealm," Lexa said. "She's in Elysian Fields, Zollah."

"Her parents disowned her. Because of me." The king cried out, and the disjointed body shifted again, his body and head twisting until the creature stood before them once more. "I will find her," it chanted over and over. "She will come back to me. The witch said. Transformed!"

"Why is he like this?" Luc asked.

"Necromancy," she said with disgust.

Both Luc and Nix sucked in a breath.

"He tried to raise her from the dead?" Luc asked.

Lexa nodded. "But that isn't all. Zollah, I want to talk to the father."

The creature shifted, its head swirling around and around out of sync with its torso, the pillar rocking with the movement so Luc feared it might topple.

When it stopped, it was on the fourth and final

face, a man older than the first, but younger than the king's face weighted with grief.

"Tell us what you did to your child," Lexa ordered.

"Azleah?" the man asked.

"That's the name," Nix said, his eyes alight with hope.

"I didn't do anything to her. She is my light. Is she here?" The man looked hopeful, his gray eyes searching. "My pride and joy."

"What did you do, Zollah?" Lexa asked.

His body and face shifted again to the grief-stricken king. "Where is my wife?"

"Where is your daughter?" Lexa pushed.

"Daughter?" he asked. "I don't have a daughter. We couldn't have children." His face shifted back to the father once more. "She is the spitting image of her mother." He beamed. "Is she here? Can I see her?"

"What did you do to her, Zollah?"

His body and face shifted again until it was the maniacal creature. "Where is she? She's mine. You can't have her. That witch stole her! Alea!" The creature screamed the words, which echoed around them in a horrible pitch that made Luc want to cover his ears, though he refrained, to keep his mouth and nose covered.

Luc watched the creature shift between beings, the man in love, the father, the grieving king, and the creature, and tried to put together Cumbria's story in the bits and pieces the soul revealed. Though confusing, it was clear that somewhere between being a husband and father, the loss of his wife had pushed Cumbria to mania, and Azleah had suffered.

"He hurt her?" Luc asked quietly to Lexa.

She hummed an affirmation.

"The witch helped you with necromancy?" Nix asked.

"Bitch. Bitch! Liar! Liar!" the creature screamed. "She stole my Alea!"

"What happened to Azleah?"

"There is no Azleah!" the creature screamed.

It twisted back to the father. "She's alone now. Her mother left her. With me. I'm alone now." He bent forward, face in hands, crying.

Then he stood back up as the king. "I'll find her, bring her back from the black world."

He twisted again.

"The witch promised. She would be reborn. I did everything she asked!" the crazed creature screeched. "Everything! The tower room. The waiting. The liar! Liar! She stole my Alea!"

Luc swore.

The creature had taken over, the other parts of Cumbria silenced by the mania.

"That is all we will get from this soul," Lexa said, and the fog and darkness swirled as she moved them into her apartment under Alabastrine once more. Luc couldn't move, and he didn't seem to be the only one, Nix and Lexa in their own heads, frozen as well in the middle of the room.

Luc swallowed, shaken by what he'd experienced.

"He hurt her," he said. "His daughter? Azleah?"

"The necromancy, along with all the other abominable things he did due to his grief," Lexa replied, then sighed. "The hearts of men can't lie." There weren't many instances in which Luc had seen his sister shaken, but she seemed as affected by what they'd witnessed as he was.

Nix was the first to move, dropping onto a couch with his head in his hands. "Who is Scarlett to that… creature?"

Luc shook his head. "I don't know. A descendant of Azleah? It would explain the godblood. The healing. Alea Maximora is in her line somewhere."

"And that… maniacal king?"

"But Azleah disappeared. From the record," Nix said.

Lexa cleared her throat. "Has anyone considered that perhaps Scarlett is Azleah?"

"What?" Nix shook his head.

Luc's head snapped toward his sister, catching Nix's movement out of the corner of his eye. He thought about what Eitan had said about Mattias disappearing.

"Good gods, no," Luc said, but he swallowed, recalling what he'd said to Brinna. Why would someone hide? *Fear,* Brinna had said. Shame, anger, danger. What if it was all of them?

He looked at Nix, who was looking at him.

"The magic," Nix said and pressed his hand to his heart. "He blamed a witch."

"Time," Luc said, now unable to shake what he'd learned about Mattias. Luc shoved his hands into his hair and twisted away from his siblings. As much as he didn't want to believe it, there was a knowing in the center of him, as if the pieces had slid into place. "Holy fuck."

"The question is," Lexa started, "who is the witch?"

The overwhelming need to see Brinna burned through Luc like a flash fire, and he whirled to Nix. "I need to get back to Brinna," Luc said, stalking to the door. "Now."

Nix watched him, his head tilting and his brows shifting on his face with a question.

Lexa's brows lowered over her narrowed eyes. "Lucian?"

Luc took a breath that didn't seem deep enough and pressed his fingers to his heart. "I mean, you know, to tell her what we've learned and see if she has any more news from the dreams. See what's happening with Aurielle."

Nix stood, clearing his throat. "Yes. I'll take you home."

"It is curious," Lexa said, those unnerving eyes still on Luc. "That you are able to Dream Walk with her." A single brow shifted over her eye.

He didn't want to think about it, still denying it was anything more than godlight and magic.

"Curious why?" Luc asked, then evaded her gaze by smoothing the wrinkles in the fabric of his shirt.

Her eyes shifted to Nix. "And you can't speak with Aurielle, Nixus, though your yoke?"

"We haven't been able to communicate telepathically since she was the key keeper," he said.

Luc felt both of their eyes on him.

He looked at Nix and thought about his brother and Auri, the connection between them, the way Nix had described it like a tether, and Luc's chest compressed with the immutable truth. One he couldn't deny any longer. He was fucking god-yoked. To Brinna Fareview.

"Brinna!" Luc's voice grabbed hold of her, tugging her back into the dreamscape. It was so far away, but still she rushed from the cottage out into the woods, which had somehow grown denser.

"Brinna!"

She could hear his panic as he yelled. The trees squeezed in around her, and though a dream in the woods, she had the impression that the trees and bushes were about to swallow her whole. The woods, she realized, a reflection of what was going on in his subconscious.

"Brinna?" He sounded strange. "Where are you?"

"I'm here," she said, and the trees relaxed, easing back to create a path, opening between where she stood and where he was a few steps away. She could feel his deep breath, experiencing his relief like swimming in the River Grimz on a hot day. "You're late."

He rushed toward her. "I am. I'm sorry."

"I thought… I thought you weren't coming back."

He didn't stop, walking right up and wrapping his arms tightly around her. Stars, it felt so good, warm, right—grounding. When he curled around her, nestling his nose into the crook of her neck, she responded by pulling him closer. The sensation of his body was as tangible as anything real.

"Are you okay?" she asked and could hear the woods closing in around them.

"I took a sleeping draft. To get to you. Are you alright?" he asked but didn't withdraw, keeping hold of her as if she was an anchor in the storm.

She hummed an affirmative, but she could hear the strain in her own tone.

Lucian drew back, his eyes searching her face. "What is it?"

"It's too much. Being here. Seeing their dreams. I can't help them." The gray of the deep sleep rose, trying to grab hold of her again. Lucian, the woods, the light retreated for a split second.

"Brinna?" he said. "What's going on?" He squeezed her tighter as if he'd seen that great gray beyond.

"They're all having nightmares. My family." Brinna looked up. "Unless you're here—it feels like a nightmare. I don't know what to do." Her eyes filled with tears. "I was afraid…"

Lucian cupped her face between his palms and swiped at her tears with his thumbs. "Of what?"

She tilted her head, releasing his gaze. "That you weren't coming back."

The woods melted to reveal Sol. They were in the atrium, just as the last time they'd dreamed together, the dream they'd kissed. Golden lanterns hung around them, torches sputtering as the water trickled.

Lucian's gaze dipped to her lips, his thumbs settling against the corners of her mouth. "I was afraid you'd think that, but I will always come for you."

"Where were you?"

"With Nix. Looking for answers."

"Did you find any?" she asked.

He blanched, his eyes flicking away.

"What is it?"

"Not yet." He shook his head, the light in his eyes dimming. Then he leaned forward and pressed his lips to her cheek as if he too needed grounding. "Just let me be here with you, first."

She could feel the texture of his lips, the warmth of his breath on her skin. Her breath caught. "Luc?" she whispered.

"Is this okay?" he whispered back, kissing her other cheek. "I haven't stopped thinking about kissing you. I haven't stopped thinking about you. There's a missing piece in my heart when I'm not with you."

His confession burst like fireworks inside her chest. She grabbed the fabric at his back, tightening the linens across his chest. "Yes. Kiss me."

He pulled back and looked at her face again, then leaned into her, pressing his lips to hers as if she was the air he needed to breathe. The soft, supple texture of his kiss felt like the comfort of coming home.

She gasped as he nibbled on her bottom lip, and she clung to him tighter. When she tilted her head, he answered in kind, tilting the opposite direction and grasping the back of her head with a hand. He tested the softness of her lips with his tongue, and she opened her mouth to let him in, her palms flattened against his back holding him more tightly. He tasted of sunshine, like sweet honey collected from a hive in late summer. The space around her heart warmed, sending tendrils of heat through her body. When she whimpered, his kiss intensified.

"Stars, Brinna, you taste good," Lucian said in between kisses.

She feared he would slip away again and didn't want to lose her grip. "Don't stop, Luc."

"Brinna." The sound of her name became more than just her name as he said it, but rather a deity to whom he offered his worship. With his mouth on hers and his hands on her hips, he walked her backwards as Sol washed away and a dark space rose around them, packed with the essence of others, crushing them together. Music pounded a rhythm that matched her racing heart.

Music, yes, but not like any she'd ever heard before.

Brinna opened her eyes and gasped, disconnecting. She was still in Lucian's arms, but they were standing in a darkened room bursting with intermittent light, flaring with the beat of the strange sounding music amidst a massive crowd of people undulating around them. Dancing. But like nothing she'd ever seen and couldn't imagine in her whole existence. In her shocked awe, she pulled away from Lucian.

"What?" he asked, still peppering her with kisses.

Her eyes skipped across the space like a stone over glassy water before stalling on a group of three people suspended above them, in a fixed cage of sorts, engaging in… an intimate act. Her breath caught at the sight. "Where are we?" She had to yell over the volume of the music.

"What?" Luc looked up and smiled, then said something. When she didn't respond, he leaned forward and said loudly into her ear, "It's a sex club. I was in one with Nix, earlier–"

Her eyes flashed to his, hurt, and she stepped back. She'd been stuck in a nightmare, and he'd been in a sex club? Her heart—still pulsing with the rhythm of the music around them—pushed against her throat with a deluge of emotion.

He shook his head. "No! Not what you think." He groaned and pushed a hand through his hair. "Shit."

The thumping music waned, the dark making way

for a new landscape.

"I didn't mean to take us there." He rubbed his forehead with his hand. "My mind is a mess."

"You went to a sex club?"

"For answers, yes. Not for sex."

His explanation made her feel a touch better.

A bright sound startled Brinna as she stood to the side of a busy, cobblestone street, busy with people, horses, and something else like a moving, covered wagon without horses but with gigantic wheels. What they were, she couldn't say. They coughed and sputtered down the roadway as people moved in concert with them, pushing carts filled with fruits, flowers, and other colorful goods for sale. Stone buildings were stacked up around her like boxes, with interesting architecture and panes of windows glittering in the waning sunlight.

When she tilted her head to look at Luc, he was gazing down at her with a strange expression on his face, but it drifted away the moment her eyes met his.

"This is a better place to talk. Looks like a city I loved to visit when I Roamed." He glanced around, then grasped her hand. "This way." He tugged her gently along the pathway. "I'm sorry about the other."

She tried to shove away the hurt, the jealous feeling curling through her, and focused on the surroundings. The women wore beautiful, slim frocks that glittered as they moved, offering glimpses of their legs as they walked past on the arms of smartly dressed men, who tipped their hats in greeting.

"Where are we?"

"A different circle in another time." He took her hand in his, the warmth of his skin like sitting by a cozy fire, filling her with comfort and contentment. Her heart answered the feeling with an erratic beat that made her eyes jump to his breathtaking face. He was focused as they darted between those moving metal beasts, his fingers tightening around hers, pulling her closer.

Once across the thoroughfare, Lucian turned to her with a smile. "Here we go." He led them between tables filled with patrons eating along the walkway… outside. Brinna noticed the din of their collective conversations, the musical clink of glass against glass, metal against glass, laughter. When they reached a table, he released her hand and pulled a seat out, waiting for her to take it.

When she did, she noticed she wasn't in the light blue dress anymore, but rather something like what the other women were wearing. The fabric was a dark aqua, the dress accented with silver sparkles and a silver bow tied at her hip. Her arms were bare but for jangling golden bangles at her wrist. "Oh," she said, smoothing a hand over the slippery fabric. "What is this?"

"You look beautiful," Lucian said into her ear.

She turned her head to find Lucian bent forward, his hands on the back of her chair, his face near hers, his lips so close to her own. She glanced at them, and he grinned as he slid a finger over the bare flesh of her arm, raising gooseflesh that raced across her skin. Then he was gone, taking his seat at the small round table across from her. Food sat in front of them, white plates dressed with curled bread, rolled and flakey, fresh fruit, and bits of cheese. There were small cups of…

"Is this coffee?"

"Would you prefer tea?" he asked.

She shook her head.

"There's cream…"

Her eyes jumped to Lucian's. "I see. Thank you. And honey." She smiled, blushing with pleasure. After adding some to her small cup, she pinched the small handle and took a sip. She could taste it even though she knew they were in a dream. "What's happening?"

Lucian shrugged. "I thought you might like to enjoy some different sites?" He smiled. "Or as close as we can get to them in my dreams for now. Is this so terrible for the time being? Considering?"

She shook her head, even if she felt a touch of guilt for being here when her family was suffering. "Why are we here, here?"

"I wanted to give you something," Lucian said, pulling out his napkin and laying it over his lap. Brinna realized he was also wearing different clothes—like the men who'd passed them earlier. His suit was a dappled, dark gray material. A matching vest covered his chest, fastened with black buttons over a stark white shirt. His blond hair was neatly styled. He always looked so handsome, and her heart compressed in her chest to gaze upon him now, so much so that she had to look away.

"Why?" she asked.

When he remained silent, she looked up and realized they were now alone on the street. Though the city remained, the outdoor space where they'd been taking their meal, the people, the bustle of the street, all the noise, was gone. It was just her and Lucian sitting across from one another. Alone. In absolute silence.

"A reprieve," he said. "For the moment, at least?"

She swallowed and nodded. The sentiment was so thoughtful, her heart pinched, and she gasped as she pressed her fingers there.

Lucian's eyes followed her movement, then jumped back up to her face. "I thought—well, I've been to many places. I thought–"

"That you could take me?"

It was his turn to swallow and nod.

Brinna noticed the way his throat bobbed, and a sound—a rushing of blood—seemed to swell inside her head, then rushed through the rest of her, filling up all the empty places she'd been ignoring for so long with warmth, light—and something else. Words struggled to form for all the feelings controlling everything else. "That's so…" She took a deep breath, moved by his thoughtfulness. "Lucian."

He reached across the table and placed a hand over hers, thought he didn't look at her, but at their hands. His fingers wrapped around hers, before he turned her hand over, palm up, then skimmed her open palm with his thumb. "Just what… a friend… should do," he said quietly.

Only Brinna knew this wasn't friendship. Perhaps she had thought they would find a way to be friends at one time but realized their interactions had never been friendly. There had always been a current running between them, a current of sparks and fire.

"Is that all we are?" she asked. "Friends? Even after those kisses?"

"I didn't want to presume." His eyes jumped back to hers.

The empty street and cafe where they sat broke apart around them.

A dense forest appeared, though it wasn't the Whitling Woods. This was something altogether different. This forest had vines like the hedge, but also giant broad leaves larger than her head, towering trees, a narrow path, and beyond them, a stone structure. It was hot, like being wrapped in a steaming, wet blanket and squeezed. It was hard to draw a breath.

"Where are we?" she asked and took Lucian's hand in hers this time. Her skin was slick.

He squeezed her hand. "A temple. Did you know that this is one thing in common across the Vasmost?"

"What? Temples?"

And suddenly they were inside of it, without needing to walk. Lucian stood so close, his hand rested at the small of her back—comforting and safe. It was cooler inside, as if the thick stone insulated the interior from the pervasive heat pressing in around it.

"Yes. Places where gods are worshiped, but rarely

the same god. Some worshiped the sun, some the moon, some worshiped various animals, and other rivers or mountains, unseen deities. It was as if there was a need in every creature to find a way to make meaning of their place in the cosmos." He paused, as if holding onto the thought for a future moment.

"I understand that." Brinna spun in place, taking in the ruins. The dark stone was overgrown with the vegetation of the forest beyond, slick with moss, some of the stone cracked apart under the influence of vines and other plants. When she tilted her head, she found a round opening built into the roof, allowing a ring of light to illuminate the floor where she stood next to Lucian.

"I bet this was a temple to worship the sun." Her eyes drifted up from the floor to look at Lucian. He was dressed once more in the light clothes she was used to seeing him in, and he was glowing in the light shining from above. "To you—god of day and light."

"What do you understand?" he asked, instead of accepting her theory about this temple.

"What it feels like to want to understand your place."

"And what don't you understand about yours?"

"I am in the middle," she said. "Each of my siblings has their purpose, and I have always thought my purpose was to take care of them."

"Noble."

"I resented it," she confessed. "I never felt like more than the one who keeps the peace."

"Is that not a purpose?" he asked.

With a sigh, she turned away from him. "It feels like a function rather than a purpose."

"I'm not the god of light and day anymore," he said. "Does that mean I have no purpose?"

Brinna turned to look at him. "That doesn't define you, Lucian, just as serving as a bridge doesn't define me."

At Brinna's observation, Luc's breath crashed into his lungs as if he'd run into a wall. He'd been wondering the same thing about himself, grappling with his own purpose. His worthiness. Even when he'd had his powers, he hadn't felt he'd deserved them, and now without them, who was he?

He'd never been tied to his identity as the god of day and light. He liked the role and the perks of his power, but he'd spent more time Roaming than seated at Sol. But until his father had asked him to commit to ascending in his place as god of the Vasmost, Luc hadn't truly had to commit to anything. He'd been mulling over why he'd been so opposed to making that commitment, and he didn't like the answer.

Because he was afraid. Terrified of letting someone down, just like he'd let down Nix.

Stay, Lucian. Stay with me.

He looked at Brinna and watched her meander around the space, inspecting trinkets, leaning to look at carvings. He'd come back to her time and again. Though they dreamed together, and Brinna was walking his dreams with him, ultimately, he was the dreamer. Old Luc wouldn't have entertained it. Old Luc would have bolted from his feelings for her, from the idea of a god-yoke, afraid.

But he was here—and where he wanted to be.

Because of her.

Even before he'd known the god-yoke existed between them.

Brinna crouched down to inspect something at the center of the room.

His chest squeezed with awareness watching her. His god-yoke. He couldn't fathom it, but knew it was true. From the very first. He didn't know when the bond awakened, but it was as if his heart had known the first time he'd seen her.

The pain inside him had been gone the moment he'd returned to her in his dreams. The realness of her walking in the dreamworld was somehow enough to keep away the effects Nix was feeling at his separation from Auri.

"I came to understand something," she said, her

fingers gently touching a stone where greenery had sprouted.

"What is that?" he asked, slowly closing the distance between them.

"Perhaps that function—the bridge—is as important as Jessamine's healing or Tarley's hunting." She stood and wiped at her clothing, looking down at them, as if just realizing she was wearing gray trousers and an ivory linen shirt rather than the earlier dress. "Oh," she breathed and looked up at him with a grin. "You dress me so nicely."

It made him return her effervescent smile. "And?"

"And what?"

"The bridge?"

"Oh. Right. Maybe my purpose was always to be a bridge between the dreamworld and the real one. To save them. That this" –she waved her hands about–"is fate somehow."

"You are incredible," he said, rubbing his chest, his heart contracting inside him with awareness—the bright heat tightening his insides—of his feelings for her. Only he wasn't sure it was the god-yoke but rather something even more.

She looked up at him as he stopped before her.

Stars, he felt hot, and it didn't have anything to do with the heat of the jungle.

She smiled.

The heat around his heart intensified, and his body woke up, his cock thickening.

"That's very sweet, Lucian," she said, oblivious to

his physical reaction to her.

The temple broke apart around them as alabaster pillars took shape, darkness framing the dais where they stood. Luc turned in a circle, taking in the risers of chairs like a small amphitheater, the dim light but for the spotlight above them, and scoffed. "Well, we're in the thick of it now." He glanced at Brinna. "The sleeping draft is messing with my thoughts." Only he knew it was a lie. He wanted her, so he wasn't surprised his subconscious had chosen this place.

Brinna's hand closed around his hand as if seeking reassurance, and he liked that she reached for him. "Why? Where are we?"

"Remember when I mentioned the pleasure ceremony, when I was eighteen?" He took her hand in his. "Let me think of someplace else."

"Wait." Brinna walked backward, drawing him with her. "What is it?" Her legs bumped up against the altar, and her knees buckled. She fell back onto the plush coverings and twisted to look. "Is this a bed?"

His throat caught, his mouth dry, thinking about her lying there, his hips cradled between her thighs as he pushed into her. His body heated, and his dick twitched. "This is where I had my first sexual experience. I didn't mean to bring—"

She turned to face him, her eyes glowing with mischief. "You didn't?"

He didn't look away from that gorgeous sight, her smile and that little divot in her cheek. Stars, he couldn't get over that smile and what it did to him. His heart slammed up against his breastbone. She was right: he'd brought her here because he wanted her, all of her, even if they were dreaming.

So rather than lie, he said nothing and waited for her to fill the silence. When she didn't, he closed his eyes. "I'll take us someplace else."

Her soft fingers squeezed his hand. "Lucian. Look at me. I don't want to go somewhere else," she said. "I want to know."

Luc opened his eyes, to find her standing before him, looking up, her expression honest and open.

"About what?" he asked.

"Everything." She drew his hand up between them and threaded her fingers with his, watching their skin connect. It was erotic, somehow. "What was it like?" She turned to face the bed, then stared out into the darkness beyond the dais, raising a hand to shade her eyes. "You were watched?"

"Yes, but not by everyone, just those in the Order."

"Order?"

"Order of Dytee. They initiate gods into their adulthood and teach the truth of pleasure."

She swallowed. "Oh."

"You don't have that in your world?"

She shook her head, glancing at him, then around once more. "No. Not in Kaloma, at least."

"Who teaches you?"

"No one. Not really. I mean, my sisters and I would talk, but none of us knew for sure. I've learned some things since…" She blushed and cleared her throat, then swallowed, smoothing her pants with her hands. Luc missed her touch. "I can't speak for everyone, but I assume that everyone explores things in their own way." Her blush intensified. "Kaloma has a skin house for that sort of thing– for men, anyway. But women–"

"Are suppressed. Yes. The barbaric state of your homeland."

"There weren't many opportunities in Sevens to meet someone."

Lucian tilted his head. "Have you had sex with anyone?" Jealousy flared through him at the idea, and it surprised him. He wouldn't begrudge her the experience, of course, but he was annoyed it hadn't been with him.

Her eyes flashed to his then away. "There was a boy I kissed outside the meeting house once."

"You had sex with him?" He ground his teeth together.

"Stars, no. He was a terrible kisser. I can't imagine what sex would have been like." She laughed. "But I'm aware of sex and how it works. I understand bodies and mechanics. I feel desire. I'm familiar with…" She stopped.

"Pleasuring yourself," he finished for her, thinking about their dream.

She walked the stage. "Is everyone required to do this?"

"No. Only those who choose it."

She turned her head to look at him. "You chose it."

He nodded, watching her move. "I wanted to learn.

Sex isn't taboo for us in Elcadia. It's a part of life, another function of our bodies, albeit a pleasurable one. And I wanted to know about myself, about what I wanted, how to communicate with a partner. How to please them."

"Did you get to choose your partner, in the Order?"

He shook his head. "They are assigned, but only after time spent learning with the Order. This is only after study and observation."

"Were you nervous?"

"Of course." He smiled. "Afraid I might not get things working properly."

She smiled in return. "Did everything work properly?"

"Quickly." He laughed.

She blushed but laughed with him. "I don't think I could do it."

"What would stop you?"

"Besides the thought of others watching? I need to feel something for my partner." She pressed her fingertips over her heart, and her eyes lifted to his. A connection sizzled between them, gripping him so hard he nearly grunted with its power. "You're an excellent kisser, Lucian."

His belly bottomed out, and his balls tightened. Fuck. "Come. Let's go somewhere else. We have to talk—"

"Wait," she said. Her chest rose and fell in rapid bursts as she moved to him. "If I chose, I would choose you. And I'd like that, right now. To choose you. I want to experience this with you," she said, a blush blooming across her cheeks.

"Even if this is real between us, more than a dream?" he asked.

"Yes, Lucian." She swallowed.

"With me?" He wasn't sure why he couldn't believe it and wanted to kick himself for questioning.

She made a frustrated noise and grasped at his waistband. "Truthfully, Lucian, our sex-dream wasn't my first with you. I've fantasized about you every night since I met you."

"You have?" Another surprise, though he'd had so many about her. He understood now.

She nodded and slid her hands up his chest. "I want it to be real. And what if–"

"Don't say it, Brin. Please. Not that."

Her body flashed for a moment, flickering into nothing, then returned. He'd seen it before—when he'd first returned to the dream. In the woods.

He grasped her face between his hands. "What was that? What just happened to you."

She stepped away and tilted her face to look into his. "I don't know how much time I have."

"What's that supposed to mean?" Fear—but not for himself—hit him in the chest.

"The deep gray sleep is tugging on me. I don't know how long this Dream Walking is going to last, Lucian."

She was waiting for him to say something, but his

heart was in his throat with all the things he needed to say. What he'd learned with Nix and Lexa about her descendants, maybe her mother. That he was pretty sure they were god-yoked. But what would she say? How would she feel? She might want to have a sexual experience with him, but was it because of him or because of the circumstances? Did he care?

"We have now," she said.

And he realized it didn't matter. He wanted to be with her. She wanted to be with him. The future wasn't a guarantee, but they had this. Now.

He grasped her face, his eyes drifting over her features. Though Nix had asked him not to complicate things by being with Brinna, this was different. This was a pulse of light encasing his heart. He knew that it might be the god-yoke, but to hear her say she'd also thought about him since they'd met, that she recognized the connection, and because he suspected there might be more, he didn't care what Nix thought. His brother couldn't be mad at him for this.

So Luc leaned forward and pressed his lips to Brinna's.

He'd kissed many. Usually a pleasant experience. There were quick kisses and lingering ones. There were kisses that comforted. There were wet and sloppy kisses, kisses with too much tongue or not enough. There were kisses that were offered and those that took. In his experience, Luc could say that he enjoyed kissing, but he'd never truthfully felt as if it left him completely satisfied.

Until kissing Brinna. Each and every time he had, the heat in his chest exploded outward the moment they connected, from his heart to his extremities. The connection swirled through him, around him, and now that he knew who she was to him, the kiss seemed to change the foundation of who he was, remaking him with contentment and joy but also deep-seated desire.

Her lips against his, her opening up to him, the ferocity of the warmth exploding inside him, the virulent need that claimed his thoughts—this kiss required sound. He moaned. She answered with her own sweet sound. This kiss, while completely unsatisfying because he needed more of her, was also the kiss to end all kisses. Brinna's kiss was the cosmos, the Vasmost. She was the final destination of his Roam.

Lucian broke the kiss, his hands framing her face between them. When she opened her eyes, they weren't in the auditorium anymore, but rather a quiet room, a bedroom with floor to ceiling windows, the sky dark beyond them but sparkling with stars and a cosmos ribboned with aqua, pink, and purple. The wooden walls, the simplicity, was familiar.

"Sol?" she asked.

He looked around as if he was unaware things had changed, and his features smoothed with recognition, then acceptance. With his content smile, his eyes sought hers. "It would seem we've come home." His voice was husky.

Her heart compressed. Home. *We've* come home. The rightness of those words filled her up with warmth and light.

Lucian bent forward to kiss her again, walking her backward toward the bed. "Are you sure, Brinna? That you want this?"

"Yes. With you," she replied between kisses, grabbing hold of his shirt.

He made a sound that was part groan, part growl, and began to unbutton her shirt.

"You can think our clothes off," she reminded him.

"Only I want this to last," he replied, sliding a thumb over her collarbone. "I want to savor everything about you. Every moment. I want to look at you with my eyes, feel you with my hands, taste you with my mouth. Every inch, Brinna." He undid another button.

She mewled, a rush of warmth between her thighs, and tugged his shirt from the waistband of his pants. "You've talked me into helping." She grinned, but her hands shook as she fiddled with his buttons.

He laid his hand over hers. "What's wrong?"

She dove into the warmth of his eyes. "I'm nervous," she confessed. "I haven't–"

"We're dreaming," he said.

"But–" She sucked in a breath. "With you, this is real."

He pressed a finger to her lips. "We're dreaming. Remember how it is in your dreams, woman?" And then he recited those words she'd said a lifetime ago. Everything he remembered about that moment she'd embarrassed herself, when she'd thought she'd been dreaming of him—it wasn't so embarrassing when he said them now, kissing her between statements and ending with, "This is going to be fun." It was sexy.

He pulled back and smiled, pushing the shirt over her shoulders, down her arms, baring her breasts to him.

His smile faded, and his eyes darkened. "Stars, Brinna." He ran his hands from her hips up her sides, stopping just below her breasts, his thumbs sliding across the skin, touching her without actually touching what ached for him.

She gasped, wanting his touch on her nipples, leaning toward him, wanting his touch everywhere and arching into it. "What if you wake–"

"Don't," he commanded and bent forward, kissing her neck, swirling his tongue across her skin, biting, then licking and kissing the spot again. He left a trail across her chest, from the top of her breast to the peak of her nipple, tight with anticipation. He hesitated, finally curling his hand around her breasts, and testing the weight of them, lifting them higher, one toward his mouth.

His tongue slid over the taut tip, his eyes on hers. He hummed, a sound of absolute appreciation.

She gasped, grabbing his shoulders. "Oh. That feels…" Her hands on him kept her steady as his tongue swirled around her nipple, drawing it into his mouth and sucking. "That feels so…" But she gasped again when his teeth rubbed against her flesh. "Good!"

He made another appreciative sound and slid his mouth to the other side, his hands and mouth taking turns.

"Yes…so good."

Wanting to be more involved in this endeavor, she grabbed hold of his shirt once more, but couldn't reach the buttons now that he was savoring her breasts. And he was savoring. "I want to touch you," she breathed.

Lucian hissed, her nipple between his teeth. "Woman. I won't last," he admitted.

"Why not? It's a dream."

He chuckled. "You're right." And suddenly their clothes were gone, and Brinna was sitting on the edge of the bed, Lucian kneeling before her. "This is about you, *mi alora.*"

"What happened to taking time?" she asked, reveling in how beautiful he was, her golden god.

He grinned, his dimples on display. "I find myself impatient," he said and lifted one of her legs, setting her foot on his thigh, looking at her sex that she could feel throbbing, ready for him.

"Stars, woman, you are" –his eyes rose to connect with hers– "beautiful." He spread her wider, putting her other foot over his shoulder. "I can't wait to get my mouth on you." He kissed her knee, slid his tongue along her inner thigh, kissing as he went, his hand following the same trail on the other leg. The anticipation made her tremble.

When he reached the juncture of her thighs, one of his hands framed her sex, while the other grabbed her hip and yanked her forward. Her thighs opened wider, and he leaned forward, sliding his tongue through her soft center. She gasped, her eyes rolling back as she dropped to the mattress on her elbows. "Oh, stars," she moaned.

"So good, Brinna."

And he savored her there, between her legs. His mouth wove a magical spell that had her gasping and mewling, unable to remain upright. He slid his tongue through the wetness, circling and sucking on her clit, then leaving her hanging on the edge as he fell away from that bundle of nerves down once more, sliding his tongue inside her, then resuming the pattern he'd created. Up. Circle and suck. Fall away just as her core tightened, ready to explode.

"Oh, please." Brinna was wild, grabbing hold of his head, holding him against her, pulsing her hips against his face. Moaning, gasping, crying out. "Oh, please! Luc!" Her cries became indecipherable as her body tightened with need.

Up.

Circle.

Suck.

And suddenly something new—he inserted a finger inside her, her body stretching to accommodate him.

"I'm…" she gasped, unsure where her words were going since there were no thoughts, only sensation, and it was all around and inside of her.

"I want to feel you come," he said against her and inserted another finger, his tongue now circling her clit.

"So. Close." She groaned, gasped, sucked in a breath. "Oh. Fuck. I'm. Coming," she panted as stars exploded behind her eyes, and her body went hot all over, rushing through her like a racing inferno so she cried out with the force of it, arching on the bed. Her legs clamped around his head as she bucked back, curling up around him.

Lucian growled. "Again." And though he slowed his attention, he began working her body expertly a second time.

She gasped. "I don't know if I can," she whimpered, her body jerking with the remaining spasm of her orgasm.

"You can," he ordered and remained between her legs, gentle and soft. "Open up. You taste so fucking good. So fucking good, Brinna." Lick. "I want to live here, between your legs." Suck. Swirl. "I have found my purpose."

The overwhelming sensations eased to make room for that addicting rhythm his mouth made. In conjunction with his words, Brinna relaxed, giving him full access, her hips finding a rhythm in concert with his mouth. Her body dipped into the calm, pleasurable waters, and they enveloped her once more, rising around her as waves of pleasure built. She gasped and moaned. "So good, Luc. So good."

"Yes. Move with me," he growled against her body,

one of his hands holding her down, his other hand worshipping her, until Brinna was crying out, her hips bucking against him once more.

"Please. Oh please," she gasped, her hands trying to find something to hold onto, his head, his shoulders, his arms, the blankets. She cried out, his fingers sliding in and out while his tongue flicked against her, offering a promise.

"Come, *mi alora.*"

"Yes! I'm coming," she cried, her back arching, her legs trying to close around him, only Lucian held her open as the orgasm tore through her, stronger and longer than the first, as the heat rushing through her body intensified.

He watched her orgasm the second time, having thought he'd mistaken what happened during the first. But this time, when that golden glow slid through him, giving him the sensations of her pleasure and lighting her up as if she were on fire, he knew. It was the god-yoke, and while he thought he would feel constricted by that idea, he didn't. At all. The pleasure was unfathomable.

And watching Brinna come—experiencing it with her—was like artwork come to life.

His cock was weeping with need.

He rose over her, slid her boneless frame up the

bed, and knelt between her splayed legs.

She smiled; her eyes closed. "Oh stars, Lucian. That was… amazing."

"Did you think we were done, *mi alora?*"

Her eyes flew open and ran the length of him.

He knelt before her, palming his cock, spreading the pre-come over his shaft, though he knew she was ready. "Are you still sure?"

Her eyes watched him touch himself, her gaze greedy. He loved it.

"Yes," she said. "But I'm afraid this will be like all my other dreams. Let me touch you."

"Not this time. I need you."

Her eyes jumped to meet his. "I don't want you to go."

"I won't," he said.

"How do you know?"

"Because I'm currently drugged in my bed. Remember? I took the draught because I was too keyed up to sleep, and I needed to see you. Nothing is waking me up." He grinned.

She palmed her tits, and he groaned at the sight. "I need you inside me." She licked her bottom lip, tilting her hips toward him.

With another groan bordering on a growl, he leaned forward, sliding the head of his cock through her slick heat. She moaned, her body jerking when he met her clit with his crown. "Fuck, Brinna."

She reached between them and grabbed hold of his ass, wrapping her legs around his hips and tilting her hips for more. "In me—"

Luc pushed into her until her body resisted. "So tight, *mi alora.*"

She gasped, then breathed. "Oh. Oh."

He slid out, her tight sheath trying to draw him back, so when he drove back in, a little deeper, her body welcomed him and adjusted. "Your cunt feels so good squeezing my cock." He pulled out again.

"Lucian," she moaned, her nails raking over the skin of his ass, his back, leaving marks.

He pushed back in, further this time. His arms shook, his body wanting to drive all the way home, but he also wanted her to enjoy it. Wanted to do this again and again. Wanted Brinna to beg. Wanted to feel her orgasm again in time with his own. With control he could barely contain, he pulled out and slid back in, this time pushing all the way in, the skin of his hips meeting the skin of her splayed thighs.

"Oh!" she cried out. "Again."

"Brinna," he gasped with her, the heat between them creating a new and forceful sensation inside of him, disconnected from the sex, as if in spite of it but stronger because of their physical link. A threading of their souls, linked with golden starlight, their godlights merging to become more.

"Lucian. I feel you. Everywhere," she moaned and let go of his ass to grab hold of her tits, tilting her hips to feel him. "More. I want all of you."

Lucian complied, pulling out, thrusting in, finding a rhythm that had them both panting, moaning, wild with need.

She cried out. "I feel so much." Her cries grew in strength, fueling him but also turning him on so that maintaining control became impossible. Though he wanted to feel her come around his cock, to feel her wring his orgasm from him, he was at risk of losing his rhythm. She was turning him inside out.

He threaded her legs over his arms, pushed her knees up to her chest, and tilted her hips so he could dip deeper inside her. "I want you to touch yourself," he growled. "Come for me."

She complied.

"Good girl," he cooed, slamming his cock into her again and again.

Her fingers slid around her clit, and he could feel her body contract around him as her cries gained strength.

"Fuck, Brinna. Fuck," he panted as his own pleasure built, tightening everything in him for the impending explosion.

Sweat rolled between his shoulder blades, down his spine as he rolled his hips, filling her, thrusting until she was screaming his name, her cunt clenching around him.

"Yes. Yes. Luc." Her body tightened with her impending climax. "I'm coming!" she gasped, bucking against him, grasping his back, digging in her nails.

As she came, Luc slammed home with a yell a few seconds later, her body gripping his, holding him hostage and milking him as he followed her orgasm with his own. Light and heat tore through him as he emptied himself into her.

Brinna screamed his name.

It was bliss.

It was everything.

When he could, he released himself slowly, and she wrapped her arms around him, pulling him down. Luc experienced the most sublime sense of satisfaction in his life as his chest heaved against hers.

Afraid he was cruising her, he adjusted his weight but remained connected.

She rolled with him until she straddled him. "Lucian?"

He opened his eyes.

"You're glowing."

The darkness in the windows made it even clearer, golden light brightening the room around them.

"So are you." He smiled and pulled her down for a kiss. When her lips met his, he felt the pull to tell her how he felt. Gods, he loved her, and his chest tightened around the awareness like a protective box. He longed to say the words, but he wanted it to be in a life awake.

"Is it the dream?" she asked.

He wanted to tell her the truth, but something kept him from admitting what he knew. He didn't understand it and wasn't sure how to process it with her. So he said, "We are a dream. You are my dream."

She smiled and laid down, her cheek to his chest.

The warmth moving through him was… wonderful. He didn't want it to end, but his mind moved to what he knew they needed to talk about. The spell.

Despite this joy, he knew where he was about to take her would probably be painful. But he needed to know if she'd discovered anything that might help him beyond the dream. More than anything he wanted her out. Awake with him.

But for the moment, he sighed and smiled, content to be with her and bask in the warm glow between them. It was the first time he could remember feeling such happiness.

There was something different about Lucian—besides the obvious—though she couldn't put her finger on it yet. Rather than overthink it, she relished the feel of his fingertips sliding up and down her spine, his body still inside her as she lay straddling him, and the warm glow between them that felt like a rare treasure. Sex with him had been more than she'd ever dreamed. Though she reminded herself they were in a dream, there was something absolute about their connection, about the experience.

She wasn't ready for the dream to end. But the gray swelled like a wave, trying to grab hold, and she felt herself flicker. It was a flash, as if she blinked, everything around her disappearing as it pulled her under.

She gasped.

"Brinna?" Lucian grabbed hold of her, and they rolled, his weight pressing her down into the mattress. His body slipped from hers, and she missed that connection.

"Don't let me go," she said, smoothing sweaty strands of golden hair from his face.

"I've got you." He pressed a kiss to her cheek.

Her heart expanded in her chest. She knew he would wake up, and she didn't know how long she'd last inside this spell without him. Didn't know how she could stop it from this side of a dream. But she knew there were things they needed to share if there was a possibility of getting out.

"Tell me what happened to you today?" she asked to take her mind off the inevitable parting, still playing with his hair.

He closed his eyes, as if relishing her touch, then lay his cheek against her chest. "Nix and I visited the Oracles again, then went with Lexa to a few places."

Her fingers slid through his hair, then down his back, and she loved that he sighed, enjoying it. "Tell me."

He looked up, his face sober. "It's… a lot."

Curling one of her legs around his thigh, she entwined herself with him and nodded. "Yes. All of this is."

Lucian came up onto his elbows, adjusting so that one was on either side of her. His fingers smoothed her hair, his eyes watching the trails he made. "I think we found your ancestors."

She pressed her head back into the mattress to get a better look at his face. "What?"

"Nix said there was a name… Az–"

"Azleah," Brinna finished, her eyes grabbing hold of his golden ones.

His eyes shifted, reshaping themselves with emotion. Sadness. "We found the name in our lineage books at the Library of Oracles."

She came up to her elbows, so Lucian had to adjust to her movement, sliding to the side. "What? How do we know we're related?"

He grabbed her hip, as if he couldn't not touch her. "A guess? Your mother–"

"She wouldn't tell us."

"Azleah is the daughter of a disowned goddess— Alea Maximora— and a mortal —King Zollah Cumbria."

"Disowned? A king?"

"And get this, Alea's power… healing."

Brinna sat up. "Like my mother?"

He mirrored her, only turned on the bed to face her. "Her powers would have been passed through her children rather than being gifted to the new god or goddess of her station."

Her mother's dreams drifted through her mind. "She dreamed of a king. My mother." Her eyes jumped to Lucian's again. "Of the death of a queen. Then, in the dream, she was alone in a stone prison of some sort."

"Holy fuck," he said and flipped around in the bed, his back to her. "Lexa was right." His head was in his hands, his hair shooting up between his fingers.

She touched his back. "What do you mean?"

Lucian swiveled to face her. "After the Library of Oracles, Lexa took us to that sex club. We were looking for a demon who could tell us about magic, about the Dream Walking, and maybe to find a way to access the human records." He swallowed, his eyes drifting away, his fingers plucking at the sheet between them. "When we mentioned Cumbria, Lexa said we didn't have to look in the records because he's in the Netherrealm."

"What?"

His eyes jumped back up to hers. "Lexa took us to speak to him—his soul, I mean." He ran a hand over his face and sighed. "It was awful, Brin."

She ran her hand back and forth over his back. "Tell me."

"I don't want to."

"Do it anyway."

He nodded, then grabbed her face and drew her closer, kissing her. "I want you with me," he said. "I want to be with you. When we break this fucking spell. Say you want that too."

"Yes. I want that too." She smiled, kissing him back, her hand curved around the back of his neck.

He pressed his forehead to hers and sighed. Then

he was quiet, and Brinna waited, understanding what he was about to tell her wasn't pleasant. "Cumbria was king, and his wife had died."

Her hand stilled.

"Gods, he loved her. That much was clear, but it messed with his head." Lucian disconnected, climbing from the bed to stand.

"Messed with his head?" Brinna watched him from the bed as he paced, processing what he'd seen. When he'd come back into the dream, she'd known he was frantic, had felt it. Now she could see it as he moved.

He nodded. "The grief pushed him to dabble with necromancy."

"Sorcery?"

"The kind that tries to conjure the dead."

Brinna swallowed. "He wanted to bring her back?"

Lucian sat next to her once more. "Brinna, he abused his daughter. Locked her in a tower prison as if she was some reincarnation of his dead wife."

Brinna's hand flew to her mouth to hold back the nausea that suddenly tightened her throat as she thought of her mother's dream. Tears pricked her eyes. She shook her head. "Azleah?"

Lucian nodded. "He had help. Kept saying 'the witch was a liar' because the daughter escaped."

Though Brinna understood that didn't make this princess her mother, she couldn't stay still and climbed from the bed, picking up her shirt and slipping into it. Even trying to deny it, her instincts prickled her skin with certainty. "There was a witch in my mother's dream. Baba." Brinna paced, the nail of her thumb in her mouth as she pondered all this information in light of what she'd seen in her mother's dreams.

"Where?"

She turned to face Lucian, her body responding to seeing him sitting on that bed. His beautiful shoulders, his chest covered with its golden hair, the gentle sway of his stomach, his slim hips. His beauty was almost too much. She wanted to climb back into the bed with him, forget all this and just exist in the dream world. But it was impossible. The gray was coming. She could feel it.

"Brinna?" he said, dipping his head to meet her gaze.

"It's hard to say," she said when she recalled his question. "The dream was muddled, but it was in the woods."

"The Whitling Woods?"

"Maybe?"

Lucian stood in all his naked splendor in front of her. "It stands to reason that's where it is. You live there. The hedge."

"And the ribbons," she said, holding up her wrist. *Until true love*, the witch had said in the dream. "True love," Brinna whispered, and her eyes jumped to Lucian.

"What is it?"

"Auri's and Tarley's protective ribbons disappeared because they fell in love—true love."

Lucian stepped closer, grabbing hold of her wrists,

folding them behind her back, then kissing her neck. "This is good."

She tilted her head, offering him more room. "Why?"

"We know where to start looking for the witch. More importantly, we know her name. Ozland, the demon–"

"At the bar?"

His tongue swirled against her skin as he hummed an affirmation. "He said if we knew the sorcerer who cast the magic, we could find a way to break the spell."

Brinna swallowed. "She's dangerous–"

"I'm a god." Lucian leaned back and looked at her.

"Without his powers," she replied.

He stepped back as if she'd burned him.

"I don't say it to hurt you, Lucian. I'm afraid for you." Her throat tightened, and she pressed her lips together, her chin quivering, but she choked out, "Look where I am."

Taking her face between his hands, he kissed her tears, and nodded, but she could see she'd hurt him, reminding him of it. He pulled her into his embrace and held her. "Nix isn't doing well."

"Neither is Auri. In her dreams, anyway. She's weak."

"The tether of their bond is tearing them apart. There's a temporary fix–" He let her go and looked for his discarded pants. She watched him slide into them unsure why they were even dressing. It seemed something to do, something to prepare for the inevitable end to this fantasy.

"Then do that."

He fastened the button of his trousers. "He won't do it."

"Why not?"

"It means forgetting Aurielle. He wouldn't want that." Lucian met her gaze. "I wouldn't want to do that either. With that kind of connection."

Brinna felt that look in her bones, as if he was trying to tell her something.

He moved once more, as if jolted back into it, then moved around looking for something on the floor. "Besides, there isn't a guarantee it will help her." When he found his shirt, he slid his arms into the sleeves.

Brinna helped him, taking the front panels in hand and fastening the buttons. "Auri would want whatever will help Nix."

He studied her face as if working to commit everything to memory. "How do you know?"

"Because she loves him. And that is what I would want." She dragged her hand down over the buttons, smoothing the fabric into place.

The gray snagged against her, tugging at her again, everything blinking away.

Lucian's eyes widened, his hands gripping her arms tightly. "I'm here."

She took a deep breath and snuggled into his arms as she resurfaced, wrapping her arms tightly around his waist. "But you won't always be," she said. "If you come back, and I'm not—"

"Don't say it. Please, Brinna. Just be here."

"Lucian—"

"Say it."

"I will do everything I can to be here," she said, squeezing him tighter.

He kissed the top of her head. "I need you to be here," he said. "I feel the pull, Brinna."

"I know."

Her heart twisted in her chest. She didn't know when she'd gone from hating Lucian to feeling like this, like she needed to touch him, wanted to hear him, found safety in his arms, but she did.

And at that moment, she realized she loved him. It wasn't the growing pains of love, but a burgeoning awareness that burst forth. That familiar heat spread through body, twisting like golden light, wrapping around the essence of her, until there was a pinch at her wrist, and then it cooled. She knew exactly what it was, knowing what she knew now.

Her ribbon was gone.

She didn't have to look to know it. She knew with every fiber that made her; she was in true love with Lucian Uraiahs.

"Hold on," he said. Then he was gone.

"Hold on," he'd told her before drifting awake. Now he stood at the window of Sol staring out the Elcadian realm, hating that he was in the real world without her. *She's stuck in a dream*, he thought and turned away, sighing. He had to find a way to get her out. They had to find the witch.

"Luc?"

He looked up at Nix, leaning against the couch. "Stars, brother. You look…"

"I'm fading," he said plainly. "I'm not sure how much longer I have."

Luc swallowed, understanding now. The moment

he'd woken he'd felt the pain. It had started slowly, coalescing around his heart, then seeping like a creeping shadow through his body. And his awareness was so new. He also had the benefit of walking with Brinna in their dreams to appease the bond. Nixus and Auri had been yoked for some time now, strengthening that bond, so that it must feel like a weight crushing his brother to dust.

"What can I do?" he asked.

Nix shook his head. "Tell me we have something we can use?"

"Brinna thinks the witch is in the woods. Baba—the name Scarlett used."

Nix's eyes brightened and he grinned, though under duress.

"Perhaps you should stay here? I will find Lachlan."

Nix shook his head. "You have no power, so you're stuck with me."

His father's words drifted through Luc's mind. *When you are ready to accept who you are and who you are intended to be, I will restore your power to you.* For the first time, Luc wished he did have his powers back. Wished he could use them to fix his brother, fix this situation. "I suppose I'll just have to succumb to Father's wishes." But the truth of it was that it didn't feel like giving in anymore, but accepting the truth, what had always been inevitable.

Nix offered a wan grin. "It is inevitable," he said echoing Lucian's own thoughts. Nix huffed a laugh. "Is

Auri…"

"She is still asleep. Still in the world." He avoided offering that she was also fading.

Nix nodded and tried to straighten as if it pained his body. "Come," he said, and Sol drifted away as he transported them to the woods.

It had been sometime since Luc had seen the hedge outside of a dream, and his renewed view of it still took his breath away. "Irrational magic."

"Most assuredly."

"Nixus!"

Luc turned, then grabbed hold of Nix, who faltered, helping to steady him. Luc swallowed the words of his concern, knowing Nix would ignore them.

Lachlan's eyes danced between them. "What's wrong?"

"Missing my love, is all," Nix said with a smile, pushing off Luc to stand on his own.

"Please tell me you've found something," the prince said, his words an echo of Nix's earlier sentiment. He shoved his hands into his hair, an action he'd clearly been perfecting, since every brown hair on his head was in disarray.

Luc thought of Brinna telling him about Tarley's nightmare and realized they were all stuck. Not just the family—though the Fareviews were sleeping—Lachlan, Nixus, and himself were living nightmares of their own, as stuck as the Fareviews behind their hedge. "Did you tell him?" he asked Nix.

"Tell me what?" Lachlan's eyes bounced between

them.

"No," Nix said. "I didn't–" He took a fortifying breath but remained silent.

"Anything?"

Nix shook his head.

Luc wondered if Lachlan—a mortal—would understand the magic, then recalled the darkling, turned to look at the hedge, and realized it was a ridiculous thought. He looked at Lachlan. "Do you have somewhere we can rest?" He glanced at Nix, then back to Lachlan.

"I don't need rest," Nix argued, but his body didn't protest as he leaned heavily against Luc.

Lachlan nodded, a quick burst of movement that shouted his impatience. "My tent!" He turned, leading them down the roadway parallel to the hedge to a small camp with members of the prince's guard. Luc didn't know any of them, though he'd seen them at the wedding. They stood stoic and observant, watching Lachlan enter the tent, their eyes steady and assessing. Lachlan introduced them: Johesha, Jude, Brendsen— obviously important since they'd followed them into the tent. Though a large tent filled with a cot, a table, chairs, rugs, it was tight with all of them inside.

Lachlan indicated places to sit before leaning against a table. "Do these accommodations meet your expectations?"

His snark made Luc smile, which seemed to irritate him further, which Luc also understood.

"What's so fucking amusing?" Lachlan snapped.

Luc held up his hands, a twinge grabbing hold of a bit inside him and twisting. He blinked and worried for Brinna, then tried to focus on Lachlan, who looked ready to shove a dagger into Luc's chest—which would work without his powers.

"No. No." Luc shook his head. "This isn't an amusing situation. And the story isn't any more amusing."

Lachlan leaned against the table once more, crossing his arms over his chest. "Tell me."

"The spell on the hedge is also on them. They're asleep in the cottage behind it."

"How do you know this?" Lachlan's brow furrowed. "There's more–"

"Yes," Luc said, sensing Nix was trying to hold himself together and couldn't find the energy to speak, so Luc told the story with Nix filling in details he failed to add. When he got to it, he added the bit about Nix and Auri's god-yoke, explaining Nix's weakened state, which necessitated sharing how they'd met.

"Is this why you look awful?" Lachlan asked.

Nix huffed an amused but weak laugh. "Thank you for pointing that out. Now my pride and vanity can take a hit along with my health."

Luc continued with what they'd learned at the Library of Oracles.

"Azleah?" Lachlan asked. He glanced at the other three men in the tent with them. "We were on the field that day. Heard that awful voice say that name. Seemed like Tomas recognized the name."

Two of the three guards nodded, the third—Johesha—just scowled.

Luc shared their journey through the Netherrealm to find Zollah Cumbria, what they'd learned about Azleah's lineage, her connection to the king, and the disowned goddess. "With the help of a witch in the woods. Which is why we're here."

"But how does this Azleah connect to Tarley? To what's happening now?" Lachlan pointed at the wall of the tent in the direction of the hedge.

Luc glanced at Nix. "We think Azleah *is* Scarlett."

Lachlan's eyebrows arched over his eyes. "Wait–" But he stopped, his brow collapsed as he thought it through.

"You said that was eons ago. How?" Johesha finally spoke.

"Time," Nix said and sighed as if it would replenish the strength used to say it.

"Time travel," Luc clarified, reaching out to lay a hand on his brother's back, wishing he could infuse him with some power and growing more worried by the minute. "It isn't an impossibility. Brinna Dream Walks. That's how I'm able to share the name of the witch."

"You've shared dreams with her?" Lachlan asked. When Luc nodded, he asked, "Have you been behind the hedge? How is Tarley?"

"I can't get beyond the hedge, only Brinna can. And Tarley sleeps." He said nothing more, not wanting Lachlan to understand his new wife's torture.

"I knew Brinna could dream–" Lachlan pushed away from the table, as if he'd been given a quick infusion of energy. "Her dream was how we knew to go after Tarley—when the darkling–" He stopped, then shook his head and looked at Luc. "The details of the dream hadn't been perfect, but it had been right. And Tarley sometimes sees things, before they happen."

"Brinna has been in her mother's dreams. It's why I think it's these woods. That the witch is here."

"But the witch… in Scarlett's dream, was a woman?"

Luc nodded. "Baba."

"A female witch?" Lachlan looked at his three guards. "But wasn't it a man's voice?"

Jude and Brendsen nodded.

Johesha scowled.

"That's what I remember," Jude said.

"Awful voice." Brendsen shuddered. "I'll never forget it. Definitely male."

"Regardless," Luc said. "It's what we have."

"Where do we go? To ferret out this… witch?" Johesha asked, his voice grim but determined. "Highness, I think you remain–"

"No," Lachlan said. "Thank you, Jo. But no. Not with Tarley stuck behind that monstrosity."

"Your highness?" a voice called from beyond the tent.

Jude left through the flap, then peeked back inside. "You might want to come see this."

Luc, with Nix leaning heavily on him, followed the prince and his guards to where another soldier held a young boy of eleven or twelve by the back of his filthy overalls.

"Found the urchin lurking behind your tent."

"I just wanted to see a prince," the boy snapped, jerking in the soldier's grip.

"Well, boy? Why did you think a prince was here?" Brendsen said.

The boy's thrashing stopped, and his bright eyes leveled on Brendsen in a way that unnerved Luc. There was something wrong about it, but he couldn't identify what.

"Rumors," the boy said, shoving his hands into the deep pockets of his pants. "Heard the prince's wife is stuck behind the hedge. And there's magic." He tilted his dirty blond head at the hedge.

"Let him go," Lachlan ordered the soldier, who complied. "It's dangerous," he told the boy. "Best you stay clear of it, yes?"

The boy's unnerving gaze slid over Lachlan in a way that made Luc tilt his head. There was something threatening in it. Something… familiar.

"Yes," the boy replied.

"Be off with you," the soldier said, pushing the boy out toward the roadway.

The boy stopped and looked at them all, his eyes jumping to each one of them, as if memorizing them. His gaze lingered on Nix and Luc for a moment longer, then he turned and ran, his bare feet kicking up dust.

"That was… odd," Lachlan said, clearly as unnerved as Luc.

"How do we find the witch?" Johesha asked, reminding them they had a task.

"Can you do it?" Luc asked Nix. When Nix nodded, he said, "He'll summon this Baba."

"Why would she answer?"

"Most magical beings can't resist a god call," Luc answered. "Especially if there's something to be acquired from the god. We'll make it worth her while."

"We should be prepared. We saw what the creature could do. In the field," Johesha said.

"Prepared for what?" Lachlan asked. "We did see what it could do. There's nothing we possess that could stop that entity if it wants to end us." Then he disappeared inside his tent, leaving that grim thought for them to ponder.

Johesha stared at where Lachlan had disappeared, turned to look at the hedge with his dark eyes, then nodded and followed his prince into the tent.

Luc, with Nix leaning heavily on him, said, "I think you should summon Lexa."

"Why?"

"For backup."

Nix nodded, then closed his eyes and was quiet, leaving Luc to worry that his brother might not make it through the day. And Luc knew right then and there that he would do everything in his power to make sure Nix would. Even if it meant making an impossible choice.

"Hold on," he'd said before leaving her, cradling her face in his palms.

Then he was gone, and his absence left her aching, as the gray world worked harder to drag her under.

Brinna reached for Auri and fell into her mind, if only to do something to keep her connected to this plane of the dream. When she surfaced inside her sister's dream, Auri laying on her back on a beach again, the sea washing over her feet, her eyes closed.

Brinna rushed to her side. "Auri. Auri," she cried out, and Auri smiled as if she could hear her. But

Brinna knew she was still just an observer in her sister's dream, walking along an invisible surface.

It didn't matter—Brinna needed to talk to her sister. "I've finally found my love," she confessed with a wan smile, sitting next to Auri even though the dream kept them apart. "It's Lucian. Can you believe it? And he's only in my dreams."

"Nix?" Auri asked, her eyes still closed. She pressed her hand to her heart. "Are you here? It hurts everywhere without you. Come back to me. I'm sorry I pushed you away."

A disjointed shadow hovered around Auri, not Nix, not anything really, but whatever was in Auri's dream. Brinna watched it float, undulating above her sister like a specter. Waiting.

When suddenly, the dark thing dove into her chest, and Auri screamed.

Brinna scrambled onto her knees and tried to reach for her screaming sister, Auri's back arched horribly in the sand, but Brinna's hands bumped up against the invisible shield between them. "Auri!" She hit the wall over and over. "Let me in!"

The shadow emerged from Auri's core, dragging golden threads connected to Auri's chest and pulling them taut as Auri screamed. They reminded Brinna of the red ribbons, only they were golden and bright. Like Lucian.

Godlight?

Brinna pressed her hand over her heart and squeezed her eyes shut.

There's a missing piece of my heart when I'm not with you.

Auri's screaming stopped.

When Brinna opened her eyes, she was in a room. "Auri," she called even knowing Auri couldn't answer. The room was beautiful, decorated in green hues with a fireplace—the fire frozen in time in the hearth—a chair and sofa on which to lounge, a window framing the inky night beyond, and central to the whole room, a giant, four-poster bed.

She looked closer and saw there was one occupant, Nix, shrouded inside the bedding. He looked wrong, as if he was a flat, two-dimensional version of himself. Auri stood bedside pounding at a transparent barrier between them. She looked wrong too.

"Come back to me," Auri was crying, hitting the glass wall. She pressed her forehead to the barrier, then screamed a horrible sound of grief mixed with frustration and terror. "Nix!" She slammed her hands against the wall. "I want the yoke. With you. I want it. Please, Nix. Don't leave me."

The god-yoke.

The fading.

"Auri?" Brinna called, but dream Auri sobbed against the barrier.

Brinna pulled herself from Auri's dream and smoothed the dark hair from her sister's forehead, then wiped the tears flowing from her eyes. "I'm here, Auri. I'll do everything I can," she said, even as she felt the gray tug against her mind. "I love you." Brinna leaned over and kissed Auri's forehead, then leaned back to see Auri's eyelids flutter, then still once more.

Brinna pressed her hand against her chest, feeling that discomfort, and she imagined Auri doing the same thing when she'd been without Nix.

Brinna's heart tripped inside her chest, and she blinked. Wait. Her mind drifted backward, thinking. She'd been with Lucian. She turned in a circle in the room, and though nothing changed, she tried to recall where they'd been.

Sol.

Talking about Auri and Nixus. When?

Before she'd gone back to the cottage. The night of the dream.

She'd been facing Lucian in the bed, trying to keep her mind focused on the story he'd been telling her about Auri and Nix. He'd been so beautiful that it was almost difficult to look at him, but she'd managed somehow to keep hold of the story. "You're telling me Auri saved the whole world?"

"Humbling, I know," he'd said with a grin, his head propped on his hand. "But yes."

"And you were there?"

He nodded. "It was terrifying. This massive, pitch-black cavern—"

Brinna had been there in Auri's dreams. She was sure of it. But what did it mean?

"Then suddenly she's there, glowing with this bright, golden light, and Lexa—my sister—and I are freaking out a touch.

Just a touch, mind you."

"Glowing?"

"Yes. With godlight."

"How, though? How is that possible? Auri isn't a god."

"She and Nix were able to communicate somehow. Nix told me once that it was like this link in their minds, that they could send thoughts and power down these threads *that connected them."*

Brinna knew now that this was the god-yoke. She'd seen those threads in Auri's dream. But it was the word Lucian had used—glowing—that stopped her heart with knowing.

"So Nix gave her godlight?"

"Yes. Gifted her his to keep it from the demon fueling the spell. She figured it out before we did, then sacrificed herself to save all of us, to keep the demon imprisoned."

"But that sacrifice broke the spell and saved everyone."

He'd smiled. "Exactly."

"Oh my stars," Brinna breathed, her hand at her throat.

There had always been the matter of why she could Dream Walk with Lucian and no one else. She'd just thought it was because he was a god, but she'd never shared a dream with another. Not like she did with Lucian.

Her eyes slid to Auri. "Could it be?" she asked her

sleeping sister, then looked at her own sleeping form, her pallor drained.

"How did you know you were yoked with Nixus?" she asked Auri, then touched her sister once more and slid into her dream.

She found herself in a room—just like the last one she'd been in with Auri, only now, instead of being separated by a wall, Auri and Nix were lying in one another's arms shrouded in a golden glow.

Brinna gasped, falling out of Auri's dream. "Oh stars." She closed her eyes and thought of Lucian, of being with him, his body connected to hers. Of opening her eyes after. Of Lucian glowing, as if lit from within.

"Is this the dream?" she'd asked.

"We are a dream," he'd replied. "You are my dream."

He knew.

They were god-yoked.

It explained everything. The pain in her heart without him. The need for him. The reason she was tethered outside the gray. She might have the ability to dream and Dream Walk, but it was Lucian keeping her there.

The gray tugged harder.

Brinna took a deep breath and imagined cutting its gray thread and strengthening the golden tether between her and Lucian.

She would hold on. She had to.

When they left the hedge behind, Luc hadn't realized he'd be practically carrying Nix through the woods, but there they were, stumbling deeper into the forest, Nix leaning against him as if Luc were the only thing holding him up. While these woods were familiar to Luc, given how many times he'd been in them, this time he wasn't alone, and this wasn't a pleasure jaunt—he was searching for Lexa.

Lachlan and his henchmen followed, making them a strange party. *Two gods, a prince, and three henchmen were walking through the woods.* Luc scoffed. It sounded like the beginning of a joke.

"How far are we going?" Lachlan asked from somewhere behind him, crashing through the underbrush.

"Has anyone ever said you're loud?" Luc asked.

"Why? Do I need to be quiet?"

"The meadow," Nix wheezed.

"When we reach the place, we'll stop," Luc called back to Lachlan, then said to Nix, "maybe you shouldn't be exerting this much energy. We can do this anywhere, right?"

But Nix shook his head. "It has to be there."

"Why?"

"I'll be where I found Auri."

Luc didn't like the sound of that at all, tugging Nix closer and readjusting to offer his brother more support. He looked up at the sky, wondering if Lexa would arrive in her dragon form, hopeful he'd see her shadow. But the sky was filled with a haze of high gray clouds.

When they finally reached the meadow, Luc helped Nix over to a boulder, then sat down next to him, unwilling to let go of his brother for even a moment. He looked around recognizing the place—it looked like a meadow. Tall grass intermingled with wildflowers fluttering like waves on the sea in the fall breeze. Around them, trees of various varieties hovered tall and imposing. Though still daytime, the clouds cast a dim, almost eerie light.

"What now?" Lachlan asked as he circled the space. His attire matched his guards', with a leather breastplate, leather bracers, and a dagger strapped to his hip, but rather than a sword like his guards, he had a bow and quiver. The prince's hair was a touch long, falling into his face so that he had to continually shake it out of his eyes. "Do we have to do some incantation?" When he turned his head to look at them, he was grinning.

With a huff and a shake of his head, Luc turned to Nix, who shrugged. "Just have to call the witch."

"Make it dramatic, I suppose," Luc said with a grin.

Nix smiled. "Baba," he intoned, his voice thick with omnipotence, "witch of these woods, wielder of magic, the god of night and darkness calls you forth."

"That was pretty convincing," Luc told his brother. "I'd come running."

"Me too," Lachlan replied, still traipsing through the meadow. "And here I thought you were just a pretty boy." He pulled up a wildflower as he said it, pressing it into his nose. For some reason, it made Luc think of Brinna, and he looked away.

Nix chuckled.

Luc looked for Lachlan's guards, finding them situated around the meadow, watchful and scowling.

"I kissed Auri here," Nix said, grabbing Luc's attention. "This place helped her remember me, when she'd forgotten." His voice drifted.

"I think it was you who helped her remember."

Nix didn't reply, just leaned into him even more.

Eventually he said, "I'm tired, Luc."

"Keep going, Nix. I can fix this."

Nix shook his head. "Not everything is yours to fix. Sometimes things happen. Good things. Bad things. Wonderful things. Awful things. That's life."

"But—"

"I'm so grateful for the spell."

Luc's stomach suspended with shock, hanging weightless in his body. "What?"

"If it hadn't happened, I never would have found Auri." Nix's eyes curled with joy, and he pressed a hand to Luc's cheek, then tapped it a few times before his hand fell away. "I forgive you, you know. I forgave you long ago. In your shoes, perhaps I might have done something similar." He paused. "Stop punishing yourself."

"But—"

"You've yoked. To Brinna."

Surprised that Nix knew, Luc didn't deny it and nodded. "I'm sorry. I didn't mean for—"

"Can't control a yoke. I should know. See what you have to look forward to?" Nix chuffed a laugh, but it quickly faded.

At a strange sound—a tumult of air mixed with the groaning and creaking of trees—Luc looked away from Nix. As the vibration in the earth intensified, birds squawked and took flight from the trees, and a breeze whipped through, carrying dead leaves and the strong odor of moist earth. Darkness spread toward them, a collection of shadows.

"Is that you?" Luc asked Nix.

His brother shook his head. "No. Pretty impressive. Perhaps our witch wants to show off?"

Luc chuckled.

A bright light appeared amidst the gray shadows, small at first, then expanding as it moved through the wood toward them. As the light grew brighter, iridescence like that of pearl shimmered, until at the core of the darkness, the pearl coalesced into a beautiful woman. Her bright white hair swirled as if she were suspended in water, her form dressed in that brilliant shimmer of light.

Lachlan's men had moved and surrounded the prince, but two of them—Jude and Brendsen—relaxed, slack jawed at the vision the woman made. Only Johesha remained vigilant between the witch and the prince.

Nix struggled to his feet. "Baba."

"God of night and darkness." She dipped her head toward him. "Your godlight is weak."

"You see it?" Luc asked, standing next to Nix.

"Your's is… different." Her brow furrowed. She looked at him, her head tilted. "Why are you here?"

"We seek answers," Lachlan said, dragging her attention away from Nix and Luc.

"You aren't a god," she said and fluttered around the perimeter of the meadow, studying them. "Answers are often not what we seek," she told them. "We seek the truth between them."

"We need a way through the hedge," Lachlan said.

Her head tilted as she returned to the earth, her form shifting from the ethereal woman into one more substantive. Older but still beautiful, she was dressed in an everyday frock, green and brown like the natural world around her, her silvery white hair in a braid. She reminded Luc of his mother—sans the preoccupation with her appearance—and she walked to a space in the meadow where she could see each of them, her eyes bouncing from man to man. Then she smiled. "True love." She made a sound Luc couldn't decipher. "I warned her."

"Azleah?" Luc asked.

The woman turned to him. "That isn't her name."

"Scarlett," Nix said.

"Yes."

"She's trapped her family. Behind the hedge," Luc said. "You helped her?"

"I gave her a potion, yes."

"You've been helping her this whole time," Nix accused.

She gave them a slow nod. "This was her last resort."

"Because you helped her escape her father?"

"Her father?" The witch's eyes burned like dark coals as she barked a humorless laugh. "No. A wretch of a different name but chiseled from the same clay."

"A different witch?" Lachlan asked, glancing at Luc and Nix.

A male voice.

"Why have I been summoned, god of night and

darkness?" she asked.

"We need to get through the hedge to break the spell," Lachlan said again.

Nix slumped against Luc. "Give her what she needs," Nix whispered. "Save Auri."

Luc's heart constricted painfully at his brother's weak voice.

Baba's eyes jumped to Luc's, and she changed, morphing from the mother-figure into an old woman leaning heavily on a thick, crooked, walking stick. "I would like a thread."

"A thread of what?" Luc asked, his fingers pressed to his heart.

"Of your yoked godlight. It's mixed up nicely with another's." She pointed at Nix. "His too, before he's gone."

Gone?

"We need to stop wasting time. We just need to break the spell," Luc snapped, sitting with Nix on the boulder once more.

"All sorcerers seek power. Even me. When I get it, I'll give you the space between the answers you seek."

"What will you do with it?" Luc asked, knowing that they didn't have much choice, but also knowing how awful it would be to learn that by giving it to her, something worse would happen. Like the spell where he'd trapped Nix.

"Immortality—or as close as I am able to get to it. That is my bargain."

Luc hesitated.

Nix huffed a breath.

"The sands are running, god," she said.

"Yes. Okay. Yes," Luc agreed.

The witch shuffled forward, and once she was close enough, held a gnarled finger to Nix's chest. As Luc watched in horrified fascination, the tip of her fingernail disappeared into Nix's chest. Nix winced and with effort, Luc kept his mouth shut.

When she retracted her finger, a small, golden thread curled around the sharp point of her nail. She held it up, studied it a moment, then dropped it into her mouth.

Luc tried not to squirm as she repeated the process with him. Where he'd thought there might be pain, he felt only a minor intrusion, but the thread being tugged from his heart felt as if a limb had been torn from his body.

"It won't change your bond," she said, holding the bright thread higher. "It is but a miniscule sliver of what is inside of you." Then she slurped it until it disappeared down her gullet, and Luc's stomach twisted at the glee on her face. She closed her eyes as if savoring the flavor, though Luc knew it wasn't flavor she tasted, but power.

"A deal is a deal," he said.

The witch inclined her head. "Listen to my words and heed them, for I will reveal the spell once: 'A drop of this potion— two, three, or four—will call to the Deep Sleep and close the door, and slip into Dreamland locked up nice and tight, with a magical beastie guarding with might. One whose heart is bound and pure will face the beastie and endure. A faithful heart will be veiled from sight to reach the dreamer bound to endless Night. Upon True Love's kiss, the spell will break, and into True Love's arms, the dreamer will awake.'"

Then, as if a door had slammed shut, she was gone, leaving the forest devoid of sound. "Seek his true name," her disembodied voice called in the eerie silence.

In the next moment, the forest came alive once more, the breeze and the sounds of birds bringing the space back to life.

"We have it," Luc said and glanced at his brother.

Nix was slumped beside him, motionless. Luc jolted forward, gathering Nix into his arms as they both fell to the ground.

"No! No! Nix. Don't leave me!" Luc yelled, shaking Nix, just as the rush of wind from Lexa's wings stirred the forest around them.

"Father!" Luc yelled, holding an unmoving Nix in his arms, as Lexa portaled them into Alabastrine. They landed exactly where he'd asked Lexa to take them—their father's study. It was a place that had, at one time, brought Luc fond memories. He remembered playing in the room with Nix as boys, their father watching them with an indulgent smile on his face, though at the moment, those memories weren't at the forefront of his thoughts. "Help!"

Ur jumped to his feet, hurrying around his giant

desk. "What has he gotten into this time?"

Luc deposited Nix onto a tufted leather sofa in the middle of the room. "Fix him," Luc demanded. "He's fading."

Ur looked perplexed, his eyes jumping between Lexa and Luc to Nix. "What is this? A new scheme?"

"Scheme? What the fuck?" Luc shouted, tears filling his eyes. "He's dying!"

"It's the god-yoke, father," Lexa said quietly, kneeling at Nix's side and moving a lock of hair that had fallen over his eyes, as if that were all that ailed him. Luc's heart pinched painfully at the sight of his brother; his skin was so pale, his eyes shut, his lashes dark against his skin.

"There is nothing I can do for–"

"You can," Luc shouted. He couldn't seem to help himself, pacing the room now. "The Order of Oracles said you could."

"I could what?"

"An *oblitorium*." Luc turned and faced his father. "He didn't ask to be god-yoked." Luc felt all the blame settle on his shoulders. If he hadn't cast that stupid spell, if he hadn't lured Aurielle...

I'm so grateful for the spell. It brought me Auri.

Luc shoved his hands in his hair, squeezing and pulling to feel the pain as he crouched down. Emotions rioted inside him, along with the constriction around his heart that wasn't only due to the god-yoke. He took a deep breath, then another, picking his way through the panic. "Prudence—the oracle—said severing the memories might help the fade, temporarily."

"There's a reason we don't do them," Ur replied.

"That could sever all of him," Lexa said, shock ringing through her tone.

"Exactly," Ur said. "I need night and darkness as is. Why would I risk that?"

Luc looked up from his cower near the floor, then stood and stared at his father. "If we do nothing, he dies. Aurielle dies. And his power returns to the cistern until a new night and darkness ascends, leaving you to deal with night and darkness in the Vasmost anyway."

"The yoke is inconsequential—"

"Maximora," Luc interrupted. "That is their godblood."

Ur swallowed and looked down at Nix. "What you're asking… Lucian. I can't."

Luc keened, a horrific sound of frustration. "What can you do?" he shouted. "Just take power?"

"Luc." Lexa glanced up from her place next to Nix. "This isn't your fault."

"Yes, it is!"

She continued to smooth Nix's hair. "When we visited Cumbria," she started.

"Who cares about that waste of a soul?" Luc huffed, turning his back on her. Though even as he said it, he recognized that without him, there was no Scarlett. Without Scarlett there was no Brinna. He heaved a huge sigh, the frustration dissipating, to leave fear and grief in its wake.

"I walked away," Lexa continued, "thinking about

was how horrible it was for him—and for his daughter—because he was stuck in his grief, stuck in the past."

Luc turned back toward her.

"He ruined lives because of it. Ruined his own." Lexa leaned down and whispered something Luc couldn't hear to Nix in that gentle way she'd always been with him. Then she looked back up. "He's stuck right now, isn't he? Nix."

"We all are," Luc replied, initially thinking about the hedge, then realized it wasn't only the spell that had done it. He'd done it himself. Perhaps he wasn't Cumbria, but he'd gotten stuck in his shame and guilt, hiding it only by Roaming. And like his mother had tried to tell him, he'd ignored the possibility to be more because of the world he'd imprisoned himself in, believing it was what he deserved.

He looked at his father. "Give me my powers back," he said quietly.

"You can't do—"

"No. But you can grant me the power because I agree to take your place. And you will do this because I ask for it."

Ur's jaw relaxed. "You understand–"

"Yes. I fucking understand. Do you want me to beg you? I will, for Nix. He deserves this from me, and maybe I don't deserve to take your place or to be god of day and light, but I will fucking do everything in my power to do what is right by Nix. And this is right. For Nix. For Aurielle."

Lexa hummed, her hand sliding over Nix's dark hair once more. "I wondered, Luc, when you would decide to step into who you were always meant to be," she said, then looked at Ur. "Father, I think you have what you want."

"Lexa, we need the Oracle, the one who knows about the *oblitorium*," Luc said.

She dissipated where she sat, leaving Luc alone with his father and an unconscious Nix.

A moment later, Luc's power filled him—a warm, quiet return like that of an old friend. Rather than say something he might regret to his father, he skirted the couch and knelt at his brother's side. "Why are you always hurt, Nix? I'm beginning to think it's a pattern, baby brother."

Only by four minutes, he imagined Nix replying.

Luc smiled.

"Lucian," Ur said, crouching down next to him.

Luc met his gaze.

"I didn't want you to beg me. I wanted you to understand you are the right god to take my place."

Luc's throat closed, but he refused to let the tears grab hold. He understood that he was as flawed as anyone else, but he could choose to do what was right, with the right intentions. Sometimes the choices were easy, and sometimes they were impossible, like now.

He looked down at his brother. "I'll do everything in my power to serve." He thought of Brinna. "To be a bridge." His heart twisted, missing her, needing her. He looked up at his father, who nodded and placed a hand on his shoulder.

"That is why it was always you."

Before Luc could reply, Lexa returned.

Luc got to his feet beside his father as she appeared, carting with her a terrified Oracle. "See," Lexa said with impatience. "I told you—"

The monk's frightened gaze took in his surroundings as he straightened, his keys clanging and jangling. His green robe sat haphazardly on his shoulders as if he'd been in the midst of putting it on. Though he was short, his face was long, making him appear taller somehow. That, and his long, prominent nose gave him a narrow countenance. "This isn't the Netherrealm?"

"I told you it wasn't the fucking Netherrealm," Lexa snapped. She growled to punctuate her frustration.

The monk dipped his head. "Almighty, Ur. Forgive me."

"We need your help," he said. "My son—"

The monk rested his gaze to Nix, then straightened. "The god of night and darkness?"

"He's god-yoked," Luc said.

The monk's eyes widened. "The fading? My brothers and sisters had said he'd come to learn about it. I have never seen it—"

"We need an *oblitorium*," Luc interrupted. "To sever his memories of the yoke—"

"What?" the monk breathed. "I know Prudence suggested it, but this," he paused. "This is magic we use in extreme cases—"

Lexa grabbed the monk's head and forcibly swiveled it to look at Nix. "Is this not extreme?"

The monk swallowed.

"Lexa," Luc said, nudging her out of the way. She was never rational when it came to Nix.

"We use it for gods who've lost their way, gods who can't control their power, those that need reformation. We've never used it this way," the monk explained. "It would rend him, and he would have to begin again."

"I was thinking," Luc said, his mind on Cumbria and the way the soul had been split into four parts, "maybe we could just temporarily sever the memories pertaining to the yoke." He looked at his father and sister, then at the monk.

"Temporarily?" The monk asked, sounding doubtful. How?"

"Lock them away instead of sever them."

"It's never been done. An *oblitorium* was designed to take them all."

"What would we need?" Luc asked. "To do it my way?"

The monk's eyes jumped to Ur.

Ur took a deep breath. "I defer to my son and sanction what is to be done."

The monk looked back at Luc. "Perhaps, with your combined godlights. We need someone who knows his memories."

Luc nodded.

"But–" the monk said.

"You are not responsible, Oracle," Luc said, "if this doesn't work. I will take the responsibility."

The room grew heavy with understanding. Regardless of the outcome, they all understood that something would be lost.

The monk nodded, slowly, his wide eyes jumping around the room. "Let's get him on a flat surface where each of you can touch him."

With Lexa's help, Luc moved Nix to the floor as Ur shoved the sofa out of the way, its feet scraping across the marble.

"We'll call upon our power, yes?" the monk said, situating himself at Nix's head, then looking at each of them, as they found a place: Ur to Nix's left, Luc on his right, Lexa at his feet. "The *oblitorium* is usually only done by a member of our Order, one with the ability to ferret through the power feeding the memory. This is my power, yes? The purpose of the procedure is to sever the power feeding the problem, then to take it so that the godblood can reset. What you're asking" –he looked at Luc– "is more complicated."

Luc grimaced. "I know."

"You will help me choose the memories."

Luc nodded.

"You" –the monk, taking charge, indicated Ur and Lexa–"will contain his power so we don't lose it and bolster the god of day and light to assist me. Don't touch the yoke's power."

"Remember, try not to destroy the memories," Luc

said.

The monk looked skeptical, but he nodded once again, then closed his eyes.

Luc did the same, and like the sensation of twirling through time and space through a portal, he felt his consciousness spiral into Nix's mind, though Luc was still connected to his physical form. His awareness, however, was strange in that he could feel the power of the others—the monk tugging him into Nix, along with the added consciousness of his father and sister. He worked to get his mind where it needed to be with Nix's.

Suddenly, a hallway stretched out in front of him, no beginning, and no end that he could see, lined with door after door, like Elsewhere Doors.

"I put Elsewhere Doors in the spell."

"Here," Luc said.

His father and sister's power drew on Nix's godlight, and doors faded, but many still glowed with bright, golden light. The yoke.

Luc reached for one and opened it.

Inside, he sat with Nix on the rock awaiting the witch. "I forgave you a long time ago," Nix said.

"This one?" he heard the monk say as if he were far away.

"No," Luc answered, closed the door, and walked forward, checking the next and the next. "But the memories are in order."

He turned in the hallway and ran in the opposite direction from that memory until he thought he'd run far enough to reach the spell, then opened another door. Nix was fucking the milkmaid in a darkened room. Luc slammed the door shut and shuddered. "Almost there."

Turning back toward the beginning, he walked a few more doors, bypassing the dark ones for those threaded with light. One was Nix walking into the trap Luc had set for him. He watched Nix walk into the spelled shed with the milkmaid, then disappear into the spell.

Luc closed the door. "Not this one," he said and reached for another door. When it opened to the meadow, Aurielle was pulling a sled, then bent to pick up the key. "This one. Here. This is the first one." His heart ached as he left the door open for detachment, knowing Nix wouldn't choose this but aware that Aurielle would.

Luc raced through the hallway, leaving open the pertinent doors for the Oracle's power and closing the door to any others that seemed peripheral.

With a glance over his shoulder, Luc watched as the door of a memory he'd selected slammed shut. The Oracle's power attached a lock to the door, then moved onto the next open door, repeating the process.

When their task was done, Luc blinked out of the trance and looked at his father, his sister, the monk, each of them blinking back into their reality. Luc looked down at his brother, who also had begun to stir, and when Nix opened his eyes, Luc smiled back.

The room spun, his vision dimming. And when

darkness overcame him, he didn't fight it, sliding straight into the abyss as it swallowed him whole.

Brinna surged up from the deep gray with a gasp.

"Brinna?"

Lucian's voice drew her, and she turned to find Lucian standing on a rocky shore, water lapping quietly behind him. She didn't have time to appreciate the beauty, but her heart relaxed, heat blooming around and through her chest as if everything was alright once more, though she knew something must be vitally wrong.

She moved toward him, only to hit a wall. It shimmered as she pushed, stretching like the membrane of an egg. No matter how much she tried, she couldn't get to him.

"Brinna?" he yelled.

"Lucian!" she cried, hitting the wall, now trapped on the other side of their shared dream, just as she'd been separated from her family's. She pressed her forehead against the wall as tears filled her eyes, then fell, flowing down her cheeks. "I know. I know," she told him, each word punctuated with a sob. "We're yoked. I know. I lost my ribbon. I love you."

"Brinna!" His hands curled around his mouth as he yelled for her. He turned in place, as if afraid to move from where he was, as if afraid if he did, she might not find him.

"I'm here!" she cried, hitting the wall again.

He scraped at the pebbles with his feet, waiting. "I had to make a choice. An awful one." He looked up. "Brinna? Are you there?"

"Tell me!" she shouted, smacking her palms against the wall. The gray tugged on her, Lucian and the comforting warmth of his dream flickering. "No. No," she cried. "I'm here."

"I had to hide his memories."

The gray grabbed hold of her and yanked. Brinna slid away from Lucian's dream and dropped into a chasm filled with nothing. She fought.

"Brinna!" Lucian shouted, his voice pulling her mind back, but she couldn't see him any longer—only hear his call from so far away.

A heated, golden thread extended outward from

her body. She grabbed hold and followed, gasping when she found herself pressed against Lucian's chest. His hands framed her face. "*Mi alora?* Where have you been?"

"It's coming," she said.

Then he was gone once more, and she was surrounded by the gray deep.

"Brinna! If you can hear me, we're coming," Lucian yelled from somewhere else, somewhere far away where she couldn't stay.

The gray yanked with a death grip, pulling her down deeper. As it swallowed her, her mind drifted into a dream where she was standing in a room, fluttering with gauzy curtains as the sun set. Alone.

"Lucian?" she called.

Only silence answered her back.

"What have you discovered?" Luc asked as he walked into Lachlan's tent.

The prince was hunched over a table in his tent with his three henchmen and looked up when he entered. "Where were my guards?"

"I blinded them," Luc said. "They didn't see us."

Lachlan straightened and sighed, clearly frustrated. "Magic." He said it like a curse.

"What the fuck is this?" Nix asked. He scoffed. "What a dump." He looked at Lachlan. "Oh sorry. Didn't mean to offend if this is"–he cleared his throat–"yours." Luc watched his brother's dark gaze bounce between them. "You must be Luc's latest lover. You seem his type."

"Nixus," Luc said, already over his brother's barbs, which had started the moment Luc had woken from his nightmare of losing Brinna to the spell. Who would have known how much better Auri had made him? Fuck.

"Well, he looks better, but what the fuck did you do to him?" Lachlan asked.

"I had to hide his memories."

"Hide?" Lachlan's eyes widened. "What?"

"Of Auri."

"Shit," Lachlan breathed.

"Why do you keep blathering on about that?" Nix said. "It's getting annoying, Luc."

Nix was right. Luc had made mention of the spell, of Auri, of the memories they'd hidden as often as it made sense to do so. "I promised I would try and help you remember, Nix. And you'll want to."

"You're being weird."

"As you have pointed out repeatedly. Just remember your older brother is the wiser of the two."

"By four fucking minutes, Luc. Four." He held up four fingers.

He was driving Luc to distraction, but then this was better than the alternative. He looked at Lachlan. "Well?"

"Between the three of us, we think we got it written out." Lachlan walked back to the table and read the spell as they remembered it.

"What are you doing?" Nix asked, squeezing in between Lachlan and Johesha. "Hello there, good sir."

The guard scowled at him.

"Well aren't you a Happy Harry," Nix said brightly.

Johesha's scowl deepened.

Luc ignored them and focused on the spell, reading over what the three of them had recalled. "I don't think the word was *bond*. I think it was *bound*," Luc said, pointing at the word.

"What's the difference?" Brendsen asked.

"Everything," Nix said.

They all turned to look at him. He was testing Lachlan's cot by bouncing on it.

"What would you know about it?" Luc asked.

"Words matter," he said. He hummed a sound. "You know what it's like when you tell a woman that you might be falling, and she makes the assumption you mean falling in love, but what you really meant was like falling asleep because you're tired after fucking. Tomato-tamato am I right?" He laughed, then scrunched his nose and continued pilfering through Lachlan's things, pressing a hand to his heart.

Luc knew the loss of his memories wouldn't hold the fade for long, but it would perhaps give them enough time to break the spell.

"Okay. The difference?" Lachlan asked.

"Bond is like a connection, right?" Jude asked.

"Or a thing that ties," Johesha said, his deep voice surprising Luc.

"And bound?"

"The idea of being destined?" Luc asked. He thought of the yoke. "Like being star-crossed?"

"Exchange vows or a commitment, perhaps?" Lachlan crossed out 'bond' and replaced it. "One whose heart is bound and pure," he reread. Then he looked up. "We're all agreed that the *beastie* is the hedge, right?"

Each of them nodded.

Luc hoped there wasn't another creature hidden in that monstrosity.

"You know, someone who is yoked could get through," Nix said, rubbing his heart.

"Like you, Nix?" Luc asked.

He made a face. "I am *not* yoked." He scoffed. "Don't be ridiculous. What a horrible thought." He shuddered and started back toward the table.

"I am," Luc said quietly, turning back to Lachlan. "And you are bound to Tarley, through your vows. So couldn't we both get through?"

"Is your heart pure?" Nix asked, looking over Johesha's shoulder. The guard was clearly annoyed by Nix's proximity, which, if Luc knew his brother, was by design.

Luc considered the spell. His heart may not be pure in many ways, but when it came to his feelings for Brinna, it was. "I think so."

Nix chuckled. "Okay."

Luc ignored his brother.

"Since words matter," Nix said, reading over Johesha's shoulder, "then those two things should hide someone trying to get inside."

"We can't risk the prince on a maybe," Johesha said.

"All due respect, Jo, do you have a better idea?" Lachlan asked.

The scowling guard swore and shook his head.

"Then we go." Lachlan patted his chest and his leather armor as if to check he had everything he needed. "Through the hedge to kiss our loves, right?"

"This, I have to see," Nix said with a grin.

Luc nodded and glanced at Nix, knowing that technically, his brother could also get through the hedge because of his bond with Auri, even if he didn't remember it at the moment. And hopefully seeing Auri would open the doors to his memories.

"And what about the others," Johesha said. "You will only wake three." He seemed excessively surly about it.

Luc hadn't realized the head of Lachlan's guard had much of an opinion about the matter.

"Do you love one of them?" Nix asked with a laugh.

Johesha scowled. "I don't know them to love them. I care about my duty to my prince."

Nix mimicked the guard, who looked like he was ready to stab Nix in the chest.

"We'll have to figure that out when we come to it," Lachlan said. "Right now, we can only control what we can control."

"Your highness," Johesha started.

"I know what you're going to say, and the answer is: I know. You can't come in with me. You three will remain out here."

"But–"

"Johesha… Tarley is mine. I am hers."

"You are also Jast's."

"Not yet, I'm not," he said. "My father still lives. My brother and sister are coming of age. Jast is covered. Tarley needs me." He ran his hand around the back of his neck. "Nothing will keep me from her, Jo. Last time, I listened, and we were victorious, but it is time you trust me. I'm not thinking irrationally."

Johesha growled.

"Did he just growl?" Nix asked, dark eyes wide.

Luc leaned toward his brother and whispered, "Maybe don't comment on it. He's already on the dark side of surly."

"I think he's way past the dark side of surly. He's something else altogether."

Luc couldn't help but smile.

Johesha offered a quick nod of deference to Lachlan. "We'll set up a perimeter around the hedge."

A few minutes later, Luc, Lachlan, and Nix stood side by side looking up at the monstrous hedge. It hadn't changed since the spell had begun, though his perception of it felt different, a little more hopeful about what lay beyond it.

Nix made a strange noise. "This doesn't look like a party. This looks like your idea of a party, Luc, a terrible spell to teach a lesson. Thanks for that."

Luc ignored the guilt, instead turning back to Nix. "How'd you get out again?"

Nix scratched his head, then his nose, then tilted his head looking perplexed. "Let me think about it. It's…"

"Forgot, huh?"

"I don't forget things, you ass. How many times to do I have to tell you?"

Luc started his reply with a hum, then said, "Let me know when you do remember, then."

Movement caught his eye, and he turned to see Lachlan stripping off his armor. "What are you doing?"

"Whoa. Are we getting naked?" Nix looked concerned. "Have you seen the size of those thorns?" He cupped his balls. "I don't want those anywhere near my nether-regions."

"I don't know… it feels right to go in just as myself." He looked at Nix. "Not naked."

"Oh thank the fucking stars. I was going to have to bow out of this little party if it was going to be naked."

Luc looked at the hedge and nodded. "Okay." He took off his jacket, sliding off any extra garments that might snag on the thorns, until all that were left was his trousers and shirt, rolled to the elbow.

Nix followed, grumbling as he did.

"Anything else?" Lachlan asked.

"I'll go first," Luc said.

"It's because you're four minutes older, isn't it?" Nix quipped.

"Exactly," Luc said and started for the hedge.

"If it squeezes you to death–" Lachlan started.

"Don't follow me in." Luc grinned.

He took a deep breath, closed his eyes, and thought of Brinna. Then he reached out and touched the closest branch. Unlike with the others, the hedge didn't try to squeeze him to death. With another deep breath, he climbed over the branch, and slid between thick vines before moving onto the next one, ducking between crisscrossed branches. He glanced over his shoulder to see Nix and Lachlan just behind him, Lachlan ducking under a vine as Nix hopped over another. All of them, alive.

The deeper they traveled into the hedge, the darker it became, the monstrosity blocking out most of the light. It was like a maze, the intertwined vines, the thorns, the darkness. It would be easy to get turned around without something to guide them. Everything looked the same no matter which way he turned. But he didn't ponder it, hopeful that they were moving in the right direction rather than the alternative. Hesitation wouldn't get him to Brinna, so he climbed, shimmied, jumped, and ducked moving deeper into the hedge.

None of them spoke—not even Nix—though Luc was certain he could feel his brother biting back the witty quips. An unspoken agreement to maintain silence seemed to have passed between.

After what felt like hours, Luc stopped. He couldn't hear his brother or Lachlan, which worried him. Though he wasn't sure if he should, he called forth his light. Opening his hand, he released a sliver of power, and a muted glow pierced the hedge's gloom. He waited; his breath caught at the stark realization he might have lost them somewhere.

But before he could panic, movement caught his eye. He squinted, and Nix appeared from one area, Lachlan from another, as if his light had guided them back. When they all stood in Luc's light, they nodded at one another—no words—and started through once more. Using his feelings like a compass, he continued through the hedge. He thought of Brinna, of her smile and her laugh. He thought of talking with her, of touching her. He imagined her under him, her kiss, and the way it felt when she'd been torn out of his arms, how he needed her in them.

Again and again, just as Luc believed he'd reached the other side—mirages of a meadow appearing through the awkwardly bent boughs enticing him—he'd burst through to find only a sea of shoots and thorns. He bit his tongue to keep from yelling in frustration and stopped, hanging his head. The pain in his chest intensified with longing, and hope waned inside of him as he stood in the pervasive, never-ending gloom.

Suddenly, he felt a hand on his right shoulder. Then on his left. Nix and Lachlan. He wasn't alone in this. Neither were they. Infused with hope once more, Lachlan took the lead, and Luc followed, Nix behind.

They took turns leading. The journey stretching on as though endless. But at least they were together. They continued—minutes, hours, days, Luc couldn't tell—until suddenly they burst through, clothes and skin torn, bodies aching from the exertion, minds exhausted as they collapsed into a heap in the meadow.

Luc rolled to his back, propped himself up on his elbows and looked up at the green monster they'd conquered. He yelled in triumph, as he fell onto his back, laughing. He'd accomplished one of the most important things he'd ever done in his life, and he glanced at Lachlan and Nix to find them smiling and laughing with him.

But the feeling of triumph soon passed, and they got to their feet, eyeing the dark cottage.

Luc saw Nix freeze, his head tilting as he stared. "I feel like I've been here before." He looked at Luc. "But that's ridiculous."

Luc put his hand on his brother's back. "Maybe you have. You just–"

"I don't forget things."

"Right. You're impervious to slips of memory."

"Exactly. I'm the god of night and darkness. I'm impervious to all kinds of things."

Luc shook his head and gave his brother's shoulder some good-natured slaps. "Okay god of imperviousness. Let's go." Though afraid of what he might find, he walked across the meadow to the cottage.

Lachlan was the first one through. "Tarley!" he called, then stopped short.

Following him in, Luc called on his light. Though

he'd never been in the cottage before, he knew it was small from Brinna's descriptions. He was unprepared for how small. A single room that housed a tiny kitchen, a dining table, and a fireplace, with a hall near the kitchen that led to a door and a set of stairs, but this was it. A cabinet used for refrigeration and a potbelly stove for an oven. No wonder she'd been in awe of the bathroom.

The dining table was set with dishes strewn across its surface, the plates with food and crumbs scattered with broken bits of glass.

"I thought your tent was a dump," Nix said from the doorway. "Who lives here?"

"There," Lachlan said, ignoring Nix and hurrying deeper into the room.

Luc watched Lachlan kneel next to a lumped blanket in the middle of the floor in front of the cold hearth. Lachlan looked up. "It's Scarlett and Tomas." He reached out and touched them. "They have pulses, but they're freezing."

"There's a sleeping man back here," Nix said from a doorway.

"Mattias," Lachlan said.

Luc started for the stairs, remembering Brinna telling him she shared a room with her sisters. "This way." The narrow stairs were barely wide enough to accommodate him. When he reached the entrance at the top, he ducked under the roughhewn frame, his footsteps echoing against the wooden floor.

And there was Brinna, curled up with her sister

Auri in one bed, as if they'd grabbed hold of each other in sleep, Tarley in the other. There was barely a walkway between the two beds, each pressed up against the opposite wall. They'd been covered—Scarlett had tried to make them comfortable, it seemed—but the room was frigid.

At the footsteps behind him, Luc glanced over his shoulder to watch Nix and Lachlan enter, hoping for a sign that Nix might remember. His brother looked around, his eyes dropping to the bed where Auri was with Brinna. His mouth opened and closed, color blooming in his cheeks as the fade receded, but then his gaze slid away.

"Well isn't this... cozy," he said.

Luc sighed.

Lachlan pushed past them to Tarley's side and dropped to his knees. He gathered her into his arms, pulling her from the bed into his lap.

"Tarley," he whispered. "My beautiful Tarley." He smoothed her hair, her face, and then leaned forward and pressed his mouth to her cheeks, her forehead, her eyelids, her mouth. "Come back to me," he whispered.

She made a noise, her eyelids fluttering open, her body starting before she realized who held her. "Lachlan," she gasped, flinging her arms around his neck.

"I'm here," he whispered.

She burst into tears.

Luc turned to Brinna, suddenly afraid this might not work. He loved her, which he knew to be the absolute truth, but he didn't know if she felt the same. They'd forged a relationship in the shadow of a dream.

There was a possibility that his kiss might not work, and if it didn't, he wasn't sure what to do. But he wasn't there to not try. He had every intention of imbuing that kiss with everything on his heart, so he pulled Brinna into his arms, and sat at the end of the bed, cradling her.

"Brinna," he whispered. "*Mi alora.* I love you. Come be in the true world with me." Then he leaned down and pressed his lips to hers. A real kiss in the waking world that felt as true as it had in the dream, and all Luc could do was believe that it—that he— would be enough.

"*Mi alora*, I love you," someone said in the distance, the sound pushing through the gray around her. "Come be in the true world with me," the wonderful voice coaxed.

She was certain she knew that voice, felt it reverberate in the deepest parts of her, bringing her pleasure and joy. She grabbed hold of the feeling, grabbed hold of the words.

"I don't deserve you," the voice whispered, "but I will work to earn your love, Brinna."

The deep gray of sleep drained away, and Brinna

came rushing back to herself, gasping as if surfacing from deep water. When her eyes fluttered open, the first thing she saw was Lucian's handsome face.

"Am I dreaming?" she asked, grabbing hold of him, anchoring herself.

He shook his head and gave her a short smile. "I'm here. In the cottage."

"I'm not dreaming?" She wasn't sure she could trust that, after dreaming so long. After meeting him, talking to him, kissing him, making love to him in her dreams.

He nodded and pressed his forehead to hers. "Truly."

She clung to his shirt, cognizant of the feelings, the textures, the sounds. Then she kissed him, unable to contain the feelings she couldn't find the words for. She found sustenance in his lips, power in that connection. A kiss in the real world. "Lucian," she breathed when she broke away. "You're here. You did it."

"We did it, Brin. Together. Both of us." He framed her face with his hands, his golden eyes darting between hers. "Brinna—"

"What is it?" She ran her palms over his shoulders, unable to fulfill her need to touch him.

He swallowed, his eyes diving to her mouth then back up again. "There's so much to say. So much I want to tell you. It's just—" He looked around.

Brinna followed his gaze. Lachlan had hold of Tarley, who was crying in his arms, but Auri was asleep.

Nix stood in the doorway, brow furrowed, staring at Auri. Brinna couldn't understand why he was frowning.

"What's wrong?" Brinna asked. "Nixus?"

His dark eyes flitted from Auri to Brinna. He offered her a tight smile. "Oh. We've met?" His frown deepened as he anxiously shifted in the doorway. "I don't usually forget things like that." He glanced at Lucian. "I don't forget things."

Brinna looked at Lucian, who pressed his mouth to her cheek and said against her skin, "He doesn't have his memories of Auri. I had to." His voice broke.

Brinna jerked back, staring at the face she'd come to love so deeply, a face that brought her joy, comfort, angst, frustration, but at the heart of all of the emotions, love. "What?"

"He was going to… die." Lucian wasn't looking at her but rather down, between them.

"Die?" She gasped.

"I had to make a choice."

"Look at me," she told him. When he raised his beautiful eyes to hers, she knew what a difficult choice it had been. Nixus's life over his memories of Auri—his joy. "You did what was right," she told him, holding his face between her hands.

Luc glanced at Auri. "What should we do?"

Because Nix wasn't moving to wake Auri, Brinna crawled from Lucian's lap to Auri's side, reaching out to touch her sister's shoulder. "Auri?" She glanced over her shoulder at Lucian. "How do we wake her up?"

"True love's kiss."

Brinna studied Lucian; his eyes filled with what she knew to be true. That he loved her. She was awake because he loved her. She glanced at her wrist, the ribbon gone, and longed to tell Lucian what was on her heart.

But it had to wait. Auri was still asleep.

She glanced at Nix, still standing in the doorway. "You love her, Nixus."

He took a step back and furrowed his brow deeper. "What are you talking about?" His gaze flew to Lucian, who stood. "I don't know her."

"Nix–"

"I mean, she's beautiful." He held out a hand toward Auri. "But it feels wrong to kiss her without her consent, you know? Like I'd be taking advantage."

"You know her," Brinna said. "She loves you. Nixus. Please."

Nix turned to Lucian. "Is this your version of a god's blind date? You set me up or something?" He grinned, but it was filled with discomfort. Pressing his palm against his heart, he winced.

Lucian sighed and slid a palm across his face. "I didn't take your memories, Nix. They're locked up. Search your heart."

But Nix shook his head. "You're being weird again. I don't forget things."

"You forgot me," Brinna said.

"I don't know you," Nix said, his ire clearly climbing as shadows coalesced around him.

Lucian stood and put a hand on his brother's shoulder. "It's okay."

Filled with fear, Brinna turned back to her sister. "Auri." She smoothed her hand over her sister's face—bright now with health. "I'm not your true love, but I love you truly." She leaned down and kissed her forehead.

Auri made a sound and shifted, then her eyes fluttered open. She sat up with a gasp. "Brinna? Oh stars. Brinna." Auri threw her arms around Brinna's neck. "I had awful dreams." She leaned back, her brow bunched with confusion as she worked through whatever was in her mind. Then she paused, her gaze jumping from the bedding to Brinna. "Mother. She slipped us something. In the tea." Then she looked around the room. Glanced at Tarley and Lachlan, Tarley muttering, "I should have known. Should have seen it…"

"She's your mother," Lachlan soothed, his tone calm and kind. "There must be an explanation."

Brinna stood.

"Where's Nix?" Auri asked her, then turned her head, and noticed him hovering in the doorway. She smiled, a radiant light on her face as she scooted from the bed. "Nix," she cried as she maneuvered through the tight space and launched herself at him.

Nix caught her, but Brinna could see his face. Confusion mired his features. He didn't know her.

Auri leaned back and pressed her mouth to his.

Nix stiffened.

Then his eyes shut, and he kissed her back, passionately, his arms curling around her.

Brinna averted her eyes and met Lucian's. He was frowning at her. She could read—could feel—every bit of regret on his face at what was happening between his brother and her sister.

"Wow," Nix said, drawing Brinna's gaze back to them. "That was quite an introduction."

Brinna saw immediately that Auri knew something was wrong. She stiffened and slid from his arms. "Nix?" She took a step away.

He grinned, a real one. "If I'd known the set up would start that way, I'd have taken better care of my appearance." His eyes jumped to Lucian, a sheepish look crossing his handsome features before he shoved his hands into his pockets.

"I'm sorry, Aurielle." Lucian looked down at his feet. "He doesn't remember."

"I would remember that, Luc," Nix said. "Seriously, you need to stop with this locking away memories thing. I don't forget things. I wouldn't forget that. Or you. What's your name again?"

Auri swallowed, looking at Nix, then took a step back, her eyes jumping to Lucian then to Brinna, who noticed the tears in her sister's eyes. "He doesn't know me?" A tear slipped down her cheek.

Nix straightened, looking rather helpless.

"What did you do, Lucian?" Auri's tone was accusatory. It was clear she was seething, her hatred for Lucian overwhelming her features.

A shadow passed over Lucian's face, but it wasn't hate or anger. Brinna knew he was thinking of the spell. That he somehow deserved it. Though she didn't know the entirety of things, she knew enough and could fill in the missing pieces based on what Lucian had told her, along with the comments Auri had made about Lucian.

"He was dying," Luc said. "I had to make a choice. To save you both."

"Because we were separated?" Auri asked, her anger doused.

"I'm the pinnacle of health, I'll have you know," Nix said.

Lucian nodded. "I wouldn't want to hurt him. Or you."

"I felt it—the fading—in the dreams," Auri replied and backed away from Nix.

Brinna's heart broke for her sister, her throat closing with tears.

"We locked up the memories. It was all we could do without severing them completely," Lucian explained.

Nix sighed. "This…still?"

Auri moved away from Nix and Lucian until she was at Brinna's side. Brinna felt her sister's hand slide into hers, and Auri squeezed with what Brinna could only assume was a need for comfort.

"They're in there somewhere," Luc said, "hidden from his consciousness. We just have to figure out how to help him unlock them."

Auri nodded, her chin quivering, then looked down as she shook her head, tears dropping to the floor.

"Where's Jessamine?" Tarley asked.

Brinna turned to look at Tarley, still in Lachlan's arms.

Tarley scrambled from Lachlan's embrace and flipped the bedding back to a starkly empty bed. "Has anyone seen Jessamine?"

The Wizard

If you take this path, you will lose, Baba had said.

The wizard frowned and looked up at the monstrous hedge before him. That fucking witch was in his head, the old crone who'd been helping Azleah all along. He shook her ridiculous prophecy from his mind and patted the vial containing the witch's thread of magic—her magical signature—in his pocket. Though he didn't like that she had a thread of his magic in exchange, he'd known getting what he wanted—access to Azleah—would cost him. He had no intention of letting the hag steal his glee at finally meting out Azleah's comeuppance. Besides, she was wrong. He was about to get everything that was coming to him.

Power.

Immortality.

Revenge.

With the witch's thread giving him access, coupled with his own magic to enhance the power, he muttered an incantation and reached out to touch a vine. The hedge shifted, vines pulsing and wreathing into a doorway. As he walked through, the hedge closed behind him, continuing to shift as it created an unobstructed passageway directly through to the other side. Once through, he looked at the lair of his nemesis, but what awaited him was disappointing.

Azleah wasn't standing there, bursting with hatred.

Tom wasn't trying to protect her.

There wasn't a glamoured castle or maze where they'd been living all these years.

No.

It was a small, understated cottage tucked up against a thicket of giant evergreens. It had a thatched roof and mullioned windows decorated with flower boxes he assumed bloomed in the spring but only contained dead plants. There was a garden, harvested now as they had slipped into fall. A barn. It looked… domestic.

He sneered and kept walking, relishing the moment Azleah would realize she'd lost.

Once at the door, he hesitated a moment, ready to

burst in and destroy the object of his rage. But when he opened it, silence greeted him, an eerie quiet that made what lay inside feel like a tomb. As he stepped inside, his boots echoed loudly against the planked wooden floor. The cottage was cold and appeared empty, as if abandoned.

But then he saw her. His nemesis, curled up asleep—a quick check confirmed—in Tom's arms, older, but still as lovely now as she'd been all those years ago, more so even than when she'd been locked in her tower prison at his mercy.

Now, it appeared, she was locked in the prison of her dreams.

The wizard crouched down and ran a finger along her cheek. "I told you I would find you," he whispered. "Now you will pay."

He stood, considering his next steps. "This" –he glanced around– "wasn't what I expected. A bit…dire and morose for my taste."

He looked back down at Azleah's face, who as just a slip of a girl had evaded him for decades. This, now, felt anticlimactic to their game of cat and mouse. Besides, he'd loved her once—as much as he could love anything. Loved her enough to desire her heart to take the place of his own. Ending it this way wasn't satisfying. He wanted her cognizant that he'd won. He was honorable, after all.

"Here's what's going to happen, Princess. I'm going to make you feel my victory. When you escape this spell, you will know that I found you, and it was because I was merciful that you are alive." He crouched down once more. "It will torture you to know what you stole was returned. To me. Then you will submit, and I will win."

With a sigh, the wizard stood and walked through the cottage.

He found the boy asleep in a bed inside the only room on the first floor. But that wasn't what he wanted. The youth wasn't hidden from the wizard's sight. Curious. He wondered if the spell had modified the protective ribbons, if the cottage negated the need for them, or if it was because he now carried a thread of magic of the witch who'd cast the spells.

He didn't linger, sure the fools he'd gained the witch's name from were trying to find their way through. Walking up the narrow stairs, he found the daughters, huddled together in their cold sleep, but he wanted only one.

And she wasn't hidden from his sight any longer.

She was breathtaking. Her dark hair, her alabaster skin, her ruby-red lips. He wondered what color her eyes were?

"My heart," he said and picked her up just as a loud yell sounded from outside the cottage.

He glanced out the single, mullioned window but couldn't see anything from his angle inside the house. While he could confront the fools, confident he knew who was outside making a racket, he needed them to break the spell. He wanted Azleah awake, and it seemed they knew how, having made it through the hedge. He would slip away, leaving Azleah to know he'd found her and infiltrated her defenses.

He smiled.

When she realized he'd taken back what belonged to him, she'd know she'd lost.

Running out of time, he carried his missing heart down the stairs and snuck out the back of the cottage—just as the front door opened. The hedge parted for him once more, allowing him passage with his precious cargo.

But part way through, the hedge began to shrink around them. The passage where he stood remained arched high above them, the original spell still answering to the thread of Baba, but soon the hedge collapsed altogether in a final, heaving puff, leaving him in the open with his still sleeping daughter in his arms.

Hurrying, he stepped into the roadway, then hesitated a moment, looking down at her beautiful face pressed against his chest, intending to spell her back to sleep. Only she didn't stir.

"Beauty," he said. "I'll take care of you now."

She didn't move.

It was a boon at the moment, for she couldn't struggle as he carried her. Getting her ferreted away to his enchanted manor was his first priority. He didn't know how to break the spell still on her, but when had something like that ever stopped him from getting what he wanted?

With a quick glance around—the roadway free and

clear—he stole down the lane toward the manor he'd taken to calling his own, cradling the treasure he'd sought all these long years, gloating that he'd finally won.

Meanwhile . . .

Johesha

Johesha Malinor, the second son of Jomiah and Rozzi Malinor, the first captain of the Prince of Jast's royal guard, had taken to prowling around the godforsaken hedge. Without his prince to watch, Johesha felt unsettled, even though Lachlan had slipped into the monstrosity without meeting his end as others had.

How long had it been? Hours? Days? Time didn't seem to be following the natural laws. He was losing track.

So faith was what was required of Johesha, only he wasn't a man of faith but of action. He paused and leaned against a tree, taking a deep breath, but grunted out his frustration. He was terrible at waiting. But he waited because it was his duty. And when Lachlan returned, Johesha would be there, tried and true. He'd taken a vow.

"Captain."

He turned his head and watched Jude move toward him using the shadows to obscure his presence. "Brendsen? The others?"

"Still at their posts, but I saw something–"

Johesha straightened at the sound in Jude's voice. "Lachlan?"

"No, sir. This way."

Johesha followed Jude back through the shadows of the woods. "A man," Jude whispered. "He opened up the hedge and disappeared inside."

"How?"

"Magic. Like the witch from the woods." Jude stopped.

"Fucking magic," Johesha swore.

"There. He went in there." The guardsman pointed, but the hedge looked like it did everywhere else. Massive twisting and gnarled branches, hulking broad leaves, humongous thorns.

"How?"

"It just… opened."

Johesha, who'd never been one to believe in such fantastical things, couldn't deny them any longer. He'd seen too much recently to remain doubtful. "And did he come back out?"

"Not yet. Not that I saw."

From the cover of the trees, Johesha watched a few more moments with Jude, then decided he needed to return to his quadrant. But just as he moved, something changed. A crackle of energy burst across the roadway, hitting him with a jolt.

"What the fuck was that?" Jude asked.

A creak and a moan rent the air, startling the birds from their nests, and the darkness of the hedge changed. A flutter of golden light drifted down, changing it back to what it once had been. Wide-eyed, Johesha stood in silent awe watching as the monstrosity shrank, then dissipate into nothing.

"They did it!" Jude smiled. "They broke the spell."

Johesha opened his mouth to reply, only to notice that something moved among the detritus of leaves now covering the ground.

Someone.

A man hurried through, carrying a bundle that looked decidedly like a person.

Snapping his hand up for silence Johesha pressed back into the shadows, Jude along with him, watching.

"That's him," Jude whispered. "The one I saw."

The man turned toward them, glanced around, then looked at his cargo.

A woman.

The man slid his hand over her face, and Johesha's heart stopped. He knew her—Jessamine. Tarley's oldest sister. Though strangely, he couldn't remember having seen her with such clarity before.

"Beauty," the man holding her said, "I'll take care of you now."

But she didn't move, didn't make a sound, and Joshesha knew she was still locked in a deep sleep—the sleep Lucian Uraiahs had described before he'd disappeared into the hedge with the prince.

The man looked around, shifted his cargo in his arms and started down the lane away from them.

Johesha Malinor was a good soldier. He'd trained his whole life for his post. He would be the Captain of the King's Guard one day.

But as he watched the man carry away a sleeping Jessamine, his instincts alerted the needed to follow. And he always listened to his instincts.

His instincts, however, hadn't ever led him away from his post.

Ever.

"What should we do?" Jude asked.

"You get eyes on the prince," Johesha said, making a quick decision. He unhooked his designated captain's metal at his shoulder and placed it in Jude's capable hands. "You're in charge until I return."

Jude's eyes widened. "What are you doing?"

"I'm going after her," he replied.

And for the first time in his career, Johesha Malinor abandoned his post.

400

The Sleeping Beauty
A Grimm's Fairytale

In times past there lived a King and Queen, who said to each other every day of their lives, "Would that we had a child!" and yet they had none. But it happened once that when the Queen was bathing, there came a frog out of the water, and he squatted on the ground, and said to her, "They wish shall be fulfilled; before a year has gone by, thou shalt bring a daughter into the world."

And as the frog foretold, so it happened; and the Queen bore a daughter so beautiful that the King could not contain himself for joy, and he ordained a great feast. Not only did he bid it to his relationship, friends, and acquaintances but also the wise women, that why might be kind and favorable to the child. There were thirteen of them in his kingdom, but as he had only provided twelve golden plates for them to eat from, one of them had to be left out.

However, the feast was celebrated with all splendor; and as it drew to an end, the wise women stood forward to present to the child their wonderful gifts: one bestowed virtue, one beauty, a third riches, and so on, whatever there is in the world to wish for. And when the eleventh of them had said their say, in came the uninvited thirteenth, burning to revenge herself, and without greeting or respect, she cried with a loud voice, "In the fifteenth year of her age, the Princess shall prick herself with a spindle and shall fall down dead." And without speaking one more word, she turned away and left the hall.

Everyone was terrified at her saying, when the twelfth came forward, for she had not yet bestowed her gift, ad though she could not do away with the evil prophecy, yet she could soften it, so she said, "The Princess shall not die, but fall into a deep sleep for a hundred years."

Now the King, desirous of saving his child even from this misfortune, gave commandment that all the spindles in the kingdom should be burnt up.

The maiden grew up, adorned with all the gifts of the wise women; and she was so lovely, modest, sweet, kind and clever, that no one who saw her could help loving her.

It happened one day, she being already fifteen years old, that the King and Queen rode abroad; and the maiden was left behind alone in the castle. She wandered about into all the nooks and corners, and into all the chambers and parlors, as the fancy took her, till at last she came to an old tower. She climbed the narrow winding stair which led to a little door, with rusty key sticking out of the lock; she turned the key, and the door opened, and there in the little room sat an old woman with a spindle, diligently spinning her flax.

"Good day, mother," said the Princess, :what are you doing?" "I am spinning," answered the old woman, nodding her head. "What thing is that that twists round so briskly?" asked the maiden, and taking the spindle into her hand she began to spin; but no sooner had she touched it than the evip prophecy was fulfilled, and she pricked her finger with it. In that very moment she fell back upon the bed that stood there and lay in a deep sleep, and this sleep fell upon the whole castle. The King and Queen, who had returned and were in the great hall, fell fast asleep, and with them the whole court. The horses in their stalls, the dogs in the yard, the pigeons on the roof, the flies on the wall, the very fire that flickered on the hearth, became still, and slept like the rest; and the meat on the spit ceased roasting, and the cook, who was going to pull the scullion's hair for some mistake he had made, let him go, and went to sleep. And the wind ceased, and not a leaf fell from the trees about the castle.

Then round about that place there grew a hedge of thorns thicker every year, until at last the whole castle was hidden from view, and nothing of it could be seen but the vane on the roof. And a rumor went abroad in all that country of the beautiful sleeping Rosamond, for so was the Princess called; and from time to time many Kings' sons came and tried to force their way through the hedge; but i was impossible for them to do so, for the thorns held fast together like strong hands, and the young men were caught by them, and not being able to get free, there died a lamentable death.

Many a long year afterwards there came a King's son into that country, and heard an old man tell how there should be a castle standing behind the hedge of thorns, and that there a beautiful enchanted Princess named Rosamond had slept for a hundred years, and with her the King and Queen, and the whole court. The old man had been told by his grandfather that many Kings' sons had sought to pass the thorn-hedge, but had been caught and pierced by the thorns, and had died a miserable death. Then said the young man, "Nevertheless, I do not fear to try; I shall win though and see the lovely Rosamond." The good old man tried to dissuade him, but he would not listen to his words.

For now the hundred years were at an end, and the day had come when Rosamond should be awakened. When the Prince drew near the hedge of thorns, it was changed into a hedge of beautiful large flowers, which parted and bent aside to let him pass, and then closed behind him in a thick hedge. When he reached the castleyard, he saw the horses and brindled hunting-dogs lying asleep, and on the roof the pigeons were sitting with their heads under their wings. And when he came indoors, the flies on the wall were asleep, the cook in the kitchen had his hand uplifted to strike the cullion, and the kitchen maid had the black fowl on her lap ready to pluck. Then he mounted higher, and saw in the hall the whole court lying asleep, and above them, on their thrones, slept the King and the Queen. And still he went farther, and all was so quiet that he could hear his own breathing; and at last he came to the tower, and went up the winding stair, and opened the door of the little room where Rosamond lay.

And when he saw her looking so lovely in her sleep he could not turn away his eyes; and presently he stooped and kissed her, and she awakened, and opened her eyes, and looked very kindly on him. And she rose, and they went forth together, the King and the Queen and the whole court woke up, and gazed on each other with great eyes of wonderment. And the horses in the yard got up and shook themselves, the hounds sprang up and wagged their tails, the pigeons on the roof drew their heads from under their wings, looked around, and flew into the field, the flies on the wall crept on a little farther, the kitchen fire leapt up and blazed , and cooked the meat, the joint on the spit began to roast, the cook gave the scullion such a box on the ear that he roared out, and the maid went on plucking fowl.

Then the wedding of the Prince and Rosamond was held with all splendor, and they lived very happily together until their lives' end.

Playlist

Found on Spotify: In the Shadow of a Dream

I Still Haven't Found You - Owsey
Nightshade - Andrew Belle
Make Believe - Shallou
Oh Baby - Ficci
Waking Up - The Light the Heat, Roary
In a Different Light - Tim Schaufers, TROVES
Above the Salt - Portrait, VERITE
Paper-Thin - OXALIS
Sleeptalking - EMBERZ, Emily Nance
With You - Faodail Remix
Klur, Kaodail
Somewhere (Acoustic) - Slow Macif, Woven in
Haitus
Raye - Sultan + Shepard, Shallou
Golden - Le Voyageur
Count On - Shallou, Colin
I'm Here - Freyr

Acknowledgements

Three books! Can you believe it? I hadn't really known there would be more than one book, but here we are, and now we have a series! I owe you an apology for that cliffhanger (covers face with hands). Truly, that was as surprising to me as I think it probably was to you. More on that in a moment.

As I was writing Dream, I knew there were things I HAD to do, namely reveal Scarlett's story and answer for the red ribbons. Creatively, I'd painted myself into a corner, but I didn't want to information dump her story through dialogue around the dinner table. So instead of that, I used what's called a frame story told through a flashback. One of my favorite authors, Judith McNaught—a romance author who wrote regency romance in the 80's and 90's—wrote Almost Heaven (1989) which is one of my favorite romance novels (also check out Kingdom of Dreams [1989]). She used the flashback as a means to offer the reader the set-up for the entire romance between her hero and heroine. So I thought, this will work. But then my amazing editor—Kate, a goddess —said: "dump the flashback."

"But... but" I sputtered, because I knew that if I didn't give readers something with this story, they were going to throw this book against the wall. But upon reflection (and another read through), I realized Kate was right. Dream provides a second-hand accounting of Scarlett's story to offer glittering gems of her secret.

Did it work? You'll have to tell me. And what happened to that frame story I cut? Keep reading.

Back to that cliffhanger.

As I wrote, Nix kept getting sicker and sicker and my heart got heavier and heavier. The god-yoke was always going to come into play for Auri and Nix. It was central to the "The Fight" story (you can find this on my website). It showed up in their "Letters" and resolved itself off the page in Hoax. But I knew that this tether was going to have an impact on them somehow, I just hadn't known how. The harsh realitywas that while Luc is responsible for so much of Nix's misery, he's also responsible for introducing Auri and Nix and as Nix revealed,

he wouldn't change that for anything. Luc's growth meant he would have to face not only the choices he'd made in the past, but also having to make another impossible choice for his brother, a sort of moment to bring him full circle. Which, I know, left you hanging gripping the side of a cliff.

For that I am sorry, but I have a plan.

I'd always known there would be four books, one for each Fareview sister. Only after writing the end of Dream, I realized there was a ton of story that needed to be written in the next one, loose ends that needed to be explored and tied up, which is why there is now a fifth book: In the Shadow of the Truth, a group of novellas written to bridge the gap between the end of In the Shadow of a Dream and the next book, In the Shadow of an Obsession. Look for Truth this year. This is where you'll find Scarlett's story and, I promise, that at least one of those cliffhangers will be resolved! In the Shadow of an Obsession is still on track for release in 2025.

There are so many people to thank for helping me get this book into your hands. Beth Stedman helped me when I got stuck, talked me through story choices and helped me see the forest for the trees. Stephanie Keesey-Phelan was a critical reader as I moved from revision to editing. And the great goddess, Kate Lamoureux, has been a steadfast editor on each of the books in this series, often helping me face narrative choices that needed a second glance. Sara Oliver has provided another amazing cover, and I am so grateful for her and the creative relationship we've built over the years. Thanks goes to my writing group—all amazing women— were instrumental in keeping me positive with forward momentum when I'd get lost in the pages. These books are better because each of these women has provided her wisdom. Thank you to all of them.

Absolute gratitude to you, dear readers. You who share your love of these characters and this story. Thank you so much for your passion.

Always, to my family: I long to make you proud.

To my savior, Jesus Christ, the ultimate redeemer, an exemplary bridge.

The Cast

in alphabetical order

Aurielle (Auri) Fairview: The fourth daughter of Scarlett and Tomas Fareview. She found an enchanted key in the Whitling Woods that trapped her in the spelled labyrinth of Nixus Uraiahs, where she was given three wishes. She fell in love with Nix and to her bewilderment, discovered they were god-yoked.

Brinna Fareview: The third daughter of Scarlett and Tomas Fareview. She is inherently good-natured and the nurturer of the family. A romantic dreamer, sometimes her dreams have seemed to come true.

Credence Crendell: Owner of the Copper Pot Inn.

Horance Forte: Brother to Credence, he helps her run the Copper Pot Inn.

Gemma Barnwell: The cook at The Copper Pot Inn.

Jessamine Fareview: The oldest daughter of Scarlett and Tomas Fareview. She is a typical oldest. A dependable and responsible daughter, she is her mother's right hand as a gifted healer in Sevens, and rarely leaves Scarlett's sight.

Johesha Malinor: The captain of the guard for the Crown Prince of Jast, Lachlan Nikolas. He is loyal, brave, and heroic. He was instrumental in saving Tarley Fareview from marauding assassins.

Keyanna Hollis: The crowned Queen of Kaloma rose to power in the male-dominated land of Kaloma. Her advisory counsel and the church of Kaloma—the Rayoran—were against her ascension and she narrowly escaped an assassination attempt on her way to negotiate a treaty with Jast—her late mother's family—for military support.

Lexa Uraiahs: Oldest sister of the twins Lucian and Nixus, she is the goddess of death and ruler of the underworld.

Lachlan Nikolas: The crown prince of Jast, he recently married Tarley Fareview. He has been tasked with remaining in Kaloma with his new wife in the capital city of New Taras to support Queen Keyanna's transition of power, a stipulation of their treaty.

Lucian (Luc) Uraiahs: Elder twin brother of Nixus Uraiahs. He is the god of light and day, but due to his meddling in his twin's life and inadvertently trapping Nix in a spell, he's been sequestered at his sky-home, Sol, until his father decides his punishment. He is the reason Auri found the enchanted key.

Mattias Fareview: The youngest child and only son of Scarlett and Tomas Fareview. At twenty, he's ready to make his way in the world.

Meera Hollis: Sister to Queen Keyanna, a Princess of Kaloma.

Nixus Uraiahs: The younger twin brother of Lucian Uraiahs, he is the god of dark and night. He fell in love with Auri Fareview when she saved him from a spell where he'd been trapped. Her sacrifice saved him and inadvertently changed the world. During their entrapment, Nix discovered he and Auri were god-yoked.

Olliander Berkman: The King of Jast's prime advisor has been sent to New Taras, Kaloma, to support Queen Keyanna's transition to power.

Poe Demertitus: Goddess of chaos and cousin to Lexa, Lucian, and Nixus, she was instrumental in trapping Nix and keeping him trapped, making a deal with a demon to sacrifice Lucian and Nixus for power. She was spared by Auri's sacrifice, but has been imprisoned for her trickery.

Scarlett Fareview: Mother of the five Fareview children and wife to Tomas, she is a healer and extremely protective of her family. She has promised her family to share secrets she's been keeping from them.

Tarley Fareview: The second daughter of Scarlett and Tomas Fareview is fiercely independent. Considered the rebellious daughter, she is often at odds with her mother. She saved Lachlan, was asked to marry him by Queen Keyanna for the treaty with Jast, but fell in love with him. Now his wife, she is finally going to leave Sevens.

Tomas Fareview: Father of the five Fareview children and husband to Scarlett, he is the voice of reason with his wife, but also unfailingly keeps her trust by maintaining her secrets.

The Darkling: a magical creature with the ability to shapeshift, it lives on blood and will imprint on its victims, choosing either to kill immediately or satiate (turn them). A darkling has the ability to see magic spells, even those that have been designed to be concealed.

Trevis: The stable boy at the Copper Pot Inn.

The Wizard: A dark sorcerer who is looking for someone named Azleah. When he appeared at the end of In the Shadow of a Hoax, he recognized Tomas—calling him Tom—when they came face-to-face. The wizard controls the darkling.

The
Fareview Fairytales
Continue…
in a book of novellas publishing 2024

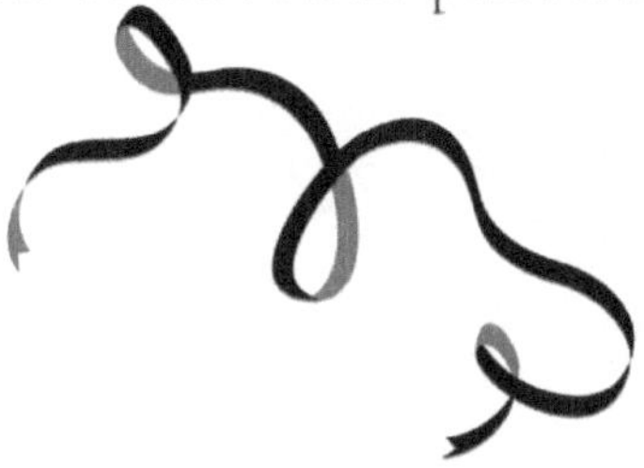

An excerpt from

In the Shadow of a Truth

By Maci Aurora

Scarlett

Scarlett Fareview, mother to Jessamine, Tarley, Brinna, Aurielle, and Mattias, wife to Tomas, and runaway daughter to the Mad King Zollah Cumbria and Queen Alea Cumbria of Echo Landing, had failed. Sitting near the fire with a blanket wrapped around her shoulders, she watched as others in the cottage spoke, could hear their voices, but nothing penetrated the haze that consumed her. Tarley, wrapped up in her husband Lachlan's embrace, clung to him as if her life depended on it. Brinna had her hand in Auri's. Mattias stood his arms across his chest, looking like the man he'd become while they'd been sleeping, talking to the gods, Nixus and his brother, Lucian a few paces away. And Jessamine... was missing.

A sob ripped through Scarlett's throat, and she caught the sound with her hand pressed against her mouth.

She'd failed.

She looked for her constant companion—the love of her life—and found him staring unseeing into the fire across from her. Tears filled her eyes and his form blurred. She shouldn't cry, knew she didn't deserve the pity rising in her heart like a raging sea, but the flood came anyway.

"I'm sorry," she whispered. "I thought–"

Tomas turned his head, his forest eyes finding hers—but for the first time since she'd know him, they were empty, as if his soul had been scooped out and discarded. He didn't smile, and that pierced her heart. He'd always been the one to smile, no matter the circumstances. He was the one who saw the world in rose, painted any situation with positivity. Now, he looked at her with hollow eyes, opening his mouth to say something, then didn't, turning back to the fire once more.

A commotion at the door grabbed her attention, along with everyone else.

A soldier—from Jast—stood in the doorway. He was tall and lean, his face pressed from granite. His features were sharp, his green eyes bright and his wheat hair short. On his chest, he wore the leather breastplate stamped with the tree of Jast, a short sword strapped to his back.

"Your highness," the man said, and ducked his head in deference.

It reminded Scarlett of a life before. Before her mother had died.

Tarley's husband, the Crown Prince of Jast stepped forward. "Jude."

The irony wasn't lost to Scarlett. No one knew her children were of royal blood, and they were also godblood descended from gods on her mother's side. She'd concealed those facts to hide them, but now that was over.

Jessamine was missing.

Scarlett knew who had her daughter, but how to find him was another matter. She didn't even know where to begin. The witch in the woods, perhaps, but the last time they had met, when Scarlett had insisted on the sleeping spell in spite of the witch's wisdom to forge another path, the witch had said it was the last time they would speak that way.

"Where?" Lachlan said, his tone loud enough to capture Scarlett's attention once more.

"He left," the soldier named Jude said, looking over his shoulder, then back.

"Johesha left? His post?"

"He handed me this" –Jude handed whatever it was to Lachlan– "and said he'd be back."

Lachlan frowned. "I don't understand."

"There was someone in the hedge when it… disappeared," Jude said.

Scarlett stood, her heart thumping painfully.

"The stranger was carrying… someone, and Johesha said he was going after her."

"Jessamine," Scarlett said and every face in the room swiveled to her. "He has Jessamine."

Emotions flashed across their faces: anger, frustration, hurt, dismissal. She couldn't blame them. She'd known this would be the case, even if her intentions had been to protect them.

She'd failed.

Baba told you it was a house built of cards.

"*He* who?" Mattias shouted. "Tell the truth. I'm fucking sick of your lies."

He was seething, shocking Scarlett. Her son, who'd always been like his father, was genial and slow to anger, but the rage in his eyes was like a living creature, breathing fire.

Scarlett looked down at the floor.

"Mattias," Tomas said, his voice a warning.

"She drugged us–" Auri snapped. "She deserves our anger, Father."

Tomas couldn't argue. Frankly, neither could Scarlett.

"Who is *he*?" Mattias asked.

The layers of spells had been broken. There were no ribbons, no hedge, no sleeping spell. Scarlett stood before her family and their loved ones completely exposed for the first time in the 28 years since she and

Tomas had disappeared behind the hedge.

Now, with nothing to hide behind, no spell to determine what she shared, there was no reason to conceal the truth any longer but for the pain it would cause her to relive it.

"Crue," she finally said, her heart racing as she did. She glanced at Tomas, whose was on her, though it slid away when her connected. It cut deep. He'd always been there to support, to bolster, to offer encouragement, but she'd hurt him deeply this time. Maybe even caused irreparable harm. "His name is Crue."

"Crue?" someone repeated.

Scarlett wasn't sure who since she was looking at Tomas, needing him.

"I don't know if that's his true name," she said, turning back to her children.

Jessamine was missing.

"True name?"

"Your given name. Like mine–" But her throat closed around the words, and she wished Tomas was standing beside her, giving her strength. But he had been hadn't he. He'd been the strong one all along and she'd failed to listen to him, failed to honor his strength and belief in her.

She tried again to say her true name, but she hadn't uttered those sounds for a lifetime, had tried to forget they existed. Her true name was attached to a promise stripped away by pain and prevarication.

"Wait. It's not–" Tarley frowned.

"Your name is Scarlett," Auri said.

Brinna was silent, but Scarlett noticed when her daughter's gaze sought the golden god's. Her dreamer.

Swallowing the sounds that cut like glass, she sighed, dug deeper for her own strength, and said, "Azleah. My real name."

Brinna—sweet Brinna—burst into tears.

Scarlett didn't understand Brianna's reaction.

The golden god—Lucian—moved to her side, and Brinna turned into his arms. His gaze looked up and met Scarlett's. She wasn't sure how to decipher his look, but she felt somehow supported.

"But why?" Auri sank to the bench near the table.

Scarlett's eyes jumped to Nixus, the dark god, waiting for him to move to Auri's side. They'd expressed their intention to exchange vows to one another, but he remained where he was, his eyes on her daughter. This wasn't how they'd been, before...

Something was wrong.

Scarlett sank back into her chair. "It's time I tell you the story, but..." She paused as the words stuck like broken glass in her throat once more. "It isn't an easy story to hear," she said, spitting them out as her chin quivered. "But it's past time you knew it."

And she started her story....

The Conclusion to
the Fareview Fairytales
Book 4 Publishing 2025

In the Shadow of an Obsession

By Maci Aurora

MP PRESS

THE
Accidental
SERAPH
A CARRAN HOLLOW FATED-MATES
NOVELLA, NO. 1

MACI AURORA

Maci Aurora has been writing stories since she was a child. At eleven, she fell in love with reading Sunfire Historical Romances about girls who made a difference in their lives while falling in love. When she discovered LaVyrle Spencer and Judith McNaught, their novels cemented her own journey to tell stories about love. Since then, she's been forever lost between the pages of a book as both a reader and a writer. While the Fareview Fairytales series is the first published under her pen name, she's written several contemporary books as CL Walters. Currently, she's busy writing the conclusion to the Fareview Fairytales series and working on some new ideas for the future. For the most up-to-date news about Maci's upcoming releases, fun extras, and behind-the-scenes bits, sign up for her newsletter on her website www.maciaurora.com.